A Certain Gentler

The Unreliable Recollections of :

Dickie Mandeville

The Chaplain's Daughter

'You shave this morning, Cadet?'

'Yes, Cadet.'

'Use a mirror?'

Dickie didn't dare look to the right. Fleming, the Cadet Captain, was 10 minutes into check-parade, and had only inspected nine juniors.

'Yes, Cadet.'

'Use a fucking razor tomorrow you clown! Drop, gimme twenty!'

'Cadet?'

'Press-ups you moron! You think I'm looking for a fucking blowjob?'

To Dickie's right, a head, enveloped in a cloud of condensing breath, labouring through press-ups. Fleming moved his attentions to the next Cadet.

'You polish those shoes, Cadet?'

'Oh yes, Cadet.'

'What did you polish your shoes *with,* Cadet?'

'Em, kiwi polish, brushes, and a chamois, Cadet.'

'Bullshit! Start running- lap the inner square until I tell you to stop! What's your name?'

'Healy, Cadet.'

'Don't bullshit me again, Healy.' It was Mick Healy, the big second-row from the room opposite Dickie. Fleming knew him well. Healy's brother was in Fleming's senior class the year before, had given him a hard time on and off the pitch. Payback time. Healy started lapping the inner square in the darkness, only the crunch of his shoes on the gravel betrayed his presence. An old man quietly forked turf into a boiler scuttle nearby, looking on in mild curiosity.

***

15 hours earlier

A pinched-faced NCO in a greatcoat picked up Dickie and two others from the train station. He introduced himself as CQMS Bailey, and ticked their names from a roll. They quietly said hello to one another, and Dickie met Paul Gavin and Paddy Doyle for the first time. Bailey led them towards a green minibus. They set off for the Curragh. The wordless NCO opened a pack of 20 Major, lit up, and fumigated the minibus with the one cigarette smoke Dickie hated above all others.

He parked outside an old, colonial-looking hospital.

'In there, wait in the room where it says 'Medicals' until you're called. If you pass, get in the bus. If you fail, someone will take you back to the railway station.'

They filed into the waiting room. Buttermilk November sun filled the room. A young man sat on a brown plastic stacking chair, looking forlornly at them.

'Failed,' he said as they said hello. They were ushered into another room by a medic, and were seen quickly by a female doctor. She checked his weight, height and scars, and passed him. The three were soon sitting back in the minibus.

A white sign at the church pointed the way to the reception in the Cadets' Mess. They entered a terrazin hallway, an enormous photo of the Garden of Remembrance on the wall to the right. A dark-haired Cadet approached in immaculate uniform, and introduced himself.

'I'm Cadet Mike Mullagh. Captain Glennon will be over to meet you in a moment. Would you like a tea or coffee?'

Captain Glennon's introduction to Dickie was short. He moved on to meet parents after a cursory hello.

Cadet Mullagh walked Dickie, Gavin and Doyle from the reception in the Cadets Mess towards the red-bricked barracks that were obviously the junior Cadets' quarters.

Atop a metal stairs, he led them into 'Pasáiste 5'. Cruciform in shape, longer in the horizontal than the vertical, there was a corridor to the left, one to the right, and an ablution room dead ahead. Eight bedrooms, two facing two, and a storeroom at each end. The glass in the unpainted sash window panes was wavy and dotted with tiny bubbles.

'That's where the details list and weekly time-table will be posted,' Mullagh said, pointing at a notice board. 'That's the annex. When you've finished unpacking, put your suitcases in there.' He opened a room numbered '4'. There were two tall sash windows either side of a silver-painted forties-pattern radiator. To the left, a metal bedside locker, desk and chair, and a bed with the blankets and sheets in a bizarrely folded block, pillows on top. To the right an oak wardrobe with double doors, and a shoulder-height chest of drawers.

'Use the sliders.'

'Sliders?'

'Small pieces of blanket you move around on to shine the lino. You tape patches to the legs of your furniture, see?' He pointed to the legs of the chair, patches of grey blanket taped in black to the base of each leg.

'Okay,' said Dickie.

'Unpack your case and distribute your clothing according to this diagram. Then leave your suitcase in the annex.' He handed Dickie a stencilled sheet showing an exploded diagram

4

of a room of identical plan, illustrating the exact contents and layout of every drawer and shelf.

The other dwellers of Passage 5 filtered in. Brian O'Shea was a well-spoken young man from Dublin, who said only 'Hi' before unpacking. He volunteered that his initials were always contracted to 'Bosh.' Mick Healy was a bluff second-row, who took the room opposite. Donal Bent had been studying law until offered the Cadetship. Alan Morgan was a cheery type from the west. Paul Gavin was a diminutive Corkonian. Henry Foster was an Offaly farmer, who had also started at Trinity, though they'd never met. Charlie Drury had completed a year of a civil engineering degree when told he had the Cadetship.

Mullagh appeared at four pm, and took them to Pearse Hall for swearing in. Lieutenant 'Smoothy' Moody (as Mullagh called him), and Martina Day, a female lieutenant, sat at two desks, a bible before each. Holding a list of names, Moody intoned 'Adrian Black'. Black stood, and walked forward from the third row of seats. In pairs, the rest followed him on cue, swore the enlisted man's oath of attestation, and signed it in front of the officer. They were officially Cadets.

***

Mullagh and another Cadet returned at 19:00, and took them into Bent's room. They went through the routine for room layout and inspection preparation. The bedding had to be folded into a layered concoction called a bed-block each morning. Mullagh had put it together in about one minute.

'It looks complicated, but you'll get quick at it.' Mullagh stated

'I'm going to use a sleeping bag,' said Healy.

'No sleeping bags allowed except issue ones, and they're only issued on the ground,' said Mullagh.

Tomorrow was going to be all one-off stuff, kit issue, fitness tests, followed by vaccinations and 48 hours ED.

'ED?' asked Gavin.

'Excused duty. You'll get vaccinations tomorrow afternoon in the hospital when you've got all your kit, then you'll be officially excused duties until Monday morning. But you'll be back here working your tits off getting your kit ready.'

'You'll find,' continued Salmon, 'the program will keep you moving and changing kit all day.' He showed them the program. 'You'll be in combats for check-parade, SD1 for morning inspection and classroom lectures, combats for weapons and tactical training, sports gear for PT, and fatigues for details.'

Their eyes started to glaze over.

'Most important, you make time for a gunge-up in the evening. Boil the kettle, Dickie.'

In Bent's room, Salmon took out a packet of biscuits.

'This is just to get you guys going, I won't be buying for you again. Pick one guy's room, have a cuppa, do your boots together, talk about the day.'

They sat about Bent's room.

'You're in for the hardest year and a half of your life, but two-thirds of you are going to make it. The six weeks to Christmas is to figure out if you want to stay. If you don't, get out. It's no fun getting fucked out of here after a year, or doing the honours course.'

'Honours?' Morgan asked.

'Getting back-classed to the juniors. Nolan out of our class will be joining you on Monday.'

They learned how to repair holes in the walls with A4 paper and grey paint; how to hide 'buckshee' kit in the attic; placing distractions for inspecting officers. How to keep "John Wayne" toilet paper in the toilets for inspection, but buy soft tissue for use.

'Why's it called John Wayne?' Gavin asked Salmon.

'It's rough. It's tough. And it takes shit from no man.'

***

The passage door boomed at 05:30 as the Cadet Captain and Mullagh hammered the doors. After almost an hour of checking every whisker and collar on the juniors' faces, the Cadets were sent back to their rooms for a bed-block inspection. Fleming and Mullagh kicked the part-assembled bed-blocks everywhere. They finished at just after seven am. B Block was in tatters.

Breakfast was not elaborate. A choice of two cereals, sweaty toast done on one side, and eggs poached or hard-boiled served by a sweaty, pimply, unkempt cook Mullagh referred to as HyGene. Tea from a large boiler tasted rancid.

***

The class assembled as instructed by Mullagh at 08:30 in front of their lines. A sour-faced NCO introduced himself as Company Sergeant Moran. He gripped a small bamboo cane with a blue pointer top beneath his left shoulder. Beside him, he introduced Corporal Curtin, who was going to look after them for the day.

In an accent licked from the cobbles of Dublin's Liberties, Corporal Curtin marched them as best as they could manage to the Quartermaster's stores.

'Army number, cadet?' the CQ bellowed.

Black didn't know it. Curtin consulted his nominal roll, and shouted out the number.

'That's the only thing I need to hear from you from now on cadet! Understood?' CQ Bailey sneered at him.

'Yes CQ!' mumbled Black.

The others quietly asked Curtin for their army numbers, and wrote them on their hands.

7

Two store men behind the CQ raced about shelves of uniform, finding or replacing shirts, tunics, trousers, boots, underwear, jumper, scarf, boiler suit, mess tins, mug, plate, knife, fork and spoon, an enormous cream-coloured mackintosh, drill rounds, a small padlock, a 'housewife kit' containing assorted needles and thread, Dickie lost track, and threw it into the bags provided. They laboured single file back to their rooms.

In Pearse Hall Moody and Day sat behind boxes full of books. They signed for their collection of weapons, drill and tactical manuals with Moody, who gave them a warning about military secrecy and the consequences of losing them.

Next, Martina Day checked their attestation details, name, height, eye-colour, religion, and scars against those entered in an A5-sized red book with a hard cover. This was their LA30, their military medical record.

It was midday. Curtin told them to get into tracksuits, and he'd be back at 13:30, to take them to the gym for their PT test.

***

'Can't do it.' Healy said plaintively as he tipped his kit onto the floor. 'Couldn't sew a fucking potato. No way could I sew tags on all this. I'm gonna call my mother.'

'You big useless turd!' Bosh was a man of mild opinion.

'Fuck you, Bosh!'

Dickie donned his tracksuit. The chart said what had to be ink-stamped, tagged, and what had to be punched.

Lunch was awful. The fitness test ahead, they weren't too inclined to eat anyway. Curtin was back at 13:30hrs.

They jogged down through the camp, down to the gym. The omnipresent CS Moran was outside smoking a cigarette.

A line of gym mats lay down the centre of the gym floor. A squat and muscular tracksuit carrying a clipboard with the class nominal roll, introduced himself as Sergeant Shaw. He divided them into two lines facing each other across the mats. Dickie had done press-ups and sit-ups before, but not burpees and stride-jumps. The exercises would start with press-ups, then the strides, then sit-ups, and finally the burpees. Dickie's one minute of press-ups were counted by Condell. He managed 34. Condell did 38. Then they faced off for the strides. From down the line there was a loud knock, followed by a howl of pain. Will O'Hara, a baby-faced Dubliner from Passage Eight had gone too close to the edge of his mat, and squatted his kneecap down hard onto the wooden floor. He screamed and clutched his knee. Dickie heard the word 'ambulance,' and he was gone from the gym.

The tests passed off without further incident. They jogged back up the camp, towards the hospital this time.

Corporal Curtin collected their LA30s and mounted the hospital steps. He emerged a few minutes later with a fearsome, bullet-headed sergeant. This was Sergeant Wendell, the most feared medic in the Curragh. He bellowed 'Black,' the first name on the list.

Black looked cadaverous, all colour drained from his lips. He turned into the annex, and passed out.

'Oh for fuck's sake!' Wendell roared, and the medic carried Black to a chair.

'Butler!' Wendell roared, eyeing his clip board again. They filed in one by one. Wendell delivered shots like darts on a Friday night in the NCO's mess. Black came too in five minutes. Wendell asked him if he'd like his shots in the arse. He raised the sleeve of his tee shirt and the job was done.

Curtin told them they were excused duty until check-parade Monday morning, and they shrank back to their rooms.

Salmon returned after dinner, and kit marking started. The veranda reverberated to the sound of polish brushes, mess tins, plates, knives, forks and spoons being stamped.

True to his word, Healy's parent's pulled up in the inner square at nine on Friday night, and he handed over anything to be sewn.

Salmon made the eight of them march up and down the passage for five minutes in their new boots before they started to spit shine them. It was a monotonous, laborious process, involving the application of small amounts of Kiwi polish on a yellow duster cloth in small circles across the toe of the boot, lubricating occasionally with spit or water.

They finished at 21:30. The seniors were to get a weekend pass after parade, their first with a junior class in the school behind them. Salmon and Mullagh filled them in on use of the Cadet's Mess for the weekend bade them good night.

*** *

Maginn's shop directly behind the lines closed at lunchtime on a Saturday, so a group of them set off for Powell's by the Post Office. With no agreement on what to watch, *Airplane II*, *Porky's* and, at Bosh's insistence, *Flashdance*, were all rented.

They watched and spit polished before the TV until midnight, pushed the armchairs and sofas back to their correct positions, and retired to their rooms.

*** *

The seniors had warned them about the Cadet Master, but nothing quite prepared them for the introduction to the man. Lt Col Oscar McCarthy Gibson, 'Oh My God' 'Oscar Mike Golf' or 'OMG' as Mullagh referred to his collective nick-names, was a barrel-chested fifty-something with a chest full of ribbons. His address to them in Pearse Hall was a stream of consciousness monologue on the honour of service, the pointlessness of viewing the Army as a career to become wealthy, the dangers of alcohol, and respect for the uniform at all times. He exited the hall so quickly afterwards that Captain Glennon was caught napping, admiring the shine on the toe-caps of his shoes.

***

In week two, they were issued a personal rifle. The Cadet School was unusual in that the amount of time juniors spent with a rifle required them to have it at all times, and store it in their rooms. CQ Bailey arrived one afternoon, with a storeman who carried a bag of chains and high-security locks. The CQ took them into the nearest room, which turned out to be Bosh's, and demonstrated the securing of the rifle to the radiator. The chain was exactly thirteen links long, and passed through the trigger guard and the magazine way before being locked with the high-security lock. The slide, top-cover, ten 7.62mm drill rounds and two magazines were stored in the cadet's locker, separately secured. They were left in no doubt of the disciplinary consequences for anyone who failed to properly secure their rifle. Dickie's rifle was numbered 1865. Bosh reckoned it was its year of manufacture.

***

Sgt Pond trotted jauntily into Pearse lines at precisely 15:00hrs. His combat tunic was immaculately tailored, the slacks as tight as was decent. Healy handed over.

'Ah. Cadet Healy M. You don't look very light. Can you float in mid-air, Cadet?'

'No, Sergeant.'

'What's wrong with Black?'

'He's gone sick, Sergeant.'

'You just told me that. With what infirmity has he gone sick?'

'I think it's a cold, Sergeant.'

'You think it's a cold. Not a very caring Company Orderly Sergeant are we? Poor old Black could be down there with gangrene for all you care- isn't that so?'

Healy had to think for a moment. The thought of Black with gangrene had a certain appeal.

'No, Sergeant.'

'Fall in, Healy.'

'Ar sodar, mairseáil!'

The class turned down towards Pearse Square and the Officers' Mess, then wheeled right for the Married Quarters, and out of the Camp. Paddy Doyle was at the front right, Pond, who thought little of Paddy's fitness, eyed him suspiciously.

'Step it out Doyle, my granny could move faster than that.' Paddy lengthened his stride, and the class moved off at greater pace for the Kilcullen road. They turned right for Brownstown. Paddy wondered should he slow down for the afternoon golfer pulling his bag across the road to their front. Pond noticed, and speeded the pace further. The golfer looked bemused at first, then hurried across the road as thirty-four in combat fatigues bore down on him.

They left the tarmac and strode onto the turf, knees and ankles found relief, but muscles groaned as resistance rose. Pond called the class to run around him in a circle about 50 metres across.

'DOWN!' They fell prone. 'GET UP!' '20 PRESS- UPS!' down again, then onwards, '20 SIT-UPS!'

They did this mini-circuit three times before he formed them into twos, and ran them up and down the tank tracks. Earth clung to their boots, as Pond ran up the hard sod to the side of the track. Up to the top, he ran them down.

Gavin was in the rear file, and under severe pressure. He fell out suddenly, and started to retch the remains of his lunch onto the plains. Pond made the class mark double-time on the spot.

'Tastes better on the way down, doesn't it, Gavin?'

'Yes, Sergeant.' He groaned.

'When you have nothing left, when you're finished, when your insignificant spirit thinks it's fucked, you want it all to end. At that moment you've done less than ten percent of what your body is capable of. Do you understand, Cadet?'

'Yes Sergeant,' Gavin groaned and re-joined the class. They set off again. Dickie's quads started to tremble.

***

Fleming and the Senior Company Orderly Sergeant marched out of the morning gloom to take check-parade. As they approached, another shape emerged from the mist. Moody, who was orderly officer, told the seniors to stand fast. He trotted up the stairs to the veranda. Moody called the cadets of Passage Five upstairs one by one. He checked that each door was locked, and that the cadet opened it with his key. He checked that the rifle was secure to the radiator, and the parts were secure in the steel locker.

The only infraction found was with Freddie Lane, who'd left his drill rounds in his webbing. Moody gave him the 'Stand House', a run to the bar at the Curragh Race track that evening in combat uniform. When Lane got there, Moody was sitting in his car, smoking a Rothmans, reading the Irish Times.

***

Later that morning was their introduction to the College Commandant, the overall boss of the Military College to whom OMG and all the officer instructors ultimately reported. Dickie had seen the clichéd Colonel Blimp characters in many films, but didn't believe they actually existed. They did. Colonel Edward Mullins, was also referred to as 'Colonel Quasimodo', or 'Charlie Quebec' due to his short stature and ample girth, and his apparent tendency to drool during long speeches.

Mullins subjected them to a 45 minute exhortation in English and Latin on the art and science of war, the need to 'maintain the aim,' the need to set an example, the need to stay fit, the importance of character and determination.

Afterwards, they marched to the Cadets' Mess for a courtesy and etiquette lecture from Lieutenant Day on table setting, the different forms of cutlery and glassware, and the order in which dishes were served at formal dinners. The lecture was far less interesting than the giggling stable girls from the local stud who had lost their way home on the plains, and trotted their mounts past the officers' mess.

***

Captain Glennon chose a Wednesday night in December to introduce the class to the RC and Anglican Chaplains. This had the added benefit that there were no work details for the night. They arrived in the mess at 19.00hrs in lounge suits. As their first 'social' evening of their cadetship, it was accompanied by a glass of sherry. The cadets were reluctant to be the first seen to raise a glass of sherry, but once Fr Campion took a sip, general absolution was granted. The Cadet Master, Lt Col McCarthy Gibson, did the introductions. It was their first time to hear him speak socially. He didn't do social.

'Maintenance of morale on the battlefield is one of the most important tasks for the commander. Spiritual welfare is an important component of morale. This evening, our chaplains are going to talk to you about spiritual welfare.'

With that, he was gone out the front door. Captain Glennon remained in the room, while the chaplains said their piece. The RC chaplain gave an amusing spin on the atheists-in-foxholes story. He told of a non-mass going Dublin soldier he met behind a sandbag wall in Lebanon, as they ran for a bunker during an Israeli shelling. The squaddie promised him faithfully he would attend mass on Sunday if they made it to the bunker in one piece. They did, and so did he.

Very Reverend Kingston said relatively little. He was delighted to have one of his flock in the class, as there hadn't been a protestant in the senior class. It turned out he was a locum chaplain, as the regular Curragh chaplain was on a sabbatical in London. The formalities over, the chaplains mingled amongst the cadets and finished a glass of sherry. Before he left, Reverend Kingston invited Dickie to Sunday lunch that weekend.

'My wife makes an excellent lunch. I understand that weekends in the Curragh are rather drab.'

Dickie's thought to decline, but he figured it couldn't be worse than spit-shining boots while watching videos in the Cadet's Mess. He gratefully accepted.

***

'La di da! Lunch with the Chaplain, Dickie? The lads not good enough for you?'

Bosh could wind as hard as he liked. Dickie didn't give a shit. There would be some tiny little bit of variety to this weekend. He said nothing.

'I hear the oldest daughter is a cracker though.' Healy added without looking up from his boot polishing.

***

Dickie got a call through to his mother from the mess payphone. The Chaplain's invitation to lunch made her day.

***

The college bicycles were serial-numbered ordnance, so had to be signed for in the guard-room. Little used, they were in pristine condition. There was a rifle-rack beneath the cross-bar. The pedals smelled of the boot-polish, with which they had been shined. The tyres had been washed of all debris, and were perfectly black. Dickie took the bike with the hardest tyres, signed for it in the guardroom ledger and cycled into a sunny, cold, December Sunday afternoon.

The Reverend had given him directions to the rectory, a modern house in Newbridge. He'd been warned not to go the old rectory close by. He parked the bike to the side of the house and rang the bell. Reverend Kingston answered and brought Dickie into the sitting room. From the magazines about the room, the Reverend was evidently a keen angler. There were family photos on the mantel piece and bookshelves, but framed photos of the full-time Reverend hung on the walls.

'Tea while we're waiting, Dickie?'

'Thank you very much, Reverend.'

Dickie surveyed the photos again when he left for the kitchen. There, close to the TV, was a photo of two girls either side of a beautifully groomed horse, which sported a red rosette. Though the shot was grainy, Healy's description of the older daughter was spot-on.

The Reverend returned with his wife, who placed a tray on the coffee table.

'My wife Esther, Dickie.'

Dickie rose and shook hands. Esther was not the clichéd notion of a reverend's wife. Slim, chicly attired in black and cream, she was a good two inches taller than her husband. She was also remarkably easy on the eye.

'Pleased to meet you, Dickie.' She extended a warm firm handshake. 'I'll have lunch ready in ten minutes, Hugh.'

She turned and left them alone. They talked for a while, the Reverend asking Dickie what service corps he'd like to be commissioned into, and what part of the country he'd like to be posted to. Dickie hadn't thought this through, commissioning being a distant, abstract concept. 'But I suppose it's all a bit early for those sorts of decisions, and they'll give you some sort of corps familiarisation later on?'

Dickie could only nod in agreement. The chaplain's wife returned, and brought them to the kitchen. Dickie heard movement in a utility room off the kitchen. A girl in tan breeches over brown Jodhpur boots pushed clothing into a tumble drier. As she leaned over the linen basket, the breeches described the most wonderfully taut and shapely legs Dickie had ever seen. He averted his gaze quickly, hoping the chaplain hadn't caught him.

'Mandy!' Esther called to her daughter in the laundry, 'Come out and say hello.'

Mandy paused, a slow, sinuous stretch at the door-jam, and stepped into the kitchen.

'Hi.' She said, extending her hand.

'Please take that sweater off, Mandy,' her mother asked. 'I can smell the horses from here.'

Mandy removed the sweater, revealing a tight polo shirt. Dickie felt even more grateful to Mrs Kingston.

'Where is your sister?'

'Still in her room, mum.'

'Would you mind asking her to join us?'

Mandy strutted into the hall and shouted 'Alison' up the stars. Overhead, Dickie could hear Culture Club on a radio. Alison slid downstairs like mucus, and fell into her chair. 15 or 16 years old, less attractive than her older sister, she oozed the aggressive boredom of the acned teen.

Mandy was studying classical civilisation and English literature at Trinity College, having started in Dublin at the same time as Dickie in October. She stayed in a flat in Rathmines Monday to Friday and came home at the weekends. Horses were her passion, and she made some money for herself riding out for the Castlemore Stud in the Curragh.

'So, what took you into the army, Dickie?' Mandy eventually addressed him directly.

'Not sure. Just something I've wanted to do since the start of secondary school.'

'And picked the Irish Army so you'd avoid anything dangerous... like the Falklands?'

Her mother shot her a look across the table.

'My cousin's in the British Army, Royal Irish Rangers. Never left Germany during the Falklands.'

'But you never felt like running off and joining the Foreign Legion or something... interesting?'

'Got a 'C' in French.'

Her mother intervened again, but Dickie could see a glint in Mandy's eye. All efforts to introduce Alison to the conversation were fruitless.

Lunch was delicious. He started to make his excuses, hoping that some other form of invitation would present itself.

'Hopefully we'll see you about, Dickie. Service in the Curragh first and third Sundays at ten.'

And that was that. Deflated, Dickie made for the door. Alison said 'bye' in the hall before slouching back up to her room. Mandy stood behind her parents as they bade farewell. She extended her hand to Dickie at the front door.

'Nice to meet you, Dickie.' She shook his hand again and returned to the kitchen. Dickie retrieved his bicycle, and waved to the Kingstons at the gate.

He stopped forty yards down the road to check the piece of paper Mandy slipped into his palm. It was a Dublin phone number, below which she had written in a very un-girly hand 'best between 7 and 9.'

***

Details on Monday and Tuesday were interminable. He got no chance to make it to the phone.

The only high point in the drudge of the week was firing the FN .22" conversion in the drill shed with Smoothy Moody on Wednesday evening. They fired from 25 yards at small targets placed against the sandbag wall.

After weapons clean-up, it was again too late to try to ring Mandy.

Thursday's details were back at the Cadets' Mess. Dickie was armed with some five and ten pence coins. The Mess etiquette was that seniors took the phone when they wanted, juniors took it when available. Woe betide the junior who kept a senior waiting. The second problem was Terry O'Byrne in their own class. Terry, whose name was already concatenated to 'Toby', was an engineering graduate enlisted as an Air Corps cadet. He'd been going out with Moyagh since she was a foetus. He hovered about the payphone like a hawk. Once ensconced, only the impolite thump of a senior's fist on the kiosk door dislodged him.

Dickie loitered with intent. Carl McGuinness, from Passage Six, was trying to get a look at Top of the Pops through the double doors of the ante-room. Twenty seniors sat in front of the TV, spit-shining. McGuinness prancing an air-guitar routine to ZZ Top's Girls. The kiosk door opened, and Mullagh emerged. Toby moved, but Dickie shouldered his way in. He lobbed in ten pence and dialled. It rang and rang. Toby shuffled outside. He rang again. It rang out again. He thumped the 'B' button, retrieved his coin, and shouldered his way past Toby.

***

'You're pulling the fucking Michael!' Morgan was incredulous.

'I'm not. We have to do it.' Healy sounded defensive.

'You're sure you heard him right?' Bosh as delicate as ever.

'Ask him your fucking self, Bosh!' Healy shouted. Bosh was silent.

Moody was orderly officer, and had returned to the Cadet Lines after Saturday inspection to inform Healy that they were to sweep up all the leaves in the wood beside the Cadets' Mess. They drew the work implements and wheel barrows form stores, and broke for a quick lunch.

The wood beside the Cadets' Mess was small, no more than fifty yards square. A stand of deciduous trees, perhaps fifteen years old, it gave some wind screening to the camp. It was piled deep with wet, rotting foliage.

A strong north wind blew across the plains. The winter solstice was close, the afternoon was darkening.

After an hour or so of labour, a few of them looked up at the stationary figure on the grass. Paddy Doyle from Passage Six stood leaning on a garden rake, smoking his pipe.

'Like the leaves of the forest when Summer is green,

That host with their banners at sunset were seen:

Like the leaves of the forest when Autumn hath blown,

That host on the morrow lay withered and strown.'

'What in sweet fuck is that, Paddy?' asked Dick O'Leary, a Kerryman from Passage Seven

'Byron. The Destruction of Sennacherib. Thought I'd introduce a bit of culture to proceedings.'

'Hurry the fuck up, lads!' Healy chided.

They had cleared the bulk of the leaves from the edge of the roadway, down the slight incline. They worked with one team in front with rakes, followed by another with brushes. A third team with wheel barrows took the piles of leaves and dumped them about 100 yards east, at the back fence of a married quarter. The floor of the wood was remarkably tidy, but every gust of wind freed another wave of leaves from on high.

'Fuck sake!' O'Leary shouted, a Rothmans Blue jammed between his lips, as more fresh leaves descended.

'What the fuck am I doing here?' Bosh's cry sounded existential.

'Because you want to fly planes, dickhead.' Commons snarled.

'It's about learning to follow orders, Bosh.' Gavin was Cadet Reasonable again.

'I get the following-orders bit, you tit.' Bosh imitated Gavin's Cork accent. 'But we're not meant to follow all orders, are we?'

'Right there, Bosh,' Morgan said, 'they strung up a few Germans for that in Nuremberg.'

Bosh revelled in the back-up.

'Yeah. We're only meant to obey *lawful* orders. Not any old shit dressed up as an order.'

'I think we'll get into lawful and unlawful orders in stage three, Bosh.'

'Shut the fuck up you silly Cork twat.' Bosh spat.

'Jesus Christ lads, it's getting dark!' Healy fretted.

'I know this is a bit mad, lads' Gavin had a plan. 'But if we shake each tree five minutes before Smoothy comes, we'll get down the loose ones, get them swept away, and he should be happy.' It was a daft plan, but the only one they had.

They kicked every tree in the wood. It generated a good fall of leaves on the bare soil.

'Right Mick, go ask him to inspect it now!' Gavin shouted at Healy.

They swept and pushed the last dusting of leaves towards the obstacle course. It took about ten minutes.

'Fall in!' they heard Healy trotting back from the Officers' Mess.

Moody trooped absentmindedly up the street, a combat jacket over his sweater. He walked into the wood, now gloomy in the fading light, and turned around after a yard or two to Healy.

'Very good, Healy. Get the tools cleaned, and carry on.'

He was already walking away when Healy called the class to attention and saluted Moody's retreating arse. Moody saluted without turning, a sodium street-light blinking on as he raised his arm.

***

Monday's details were back in the Cadets' Mess. Everything had to be in place for the cadets' Christmas Dinner.

When they finished, senior cadet Murnaghan fell them in before the main door and asked if any of them had done any debating. Dickie had gone as far as his maiden speech in the Trinity Phil before he came to the Curragh. Gavin, Peter Clay and Dickie raised their hands.

'Great. Be here at 18:00hrs in lounge suit on Wednesday. Freshers' debate in TCD.' Murnaghan jotted their four names down in his notebook and disappeared.

Dickie ran into the mess. He could hear Fleming in the kiosk. He hovered, hoping no other senior appeared. Fleming exited the kiosk and shot Dickie a dirty look. Dickie put the warm receiver to his ear, and shoved some coins in the phone. A female voice answered.

'Mandy?'

'No. Can I say who's calling?'

'Dickie.'

'Hold on.'

The wait seemed long.

'Well hi there, Cadet Cool,' came the eventual response.

'Hi Mandy. I tried to call last week.'

'Sure you did. We're just heading out. Pity you're not here.'

'I'll be in Trinity on Wednesday evening. At the Phil. Hopefully you can make it?'

'I'll see. I'm studying awfully hard.'

'Oh.' He was unsure how seriously he should take her.

'But I'm sure I'll make it out for a while.'

The phone peeped for more money. He had none.

'I'll see you then. After seven.'

He heard no reply as the line went dead.

***

'Taking you a stage further in your arms drill, I will now demonstrate the 'Fix Bayonets'.' Corporal Curtin roared at Dickie's section, which was Passage Five.

Depending on the subject matter, the class was divided into either four sections of eight, two 'platoons' of sixteen, or the full class of 32 together, though O'Hara was still in hospital. For square bashing, the class took up separate corners of Pearse Square as the four corporals bellowed at them.

It was hilarious, tedious and monotonous. If they got as far as September, their 'Method of Instruction' training would require them to do exactly the same thing.

The neophyte cadets had no understanding of the ways of the military world as yet, but Curtin did. He'd taken a posting from Dublin to oversee these snot-nosed, pimply-faced kids who wanted to be officers. It wasn't to the taste of many junior NCOs, but Curtin knew that a couple of years here would get him a third stripe, maybe more. And unlike some, Curtin enjoyed the job.

He was a good NCO, and he knew it. He'd get to mould, to shout and roar for a full year at these presumptive little shits who would be officers. As soon as they were commissioned, he'd move onto the next batch. He was a man at ease with his lot. Deep down in his marrow, he knew his was the most important role in any army. Sergeants and generals were the stuff and stars of war movies, but the corporal was chief of the section, the atom of warfare. More senior ranks led leaders. But since the first Harappan warrior raised his spear before his ten comrades, the corporal led the ordinary man in war. He was the engine of the battlefield. It was no accident that both of Moscow's brushes with destruction were at the hand of those who had risen from the lowest military rank.

***

The minibus was outside the Cadets' Mess at 18:00 sharp on Wednesday. The seniors were already inside, dressed in their blazers. The juniors had marched down in their lounge suits. Moody took his seat at the front of the bus, and chatted casually to the driver. They arrived at Trinity after seven.

Murnaghan had some admin with the senior class speakers, before all took their places.

24

Dickie's eyes patrolled the lecture theatre looking for Mandy, of whom there was no sign.

Murnaghan was already seated, and McCoy about to start, when she walked into the rear of the theatre. She stood in the doorway, momentarily framed in yellow light, an eighteen year old Rebecca de Mornay with dirty-blonde hair. She wore a brown over-coat over a cream-coloured roll-next sweater. She slid into the row beside him.

After half an hour or so, she nudged him and tipped her head towards the exit. They walked out onto Library Square. She turned, put her arms around his neck and kissed him hard on the lips. Her tongue tasted vaguely of food, a residual sweetness.

She took his hand in hers and pulled it slowly down, opening her coat. She lifted it beneath her sweater, and placed it on her uncovered breast, and squeezed herself tightly to him, their intimacy invisible to the casual strollers.

Dickie lost all track of time. They might have kissed for 30 seconds, or 30 minutes. She moved gently away.

'I have to go now. You in the Curragh this Saturday?'

'I'm in the Curragh every Saturday.'

'I might drop by, on my way home from Castlemore. Say around six?'

'How...?'

'I'll ring you. It's in the phone book, isn't it?'

'It is.'

'See you Saturday,' she said with a lop-sided smile, and was gone. At eighteen, she had already mastered the art of giving a little away, while keeping it all for herself. Dickie didn't care. He'd already fallen for the Reverend's daughter.

***

Saturday morning's inspection passed as usual, and no one was thrown off the square. It was the last Saturday before Christmas leave.

They were detailed to rebuild the sandbag wall in the Drill Shed after parade. It had received only the most minor damage during the range practice with the .22" FNs.

It was filthy, back-breaking, dirty work, after which the Drill Shed had to be swept from one end to the other. Sergeant Pond was on hand at 15:30hrs, to pronounce himself satisfied with the job. They went back to their lines and showered. The removal of gun oil, floor polish, Kiwi, Blanco, Windolene, Brasso, sweat and dirt that had accumulated over the previous 24 hours was a liberation.

They got into civvies, had dinner, and went to Powell's. The seniors weren't on pass that day, so the rigid hierarchy of seniority applied. Seniors took the front two rows of seats in the ante-room, and it was first come, first served for the chairs behind those.

These few hours spent in the Cadets' Mess at weekends were some of the few interactions they had with the wider class and the seniors. As they tip-toed gingerly in the main ante-room door, a shout of greeting went up from one of the seated seniors.

'Come in! Come in! Be seated, gentlemen!'

It was Eamon Cole, the six-foot-four Kerryman and footballer. He was fourth of an unbreakable quartet known as the fearsome foursome with Brian Arnott, Robbie Lyons, and Jack Corrigan. Lyons was the loudest, Cole the biggest, Arnott the maddest. Lyons was christened 'Teabag' in honour of the manufacturer of the same name. And then there was Corrigan. Corrigan seemed unremarkable in every respect. He was of average height, and was squarely in the centre of the front rank on parade. No star sportsman, he was a permanent fixture on every team of every code the Military College put on the field. Placed fifteenth out of thirty in his first class placing, he'd never strayed a single place higher or lower in the intervening twelve months.

He would pass for the invisible man were It not for his nocturnal 'coming out.' He became a class legend the previous May when he propositioned Moody's girlfriend at the pre-commissioning ball. She laughed off his advance. Moody was too smooth an operator to react. He filed away the episode for future reference and retribution. Corrigan had laid down a marker. He was eighteen years old and would let no convention stand in the way of approaching any woman.

As Lyons later remarked 'You wouldn't you trust him with your sister! You wouldn't trust him with *his* sister!' He acquired the nickname osmotically. The legend of 'The Scut' Corrigan was born.

'You've met the Cadet Captain. Sit down here for real education!' Lyons shouted.

The juniors sat down to watch the senior-selected videos, the smokers forming little circles about the few ashtrays. Dickie sat at the rear, ear cocked to the payphone in the hallway. A steady line of cadets made their way to the kiosk, ringing home.

Six p.m. passed. The phone rang. Dickie hopped up and went to the kiosk. It was Toby's girlfriend. Dickie muttered about expecting a call from his grandmother. Toby was still twenty minutes on the phone. 18:45, it rang again.

'Dickie?'

'Yes. Mandy, where are you?'

'At the payphone, by the post office.'

Probably the only place in the Curragh she knew.

'I'll be there in five minutes.'

He got his coat, went out through the pantry door, past the turf shed, and turned right. It was dry, but the Curragh wind was biting. He made the cross-roads in the camp in five minutes. She was standing in front of her father's church, wearing the same clothes he had seen a fortnight before, plus a Barbour jacket and a woolly hat.

Dickie hadn't figured out where he was going to bring her. Mandy might find being shown into the mess Trophy-Room off-putting.

'Hi.'

'Hello, Mandy.'

They stood alone in the middle of the Curragh Camp, sodium lighting their only company.

Dickie, who'd thought of little else since Wednesday, didn't know what to say or do.

'Where's your room?'

They walked slowly up the camp to the Cadets' lines. Dickie parked her bike beneath the stairwell by the admin office. He unlocked the main passage door, she headed for the ablution area.

'Jesus, does anyone live here? It's spotless!'

'Yeah. It's a labour of love.'

'Or a love of labour. Is that immersion heater... polished?'

'It's a bit strange. But we have to do it.'

Dickie worried she'd find this too bizarre. He led her to his room.

'What are those... things... on the floor?' she asked, looking down at the woollen sliders.

'They're to protect the floor.'

She snorted.

'What's that?' she pointed at the bed.

'Bed block. Have to make when we get up each morning.'

'*101 Uses for a Dead Cat*?' she asked, holding a cartoon book his sister had given him.

'Distraction when they're inspecting the room.'

'I see. What's the chain for?'

'Chaining clergymen's daughters to the radiator.'

'What if she's Catholic?'

'I'd need another chain.'

'Catholic girls harder to lie down?'

'Don't know. Haven't tried it.'

'We haven't much time.' She said. 'I told my parents I'd be home by nine.'

Dickie closed the door and turned out the light. They kissed in the centre of the floor, shedding clothing as they went. Dickie literally couldn't contain his excitement, which jutted prominently forward in his flannel trousers. She pushed herself gently against him.

Dickie put the bed-block on the floor. They fumbled with each other on the bed. Mandy, topless over her breeches, stood up and grabbed the sheets. Dickie pulled off her Jodhpurs and breeches as they crawled into the roughly-made bed. Mandy's panties were still firmly in place. Dickie wondered how far proceedings would go.

This was his first sexual experience in an actual bed, something he'd never admit to her, or his comrades. He was impossibly aroused, erection was as hard as the leg of the chair. Every drop of blood in his body had migrated to his groin. He felt faint.

'My coat! My coat!' Mandy started to grope about the floor. Dickie felt a fleeting horror that she was going to leave him, throbbing and unsatisfied. He spied it in the sodium gloom. She retrieved it, working through the pockets. She found what she was looking for, and worked her panties down to the floor. She stood momentarily over him, naked and silhouetted by street light. Dickie thought he was going to climax there and then looking at her. She pulled his underpants down, easing them over his problem. She opened the condom, and slipped it quickly onto him. He thought of Corporal Curtin, sweeping woods, combat PT, anything to avoid ejaculating in her hand.

She slid into the bed beside him and pulled him on top of her. It was all over farcically quickly; Dickie heard the hint of irritation in her voice. He moved the condom and its pendulous contents, knotted it, and dropped it on the floor.

'Bit of an eager beaver, aren't you Dickie?' she whispered in his ear.

'I, well, I...'

29

She put her finger on his mouth. She stroked his chest and stomach, moving her hand downwards.

'I've got one more. You're going to have to be much, much slower this time.'

Afterwards they dozed for a few minutes. His mind raced, not knowing what to say.

'I have to go home now.'

'When will I see you again?'

'Service. Tomorrow morning. St Paul's.'

She got back into her clothes, Dickie following. He opened the passage door, listening for any footfall. It was quiet. They retrieved her bicycle, and walked out onto the street behind the lines. He kissed her hard on the mouth, her hands stayed on the handlebars.

'See you tomorrow,' she said, and she set off into the gloomy Curragh night.

***

Reverend Kingston was delighted to see Dickie at Holy Communion the following morning. His daughter wasn't there.

***

The six weeks from enlistment to Christmas leave ticked by. There was nothing too academic on the syllabus. He was able to stick with his classmates through the physical training. The weapon training was relatively simple.

The schedule kept them in a perpetual, blind stupor of exhaustion. The less organised were struggling to get to bed before midnight from Sunday to Thursday, and were barely getting to bed at all on Friday nights. Though seventeen or eighteen hours long, each day seemed to last far longer. Sunday morning was the only real break from kinetic monotony.

They had to parade on Pearse Square for Church Parade, Dickie included, after which he was free to make his way to service in St Paul's, or retire to the lines. After lunch, there was generally sport. Dinner on Sunday evening signalled the onset of preparations for the long week ahead.

***

The College staff made crystal clear their determination to get rid of Cadets who weren't sure of their 'vocation' before Christmas. Any later, and the College was not allowed to fill the vacant place in the class. Methodologies differed. On the one hand, there was the careers-guidance approach. The other approach was screwing cadets into the ground. If the softly-softly, educationalist did not succeed, then puking your guts all over the Curragh Plains would do the trick.

The combination of the two was effective. It was only the second week of December, five of the 32 had left, and were replaced.

The short-listed arrived in the Curragh liked wide-eyed virgins. Dickie couldn't be sure if they were getting the easier time of it, having a shorter run to Christmas, or whether they'd suffer for their ignorance.

***

Captain Bohan strode into Pearse Hall for his lecture on Military Writing. Black was company orderly and handed over the class.

'Sit down, Black,' Bohan snapped, and walked over to the overhead projector to commence his lecture.

'Many of the submissions made following Tuesday's class were unacceptable. The rules are simple, and are clearly expressed in your manual of staff duties. Any further errors in submissions and I will be taking corrective measures. Understood?'

'Yes, sir!' chimed the class.

Military Writing was a new form of communication. It was English shorn of adjectives and all descriptors, bar objective ones. There was no 'big' no 'small', no 'near' or 'far.' Size was quantified in area, volume or number. Distance was quantified in metres. Conjecture did not exist. Something was, or it was not.

Bohan was expounding on the rules for map overlays, a peculiar way of representing friendly and enemy forces.

'The main areas of error are getting your force strength indicators incorrect, and running boundary indicators through your force indicators. Understood?'

'Yes, sir!' and Bohan got on with boring them senseless for the following 45 minutes. Dickie looked left. Paddy Doyle was drunk with sleep, eyes starting to roll upwards, chin bobbing down. Like a heart monitor on a dying man, his pen was flat-lining as he took notes, and was slowly inching towards the edge of the page. Bohan didn't see him, and paced the hall as he got the class to mark an offence trace. No infraction was too minor to escape a yapping comment from him.

'What colour are enemy mines, Black?'

'Green, sir.'

'Then why are yours black... Black?'

'Mistake, sir.'

'What's that, Gavin?'

'Concertina wire, sir.'

'Why does it look like a pig's tail then?'

'Erm, line through the centre is missing sir.'

'Then bloody well put it in!'

'Yes, sir.'

'What's that, Cadet?' Bohan had forgotten Loftus' name.

'HQ of 7th Brigade at 20:00hrs on 29th September, sir.'

'What does the question say?'

'*Future* HQ of 7th Brigade, sir.'

'So what should the unit designation look like, Cadet.'

'Dashed box, sir.'

'Well change it, Cadet!'

'Yes, sir.'

There was consistency in the monotony of Bohan's interrogation.

'The six characteristics of a military paper?' Bohan started to indicate individual cadets, not bothering with names. 'You!'

'It should be accurate, sir,' Clay getting out the easiest one.

'You!'

'Should have a clearly defined aim sir,' fair play to Condell.

'You!'

'Brief, sir,' shouted Hackett.

'You!'

'Clear, sir,' said Morgan. Getting into trickier territory now Dickie thought, trying to find the right page on the precis in front of him.

'Concise, sir,' McGuinness shouted, delighted with himself. Dickie couldn't remember any more.

'You!'

A moment of panic on Dickson's face.

'It should have a...' Bohan batted him away.

'You!' jabbing at Kennedy.

'It should have a clear introduction, main body and conclusion.'

'Yes!'

Doyle had fallen asleep. Dickie wondered if he would escape Bohan's attention again. He didn't.

'Cadet Black will call the class to attention. I want everyone in the hall to remain seated. Cadet Black, loudly please.'

'Seomra Aire!' roared Black, too loudly. With pitiable determination, his chair scraped backwards, and Doyle rose to attention.

'Doyle! Outside now! Wait for me at the school office.'

***

The Wednesday before Christmas leave was the night of their Christmas dinner. They finished a map-reading lecture at 16:30hrs, and were allowed repair to their rooms to get ready for dinner at 19:00hrs. Cadets didn't have a proper dress uniform, so juniors wore a white shirt and bow tie under their greens, while seniors wore the same under superfines. The junior officer instructors for both classes arrived at 19:10hrs, Colonel Quasimodo the College Commandant, OMG the Cadet Master and Chief Instructor at 19:20. The juniors loitered carefully back from the sherry reception, though Fleming made clear to them that they were now 'social' and should participate.

Lieutenant Day's Courtesy and Etiquette course suggested they take one sherry and nurse it all the way to dinner time. Lane downed four, visibly merry. Dickie was the nominated junior to say the 'Grace before Meals.' They sat for their turkey and ham.

Quasimodo rose to speak. Salmon had warned this could take quite a bit of time. At the Officers' Mess Christmas dinner, he had advised the diners that there would be an interval after his first forty minutes.

He started with a reference to the training from an early age of the young men of Sparta. He moved to some key learnings from some of the students on the Command and Staff Course. He drooled slightly. Dickie felt his bladder distend, but knew that rising was strictly *verboten*. The speech ended at ten.

They retired to the anteroom for drinks, where both fires were roaring. Gavin had Cole, Lyons and Arnott of the senior class in a corner, interrogating them about the exercises in the Glen, which was toughest, and asking them how they got through SCRATCH, fishing for tactical hints.

'SCRATCH is all in your head, Gavin!' Cole held a pint of Guinness like a thimble in his hand, and tapped his temple with the other. 'It's like a three-hour long football match, and then it's over. The dig-in is tougher. AUGHAVANNAGH is tougher. You just keep going!'

Quasimodo gave a theatrical 'harrumph' at eleven, and the senior officers exited the mess. Smoothy really relaxed with their departure, joking away in the bay window with seniors and juniors alike.

The junior officers exited *en masse* half an hour after the seniors. Cole, Lyons and Arnott emitted a loud 'Yahoo' when they were a safe distance out the door.

'Save the uniforms, lads! Save the uniforms!' Cole roared.

In seconds, he, Arnott and Lyons had stripped off their tunics and trousers, threw them over the back of a couch, and stood drinking in shoes, socks, white shirts and bow ties. Cole wore army-issue Y-fronts, and luxuriated in the removal of the tight-fitting superfines by jiggling his wedding-tackle, shouting 'the freedom! the freedom!' at Arnott.

Despite the departure of the barman, the seniors had a plan for alcohol. They'd been drinking bottled beer since they retired to the anteroom after dinner. In groups of two and three, they had been buying multiple rounds of bottled stout and lager, and secreting a stash in the trophy room.

As the juniors filtered out of the anteroom, Cole stood, heroic, in the centre of the floor. A large bottle of Guinness held aloft in his left hand, his scrotum cupped in his right, he roared, 'Remember what the Colonel said, lads! *Sic vis pacem, para bellum*!'

***

O'Hara returned from his six weeks in the garrison hospital the night before they were due their Christmas pass.

'You poxy bastard!' Healy roared at him. 'Six weeks in bed and you're going home in the morning!'

O'Hara looked anything but happy. 'I have to get a rifle for the inspection in the morning- can someone help me with it?'

Dickie was platoon orderly sergeant, and stuck his head out of his doorway.

'We'll go to the guardroom in ten minutes, Okay? Meantime, get working on your room.'

O'Hara looked more frightened.

Bosh's ghetto-blaster was set to eleven. No other radio could be heard. He was whirling about his room on sliders, and seemed far ahead in his preparations.

The night wore on, the Cadets finishing their rooms, uniforms and rifles before tackling their passage details. Everyone stopped for a gunge-up in Gavin's room at 23:00. Despite the energy boost after the gunge, tea and coffee, the communal volume dropped, and each cadet retreated into himself as he struggled to finish and get a little sleep. Bosh announced loudly that he was starting the brasses at 01:00, his personal chores complete. He went to the latrine and began polishing the pipework. He draped small sheets of John

Wayne toilet paper over the pipes where there was a gap between the sinks above them. He was finished by 01:30hrs.

'Now keep the fucking music down,' he shouted, and turned off Madonna in his room.

Dickie looked across at Healy, who shook his head and said 'wanker' to himself.

The talk decreased further. They focussed on their own tasks, longing for precious sleep. Dickie pulled his bed out and rubbed mansion polish onto the floor. He polished the soles of his boots with liquid polish, and propped them on the end-poles of his bed to dry. He polished the mirrors and checked his rifle one last time. Sights brushed with a toothbrush, holes in the flash-hider cleaned with a cotton bud. Grenade sights polished with a cloth. Magazines stripped and springs dusted. Gas rings on the piston polished, always a bastard. Inside of the pistol grip wiped dust free. Drill rounds polished and slid back into their clips. Webbing dusted and stacked per regulation on top of the wardrobe. Rear of wardrobe, dresser and bedside locker dusted. All shirts and underwear folded and squared away. Bookshelf, window frames, top of mirror, top of door, central heating pipe and chair dusted with damp cloth. Beret dusted with black boot polish brush. Blanco belt reassembled. Back to the latrine for Dickie's passage details: he was on sinks this week. Everyone hated the sinks. Couldn't finish them until everyone had finished shaving. Someone had cleaned a mess tin in the first sink; there was the tell-tale black mark of aluminium on enamel.

'No mess-tins in the fucking sink!' he shouted into the passage loud enough to wake Bosh, hopefully. He scrubbed it clean with Brasso.

The night train sounded in the distance on the Kildare line, the DJ rumbled from Dickie's radio.

***

37

Check parade no longer provoked the absolute fear of six weeks previously. He passed Dickie without comment, but a casual question to O'Hara on his shaving provoked a shiver. Home for Christmas today, thought Dickie, as the orderly sergeant marched the class to breakfast.

The senior class lightened the mood on a Saturday morning. Cole, Arnott and Salmon bellowed out the orders for right-dress. Salmon never said anything particularly funny, but his baritone could frighten horses two miles away.

Cole affected a Louisiana accent, sounding like he was shooting the rape sequence from *Deliverance*.

Arnott, under the decibel cover of the other two, deliberately mangled the Irish drill commands, in a solid Terry Thomas impersonation.

'Oh yesss… It's ME!' for the right dress, 'Daaartry ROAD!' for the eyes front. 'A Rash, Begorrah!' and 'A Ride, Begorrah!' as he inched his rank back or forward.

From the corner of his eye, Dickie saw CS Moran marching towards them in SD1. Not good. Bosh mouthed a 'who?' to him. He mouthed 'Moran' back. Someone whispered 'Jesus' from the rear rank.

'March off the senior class, Cadet Salmon!' he shouted, walking past the seniors. He went straight to the junior class.

'Ah, Cadet O'Hara, we haven't seen you in a long time. How long is it?' Moran was at his most menacing when light-hearted and casual.

'Six weeks, sir.'

'And what misfortune befell you to miss six weeks of training?'

'I was in hospital, sir.'

'Why?'

'Damaged my kneecap during fitness testing, sir.'

'You damaged your kneecap during one of the least physical tests you will be subjected to in 18 months here, and you spent six weeks in hospital.'

'Yes, sir.'

'What would that be in percentage terms, O'Hara?'

'I, think, about…'

'I would make it almost eight per cent of your total training, were you to make it as far as commissioning, O'Hara.'

'Yes, sir.'

'Does that bode well for you as a leader of men?'

'No, sir.' O'Hara was a beaten man.

'At least you're honest. I agree with you, O'Hara. Does that please you?'

'Yes, sir.'

Moran leaned into O'Hara's right ear and whispered.

'Soon after this parade, O'Hara, you'll get your little hands on your Christmas leave pass. It will allow you home to the bosom of your family. On it will be the date and time of your return here. I want you to look at that pass every day, O'Hara.'

Moran slowly pronounced every syllable. 'As you eat your Christmas turkey, look at that pass. As you drink and make merry with your friends, look at that pass. Each day, you'll know you're one day closer to here. Picture the man who will be waiting for you when you get back. Because, Cadet O'Hara, I will be that man.'

'Yes, sir.' O'Hara had shrunk in on himself like a pale, inflatable mannequin, leaking his stature away to the December air.

Moran regarded O'Hara with a flicker of satisfaction. Job done.

***

The senior class was long gone when they went to the Admin Block to collect their passes. Moran stood with the pass book handing them out with his dead-eye smile. They were free to go home for Christmas.

***

Dickie's week at home in Wicklow consisted mainly of school friends marvelling at his crew-cut. He couldn't explain what it was like, he knew it would all flood out as drivel, so he said it was 'interesting.'

He wondered should he run during his ten days off, but decided against it. The ten days passed quickly. Unlike his solo arrival in November, his parents were able to drive him back in January.

They watched in silence through the car window as he signed off pass. True to his word, CS Moran was there. Dickie paused for a moment, then waved his parents goodbye.

***

Thursday 3rd January

Despite the presence of CS Moran, O'Hara stayed put. In the morning however, he dressed in civvies for check-parade, and told Fleming what he was doing. He went to the office after morning parade, and signed his discharge.

His parent collected him at 10:00hrs. He would be the last leaver to be replaced.

***

A new instructing officer arrived in January. Dennis Brown sported an attempt at an Errol Flynn moustache above his lip, and a Ranger tab on his shoulder. For a man who affected military gravitas, his first inspection was pantomime.

He finished on the square without kicking anyone off, and commenced a forensic room inspection. He ordered the movement of furniture, to check the lino beneath had been polished. Dickie handed over his room, as Brown looked right towards the dresser. Dickie feared he'd spotted a stain, then figured Brown was simply admiring himself. He turned to Clay, the company orderly.

'Cadet Clay, I notice Cadet Mandeville has a Tiny Tim air freshener on his dresser'.

'Yes, sir,' replied Clay, confused.

'I also noticed that Cadet O'Shea had a Tiny Tim, but Cadet Healy had none.'

'Yes, sir.'

'I also noticed that Cadet O'Shea's Tiny Tim was placed on the left of his dresser, while Mandeville's here is placed on the right.'

'Yes, sir,' said Clay, uncertain.

'Cadet Clay, at this early stage of the rooms' inspection, are you telling me we will find Tiny Tims, or any other proprietary air fresheners, randomly scattered about some rooms, and none in others?'

'Perhaps, sir.'

'Were Cadets issued with a room layout diagram, showing where all issue and personal items were to be placed?'

'Yes, sir.'

'Were Tiny Tims displayed on that diagram?'

'No, sir.'

'Then how do you, as orderly sergeant, account for this lack of uniformity?'

'It's quite an old diagram, sir. I don't think they had Tiny Tims back then, sir.'

'They didn't, Cadet. That is the point. All Cadets will have Tiny Tims, or none. If all Cadets have Tiny Tims, they will be located in the same place in the Cadet's room. We can't have Tiny Tims randomly scattered about. It's about uniformity.'

'Yes, sir.'

Clay and Brown entered Bendy's room next door. Across the corridor, Healy was vigorously masturbating his bayonet.

***

Another Saturday, 08:30hrs.

As usual, Passage 5 was first passage in line for room inspection. First passage meant there was no cleaning that could be left until after parade. The inspecting officer followed the Cadets back up to the lines, one or two minutes after the parade marched off the square.

The upside was that after inspection, cadets could begin the post-inspection routine straight away. Start packing a bag if it was a weekend pass. Assemble rifle for return to the armoury. Get a cup of tea in the annex while the officer inspected the following passages. Pain in the arse as it was to be inspected first, the pros outweighed the cons.

There was a collective groan of disappointment when they heard Lt Moody's shoes clatter away from them as he topped the stairs, and Nolan shouted Passage 8 to attention.

The groan from Bendy's room was more pronounced.

'Oh Jesus, I'm not going to make it...'

'You'll be fine for fuck's sake.'

'Not the room, I need a shit!'

'You're not shitting in my jacks.'

'I have to, Bosh.'

By now all in Passage 5 had come forward to their doors and were leaning into the hall.

Bendy was doubled over, holding his stomach.

'Fairness Bosh, he's sweating,' said Healy, the voice of reason.

'He won't be here for an hour. I'll have crapped myself by then.'

'I don't give a fuck Bendy, you're not crapping in those jacks.'

'Christ, Sgt Pond!' Bendy pointed out the window. Bosh turned on his heels to look. Bendy ran out into the toilets.

'Dickhead!' Bosh shouted as he followed. 'Get out of there!' and started banging on the cubicle door. Bendy uttered a long moan, a mix of pain, layered on pleasure. For so long a prelude, it was all over pretty quickly. They heard him tearing off a few sheets of John Wayne, and pulling up his pants. A flush, then nothing.

'What the fuck are you doing in there Bendy? Get out!'

The cistern filled, another flush.

'Just a minute. Bit of a problem.' By now all seven others were in the latrines, wondering what was going on. The smell was toxic. They could see Bendy's boots moving frantically beneath the cubicle door. 'Can someone boil the kettle?' he asked from inside.

'You want a cup of fucking tea?'

'I reckon if I pour boiling water on it, it'll melt.'

'What?' Bosh was starting to look worried. 'Open the door!'

Bendy emerged sheepishly. He had deposited a ruler-straight turd in the bowl. It stood vertically from the bottom of the u-bend all the way up to the wooden seat. The heavy fug of his innards stank the latrines.

'Pick it out of there, you filthy wanker.'

'And what the fuck will I do with it then you clown?'

The two of them spent the next few minutes pouring boiling water over the offending turd ineffectually. Finally Bosh stormed off and retrieved a wire coat hanger. He severed the turd in three, and flushed it away. He handed the soiled hanger to Bendy.

'Get rid of this, and clean the seat, you twat.'

Bendy opened the latrine window and jammed the hanger into a gap in the brickwork. He wiped the wooden seat clean, then sprayed air freshener furiously. They could hear Moody walk into Passage 6.

***

The seniors had already left on the bus for a weekend pass. The choice of videos for that night was contentious, but they eventually settled on *The Blues Brothers*, *Apocalypse Now*, and *Stripes*.

***

It was a crisp but freezing morning at they rode their bicycles down to the gas chamber at the far end of the camp, near the ammunition depot. Cheeks were raw in the frigid air. CS Moran was already there, standing by his Ford Fiesta, smoking a cigarette in full NBC gear. On the roof of the car was a wooden box, covered in hazard markings.

The gas chamber was no more than an old boarded up red-brick building. The class parked their bikes to the side, and fell in facing the gas chamber door.

'We will test the integrity of our respirators, before going into the gas chamber.' Moran took his respirator, and checked that the gas filter was screwed fully home. He then drew it quickly over his head, then exhaled, shouting Gas! Gas! Gas!

'With the respirator in place over my face, I can check the integrity of the mask by blocking the air filter, and inhaling- like so.' With his palm over the front of the respirator, he inhaled, sucking the mask onto his face. He ordered the class to check theirs.

'Satisfied? Good. We will check them for real in a compound smoke atmosphere.' Moran could make a grocery list sound menacing.

'We will enter the gas chamber in groups of four, with our respirators secured in their pouch. I will introduce CS gas to the atmosphere and we will conduct our gas drills. Understood?'

'Yes, CS.'

'Cadet Condell,' he said, addressing the orderly sergeant, 'You will keep a roll of those who have completed.'

'Yes, CS,' he replied, clip board in hand. The first four walked into the gas chamber after Moran. Dickie checked his respirator, and placed it carefully in his respirator pouch. They stood at ease outside the chamber and waited.

Thirty seconds later, Black stumbled out, spluttering, drooling saliva, and dry retching.

'Condell!' Moran roared from the gas chamber, 'Black hasn't completed his drills, he will come back with the last group!'

'Yes, CS!' Shouted Condell, marking the nominal roll. Black was standing against the wall, scratching at his collar.

'Stop scratching yourself, Black,' Gavin intoned, maternally 'It'll only make it worse.'

'Fuck off, Gavin.' Black blurted.

The rest started to come out, one by one. Eyes flooded, faces contorted in pain, dripping thick, viscous phlegm. Those who had finished converged at the gable, exchanging experiences. Black waited, disconsolate, for his second appointment with Moran.

It took almost fifty minutes for Dickie's turn to come. He has in the last group, with Black. The chamber was unlit. The effect, as CS Moran closed the door, was to render them blind.

Moran took his cigarette lighter to a gas pellet, throwing yellow light on the walls. Though the gas pellet was only starting to smoke, the chamber was already thoroughly acrid with CS Gas. Moran, in full NBC kit, was very clear and precise through his respirator.

'The vapour is just developing, no one is to don their respirator until I give the order.'

'Yes, CS,' the four replied.

Dickie took a breath or two quickly, before the gas dispersed. Not too deeply; he could detect the irritation already. The dispersal was rapid. Dickie wondered how long Moran would let them linger in the gas. He could feel the gas begin to scrape at the surface of his eyeballs.

'Gas! Gas! Gas!' he shouted quite suddenly. Dickie opened his respirator pouch, and pulled it out by its back straps. He pulled it quickly over his head, and exhaled hard, shouting Gas, Gas, Gas. He could hear the others as they completed their first gas drill. So far, so good.

'Name, Cadet?'

'Cadet Hourigan, CS.'

'Test the air tightness of your respirator, Cadet.' Hourigan placed his hand over his filter and inhaled. His mask sucked inwards against his face.

'What is your home address, Cadet?' Hourigan recited. 'What is the cyclic rate of fire of the Gustav sub-machinegun?'

'Six hundred rounds per minute, CS.'

'What is the tracer burn-out range of the .50" HMG?'

'Eleven hundred metres, CS.'

'Name the normal types of ammunition for the 84mm recoilless rifle.'

'HE, HEAT, smoke, illumination and TPT, CS.'

'Very good, Cadet Hourigan,' and he moved on to interrogate the other three in their turn.

Black was beside Dickie on the right, second to be questioned, and got all correct. Dickie, and finally O'Leary, were questioned and passed. His interrogation complete, he returned his attention to Hourigan.

'Hourigan, remove your respirator. I am about to ask you some questions in a contaminated atmosphere.'

'Yes, CS,' he said, as he removed the mask and held it in his left hand.

'Open your eyes, Cadet.' Hourigan opened them to narrow slits.

'Number rank and name, Cadet.'

'Eight-four-oh-three- cough-cough-cough.'

'I didn't hear you, Cadet.'

Hourigan repeated his number, gasping.

'Your height in centimetres, Cadet?'

'One eight seven, CS.'

'That's very tall, isn't it, Cadet?'

'It is, CS.'

'Out you go, Hourigan.' The daylight was blinding as Hourigan staggered out, and the inky blackness was almost physical as the door closed again. 'Cadet Black, are you feeling better now?'

'Yes, CS.'

'Remove your respirator.' Black said nothing as he lifted it over his face. 'What does the military acronym METTS stand for, Cadet Black?'

'Mission, enemy, troops, terrain, space and time, CS.'

'Very good, Cadet Black. You're somewhat more collected this time, aren't you?'

'Yes, CS.'

'What does the acronym COCOA stand for?'

'Cover and concealment, obstacles, critical terrain, observation, avenues of approach.'

Black was gasping and whimpering at the same time.

'Outstanding, Cadet Black. There is nothing so painful as the anticipation of pain itself. Is there?'

'No, CS.'

'You allowed your fear of the gas overwhelm you the first time in the chamber, didn't you?'

'Yes, CS.'

'Not as bad when you've steeled yourself for it?'

'No, CS.' Black was bent forward, sobbing.

'Out you go, Black.' Black staggered to the door, fumbling to find the handle, then walked out, retching. 'Who's next?'

'Cadet Mandeville, CS.' Dickie concentrated on breathing as deeply as he could, saturating his lungs, to be able to breathe as little as possible.

'Remove your respirator, Cadet.' He inhaled hard and pulled the canister up and over his face. The effect wasn't immediate. Like a pinch of fine white pepper in the eyes and nasal lining. His sinuses began to fill with fluid immediately, and his eyes started to stream. In the throat, an intense itching sensation. He wanted to stick his fingernails in his mouth and scrape. He could feel his saliva thickening, and the muscles in his trachea contract. 'What is the magazine capacity of the Gustav sub-machinegun, Cadet?'

'Thirty-six rounds, CS.'

'Very good. How many mils are there in three hundred and sixty degrees?'

'Six thousand four hundred, CS.'

'In one hundred and eighty degrees?'

'Three thousand, two hundred, CS.'

'In two hundred and seventy degrees?'

Oh Jesus, thought Dickie, he couldn't remember, and was multiplying 1,600 by three in his head.

'Hurry up, Mandeville.'

'Four thousand…' His throat felt like he was pulling a string of fish hooks through it. He could feel the panic well inside as his lungs begged for air. '…eight hundred, CS.' Like all the others, he found himself pitching his torso forward, trying to curl up, hands involuntarily drawn up to his face, wanting to rub his eyes and itch his face and neck.

'You don't appear to be enjoying yourself, Mandeville?'

'No, CS.'

'Do you consider Compound Smoke to be an effective crowd control agent?'

'Yes, CS,' Dickie rasped. His hands clutched his throat as the noose inside it slowly constricted. He wondered how long more the CS would keep him here. He took a shallow puff of breath through his mouth. It squeezed his throat further.

'And would you use a CS grenade indoors, Cadet?'

'No, CS.'

'Not unless you intended to kill someone?'

'No, CS.' Dickie felt his chest start to spasm as he resisted taking another breath.

'Out you go, Mandeville.'

They congregated outside while the CS doffed his NBC gear and stowed it in a black bin-liner in his car.

'What's next on your program, Cadet Condell?'

'First Aid, Pearse Hall, CS.'

'Very well, carry on.' The CS lit a cigarette and watched them as they cycled off back up the Camp.

Dickie was glad of the chill air blowing over his combat uniform as they went, and like the others, he breathed as hard as he could, trying to rid hid lungs of the acrid tang of the gas. There was no change of dress. They'd have to stay in their contaminated combats until lunchtime. They marched to Pearse Hall, for an hour of Sgt Wendell on field dressings,

49

splints and stretchers beckoned. No one would fall asleep this morning. Their hands and faces burned with CS gas.

***

The seniors were on the final furlong now. A few GTs, the final class placings, corps and unit allocations. Socially, the (accompanied) pre-commissioning ball, and the (stag) pre-commissioning dinner were next on the calendar.

When he eventually phoned her, Mandy agreed to accompany him. They were released for a weekend pass that afternoon. He took a taxi to the rectory, picking Mandy and her little clutch bag up at seven. The reverend wasn't there. Her mother waved her off.

'You look stunning,' he told her truthfully in the taxi to the College.

'Thank you, Dickie. You look pretty dapper yourself,' she replied.

He didn't. Bow-tie with green uniform did not go.

'Where are you staying tonight?'

'The Keadeen.'

'Oh. Not in your little room?'

'We're not allowed stay there the night of the pre-comm. In case of nefarious goings-on. We're on pass.'

'I see,' Mandy said, non-committal.

She was the best looking girl there, and revelled in the attention. Working the room like a politician's wife, she said hello to everyone. Dickie caught Moody giving her a forensic once-over, before returning to his fiancée. Everybody loved Mandy by the end of the night.

They took a taxi to the Keadeen at two thirty.

'Are you coming in?'

She sat motionless for a moment, and then, without a word, followed Dickie into reception. He'd brought his key with him. There was no awkwardness with the night porter.

She went first into the room, turned on a small table lamp in the corner. She took Dickie by the hand over to the bed. They kissed, and she turned around, inviting Dickie to open the zip at the back of her dress. It fell away to the ground to reveal a strapless black bra and panties. He could see her clearly now, having only glimpsed shadows in his room before Christmas.

Afterwards, he lay spent on the bed, looking at her sleep. Her eyes opened, she turned towards him and smiled.

'I'm really tipsy!'

A surprise to him. She's barely had two glasses of white wine all evening. She leaned towards him and kissed him hard on the mouth, got out of the bed, and started to dress.

'I have to go. Didn't tell them I'd be in a hotel tonight.'

'Of course,' he blurted, and started to get up. 'I'll take you back...'

'Dickie, it's just a mile away. I'll get a local cab. Please.'

He sat transfixed, looking at her perfect form. She kissed him warmly on the cheek. She opened the door quietly, and was framed by the bright light in the hotel corridor. Her face was almost in silhouette, like the night in Trinity College.

'Bye, Dickie.'

If he'd known it was the last time he would ever see her, he would have begged her to stay just a moment longer, bathed in soft yellow light and dazzling. He drank in the smell of her, still on his face and chest, as she pulled the door quietly behind her.

A Religious Experience

'That's preposterous, Mandeville! You're bloody Protestant!' Lt Col McCarthy Gibson fulminated. 'Isn't there some rule forbidding you people from going?'

Dickie had been summoned to the Cadet Master's office to explain why he'd volunteered to go on the Military Pilgrimage to Lourdes. McCarthy Gibson saw no merit in the Pilgrimage from any perspective. There were rumours Scut Corrigan had propositioned a postulant nun at the grotto the previous year. He'd spotted the 21 year old Spaniard at the rear of the congregation, and made known his views on good-looking women dedicating themselves to celibacy. Though not fluent in English, she understood sufficiently to be offended. The subsequent investigation by the officer in charge yielded nothing actionable, but word got back to McCarthy Gibson.

Corrigan claimed the postulant was a dead ringer for Isabelle Adjani. He considered it immoral that any woman, other than the morbidly obese, or the hairy-knuckled Guinness-drinking lesbian variety, should be celibate.

'No, sir. In fact the Chaplain said all were welcome, not just the RC faith. And Reverend Kingston told me...'

'Stop! Stop! I don't want to hear it. It's bad enough eight more want to go. But they're bloody Catholics! They have an excuse!'

'Father Clarke said it was well attended by all denominations, sir.'

'You know you're coming straight home to the Glen? We'll have to lay on a special Exercise SCRATCH!'

'Sir, if you wish me to withdraw...'

'Oh shut up, Mandeville!' The RC Chaplain had told Dickie that the Head Chaplain had written personally to the Chief of Staff to ensure that Cadets would travel. Dickie knew that withdrawal of his name would reflect on McCarthy Gibson; his offer was a non-offer.

The Colonel dismissed him with a swat of his hand. Dickie saluted and marched from the office.

***

CS Moran strode out onto the square, in spotless SD1, a rifle tight by his side.

'You people may, like the cadets of the 37th Class, be fortunate enough to enjoy the assassination of a US President during your time here. You may even be so lucky that the newly single First Lady friskily requests your attendance at the funeral.' He paused theatrically.

'I wouldn't let you rabble attend the obsequies of a gravedigger's dog.'

Moran surveyed the ranks for a smile or smirk. Dickie bit the inside of his left cheek.

'It is unfortunate for you, for me, and the Defence Forces, that the syllabus requires you to learn funeral drill. We will spend days together on this square until you can perform it without dropping your rifle.'

He marched towards the centre of the company, and executed a right face towards them. It wasn't his style to stand a class at ease. They stood rigidly to attention for his demonstration.

'All funeral drill commences from the salute.'

Detest him they might but his drill was perfection. He executed the five distinct movements with robotic precision.

'Does everyone understand how to execute an *Aisiompaíg Airm*?'

'Yes, CS!' they shouted, clueless to a man.

The CS proceeded through the movements, which had found such favour with President Kennedy during his 1963 visit that his widow asked for it at his Arlington funeral. The rifle had changed from the Lee Enfield to the FN since then, but the drill was essentially the same. Moran gave the slow, arcing, vaguely Nazi salute of his right arm to the right, down to rest on the butt-plate of the rifle, followed them same salute to the left, and finally, with both palms rested on the butt, he lowered his head.

He lifted his head and scowled at the class. Behind him, four sheep had meandered past the guardroom on the right, and started to graze about the base of the flagpole.

'Loftus! If you find grazing ruminants attractive, save it until your next weekend pass.'

'Yes, CS.'

Moran, no longer the mannequin, paced up and down the ranks as they carried out the movements by parts. Time dragged interminably. The lessons were 45 or 60 minutes long, but felt like hours. Moran left them standing in the most painful, awkward position possible. He particularly enjoyed stopping them after the third movement, the rifle held at arm's length in front of their chests, while he checked they were vertical. Dickie's right bicep started to twitch involuntarily, causing the butt to shake.

'Cold, Cadet Mandeville?'

'No, CS.'

'Well stand still man!'

Gavin in the front row grimaced in pain, arms in spasm as his small frame held the rifle to his front. Everyone was leaning back a little to counterbalance the load.

Dickie's mind drifted up from Pearse Square, through the clouds, and into a café bar in Lourdes, a beautiful French girl sitting at his table. The burning in his forearms faded into the distance.

***

After a nine-man audience with OMG, during which he roared at them to wear the uniform with pride, the minibus took them and their luggage to Dublin Airport. There they met the wider travelling party, which included an FCA Pipe Band. There were thirty in the Irish party. They arrived in their hotel at 19:00 local time.

A DFHQ captain in charge of the travelling party took them to one side in the hotel before dinner. In what seemed a pretty aggressive briefing, he laid down the law as to what behaviour was expected, and he sketched out the ceremonies the cadets would be officially involved in. They had dinner with the travelling party in the hotel, and then ventured outside.

Lourdes was put under military law for the duration of the military pilgrimage. French MPs took no half measures. An unfortunate paralysed paratrooper was left helpless in his wheelchair some years before when they tear-gassed the bar he was drinking in.

The bars were full of soldiers of every European nation, and quite a few from the Americas. Spirits were high, aided by the fact that the bars sold beer in one-litre tankards known locally as *Formidables*. The French considered these a novelty, but for a town temporarily inhabited by 40,000 soldiers they were obligatory.

The town was a kaleidoscope of military uniforms, the French predominating. Austrians circulated in their ominous coal-scuttle helmets. Americans, their uniforms not as perceptible as their voices, were everywhere. The Italians had simply transferred the *passeggiatta* to the French town, the plumes on their caps identifying them from a distance. In another bar the cadets passed, a group of Liverpudlian Foreign Legionnaires was already drunk, and shouting loudly at any who paid them attention. A small knot of Norwegians stood outside a café, taking it all in with a bemused, dissenting look.

They walked on until they heard the unmistakable drone of the bagpipes. A large crowd had gathered outside a café by the river. A clutch of young women were gathered round, particularly fascinated by these Irishmen in skirts. The cadets broke the round up into three calls of three *formidables*.

Dickie shouted for *trois formidables* across the heaving bar, and pulled the little wad of fifty franc notes from his wallet. At the bureau de change in Dublin Airport they had devised the mantra 'divide by eight' to figure out the conversion rate. He hadn't a clue how many to offer the barman. He peeled a fifty off and handed it across. He received small change.

The pipers took a break. Clay went over to enquire who they were. From a Wexford unit, this was the first time they had taken their talents abroad. One was a farmer, the other a car dealer.

'Are you wearing jocks under those kilts?' Gavin asked. The two reservists looked at one another and started laughing.

'We were wearing them on the way over.' Said the farmer.

'But it was obvious we weren't expected to.' Said the car dealer. They were laughing by now.

'So we went to the toilet and fired the jocks in the bin!'

'Have to give the fans what they want!' The car dealer declared, as a young French soldier, in a khaki uniform that left not a single curve to the imagination, came over with two tulips of *Stella Artois*. In a heavily accented voice, she pronounced their music 'beautiful'. Neither of the pipers would grace the cover of Esquire magazine, but had just become the rock stars of the Irish party.

The pipers played a set of another ten minutes or so. There seemed to be a gathering group of French female soldiers in front of them. This had not gone unnoticed by Black. He was suddenly familiar with them. In charge, even. Dickie looked at him and wondered if all graduates of Gonzaga were as overbearing and smug. Some of the impressionable French soldiers were being taken in, especially as Black was converting what little he remembered of his school French into conversation. This was annoying, as the six French soldiers were all attractive, two of them stunningly so.

'*Vous êtes d'ou?*' one of the taller, more attractive brunettes asked Black.

'She says you're sweet,' Gavin quickly translated for him. Black fell for it, his chest swelling.

'*Et vous aussi.*' Black replied, to the puzzled French girl. Commons and Clay, started to belly-laugh, to Black's annoyance. After half an hour of ribbing, he stormed off in a huff.

The other French girls peeled away, leaving Julie and Catherine with Dickie and Gavin. Julie was the tall brunette, twenty-two and from Mulhouse. Dickie's French improved with every *formidable*, though he wasn't quite sure what he was saying.

Their friends eventually retrieved the two girls close to one am. Julie volunteered to Dickie that they were staying at the *Mediterranee*, and they left. He and Gavin joined the others, assembled by a group of American Airborne and Italian troops. One of the Americans was in full 'back in 'Nam' mode. Gavin decided to intervene.

'So when you guys are finished fighting, do you, like, parachute back out again?' He enquired, in the most beautiful Corkonian innocence. The American swivelled towards him with a baffled expression, minimally alert to the possibility he was the butt of the joke.

'No, son. Parachutes only work downwards.'

The cadets, and the Italians nodded sagely, with straight faces. The American was a pretty big lad.

The night wore on until Hackett pointed out they were on a guard of honour in the grotto in the morning. They wouldn't get five hours sleep. They headed back to the hotel. On the way, Dickie and Gavin took a detour to find the *Mediterranee*, to no avail.

***

The march to the grotto the next morning was uncomfortable. Dickie was trying to remember how many *formidables* he'd had. Was it four or five litres?

They formed up outside the hotel for the parade to the grotto at 08:00. The ceremony was held early in the morning because of the stifling temperatures in the enclosed arena. Participating in RC religious ceremonies was part of the gig when he signed on for the pilgrimage.

Neither the appearance nor the smell of the cadets appealed to the captain. He warned that no one was to faint in the grotto. Anyone feeling ill was to fall out to the right, and one of the other four was to march in and replace them.

An advantage to having a pipe band was that it cleared pedestrians from the route all the way to the Pyrenees. The downside was that nursing a hangover through bagpipes was like having a cat scrape its claws slowly along the inner lining of Dickie's skull. He ground his molars together and marched on.

The band fell silent as they entered the grotto. The captain chose his guard for the ceremony. Dickie and Clay to his left and right, Commons, Gavin and Black to the rear. He marched them into position in the grotto, and stood them easy for the start of the ceremony.

A French chaplain was leading the service, with occasional assistance from a Spanish and an Italian chaplain. Though not every line was getting a three-way translation, the ceremony was going to be considerably longer than Dickie had thought.

Clay was the first to waver. It started with a gentle forward and backward rocking. Dickie thought he was stretching his toes. So did the captain, until Clay took a forward pendulum that almost brought him on top of the steel barrier. The captain whispered 'fall out and fuck off.' Clay executed a competent right turn, and marched away. Butler quickly marched into position. Can't be too much longer, Dickie thought. Next came a strange, gurgling groan from behind, where Commons stood. Was he going to puke on the back of Dickie's uniform? He emitted a low moan, the early phase of a retch. The captain responded with a ventriloquist's growl, through pursed lips. Commons turned left. Nolan quickly stepped in. The ceremony droned on. The sun climbed higher. Dickie felt a bead of sweat onto the collar of his shirt. He'd been under pressure, but it was fading now. A few thousand pilgrims were before him, worshiping, praying, smiling, feeling the love. So this was what Catholicism was really about. His father had never told him. This was good. The crowd moved in front of him. Little stars of pink and yellow, and other, beautiful, indefinable colours started to flutter from the sky onto the heads of the faithful. Only McGuinness, standing in front of him with a fat, worried face, struck a discordant note.

Something deep in his subconscious told him to throw his left leg forward. He stopped just short of the crash barrier. He wobbled out of the grotto. McGuinness was already marching his way in.

'We're fucked, Dickie!' was all he could whisper as he passed him on the way towards the colour party.

Dickie looked at his watch. They'd only been in the grotto for ninety minutes. It felt like hours. He joined Commons and Clay, about a hundred yards away and out of sight of the colour party. Clay had recovered his pallor. Commons was Martian green. His cap was pushed back on his forehead. He hunkered down on the plaza and started to retch. A small group of nuns watched in concern. One of them approached Commons with a glass of water.

'Take this young man. It's water from the grotto. You'll feel better.'

'Fuck off, nun! Can't you see I'm puking?' Commons growled. The shocked nun skulked away.

***

The bottling session lasted a good twenty minutes. The captain had never seen anything like it in his life. Three of five of a guard of honour had passed out. It was a disgrace. Most of it went over their heads. They'd heard far worse in the Curragh. The threat to go to Captain Glennon was different, though. That would make life far more unpleasant on their return. If it didn't permanently foreshorten their cadetship. They resolved to take it easier that night.

The afternoon was devoted to taking some of the invalids in the pilgrimage party along the *Chemin de Croix des Maladies*. Pushing the wheelchairs up the incline was hard work, but four female UCD students, all very gentle on the eyeball, eased the load as they accompanied a group of invalids from Dublin. They agreed to meet later in the Irish hotel.

***

'These *formidables* are fucking lethal, guys.' McGuinness reasoned, before they hit the first bar.

'Shut up, Carl,' Clay replied.

'Just saying we'd be better off with something smaller than rounds of litre pints.'

'No such thing as a litre pint,' Gavin corrected him.

'Fuck off, Gav!'

They surveyed a few bars on the Rue de la Grotte.

'Sounds like the sort of place you'd pick up a bird, McGuinness!' Black chuckled, pleased with himself.

'And give her to you for sloppy seconds, Black.'

They found a small bar overlooking a square.

'Le Cardinal. This sounds pretty senior,' said Condell.

'Almost papal.' Morgan declared.

'Those guys are drinking out of smaller glasses,' said McGuinness. A group of Austrians drank Stella Artois from goblets.

'Anyone ever hear of *Stella Artois*?' asked Commons.

'You've been drinking it for two days.' Dickie reminded him.

'Can't be worse than Harp.' Clay said, and ordered a round of Stella, in smaller glasses.

The Austrians were agreeable company, not as austere as their nationality suggested, bordering on Irish, Dickie thought. They were about an hour in Austrian company, when a loud 'Ah Jaysus!' was heard from the square outside. About twenty British soldiers, led by a senior NCO and a lieutenant, entered the bar. The soldiers following behind looked a deal less comfortable than their leaders.

Lieutenant Mike Hardiman and Colour Sergeant Tom Byrnes were the only two Catholics in a group of soldiers from the Royal Irish Rangers, stationed in Germany with the British Army on the Rhine.

Neither knew Dickie's cousin, but the query was an ice-breaker. They settled in quickly amongst the Irish and the Austrians. It was clear the Royal Irish squaddies, all from East Belfast, had never been in the company of so many Catholics, still less in a Catholic Shrine on a military pilgrimage. As a relatively recent graduate of Sandhurst, the cadets were as eager to hear Hardiman's exploits as he was to share them.

'So the Sergeant Major told me I wasn't permitted to speak on the parade ground. I was to go over to Queen Victoria's statue and apologise to her. When he saw me going back to my room after speaking to Queen Vic, he roared at me to asking what I was up to. I told him I'd apologised to Queen Victoria, and she said "That's perfectly alright, young man. Take the rest of the day off!"'

Even some of the Austrians laughed at that one.

***

They had mastered the art of pacing themselves by the third night. Dickie and Gavin still hadn't found the *Mediterannee*, and Dickie was wondering if the place existed at all.

They found a heaving bar close to the river, and settled in. A group of Belgians were singing loudly. The place started to thin out early, though. Gavin enquired what was going on. One of the Belgians told him 'everyone is going to the Irish hotel,' as the pipers were topping the bill. They got back just short of eleven. There were already substantial numbers in the lobby. Of the young female French soldiers, there was no sign. However two of the UCD students, Rachel from Mullingar, and Helen from Limerick did appear with their charges in wheelchairs. The British platoon was already there. The colour sergeant, or 'Scarf' to his men, had just regaled the crowd with 'The Auld Triangle.'

It was standing room only. Dickie, Morgan and Gavin were wedged into a corner of the lobby, trying to find room to raise a glass to their lips. The Irish Chaplain sat cosily beside a French warrant officer, mid-forties, with a remarkable figure.

Clay finished a rousing version of 'Johnny Jump Up', when Scarf Byrne of the Royal Irish Rangers turned to a reservist captain from Cork, and put his arms around him.

'Jaysus, man, you can't beat the Irish for a song!'

'You're no Irishman,' the Corkman spat. 'You took an oath to the fucking Queen!'

The silence was palpable. The assorted Billies and Sammies of the Royal Irish placed their glasses down before defending their Scarf. An Austrian thrust a *formidable* high into the air and commenced a drinking song, and the moment passed. As Dickie turned back to Gavin and Morgan, he noticed the chaplain and warrant officer were gone.

***

Dickie and Gavin packed their bags silently on the last morning in Lourdes. If they returned to Ireland in time, they would commence Exercise SCRATCH that evening in the Glen.

As he put his few things into his bag and closed it, a red light, fading in the morning sunshine, caught his eye.

'Gav, look out there.'

Gavin went to the window a fresh Pyrenean breeze blowing in the curtains. A hundred yards away, its night time neon light still flickering, was the *Hotel Mediterranee*.

***

The travelling party went their separate ways at Dublin Airport. The cadets worked every ruse to delay return to the Curragh. They heard in the orderly room that two of the class were in hospital with injuries sustained during SCRATCH. They hung up their abused superfine uniforms, and got into combats. They brought their overalls as well, SCRATCH would be carried out in overalls to protect their combat uniforms.

The truck for the Glen of Imaal left Pearse Square at 17:30hrs. They could delay no longer. Their packs formed a pile in the centre of the floor. There was little talk. Rob McGuinness sat at the rear tailboard, smoking furiously.

The truck passed through Dunlavin. Ian Butler broke a long silence.

'I think we should say a decade of the rosary. You can join in if you want, Dickie.'

It was the first time Dickie had ever heard any of them propose prayer among themselves. He said the Lord's Prayer and mumbled his way through the rest. It took them as far as the Glen Lounge.

They got into Coolmoney Camp at 18:15. Their classmates were in a stupor, having carried out section-in-attack drills after completing SCRATCH. They got some forewarning of what lay ahead. The part that had done the injuries was leopard-crawling in the armoured car pool. The covering of muddy silt on the bottom of the pool held a layer of sharp granite pebbles. The pilgrims raided an empty billet, and stole a few of the heavy grey blankets.

They cut them into one-foot strips, which they could tape around their knees and elbows.

They went to bed listening to the agonised groans of classmates clutching hamstrings and

calves.

***

'Hands off cocks, on with socks!' Sgt Richards kicked the billet door in. It was 05:30hrs.

While the rest of the class went away for section-in-attack drills, the nine pilgrims would

carry out SCRATCH. They ate very little for breakfast. They drew their rifles from the

guardroom, and fell in before their billet. An enormous, gorilla-like captain who'd joined

the school staff while they were away introduced himself.

Captain Collins was six foot two, barrel-chested, and sported a Ranger tab on his combat

tunic. He spotted the bulging at the knees and elbows, but said nothing. Black took no

precautions. He figured the padding would slow him down.

'I don't know if you had a religious experience in Lourdes, but I can promise you that

you're going to have one now!' He faced them left, and doubled them into the woods.

There was no tactical element in SCRATCH. It was no more than a three-hour screwing

session. One completed it, or failed to complete it. It was a test of will, of mental and

physical endurance, with its own myths and legends over the years of inclusion in class

journals. It was a rite of passage, the beginning of the end of Stage I training. You're in the

army now, boy.

They doubled out of the northwest corner of the camp into fields of sedentary sheep.

Sergeant Richards and CS Moran joined them. The first section required them to fix

bayonets and stab straw-filled tunics to death. They doubled onwards to a section of

rutted track. They leopard-crawled it, doubling back over it each time they made it to the end. They ran on. Towards an innocuous looking ditch that Collins ordered them to vault.

Beyond lay a stagnant pool of reeds, rainwater and dung. Dickie and Clay exchanged a

momentary glance before Collins roared at them to continue. They jumped. Both tall, with

Clay the taller man, Dickie found himself up to his chin in the fetid liquid. After a moment

of panic, his feet found purchase on hard ground at the bottom, and he pushed forward. It

resisted like quicksand. Behind them, Gavin didn't even look before leaping, and vanished

below the surface, Dickie and Clay put their arms back into the mire and found his

shoulders. They pulled him out. He was already too exhausted to care. Black, following

close behind, flinched at the disappearance of Gavin. In mid-air he threw his rifle to one

side. Collins screamed at him as the rifle started to bubble and disappear below the

surface. Morgan spotted it and got a hand to the muzzle.

As the nine gathered beyond this water hazard, Collins walked menacingly towards Black,

and grabbed his rifle.

'This rifle has a serial number stamped on it Cadet. It has value. You don't. This rifle has

served the army for more than twenty years. You look fucked already. Do you want to fall

out?'

'No, sir!'

'Are you sure, Cadet? You look tired.'

'I'm not, sir!'

Collins didn't wait on the reply. His finger pointed the route for them to follow. He was

running at three-quarter pace down to the river. Gobs of mud and dung started to fall

from their overalls. Dickie felt the strips of blanket loosen slightly, but they stayed in place.

They reached the river at a point at the far west of the camp. They crossed the river a few

times, the clean mountain water a cooling relief. They realised they were heading down to

the armoured car pool. A concrete-walled pool about forty yards square, it could be flooded to fashion a four-foot deep pool where armoured car drivers could practice water manoeuvring.

They could see the ragged trails left by their comrades the day before. Collins stood at one end and told them to leopard crawl towards him. Morgan, Clay and Commons made the far end of the pool first. As the other six pilgrims crawled towards them, they held their rifles aloft, doubling on the spot, shouting 'Hurry up! Hurry up! For fuck sake hurry up!'

Once all nine gathered at the end of the pool, they went back to the far wall and did it again. Black emitted a strange, high-pitched shriek as he fell to his knees. Dickie felt the woollen protector on his left knee slip, and the bite as gravel penetrated his overalls. The instructors screamed at them to keep their weapons out of the mud, but Dickie's rifle, like the rest of them, was but the rough outline of an FN.

Leopard crawling looked so easy when you were standing up. They were no longer crawling smoothly. It was left knee, right elbow, and splat. Right knee, left elbow, splat. CS Moran was banging loudly on the helmets of the nine with his cane.

Collins shouted 'UP!' and they doubled back up the hill. Ahead they could see another tree line. Another soprano cry from Black, he started retching.

'Tastes batter on the way down, Cadet!' Collins roared at him.

'Yes, sir!' Black mumbled.

The rest kept up their running on the spot, 'Hurry up! Hurry up! For fuck sake hurry up!'

'Hurry up! Hurry up! For fuck sake hurry up!' Black was taking his fucking time wiping his mouth too, Dickie thought.

The sodden trudge started again. They got to the tree line. They might have been two hours on the go, or 45 minutes. He had no idea. He saw where Collins was headed, though. There was another deep ditch ahead, cut up from the exertions of the rest of the class yesterday. It was about ten feet across, and forty yards long. Clay, the tallest, reached it first. Dickie was alarmed to see most of him disappear into the ooze. He couldn't decide if it was best to follow directly in Clay's path, or if the ooze would be firmer to the left or right of Clay's trail. He decided on the former. Wrong decision.

It must have rained the previous night. The mud was viscous like cold treacle. The bottom wasn't firm. Dickie tried to crawl, but there was nothing below on which to gain purchase. His elbows and knees simply moved backwards. It was more treading water than leopard crawling. Somehow Clay was making progress.

Moran's bayonet clanged off the top of his helmet. He figured out what Clay was up to. He was sticking one toe down into the bottom and pushing forward, followed by the next. More a climb than a crawl, but it started to work for Dickie.

It was such a short stretch of ditch that, nose to tail, they occupied almost half of it. Behind him, attention had shifted to Gavin. Gavin had crawled into the ooze, and was entirely covered bar the muzzle of his rifle. He was making no effort to emerge after ten or fifteen seconds. He seemed to be trying to crawl along the bottom. Collins and Sergeant Richards reached into the mire and grabbed his shoulders.

'Army number, Cadet?' Collins shouted in his face.

Gavin mumbled a response, eyes in a fixed stare ahead.

'What's your army number, Cadet?'

Nothing.

'Take him to the MAP.' Collins said to Richards. The sergeant started to walk Gavin back to the camp. Eight pilgrims left.

It took them an eternity to reach the end of the ditch. They had to double on the spot as Black dragged himself to the end. Collins brought them back to the start of the ditch again. Dickie's heart sank. Captain Bohan had joined the party, jogging down from the camp to replace Sergeant Richards. Clay entered the mire again. Dickie kept as far to the left as he could, and found the going easier. Towards the back, Black was whimpering. The tail of the line was not a place to be. The instructors concentrated on those in the rear.

68

'There's no point getting in there, Black. You'll kill yourself.' Bohan said, feigning concern.

Black got into the mud, and started to flail uselessly.

'Come on, Black. Nice ambulance on the road. Fresh water. Warm blankets.' Bohan continued. Black started to cry. Bohan, a teak-tough hurler from Tipperary, was as far removed from Black and his affected, Gonzaga, South County Dublin, Camel-smoking, self-regarding ways as could be. He despised him, and success was within his grasp.

'Had enough Black, haven't you?'

'Yes, sir!' Black simpered, and Bohan nodded through the trees for him to leave the exercise. They finally made it to the end of the ditch. Collins doubled them towards the camp. It was over.

It wasn't. Collins doubled them past the cookhouse. He ran past the bayonet dummies. Towards the deep ditch. They were doing the whole circuit again. Dickie felt panic rise in him. He put one foot in front of the other, but didn't seem able to run. Everything was laboured.

They jumped into the muddy pool, exiting as quickly as they could. They didn't run straight to the river. Collins lay them down in a line. They had to leopard crawl a hundred yards towards him. Each thrust of a limb required mental as well as physical effort. Like a baby learning to walk, he had to think of which body part to move next. He looked at McGuinness, whose face was deathly pale, and eyes wide. Collins spotted it too.

'What's your army number, Cadet?'

'Cadet McGuinness R, sir.'

'What's your *army number*, Cadet?' Collins repeated, roaring.

'Cadet McGuinness R, sir.'

'Back to camp, McGuinness!'

Initially McGuinness didn't move. Collins nodded to CS Moran, who turned McGuinness bodily and walked him back to the camp, opening his overalls to the cool air.

The six remaining pilgrims made their way towards the armoured car pool, resigned to their fate as condemned men.

Collins lined them abreast at the end of the pool. They started to crawl. Dickie was no longer crawling, just flailing about. The gravel bit into his injured left knee again and he flinched.

'Stand up, Mandeville!' Bohan roared at him. Dickie slowly got to his feet. Bohan and Collins looked at his legs. Dickie looked down and saw a hole in the boiler suit on his left knee. His woollen protectors rested uselessly on the tops of his boots. Blood oozed out of his knee.

'Stand up the rest of you!' Bohan shouted, staccato.

They shuffled upright. Morgan and Nolan were also bleeding.

'*Ar sodar!*' Bohan ordered, and they doubled back up towards the lines.

He stopped them outside their billet.

'Get cleaned up. Mandeville, Nolan, Morgan, go to the MAP for dressings. Tactical training starts at 14:00 hours!'

Exercise SCRATCH was over.

***

The officers and Sergeant Richards doubled away. They shuffled into the billet. It was done. The six of them had completed SCRATCH. All 26 of the rest of the class had finished, but five days of debauchery in Lourdes had taken its toll on the pilgrims.

Dickie wanted to run naked over to the shower block and clean himself, but they had to be covered at all times. He pulled on track-suit legs and a vest, took a towel, and carried all his gear, rifle and all, into the shower block.

'What are you doing, Dickie?' Morgan was already under the hot water when he saw Dickie bring in his rifle.

'No fucking point in doing anything else!' he replied, and threw everything in a pile below the shower head.

Morgan jammed his index finger against nose and evacuated the right nostril. A pellet of sheep dung shot out into the gulley.

Dickie rolled everything under the warm water, starting with the rifle. The steel and wood emerged quickly as the grime fell away. He showered the helmet, boots and overalls, finally himself. He allowed the hot water into his mouth. He still had the rancid tang of sheep shit inside his cheeks.

He got into combats and went to the MAP. Nolan was having an elbow patched.

'Don't want to do that again.' Dickie said.

'Try doing the fucking thing twice!' Nolan, the honours student, laughed back.

***

His recce patrol left the base camp at 03:00. He was to recce a forest junction for a fighting patrol later that day. He followed the phosphorescent spots in Healy's footprints in the boggy ground. He never knew that boggy soil glowed like that until this very night. They found the objective at 05:00. His OP was set up by 05:30. Dickie took Pond's silence as a tacit endorsement. Nothing much happened. He had to sketch the junction, and bring back a brief to a fighting patrol.

From the valley below, the whine of a forage harvester drifted up. The smell of diesel and freshly cut silage reached his nose. The sounds and smells of summer on the farm, where his father and big brother worked on without him. He looked at the map. He was less than 20km from home as the crow flies. Perhaps his father was cutting silage this morning.

Dickie lay in his shell-scrape in the dark. Cold, hungry, he wondered how he was going to stay awake until he woke Clarke for the next watch. It was three am. Sun-up in less than two hours, but it wouldn't brighten inside the forest for four. There was one patrol out, not due back for an hour. Brown was DS for the night. Dickie fingered the plastic on his ration issue packet of 'Biscuits Brown.' Hungry as he was, he didn't want to eat them, as he had no water left. He longed for the relative luxury of a 'Biscuit Brown AB', not much of a greater comfort than its plain brown cousin, but sweeter, with the occasional raisin.

How to stay awake and not eat a biscuit? He didn't know what 'AB' stood for, so tried to think of as many solutions as possible.

Absolute Bollox. All Bad. No. Absolutely Badger. This was hard. He recalled that a sign of genius was to come up with fifty alternative uses for a coat-hanger or something like that. Acute Botulism. Yes, better. Actually Bovine. Arse Beetle. Was that a dozen? He couldn't remember. Amoeba Burp. Anus Belch. Definitely. Alcohol Better. Attractive Beaver. Aureola Breast. Yum.

***

Mandy Kingston's fragrant breasts smothered his face. He tugged urgently at her panties. She giggled. She kissed him hard and long, biting his lower lip. His right hand wandered down her crotch into wondrous warmth.

He felt an immediate throb in his pants as cold earth beneath the poncho resisted his erection. He rolled to his left to relieve the pressure.

'Ah, Butler, you awake?' It was Brown, he'd crept up from Dickie's right.

'It's Mandeville sir, Butler's finished watch.'

'Why didn't you challenge me, Mandeville?'

'You were inside the perimeter, sir.'

'Could've been the enemy. Crept inside the perimeter. Have a MAG now inside the patrol base. One belt of 7.62. Kill everybody.'

Dickie marvelled at Brown's English, wondering what hedge school in Ballygobackwards had produced someone with no personal pronouns.

'Sir, you were inside the perimeter.'

'Shut up, Mandeville,' Brown grunted, then walked off along the path to Dickie's left.

The rest of his watch passed uneventfully. He heard the patrol come back through the ten o'clock position. Tired bodies made their way back to shell scrapes to get some sleep. Foster was coming back to Dickie's shell scrape. Would this fucking watch never end...

Condell relieved him, ten minutes late. Dickie was about to shake him awake when he heard him scraping along the perimeter. Keen to get a full handover, arcs of fire, and all that bollocks, Dickie told him to fuck off, gave him the password, and went to his shell scrape. If he wanted the full Military Monty, he should have been on time.

Foster was already unconscious beneath the poncho. Exhaustion sucked at Dickie's body. He knew he'd be asleep in seconds. Or so he thought. Foster gave the first shudder. Dickie thought he was masturbating, and admired his energy. But the shudders were violent, and shook his whole body.

'Henry, what's up?'

Nothing. He rolled to the left, nudging Foster in the shoulder.

'Henry, you Okay?'

'Ggggrand. Bit cold. Fell in river. Ss Ss Sleepin'...' Foster rolled away and went back to sleep. But the shaking continued, more violently. He wondered if Foster was having some sort of seizure. His body contorted in spasms. Then the groaning started, a rhythmic 'nnn...nnn...nnn...' that matched the twisting of his body.

'Henry!'

Silence, broken by the soft recurring 'nnn...nnn...nnn...'

'Henry! You've hypothermia!' He kneed Foster in the back.

'Fuck off! I'm slee...' Foster was incoherent. The spasms continued like an epileptic fit. A tiny part of Dickie was concerned that Foster was ill. Mostly, he wanted to sleep. He waited another few minutes. The spasms deepened and came closer together. Dickie got out of his sleeping bag, and started to drag Foster out of the shell scrape. Foster got an arm free and took a swing at him.

'Leave me alone!' he pleaded, just as Corporal Curtin came down the track.

'What's goin' on?'

'I think Cadet Foster has hypothermia. He's shaking.'

Curtin grabbed Foster by the epaulettes of his combat jacket.

'Foster! Count back from a hundred in sevens!'

'Ninety three!' Foster whispered with great conviction. Then stopped, body going into another spasm. 'Eighty two!'

'You're fucked, Foster! I'm taking you outta here!' He turned on his torch, illuminating Foster with its red-filtered glow. 'Mandeville- pack him up!'

'No Corporal, I'm fine!' Foster pleaded, as it dawned on him he wouldn't finish EX AUGHAVANAGH.

Curtin went to alert Lieutenant Brown as Dickie rolled up Foster's sleeping bag.

'You prick, Mandeville! I'm Okay!'

'No you're not, Henry. You're fucked.'

Foster struggled to close the straps on his webbing. Dickie was glad- he would have been pissed off if there was nothing really wrong with Foster.

Brown arrived on the scene. He harrumphed meaninglessly as the Corporal escorted Foster out of the base camp, and down to where the emergency Land Rover awaited. Dickie could hear the crackle of twigs as they walked away. A midge buzzed about inside the shelter. He couldn't care less. With one deep breath, he was asleep.

***

Black's fighting patrol O-Group took place on a ditch-line behind their dig-in position near the River Slaney. It was the third day of the dig-in. Tonight would be the last patrols, tomorrow they would fill in the trenches and head back to camp. It had rained solidly for three days. Some of the trenches had inches of water in them. A dozen soldiers from the 3rd Battalion, who were supplying manpower for the exercise, had already gone sick. Dickie looked at his hands. The soil and grit of the Glen was by now buried deep in his epidermis, like a tattoo.

Moody was the DS for this patrol. He sat on the ditch in expensive Helly Hansen rain gear, cupping a cigarette. Black fidgeted nervously about his model, a poncho held down at the corners with large rocks. His blue chalk line representing the Slaney was already fading to a small blue puddle in the rainfall. Everyone knew he was under pressure for this, his set-piece leadership role in the first Glen. His section-in-attack had been comical, his overall performance suspect. No interaction with a DS seemed to pass without negative comment. It was unfair in a way. He made a slip here, an error there, and soon he was under the microscope by every DS during every exercise. Unfair or not, this was his for redemption.

He began. Black went into detail on every single phase of his patrol. Too much detail. Start to finish, he took fifty minutes to give his orders.

'Final rehearsal 21:30 hours here. H-Hour 22:00 hours. Questions?

It was Moody's turn. Moody was the fairest of the DSs. He didn't stick the boot into Black in previous exercises, even when he should have.

'First thing, Black: when you're delivering an O-Group in a monsoon, you don't use a chalk diagram. Use stones and wood. Our position is on elevated ground. We can see it two clicks away. Your route out is almost the same as your route back. You better hope the enemy doesn't decide to ambush you. You've given yourself the easy river crossing on the way out, and the hard one on the way back. Let me know if you want to do any revisions to your orders when you do your rehearsals.'

He got up, and walked away. Black's fighting patrol looked at him; a picture of misery and defeat before they'd moved a foot.

***

The patrol was worse than his orders. Moody was about to cancel the exercise at the point where they crossed the River Slaney. Black missed his fording point. They had to traverse a torrent of ice-cold mountain water, still within a kilometre of their own position. The assault was a comedy of errors. There was an inevitable ambush on the way back. Moody, to be fair, had warned him to change his orders. They got another drenching in the Slaney coming back at 02:30. Dickie got into a damp sleeping bag for an hour in his trench, and tried to coax blood flow back to his feet.

Black was officially in-the-shit.

***

The Kingston's phone answered on the third ring. With no seniors in the Cadets' Mess, the only obstacle to the phone was Toby and his interminable girlfriend. Mandy's mother answered.

'Hello, Mrs Kingston, Dickie Mandeville here, is Mandy there?'

'Dickie, no. She didn't tell you? She's gone inter-railing with her friends for the summer. She's transferring to the University of Edinburgh in September.'

'Oh.'

'Shall I tell her you called?'

'...Yes. Please.'

***

The NBC training started after their return from the Glen. Instruction was divided between Smoothy Moody, who did the academics, and CS Moran, who did the practical. As both had completed NBC warfare instruction courses in the UK, the module was covered in particular detail. Officially, this was about survival in a contaminated battle-field. Unofficially, it was hell. Every hour in full NBC gear was as tough as four hours in standard combat gear.

Smoothy was a science graduate. He went into detail on the neurological effects of nerve agents on the body. He explained every facet of the effects of blood, choking, nerve and blister agents on the human system. He described how to self-diagnose if attacked. The nuclear warfare section explained the science of killing people on population-level scales. Moran majored on the practical measures to counter nuclear, biological and chemical weapons. Central to everything was the 'Chemical Safety Rule.' Moran repeated it in his John Wayne drawl as they formed a circle around him in with their full kit in the Drill Shed.

'IF you experience BOMBARDMENT of any kind,

SIGHT hostile or unknown low-flying aircraft,

SEE suspicious mist, smoke, droplets or splashes,

SMELL anything unusual,

NOTICE symptoms in yourself or others such as dimness of vision; irritation of the eyes;

sudden headaches; tightness of the chest; running nose or intense salivation,

Or HEAR the alarm,

ASSUME it is a chemical attack,

And carry out the CHEMICAL IMMEDIATE ACTION DRILL.'

Which was the army way of saying 'put on your respirator.'

Freddie Lane figured the IA Drill justified staying permanently in a respirator when on exercise. Paddy Doyle reckoned the smell from the Passage 6 latrines meant he'd been under sustained chemical bombardment every day since they arrived in the Curragh.

***

There was a change of School Commandant in the summer. The class bade farewell to Lt Col McCarthy Gibson. His departure prior to taking a battalion to Lebanon was welcomed by all. There was a stand-down parade on a Thursday afternoon and OMG was gone. 'Oh my God, he's gone' became a catchphrase for a few weeks.

His replacement, Lt Col Terry Quinn, was a different character. Soft-spoken, punctilious, and pleasant. A single man, his reputation preceded him. He was a Congo veteran, whose company had suffered the humiliation of a surrender after a prolonged siege. Not before they had despatched several hundred Katanganese rebels and Belgian mercenaries and wounded a thousand more.

The End of the Beginning

There best thing about moving down to the Cadets' Mess was that the dreaded rifles were gone. Tactical training was finished, and in any case the Mess wasn't centrally heated, so there were no large cast-iron radiators to chain an FN rifle to. Morning parade was in uniform only, Saturdays included. The downsides were that they slept two to a room, and had to heat the place with turf fires. Dickie was roomed with Bosh.

The place was enormous, with a multitude of rooms and annexes that required cleaning for Saturday mornings. They looked forward to the arrival of the juniors in a few weeks to take care of that.

***

'Healy! You're a completely useless cock-wank, you know that?'

They could hear the fight upstairs. Worse was the fact it was Dickson, the quietest man in the class doing the shouting. It was an emergency rehearsal of their history syndicate on the Battle of Kursk. The other three had spent their hours in the library, finished their OHP slides, written their scripts, and learned by rote. Healy had done no work on his section, an analysis of the strengths and weaknesses of the opposing Russian and German main battle tanks. What little he knew was consigned to a few A4 pages of his illegible cursive.

It was pantomime of the purest quality. Foster had gathered a small crowd outside the library door, doubled over in suppressed laughter. Dickie came downstairs to check the commotion.

'The Panther ran on petrol, the T34 ran on diesel!' Nolan was roaring. 'I know that and I'm not even covering the tanks! And it's the Battle of KURSK, not fucking KRUTSK! Stop fucking saying that!'

Foster fell forward laughing, banging his head into the door. Healy came out, head flushed.

'Fuck off back to your rooms! Leave us alone!'

The other three members looked balefully out the door. This syndicate was a millstone taking them down.

***

It wasn't that they were smug following the end of the second Glen; more a feeling that the worst was behind them. They were on the home stretch. A certain worldly wisdom infused the class. Out there in the world, the Army was interviewing the next batch. Soon they would be the senior class.

Perhaps this was on Moody's mind as he took the first class PT after the second Glen.

They headed for the tank tracks, at a good pace. At Donnelly's Hollow, they did push-ups, sit-ups and burpees. Moody did three sets of repetitions, before taking them to the tracks. The tracks were tough at the best of times, but after three reps of burpees, the quadriceps started to burn. At first the class did a small circuit that took them up and down a series of tracks. Then Moody doubled them to the highest track.

'Pair off! Piggy back!' he ordered, and the class dutifully paired off with Cadets their same size. All thirty-two were on PT, sixteen pairs set off up the track. Dickie carried Black up the track first, then down the far side. The exertion on the way up was bad, but the way down was harder. Each step down was a standing squat, with a dead-weight Cadet on the back. Black snorted in his ear as Dickie slogged his way down the slope.

'Change round!' Moody ordered from the top of the track, and Dickie hopped up on Black.

'Jesus Christ Mandeville, you're a fat bastard!' Black spat as he trudged up the track. Black huffed and puffed theatrically as he picked his way down the far side.

'Change round!' came the order from the top of the hill. Dickie set off up again. He could feel the lactic acid burn. Black grunted and exhaled as Dickie bounced him upwards. He sounded ill.

'Don't puke in my ear, Black!' Dickie hissed.

'Fuck off, Mandeville' Black groaned back at him.

'Quiet down there!' Shouted Moody.

They changed round again. Black was making slow headway back up the track when Moody rounded on him.

'You're not very happy, Black'.

'No, sir.'

'Perhaps you should head back to the lines, throw in the towel?'

'No, sir.'

'Well get up that fucking hill, Black!'

'Yes, sir!'

Black started upwards, slowly picking his footfalls on the track. They reached the top of the hill and went down the far side.

'And again!' Moody roared from the top of the hill. Black was silent as he got up on Dickie's back. Dickie wondered if it would a fourth time. His leg muscles were screaming. As he crested the hill, he his legs started to spasm.

'Move it, quickly, come on!' Moody was waving them up the hill. Black managed four or five steps up the hill and started throwing up. He released Dickie's legs, and fell. Dickie slid to the ground, and started to walk solo up the hill.

'What do you think you're doing Mandeville?'

'Continuing, sir.'

'Wait till Black finishes his lunch, then get back up on him.'

'Yes, sir.' Dickie looked over at Black. He stood, hands on knees, purging the bottom of his stomach. Dickie climbed up on him again to complete their torture.

They reformed at the bottom of the hill, Moody ordered them into three ranks, and they were heading back. He directed them down the road to the racecourse. They approached the crossroads. Left back to barracks; right, to the graveyard; straight-ahead, to the racecourse. The trick, Dickie knew, was never to slow down coming to an intersection. Never anticipate the command to turn for home, or it would not come. Dickie looked up the file, and saw that Mick Healy was front and left. He was lengthening his stride slightly, increasing the speed. Good man Healy! Dickie thought- fuck you Moody, I'm still up for it! I'm taking you all the way to the fucking racecourse unless you turn us now. Fuck you!

'*Clé chasaigh!*' Moody shouted from the back, and Healy wheeled them left, towards the football pitches and home. Moody started some sprints as the road entered the wood, rear file sprinting to the front. Whether it was the bonhomie in Moody's voice or the smirk on his face, Dickie felt uneasy. Condell and Gavin were relaxing, arms dropping, as they passed the guardroom. Moody ran past Condell who was front and right.

'On me now!' he shouted, and strode out. His pace was nearly a sprint. Condell almost fell. Gavin let out a whine. Moody didn't hear it, he had turned left on McDonagh Terrace, and was heading back out on the same circuit again.

Moody's legs weren't tired from the tank tracks. Condell started to fall back, Dickie couldn't believe he was outlasting Condell. He was staring aimlessly into the trees. To Dickie's right, Black uttered a simpering sob. He fell out from the back and started dry retching at the side of the road, nothing but clear spittle trailing from his mouth.

Moody was about twenty yards in front, and turned around.

'Leave him!' he shouted as Morgan tried to pull Black along. Moody swung left to the rugby club, past the obstacle course, and across the field up to the Cadets' Mess. They slowed to the double, and reformed ranks. Moody dropped to the rear again.

'If you intend to be officers, you have to be able to command. You have to lead. You have to be fit to lead.' He didn't wait for Black to catch up.

Moody wheeled them back to the lines. He turned his back and trotted down to the Officers' Mess before Hourigan could call the class to attention.

***

There was no let-up in the Saturday inspections, either. Moody and Brown went through the rooms and passages with a toothcomb. The first weekend pass after the second Glen saw only twenty get to Dublin. Dickie joined eleven others, looking forlornly as the bus pulled away from Pearse Square. Fuck it. They'd watch a few vids and have a gunge-up in the mess tonight.

***

Black, and Gander from Passage 7, were ordered to Glennon's office on Monday afternoon. The class had finished lectures and were on the way to the cookhouse when they reappeared from the admin block. Bosh shouted to Black from the veranda.

'Is it good news for you, or good news for us?'

There was no response.

Gander would join the junior class. Black was discharged. 32 had become 30.

***

Thursday afternoon arrived with a new matinee buzz. Healy's syndicate were presenting the Battle of Kursk in Murphy Hall. The whole class, other than the syndicate, had been looking forward to this one. Past the half-way stage, every exercise, task and appearance was a performance to be marked and graded for class placing.

Kennedy's group played Elgar in their presentation on Verdun. Bosh's group had chanced showing a slice of *The Battle of Algiers* using a College projector of dubious reliability.

The Cecil B DeMille theatrics required of each group in the presentation of the syndicate opus was one thing, but the Kursk group were in costume. They wore Equitation School cream roll-neck sweaters, together with jodhpurs, and riding boots they had purloined from CQ Bailey. Healy insisted the class remain fallen in outside Murphy Hall while they awaited Moody.

Moody looked bemused as he approached, expecting to be last in. Instead, Nolan saluted him and showed him inside. The rest of the class were then admitted, the four members of the syndicate screaming at them, in an attempt to channel the treatment of the Soviet conscript by the NKVD police battalions. O'Leary enjoyed the pathological shouting, whacking a riding crop wildly. Dickson looked uneasy. From his embarrassed mug, Nolan was clearly the originator of the spectacle.

Nolan started off, setting the scene, the retreat from Stalingrad, the political situation, Von Manstein's strategy for *Citadel*, and Army Group South. Dickson had been given the heavy lifting, comparison of overall strengths, and the Soviet defensive strategy. They were about an hour and a half into the great Syndicate of Kursk. Healy stood up, third man. Healy was just going to talk about relative tank capabilities and strengths. Damage limitation.

His three teammates stood conspicuously about the stage, ready to reveal or occlude visual aids.

Healy clung manically to his A4 notes. These he occasionally shuffled, causing his teammates alarm. A brown moth fluttered onto the OHP as Healy described the relative tank strengths prior to battle. Healy swatted it away with his notes. A snigger from the class startled Dickie from an embryonic snooze. Healy turned off the OHP, the moth disappeared. Dickson and Nolan manned boards with exploded diagrams of the Tiger and Panther tanks. Healy explained the technological advances in the latter, and why the Germans were happy to wait for them at the front. He expounded on transmissions, turrets, armour, fuel tanks and main guns. The cracks began to show. Nolan pointed to the main gun on the Panther. Healy, glued to his notes, referred to the '88mm main armament' and turned around to see Dickson with his pointer at rest, and Nolan indicating the Panther.

'No, no, the 88mm gun is on the Tiger!' he blurted, as Nolan lowered his arm and Dickson quickly raised his to the Tiger. Magicians they weren't. O'Leary stood in concentration on the opposite side of the stage, before a T34 diagram. The spotlights and projectors warmed the room and the audience. A bead of sweat rolled down O'Leary's cheek.

Long pauses followed as Healy flailed through his A4 sheets. Moody tapped a biro loudly on his notebook at the back. Healy shouted directions at teammates unable to predict which stage-aid he would indicate next. He moved onto the manoeuvre tactics of Von Manstein and Model, Zhukov and Rokossovssky. This was the cue to O'Leary to turn on the epidiascope, throwing photos of the Generals onto the screen. Nolan turned off the auditorium lights. While the OHP bathed the speaker in light, the epidiascope emitted little. Healy tried to read his notes in the sliver of light from where the history book was inserted. Bent over, trying to read his notes along a narrow beam, Healy gave up and returned to the lectern's reading light. He recovered his composure as he regained his position in the script. Dickie saw the moth flutter down from the ceiling. It corkscrewed its way towards the light, and landed on the projected page. It walked slowly onto Field Marshal Model's chest. There it halted next to his Iron Cross. O'Leary, Dickson and Nolan stood, backs to the screen, oblivious to the pantomime projected behind them. The sniggering started again. Healy grew testy, and fidgeted with his notes.

Healy was twenty minutes in at this point, and might have survived, had the moth not decided to fly closer to the light. Ignorant of the thermal qualities of the epidiascope, it fluttered upwards, landing on the scorching lens below the lamp. Sticking instantly to the glass, its innards boiled. In a silent act of lepidopteral *seppuku,* its abdomen burst. The grunts of laughter were audible from the class. Tears formed in Dickie's eyes. Healy struck on grimly. Nolan, Dickson and O'Leary, convinced the class were laughing at Healy, misread Foster's frantic pointing at the epidiascope. Foster pointed instead at the screen. Nolan turned around in time to watch, horrified, as the moth's torso crenelated and its wings shrivelled up, burning to a crisp in a wisp of smoke.

O'Leary whipped the history book from the epidiascope, but the moth was stuck to the lens, not the page. Moody stood up loudly.

'*Áth-dhéanamh, Dalta*!' he roared in Healy's direction. Moody didn't normally break into Irish. The class sprang to attention. Though he sounded livid, Moody too was suppressing laughter. He knew better than to look back as he marched out of Murphy Hall. The Cadet audience burst into uncontrolled hysterics.

O'Leary broke from his position by the epidiascope and went for Healy.

'You stupid fucking wanker, Healy,' he shouted, grabbing him by the sweater. Nolan stepped in and pushed them apart.

'Fuck you, O'Leary,' Healy shouted back, and the two squared off. Dickson crouched down at the rear, disconsolate. Morgan, the company orderly sergeant, bellowed them to fall in outside. No one was sure what they'd do for the next hour, which was still programmed for the syndicate.

Foster shouted back at a resigned Healy. 'Mick! Pure class! First there was *The Terminator!* Now there's *The Incinerator!*'

***

The appearance of the nominal roll for the new class was a memorable day. The juniors would arrive tomorrow. Adding to the general mirth, there was a 'Cadet Bond' among them, to whose army number some humourist had given the last three digits '007.'

Hours of fun for the poor bastard, Dickie thought, the NCOs would be planning them now.

'Would you like your tea shaken or stirred, Cadet Bond?'

'Any chance of an Odd Job, Cadet?'

'To you, Cadet, she's a Bond-girl. To me, she's a sheep.'

Oh yes, there would be hours of fun.

***

There was a spring in the step as the class marched up to check-parade, the first for the juniors. Toby and the School Orderly had an early start. A light mist rolled across the Camp, making the turf smoke moist on the face. As they entered the inner square, they could see the ghostly line of mufti-clad juniors shaking under the dim lighting of the veranda. Toby was bollocking them in his gutless, perfunctory way.

'You shave this morning, Cadet?'

'No, Cadet.'

'Why not?' he snarled.

'I'm a... female, Cadet.'

***

The next interesting nugget Toby brought them concerned fatigue details. Captain Bohan had concluded that skivvie details were not part of the military syllabus. Details for the junior class would be minimal, and focussed on their own lines in Pearse Square. Well done, Bohan, was the first reaction. Their presumption was that Glennon would rethink the division of labour in keeping the mess clean. They were wrong. The senior class would now have their own evening details in the mess.

There was admiration for Bohan's stance on his class, and a feeling that Glennon was disloyal to his.

The consensus was that the first junior who appeared in the mess before seniors had completed their details, was a dead man.

***

They enjoyed a drunken day-pass to Dublin that Saturday, their first as seniors. Come Sunday, they were the ones in the front row in the Cadets' Mess. Sullen juniors picked a seat behind them and muttered darkly to one another.

Twelve months before, Dickie had sat there, looking for a friendly smile from a senior. He felt no urge to extend support now. He had made it to here in this Darwinian place. Only they could forge their way through the next year.

Terminator was on the menu again, as was *Ned Kelly*.

Ned Kelly came to an end with a groan from both seniors and juniors. A bit too art-house for most.

'Shit film, Foster, but Jagger's cool as penguin piss,' announced Bosh.

'He's a better actor than a singer!' was Foster's view.

'Bollox! Jagger's the man. He'd drown in a tsunami of pussy if he wanted.'

'No doubt. World's full of slappers like your sister who'd fuck a skinny twat with a microphone.'

'And he nicked Bryan Ferry's bird.'

'See what I mean?'

'You're killing your own argument, Foster.'

'No I'm not! Jagger's the slapper-king. But if you want a man that'll walk out of a bar with the classy chick, who rides reverse-cowboy and smokes Gitanes, Ferry's your man.'

Dickie nodded sagely. He didn't know what 'reverse cowboy' was, but it sounded interesting.

***

A new officer instructor arrived for the junior class, and took their Monday morning inspection. Lieutenant Bishop was a wiry, UCG graduate, and spoke with a pronounced lisp. He worked his way along the front rank of the juniors until he got to one Cadet Donal Denny. The unfortunate Denny had been christened 'Sausage' the day of his arrival, not just because of his surname, and the fact he was somewhat porky, but because he too had a lisp.

'What's your name, Cadet?'

'Cadet Denny, sir.' Denny's lisp was even worse than Bishop's; he struggled with 'D's, soft 'G's, 'X's, as well as 'S's.

'You pulling the piss out of me, Cadet?' Bishop interrogated, spittle flying.

'No sir, I really speak like this!'

***

The class counted down the days after their Christmas leave to IS week. As juniors, IS week was a bit of fun, occasionally playing prisoners or terrorists. The riot exercise was the chance to settle old scores, a punch in the face, or knee in the balls, just reward for the seniors who had made their life hell. All under the watchful eye of the DSs, all legal.

As seniors, it was a different story. Though not as physically intense as the tactical training in the Glen, the week was run at a frantic pace, sleep-disrupted. IS scenarios took pace at any hour of the day or night. They were removed from the Cadets' Mess for the week, and billeted in two section rooms in the Weapons School on camp beds. Their weapons were with them all the time, including meals and ablutions. They had to maintain a permanent watch on a 77-set and a field phone, from which taskings would come from 'Army HQ' or the local 'Garda Superintendent.' The officers and NCOs playing Gardai were particularly obtuse, testing the Cadets' knowledge of their DFRs on Aid to the Civil Power.

Al Morgan was first up, in charge of a patrol to attend the scene of arrest of a 'militant.' The arrest had apparently gone wrong, and a 'Garda' had been taken hostage. The call came over the landline, and gave a grid and junction reference for the house. Morgan had to give a rapid 'O' Group, and then they were off, in two Land Rovers.

It was a red-brick two-story house, looked like an old British married quarter. The downstairs windows were boarded with plywood, the upstairs windows were gone. Moody was there, standing by his car, and identified himself as 'Inspector Murphy'. He gave his usual smooth est-of-sit to Morgan, which involved Sergeant Pond as the militant screaming out the doorway, a Browning stuck in the face of 'Garda' Bailey. The CQ was uncomfortable, Pond's headlock looked tight.

The 'Inspector' told Morgan there was an imminent threat to the life of 'Garda' Bailey, he was authorising him to use force. Dickie shot Morgan a look, wondering if this was some sort of trap. Wasn't an authorisation to use force meant to come from a Superintendent? But the rule book was out the window when a member of the security forces was in immediate danger, so all options were on the table for Morgan. He barked a few orders, taking Condell and McGuinness towards the house with him. He shouted at Pond to drop the weapon. Pond loosed a string of imaginative republican obscenities at him, and started to retreat into the house. Morgan cocked his Gustav, and followed him through the door. His frame filled the entire doorway as Condell and McGuinness trailed behind.

Dickie could see nothing as the confrontation moved into the sitting room, obscured by plywood. He drew back the butt of his FN, and swung hard into the plywood. The sheet flew off its wooden frame and landed on the floor inside. Pond, Bailey, and Morgan all jumped as the room filled with light.

Pond dragged the CQ by the neck into the kitchen. Dickie was about to jump through the window when he saw light behind Pond. The back of the house was open. Moody looked impassively at Dickie, exhaling cigarette smoke. Dickie ran to the back of the house. Pond inched towards the scullery door. Dickie poked him hard in the ribs with his rifle.

Pond pushed backwards against Dickie's rifle. Morgan came forward, the muzzle of his Gustav trained on Pond's face. A Mexican standoff developed in the back yard. Morgan tried to sound authoritative, shouting at Pond to drop his weapon. Dickie pointed his rifle at Pond's ear, touching the lobe. If a blank went off this close, it would leave him lobe-less.

'Endex! Endex!' Moody shouted, and that was it.

Success in an IS exercise was mainly not fucking up. There was no 'victory,' Dickie thought, no tactical brilliance. Just reaching the end of IS week.

***

The riot was programmed the following afternoon. The juniors had been throwing wise-guy looks; some felt they were going to get even.

The situation was a protect-the-British-Embassy scenario. Someone had obligingly dropped a half load of turf clods at the side of the track. The class was kitted out with one section with full-length shields, the rest with the shorter shields.

Gavin was the platoon commander. He was laden with his normal gear, short shield, baton, Gustav across his back, and a large loud-hailer strapped around his neck. Lt Brown was grinning manically as the juniors closed in on the riot platoon. Two small gate pillars, long ago shorn of their gate, marked the 'entrance' to the British Embassy. Brown sneered at Gavin to 'take control' while the juniors were still 100 yards away, doing nothing more sinister than looking sinister.

The platoon had to escalate slowly through the permitted degrees of force, just so far as to restore order. They could fire CS gas canisters or rubber bullets before resorting to rifle fire, which was really game-over and time to exit stage left. Because of the proximity of race horses and sheep, CS gas wasn't permitted, and firing real rubber bullets at junior Cadets remained frowned upon. So the most the senior class could do was beat the crap out of them, throw smoke grenades, and fire a blank round or two.

McMahon and O'Brien were throwing shapes at the front of the junior rioters. Just like his class had been briefed last year, they were trying to get someone to lash out violently. McMahon had his hair shorn specially for the day.

The first turf-clod sailed over their heads and clobbered Nolan on the top of the helmet. He fell on his arse as Brown roared at Gavin to get the shields overhead in the second and third ranks. The juniors reacted by flinging turf with abandon. Turf was used so as not to cause too much injury. But the stuff thrown high was inflicting proper punishment. Morgan shouted 'HEADS,' and Dickie raised his long shield. The clod struck at face height, and broke the shield in two. A massive cheer went up among the juniors. Dickie pushed away the useless piece of plastic, and they started to pelt his exposed torso directly.

Brown was shouting at Gavin to get a grip of the situation. Gavin gripped his loud hailer, and ordered them to disperse. He ordered them forward five paces, to regain the ground they'd lost as the juniors compressed them. They pushed the juniors back. One of the juniors grabbed Dickie's shield by its broken top and tried to pull him out of the front row. He jabbed his baton down on the fingers, and the junior shouted in pain.

Gavin announced he was about to throw gas, which meant the seniors had to quickly don their respirators. Since it was only smoke, not gas, and as the respirators reduced their visibility and ability to communicate, the threat of 'gas' was loudly welcomed by the rioting juniors. Someone lobbed a couple of smoke generators onto the road to the front. In the near windless atmosphere, thick white smoke developed quickly, and hung like a fog about the fighting cadets.

The exercise descended into a melee. Hackett decided to take the initiative. 'Forward lads' he rasped, pulling Gavin alongside. The front rank moved forward half a dozen paces. The formation loosened a little, allowing a few juniors, including McMahon and O'Brien, through the first rank of the riot platoon. Hackett, Healy and Morgan, who Gavin had been holding back for a baton charge, got a few of them on the ground. Unseen by the staff, they thrashed them. Two more were trussed up with nylon cord and left at the side of the track. One of the juniors made a running jump at Dickie, trying to finish off with a flying head-butt. Dickie dropped his chin. The junior's nose slapped loudly into the roof of his helmet. The riot had degenerated into a serious of beatings, with the seniors coming off marginally. But with respirators, they were striking out half blind.

Gavin shouted a respirator-muffled order to pull back to the gate. Brown intervened, trying to restore order. Through clearing smoke, Dickie was pleased to see a few torn tracksuits, bleeding lips, and sheep-shit on faces.

Brown gave a stream-of-consciousness debrief, and Gavin's appointment as riot platoon commander was over. They marched back to the Weapons School, happily pounding out the cadence with their batons.

***

The arrival of the College football team from West Point was a high profile affair. They came to play an exhibition match against another college team in Dublin, and were to be billeted in the Curragh for a week.

***

'So you're the Cadet Captain?' Paddy asked the loud American at a Mess reception.

'Sure am. Called First Captain at the Point.'

'You're the top of the senior class.'

'Yup.'

'In charge of all the other Cadets.'

'That I am,' he replied in that pathologically optimistic, irony-free tone, devoid of depth or reflection, reserved by Americans alone.

'How many of you?'

'About fourteen hundred enter as plebes, about a thousand graduate.'

'You guys are regarded as the best in the US Army?'

The American thought for a moment. 'Once you omit the words 'regarded as', that statement is accurate,' he pronounced.

Paddy smiled and took a deep draw from his pipe. 'So how many officers does the US Army commission each year?'

'Oh, some five thousand in total I guess.'

'So you guys are the top twenty per cent.'

'Absolutely.' The American said, proudly.

'Jesus,' said Paddy, pulling the pipe out of his teeth, 'you're telling me there's five thousand nine hundred and ninety-nine fuckers dumber than you in the US officer corps!'

The American dropped his beer onto the bar, right fist winding back. Healy stretched his arm out across the American's chest. 'Easy now, only a bit of ribbing,' he said, as Paddy turned away laughing.

***

There were four successive mid-week evening passes to various events while the 'Yanks' were in the Curragh. Not all the class were allowed out of course. Glennon divided the passes up amongst the class. Dickie enjoyed the attention he and his seven colleagues enjoyed in Dublin on the Thursday evening before the match. Cinderella-like, they had to be on the bus back to the College at 23:30.

***

Dickie, along with the Cadet Captain and Paddy Doyle, were chosen to accompany the West Pointers back to Dublin Airport on their departure. Paddy was promised to be on his best behaviour.

The Americans slowly checked in, the vast quantity of sports and personal gear taking a long time to tag. They eventually made it to security. The First Captain was last to go through the barriers. He paused before he went through, turned to the Irish cadets and shouted across the departures lounge.

'Way to go on commissioning, guys!' Keep shooting those fucking Brits! Up the IRA!'

***

96

The departure of the Americans was Glennon's cue to deliver another fear-of-god address in Pearse Hall. His apparent fear was that things had relaxed too much during the West Point visit. They still had their Border familiarisation, and Weapons School sub-course to complete.

Glennon was warning them that the slope to the finish line was angled upwards, not down. With two gone from the class, they needed little reminding. Dickie knew the day passes following Saturday's inspection would be filleted.

***

They heeded the warning signs, working late into Friday night and Saturday morning. No fires were lit, so that the fire places would be spotless.

As Dickie and Morgan slid silently around the lino floor of a disused ante room in the West Wing, Dickie lamented that seniors had a Mess to clean, while the juniors had a single room and a few passage details. If Glennon wanted to concentrate minds, he could just cancel the day pass for the whole bloody class and have done with it. He realised he was grumbling out loud. Morgan was looking at him, sucking fiercely on a Silk Cut.

Floor polished, they slid furniture back into place. It was 01:30hrs. They trudged upstairs without a word.

***

Dickie survived without comment from Glennon on the square inspection. Glennon has to inspect the junior lines before the Mess. An hour and a half passed before he came down to the seniors.

Dickie heard him walk along the corridor, inspecting room by room, the mutterings of infractions noted. Glennon liked to affect a casual look as he went about, but his eyes gave the game away. He strolled into Dickie's room, and despite a slow, forensic look about, walked out again. Dickie dared to hope. The seniors filed out of their rooms to their details downstairs. Glennon arrived twenty minutes later. He walked slowly around, rubbing his glove along the mantel piece and the sash windows. All clean. He checked the bookshelf in the corner. He pulled the easy chair out, and extended his index finger along the leatherette at the back. He spun it around to show the two Cadets. His finger described a clear line in fine dust. In the orange light of the single lightbulb the night before, Dickie had missed it.

'Who is responsible?'

'Me, sir.' Dickie intoned, already considering his video choices for the night ahead.

***

Moody was orderly officer in the College on the Sunday afternoon when the class headed for Border familiarisation. A week of duties and patrols, but a freedom to go to Dundalk each evening was a sweetener. And the class officers would not be about.

A gruff 27th Battalion sergeant was BOS, and showed them to their allotted lines in a block overlooking the main square. There were between three and six double bunks to a room, and spotless ablutions in the hall-way. They were permitted to exit barracks until 23.00, signing out and in at the gate.

***

They lined up for breakfast at 07:00, attracting curious looks from the soldiers of the 27th.

They drew rifles and ammunition for parade at 08:00.

Commanding the square was a fearsome Sergeant Major, whom Dickie put at 45 years or so. His roaring growl had corporals and sergeants scurrying around into their respective duties. The only Border patrol that seemed to excite the soldiery, was the foot-patrol of Colman's Island. A blister of the Republic squeezed into the North, there was no road access for the Irish Army. Patrols were inserted exclusively by helicopter. But the daily taskings for the Alouette chopper allocated to the 27th Battalion meant that these patrols were irregular.

The other unusual characteristic of the Border patrols was that they were typically armed with a MAG and two hundred rounds of belted 7.62mm.

Dickie was detailed with Healy, Gavin and Bent to checkpoint duty with Gardai at Hackballscross, at the concession road border crossing. It was as exciting as it sounded. A barrel-chested Garda in a heavy greatcoat stopped cars entering the Republic, of both Northern and Republic origin. He seemed to know quite a lot of them, saluting some, asking others how much booze they had in the boot of the car. The cop called a halt to the checkpoint after thirty minutes of rain. They returned to Dundalk for lunch.

That afternoon, a sergeant took a larger group of them on a two-vehicle 'fly-the-flag' patrol. Cleary, Doyle and Drury joined Dickie's group, Cleary carrying a MAG. Other than the odd piece of republican graffiti, there were no obvious signs or markings that the border bisected a road.

Dickie ended up in the rear of the sergeant's FFR, with a monosyllabic private from Monaghan who had seen it all before. As a miserable February evening closed in, Dickie was glad of any time the Land Rover was moving, venting the soldier's poisonous smoke out the rear.

The sergeant pulled the convoy to the roadside about 500 yards short of the border, and ordered the Cadets out.

'This is the Carrickmacross Road. We have to take this road to get to the other Border crossings. We can't access them on the Concession Road.'

It didn't seem like too much further, less than a mile, when the sergeant gestured to the driver to turn right.

'This is Blackstaff', he said, presumably to Dickie, but didn't call the driver to stop. They drove on a little more, before turning right again.

The sergeant gestured to the driver to pull in at some old stone buildings and dismounted. The Cadets joined him.

'The old mill here is on our side of the Fane River. The Border goes through the idle of the bridge.' The Cadets walked absentmindedly about the bridge. The sergeant went to the middle of the span, and paced over and back. 'Northern Ireland, Republic, Northern Ireland'.

Below, Dickie could see the February current ripple quickly through the arch of the mill race. Twenty yards away, they heard the whine of the 46-set in the FFR. The sergeant's ears pricked up.

'What's up, Harris?' he shouted at the signaller.

'Incident in Crossmaglen, Sarge. They think the lads might be making a run across the river.'

'Do they know where we are?'

'I radioed the crossing to them, Sarge.'

The sergeant looked displeased.

'And they know we've no cops with us?'

'Yes, Sarge.'

Dickie watched the sergeant's brow furrow as he put his plan together.

'Right, Seamie,' he nodded to the corporal, Healy and Gavin and one of the privates, 'you take them to the bridge. Make sure you've got Harris on the radio,' he said. 'We'll cover the river.'

They drove back down the road a little. The sergeant pulled the Land Rovers into a gateway.

'Right lads, this farmer isn't too keen on us,' he pointed at the farmhouse and out-buildings. The signaller manned his radio as the sergeant, Cleary, Doyle, Drury, Bent, Dickie, and two privates headed for the farm gate.

'We're goin' down here a hundred metres to cover the river. We've no cops. We're flyin' the flag only. Do nothin' unless you hear it from me. Understood?'

'Yes, sergeant!' they all chimed, and started across the gate.

Cleary made a big deal of wrapping the belt around his MAG. He was pricking about with the top cover, removing and replacing the belt. Bent asked him if he needed a hand. He shook his head.

The patrol walked through the farmyard. It opened through a hedgerow into a small field, dropping down to the river. The sergeant halted them.

'That hedgerow runs down to the Fane. That's the Border. There's an old ford down there. We'll cover that.'

They walked towards the hedgerow. Dickie heard noise behind. The muffled clatter caused the patrol turn around. In seconds, a British Army Puma screamed through the air above their heads. Dickie recognised the size and shape of the thing, the Air Corps had a single specimen in Baldonnel. Time slowed down. The staccato WHAP-WHAP-WHAP battered their ears. Dickie figured it was no more than forty feet above. The wheels were down.

The pilot was using the Fane for navigation, Dickie reckoned, but he was in the Republic.

Cleary stood framed in the evening sky, MAG trained skywards.

'COVER!' the sergeant roared, and the patrol ran to the hedgerow. The sergeant was first to hit the ditch, as the Puma banked left, and flared above a field in the North. Dickie could clearly make out the fully tooled-up British soldiers, back-packs on, ready at the open door.

Cleary got into position with the MAG, dropping the bipods, and releasing the belt. The Puma steadied above the field; earth and debris flying as the big chopper settled to land.

BRUUUP! It took a second for Dickie to realise the machinegun fire had come from his right. The tracer round flying over the tail boom of the Puma came from Cleary's MAG. Was it four, five rounds?

'Jesus fucking Christ!' Dickie shouted at Cleary, who lay behind his MAG in manic confusion.

'Who the FUCK?' roared the sergeant, before running towards Cleary. 'Keep your fucking heads down!' he shouted.

The pilot applied full power, the Puma screamed and started to rise. It roared off northward again.

The sergeant crouched low beside Cleary, pinning him hard by his right arm.

'What the fuck d'you think you're doing?'

'Sarge, I, I....'

'Shut the fuck up! Back to the cars!' They got up and doubled across the field. The corporal, Healy, Gavin and the soldier, were sprinting back down the road from the bridge.

'We heard shots!' the corporal shouted. 'Fuckin' Puma nearly took the head off us!'

'Our fire Seamie. You!' he shouted at Gavin, who was standing beside Cleary. 'Clear that fuckin' MAG!'

Gavin knelt down, and warily cleared it. He was about to put the belt back on when the sergeant roared at him, 'Leave that fucking belt off!'

He motioned Gavin into the FFR with his own rifle and the MAG. The two cars sped off down the road, Cleary in the back, unarmed.

Healy looked around the faces in the back of the GS. The two soldiers were sitting forward, closest the corporal.

'What the fuck happened?' Healy asked quietly. Cleary said nothing, looking at the floor.

'ND from the MAG.' Bent half-whispered, brushing the side of his nose towards the local soldiers.

The two Land Rovers pulled into the side of the road. The sergeant dismounted, and ordered the Cadets and the corporal out. The privates were told to stay put.

'You some sort of undercover Provo, or just a stupid cunt?'

'Sarge, I... thought...'

'The reason we're standin' here like fucking bell-ends is because you didn't fucking think! Was the safety catch on or off, Cadet?' Straight for the jugular, thought Dickie.

'I... I... can't...'

The safety on the MAG could only be set if it was cocked. If he said he'd set it, he was admitting cocking it without being ordered. If he said he didn't, he was admitting he hadn't a clue how his weapon was cocked.

He was either insubordinate, incompetent, or guilty of serious negligence. Or was it worse? Dickie looked at Bent. Both were recalling Cleary's fucking around with the belt at the farmyard gate. Had he cocked it then?

'What's your name, Cadet?'

'Cadet Cleary C, Sergeant.' He whimpered.

'Well Cadet Cleary C, I'll tell you what's goin' to happen next. We're goin' back to Dundalk. I'm goin' to charge you with negligence, or a Section 168. And if you get away with just a charge from me, instead of a full fucking Court-Martial and a bunk in the Curragh prison, you're going to suck my cock. You are goin' to plead guilty, son. Corporal O'Doherty here is goin' to say a few nice words about ye, what a nice young lad you were.'

The corporal nodded sagely. Dickie noticed the Dundalk accent was much more pronounced now.

'If you have a problem with that, better make yourself fuckin' scarce. Coz I will personally fuckin' plug you. Understand?'

There was no sympathy for Cleary. They were lucky the Brits didn't return fire. They were lucky if any of them got commissioned after this. Cleary had had one chance too many.

'Yes, Sergeant.'

'Stay there, the fucking lot of you.'

The NCOs returned to the FFR. The sergeant took the handset, the signaller composing a Griddle message for him.

They were back in Dundalk 40 minutes later. The barracks was emptied of soldiers' cars, but the Adjutant and Sergeant Major awaited them. The Sergeant Major accompanied the patrol back to stores, where the weapons were handed in. All bar the MAG, which a Military Police sergeant took custody of. The QM asked Cleary for the ammunition. Cleary handed back three full belts of fifty rounds, and one belt with five empty slots at the end.

'How many rounds were you issued with this morning, Cadet?'

'Two hundred, CQ.'

'How many are you returning to stores?'

'A hundred and ninety five, CQ.'

The CQ looked up at the Military Police sergeant, who jotted in his notebook.

The others handed in the rifles and ammunition. The sergeant marched them over to Battalion Operations. The Adjutant was there, the Ops Officer was there, the CO was there.

They were then shown to an annex to the Ops Room, and told not to speak. The sergeant was called out first by the MPs. He was gone about an hour when an MP returned, calling out Cleary this time. It was 8pm.

The rest sat nervously looking at each other. Cleary was gone an hour when they heard the whine of a Gazelle helicopter land on the square. Two DFHQ-types in working dress emerged. Then they saw Captain Glennon getting out of his green Ford Escort. Things were going from bad to worse.

A rapid succession of short meetings followed, interspersed with the tap-tap-tap of officer pattern shoes moving between Battalion Ops and the CO's office. The Sergeant Major returned, and ushered the privates out. The Cadets could hear authoritative voices followed by loud 'Yes, sirs!' And then the soldiers were gone.

Another wait. It was 9.30pm. They could hear the Sergeant Major and sergeant outside, smoking.

'Fair fucks to you, Hughie!' laughed the Sergeant Major. 'The pints are on me tonight!'

Silence hung like a smell in the room. Dickie watched the minute hand of his watch inch towards 9:45pm. Tap-tap-tap outside in the corridor, and Glennon, the Battalion Ops officer and the two DFHQ types walked in. Glennon took up a sheaf of A4 paper. Cleary entered the room and stood to attention with his classmates. He looked ashen. Glennon read aloud.

'During a Defence Forces patrol of an area south of the Fane River this afternoon, five rounds of ammunition were discharged in error, striking the ground. No one was injured in the incident. The circumstances of the incident are deemed to come within the terms of the Official Secrets Act 1963. They may not be disclosed by you to anyone. Breach of this order by you, whether as an enlisted man, a commissioned officer, or as a civilian, is punishable on conviction by Court Martial or a civil court with a sentence of up to seven years penal servitude. Do you understand what I have explained to you?'

They shouted their agreement. Glennon told them to append their signed names and serial numbers to the typed sheet. He directed a look of pure venom at Cleary and exited the room with the two DFHQ staff officers.

The Battalion Ops officer remained behind. He too had a sheet of paper. With the glimmer of a smile, he read aloud.

'The following was issued by the British MOD at 17:00hrs through their Military Attaché in Dublin. "This afternoon an attempt by PIRA to mortar the army base at Crossmaglen was foiled. The suspects escaped south after mortars, hidden in the back of a truck, failed to fire. Members of the PIRA team fired on a British Army helicopter which was in pursuit. The MOD expresses its appreciation for the speed with which an Irish Army border patrol on the Culloville Road responded, forcing the PIRA suspects to flee the scene."'

He looked up from his notes at them and continued. 'That information is in the public domain, and will be in tomorrow's papers. You may not link it in any way with what happened today. You may not discuss it with anyone, fellow Cadet, family member, Military College instructor, no one. Understood?'

They affirmed, and he directed them to the cookhouse. Glennon had assembled the rest of the class. He told the class there had been an incident during a patrol, which was subject to the Official Secrets Act. They were not to ask questions about it, or converse about it, ever. He walked out, fired up his little Escort and was gone.

***

The remainder of the border familiarisation proved mundane. Dickie and Morgan still required girls for the pre-commissioning ball in April. Glennon's arbitrary cancellation of passes meant that the eight weeks between now and the ball could be spent confined to barracks, but the coming few nights out in Dundalk were subject to no passes or restrictions. It was time to make hay while the sun shone.

Dundalk did not disappoint.

***

The support weapons sub-course hadn't warranted much comment from their senior class. There were no war stories or horrific tales. Just a few reasonably relaxed weeks, and they would be qualified instructors in the MAG SF, the 60mm mortar, and the 84mm anti-tank.

CS Richards, late of the Cadet School, had other ideas. He had left the Cadet School as a sergeant in September. He'd taken a CS vacancy in the Weapons School next door. Though a relatively junior Sergeant, he'd got the promotion. As a CS at 33 years old, Richards was placing himself to be the youngest sergeant major in the Army.

Crew-served weapons generally required three soldiers. This gave Richards a chance to indulge in some old-fashioned gun drill. The CS was fond of drill.

As instructors, they were required to know every piece of information on weight, specification, ammunition, and performance that any soldier would ever ask.

Gun drills took place after a run far out onto the Curragh Plains, carrying tripods, belts, boxes and other paraphernalia. Lesson planning was endless. Gun drill had to be carried out smartly.

Richards didn't know when to stop. Before they knew it, they were marching around the camp, roaring their heads off like spotty recruits. 'Square bashing with mortars' Foster christened it.

Matters came to a head on a Thursday afternoon conducting machine gun drills. The class were insufficiently kinetic for Richards. He began a tirade lifted from some movie about Marine Corps Drill Instructors.

They stood at the roadside, civilians passing them on the way to the golf club. Someone shouted 'Suas!' It spread like a virus through the class, everyone roared their lungs out like juniors.

They stayed in for the weekend and watched the juniors leave on pass.

***

The final exercise prior to completion of the weapons course was a live-fire 'advance-to-contact' in the Glen. The class split into three sections, each of which would carry an SF, and 84mm anti-tank gun and a 60mm mortar, and full first-line ammunition allocation.

Dropped at the far side of Lugnaquilla Mountain, they had to force-march up to Table Mountain, and back down into the Glen of Imaal to their firing point at the range below Cemetery Hill. Each section had to engage targets with all three weapons. The SF and mortars would have to record targets, dismount their weapons, remount and hit the targets on bearings alone. All this against the clock.

CS Richards announced that the winning section would get a day-pass to see Ireland versus Scotland in the rugby championship the next day.

Captain Glennon and CS Moran joined them, to further lift morale. CS Moran travelled with Dickie's section.

Dickie's section commander for the exercise was Hourigan. Dickie carried an SF; Gavin and Nolan making up the crew. The thing that surprised everyone was the weight of a full ammunition load. Full 200-round boxes of 7.62mm weighed plenty. They also had to carry six rounds of 84mm anti-tank, and 30 mortar bombs.

The sections set off in 15-minute intervals from Glenmalure, Dickie's section third and last at 08.00hrs. CS Moran set off at a blistering pace. They rose higher. The road became a track, and then disappeared. After an hour, they overtook the second section. Dickie was sweating madly. He opened his jacket, his shirt, and his fly. It did little to stem the flow of perspiration. Hourigan was up front with the CS, a battle of wills to see who would crack first under the pace. The CS was 45 years old, and a smoker, but he wore only a belt and water bottle. Hourigan carried his 84mm gun with the rest of his kit.

The forest gave way to open ground, peaks rising to their west, north and east. Dickie's head dropped, his mind retreated into its own little space. They had done about six kilometres of fast ascent in an hour and a half.

They crested the saddle below Table Mountain, and descended into the Glen. Dickie could see the first section less than a click away. They speeded up. Tired muscles twitched as they headed down.

They overtook the first section. Hourigan had them in a 'scout's pace,' doubling for a dozen paces, then fast walking for another dozen. They could see the trees of Cemetery Hill in the distance.

They took the bridge over the Slaney, and trotted to Cemetery Hill. They reached the range at 11.15hrs. They dropped their kit at firing positions, and drank what water was left. The clock was ticking. They set up their firing positions.

On the far left, the instructor was moving the tank target on its railway 300 metres away for the 84mm. 50 metres away, the mortar crew were digging in their gun. Dickie and Gavin dug in their tripod legs, and prepared the GPMG. Nolan set out the aiming post while Dickie attached the dial-sight.

The sergeant indicated a white-washed rock in the distance. None of them had fired at such a long range before. They agreed a 'class average' range of 800 metres to target. Dickie set the range and adjusted the iron sights onto the rock.

Dickie fired his first long burst. The tracer arced gracefully up the valley. They watched as the rounds dropped short of the target. Dickie set the range for 1,000 metres, close to the tracer burnout range. Another long burst. The bullets landed near the rock, about eight o'clock. Dickie checked his sights. The foresight was bang on the centre of the rock. He noticed the gentle breeze from the southwest on his cheek. He adjusted the tripod until the foresight sat on a patch of grass at two-o'clock. Another long burst. The trail of tracer rounds landed on the rock, spouting dust and rock skywards. Seconds later, they heard the musical whine of the ricochets.

Dickie shouted 'On!'

He focussed the dial sight on the aiming post, and shouted the bearings to Nolan. He fired another long burst at the rock. The rounds hit as before. Nolan checked the bearings and the aim onto the aiming post.

'Target recorded, sergeant!' Nolan shouted, and the sergeant looked at his watch. It was 11.40hrs.

The other two sections had arrived, and were setting up. They could fire as soon as they were ready.

Their 84mm crew were down to their last round. They had hit the tank moving from right to left, but had yet to hit it once moving left to right. They watched as Clay took aim with the last round. The target wobbling its way along the rails. Clay fired, an enormous spout of flame and dust lifting from the ground behind. The tracer converged with the moving plywood 'tank.' Closer. The shell slapped into the back of the target. Dickie's section cheered. Not pretty, but a hit was a hit.

The 60mm crew were slowly adjusting fire onto a ditch junction about 1,500 metres away. McGuinness shouted 'Three rounds fire for effect!' and the crew lobbed the bombs down the tube. Three brown puff-ball bursts told them the target was hit.

The machine gun and mortar crews had to dismount and remount their guns, and hit their targets using recorded bearings only. Dickie detached the gun from the tripod and placed the little triangle in the ground marking the centre of the tripod.

They lifted the tripod and placed it beside the gun. The taped sergeant the SF's iron sights fore and rear with black tape. He checked his handiwork, then nodded to CS Richards.

The sergeant told them to mount the gun again. Gavin placed the tripod over the triangular marker. Dickie and Gavin dug the tripod feet in with their boots, into the same depressions from which they'd pulled them. The dial sight on, Dickie applied his readings and took a bead on the marking post. He loaded a belt and fired a long burst. The trail of rounds sailed into the Glen, and bounced off the rock. He expended the rest of a 200 round belt at it.

The 60mm bombs landed sweetly on target. They looked at each other in satisfaction. With the time advantage they'd taken into the Glen, and the fact they had hit all their targets, there was no way the other sections could overhaul them now. They had won. Lansdowne Road beckoned …

They cleaned their weapons and packed up. The transport awaited and took them back to the Curragh. CS Richards pronounced himself satisfied with the cleanliness of the weapons, and they were returned to stores.

They marched back up to the Cadet School lines. The College staff had thinned to nothing on a Friday afternoon. O'Leary went to Glennon's office to check arrangements for day passes for the victorious section. No arrangement had been made. He wasn't going to allow a pass. O'Leary broke the news before they marched back to the Cadet's Mess. Dickie's section were gutted. Fuck them. Eleven weeks to commissioning.

***

Despite efforts by a minority of the staff, class morale improved. They completed the more gentlemanly subjects in class, such as Military Law, Economics, Politics, and Administration. They commenced sword drill with Smoothy Moody in the drill shed. He at least had adopted the mien of one who expected to socialise with them after they were commissioned.

Appalled at the senior class throwing their caps skywards in front of the dignitaries the previous year, Glennon decreed that caps would remain firmly in place.

The class split on observance of the diktat. Hackett, the first Cadet Captain, was of the view that there was nothing Glennon could do about it. Toby took the view that they might as well humour the bastard one last time before they went their way.

***

Dickie was excused participation in the pre-commissioning religious retreat. He was told he could remain in the College for the three days, and spend time in the Library or on details.

Dickie had heard that the retreat was a relaxed affair, religiously speaking. Most importantly, they were free to leave the monastery in the evenings. If he could go to Lourdes, he could go anywhere.

Before departure, another Glennon briefing took place in Pearse Hall. The purpose of the retreat was to reflect on one's time in the Military College, forgive-and-forget, and contemplate life as a commissioned officer. Nothing excessively papist, Dickie concluded.

***

Dickie read the newspaper in the sitting-room while the remainder attended confession.

Freddie Lane appeared, in an excited state, sporting a bruise to his left cheek and eye.

'What happened you, Freddie?' Dickie asked.

'Bit of a row in the oratory, Dickie,' and Lane was gone.

Others started to file out, a shocked priest following them.

'Never...' blurted the old priest, 'Never have I seen such *wanton* disrespect for the sacrament of confession!'

Foster filled him in.

***

Lane, arriving in the oratory early, saw three classmates outside the priest's confession box, and that the confession box opposite was unoccupied. He slipped in unnoticed, and switched on its 'occupied' light. He heard a more cadets enter the oratory kneel outside.

First in to Father Lane's box was Gavin. He was two or three minutes in there before he heard giggling from the priest. He left the confessional box just as Lane rolled out onto the oratory floor laughing. Gavin started thumping Lane on the ground before his classmates intervened.

***

Dinner was invigilated by another priest, who wisely stayed off the topic of confession. They had a 'meeting of reconciliation' afterwards, which finally drew to a close a 21:30hrs. They got out of the monastery and walked to the pub at ten.

Proceedings were civilised, Gavin and Lane sat separately. Gavin nursed a pint of lager silently. The barman indicated his intention to close at half eleven sharp. Hackett stood up and demanded to know what Gavin had confessed in the box. Gavin pushed his pint out of the way. A few colleagues muttered 'take it easy' to him. At the far wall of the pub Lane stood up solemnly. Dickie wondered the first all-out bar-brawl in class history was about to start. Lane raised his right hand, making the sign of the cross with a grand vertical and horizontal sweep.

'Gentlemen, it was told under the seal of the confessional!'

***

Dickie's date for the pre-commissioning ball was, in truth, just fulfilling the fixture. He'd asked her on his last night in Dundalk, desperation stakes. She had promised him she would attend. He collected her at the railway station in Newbridge, and installed her in a room in the Keadeen Hotel for the night. At the sight of the double bed, she made it clear there would be no 'hanky-panky.'

She was a woman of her word.

***

Three weeks out from commissioning came the reception in the Cadets' Mess for their corps and unit assignments. Glennon first announced the prize for top cadet of the class, which, to no one's surprise, went to Toby.

The announcements of corps and postings were made in alphabetical order. Dickie was posted to B Company of the infantry battalion in Killimore. He rang his parents after the reception, and asked his father what county the town was in.

***

Their last significant social event was the pre-commissioning dinner. With four women in the junior class, it couldn't be called 'stag' so they reverted to the term 'unaccompanied.' Quasimodo's speech was a more manageable 25 minutes. The atmosphere among the senior class was giddy. Even the junior class looked pretty happy. Only Gander, sitting forlornly among his new junior classmates, struck a sad note.

The instructors were game for the ribbing after dinner. Brown, pain in the arse on the job, was quite the *bon viveur* in a social setting. Bohan, tea-total and normally as stiff as a plank, was relaxed, standing at the fireplace with his orange juice, fielding ripe questions from Dickie's classmates.

The officers were all gone by 23:15. The cadets retrieved their hidden stocks of hooch. Some of the juniors joined the action.

'Dickie, can I have your room when I get down here?' Cyril McDuff enquired loudly. McDuff was one of the more 'entertaining' members of the junior class. Dickie's room was one of two above the anteroom, benefitting from the heat below.

'If you make it that far, McDuff!' Foster shouted at him.

'Bohan'll give you batmen to clean the place,' Dicke remarked loudly.

'He's talking about it alright,' McDuff countered.

'We're ripping the uniforms on Friday. I swear one of us should run a fucking boiler suit up that flag pole,' Dickie said.

'Should've put a boiler suit on your class pennant!' McDuff shouted. Even the juniors thought Glennon screwed the senior class.

'Go fuck yourself, McDuff.' Healy grunted. McDuff waddled off to the bay window with another classmate, Billy Cummins. The four females were gathered there, trying to fend off Gander's extremely polite advances.

Toby started huffing to get the juniors moving. Gander was already gone, escorting Olive the pretty, blonde junior, back to the lines. They were all gone half an hour after midnight, leaving the seniors to their devices.

***

The orderly officer showed up in the cookhouse for breakfast, looking for Toby. Toby was already sitting down to a plate of fried eggs and rubber toast. The captain took him outside in a less than cordial manner. Toby returned and addressed both classes.

'He wants to know who ran the boiler suit up the flag pole. He's going to Captain Glennon as soon as he gets in.' Toby returned to his eat and finished his breakfast.

Several pairs of eyes swivelled towards Dickie, including Foster and Healy.

'I didn't do it!' Dickie glowered.

'Your fucking idea!' Healy spat at him.

Dickie looked at his watch. 07:30. Flag up was at eight, so the guardroom must have alerted him. Which was pretty stupid; the offence must have happened under the nose of a sentry. Sun-up in mid-May was just before six. Whoever did it must have been there at least an hour earlier. Or after dinner...

Morning parade was changed from greens to boiler suits. Instructors focussed purely on the rear collar of the overalls. Looking for the stamped service numbers. Toby's boiler suit was impressively unblemished. Moody checked it anyway. The check was pointless. Most kept a buckshee set of overalls for permanent display in their chest of drawers. Dickie figured the boiler suit that had come down the pole had no service number on it, or had a service number from Dickie's senior class.

The inspection yielded nothing.

In a change to the program for both classes, the College Commandant was going to speak to them in Murphy Hall at 09:00. For the senior class, this meant a late start for their lecture from the Command Legal Officer. No one cared. The CLO's relatively limited experience as a barrister had earned him the sobriquet 'Necessity,' as in 'Necessity knows no law.'

***

Quasimodo wobbled into Murphy Hall at 09:10. Glennon and Bohan stood at either side of the stage.

'A certain gentleman has decided to denigrate the National Flag, the Military College, and the Defence Forces ...'

Dickie was tempted to point out there were four female juniors, in whose class the perpetrator probably resided.

The College Commandant wrapped up in a curt ten minutes.

'I expect the responsible party or parties to admit their actions, and face the consequences.'

Both classes reverted to program. After lunch, Bent appeared from the orderly room.

'Glennon wants to see you, Dickie.'

'For what?'

'Didn't say.'

He marched into the class captain's office. Glennon sat behind his desk, the class diary open on Dickie's page.

'You proposed the idea of running the overalls up the flag pole.'

Dickie was stunned. There were few enough who'd heard him say it. And even fewer who had spoken to an officer since then.

'I did, sir. As a joke.'

'And a few hours later, they were found on the flag pole. Own up to it.'

'I would if I did it, sir. I didn't. The juniors left the mess 40 minutes after the officers. We were up another hour or so. Cadet O'Shea can vouch for the fact that I went to my room.'

'You'll probably still be commissioned. There isn't the time for a Court Martial. It's likely to be just a Section 168 charge. Summary disposal.' The word 'probably' had never been so loaded.

'I can't take responsibility for something I haven't done.' Dickie glowered at him.

'Get O'Shea for me.'

Dickie saluted and left. He called Bosh out of Pearse Hall. There was consternation when Dickie told the class of Glennon's accusation.

'You're a fucking rat, Toby!' Healy spat at the Cadet Captain, who tapped his pen on an A4 pad.

'I said nothing.' Toby retorted unconvincingly.

Bosh added nothing to Glennon's case. Glennon could do nothing without a confession or red-handed proof. He'd get neither.

Thursday passed. Friday. Last lecture was at 15:00. They returned their manuals to Pearse Hall. They drew their swords from stores for a last polish before the ceremony. The CQ sent down large canvas sacks into which old uniform was to be placed, destined for the rag pool.

***

The mess descended into childish chaos. They started ripping the arms off their greens, stabbing and slashing them with swords. Foster stood as a matador, his tunic a cape, while Condell charged it with his sword. Healy started the wedgies. Anyone misfortunate to be wearing army issue Y-fronts suffered greatly. In Gavin's case, they didn't yield at all. He screamed as Healy and Morgan tried to rip the jocks off him. Hackett and Clay had a sword fight in the main hall.

The juniors appeared, desperate to salvage buckshee uniform. They took old combats, spare boots, and overalls that weren't already in shreds.

Saturday morning inspection by Moody was cursory.

'Ever been to Killimore, Cadet Mandeville?'

'No, sir.'

'Fine town. You'll enjoy yourself.'

Technically they were enlisted men only until Monday, when they were to be discharged. They were on pass until Tuesday, returning to the College as civilians in the afternoon with an over-night bag and uniform only. Their parents started to arrive by car from midday onwards, and they left the Cadets' Mess as cadets for the last time.

They had done it.

The Unknown Soldier

Killimore Barracks

Monday, 19th May

The driver picked Dickie up from the train station at 10am, and took him in a Land Rover to the barracks. It was accessed through a gate on the west, and internally divided by a terraced row of soldiers' single quarters. A path to the front door of the officers' mess bisected a rose garden and lawn.

A soldier stood in working dress at the end of the path as the Land Rover pulled up.

'Private Shivnan, sir,' he saluted smartly, and went to the tailgate of the Land Rover to remove Dickie's cases.

'I'll take you to your room, and then to the adjutant's office.' Dickie followed him through the front door, and up the broad stairs immediately in front. Shivnan brought him into a small bedroom, furnished much as his room in the Cadet's Mess had been.

***

The next morning, Dickie was picked up by Pte Wilson, for his meeting with the GOC in Command HQ. All six newly commissioned officers were due to meet the Brigadier for what was known as 'the morality talk'. Wilson saluted Dickie as he approached the Land Rover. He was the barrack commander's driver, and considered the transportation of subalterns be beneath him.

'Morning sir, the boss is on leave today, I'm taking you to Command', he said, more by way of complaint than by explanation. Dickie settled into the passenger seat for an hour and a half of Wilson's philosophising.

A red-cheeked colonel marched them into the GOC's office, ordered the salute, and stood them at ease. The GOC started in breezy terms about how lucky the six of them were, commissioned into the army in the prime of their young lives.

Dickie noticed the paintings behind the head of the GOC as he droned on. One was a pastoral scene, another of soldiers manning a checkpoint in Lebanon. He wondered how long it would be before he would get posted to Lebanon.

He reckoned the general had been at it for ten minutes. Out of the corner of his eye, Dickie could just make out Morgan, who had a placid smile about his face as the lecture wore on. The occasional groan of a truck passing below, or roar of a Training Depot sergeant on the square, punctuated the monotone coming from the GOC.

Morality, mess bills, respect for women, treatment of the men, decorum in the mess, pregnancy (avoidance of, through abstinence, acceptability of, through marriage), personal appearance, place in society, punctuality; Dickie started to lose track of the injunctions. His attention was drawn to the GOC's eyebrows, long grey metallic things, untidily planted about the man's forehead. One in particular overshot the side of his head by about half an inch. As he emphasised points of lesser and lesser interest, the rogue follicle undulated up and down, a natural sine wave. Dickie resolved to avoid staring at it, yet found his eyes rolling back involuntarily.

The day was warm, and the colonel opened one of the sash windows. Dickie could see a few officers converging on the mess for coffee. Nearly eleven o'clock. That meant the GOC had been at it for 45 minutes. Morgan's head seemed to sway slowly forwards and backwards.

Dickie flexed his toes, and moved his weight fore and aft on his feet. A long deep breath in through his nose, and he felt better.

The GOC completed a three-minute spell on the importance of accuracy in the weekly ordnance check when Morgan arced forward, head-butting the desk violently. The GOC started with a high-pitched squeak. Morgan's hands were still clasped behind him in the at-ease position. Blood flowed from a gash across the bridge of his nose. Dickie and the colonel hauled him into a chair and stuck a handkerchief in his face to stem the blood flow.

'Well gentlemen, this is most unfortunate', the GOC spluttered. 'I'll postpone the rest of my briefing to another day.'

'*Seomra aire!*' the colonel called, as the GOC walked out. Morgan, still prostrate in the chair, began to come too.

'Fair fucks to you, Morgan!' Healy declared, after the colonel left. 'I was about to go myself.'

***

Captain Caple called Dickie into his office after morning parade, and introduced him to the only other lieutenant in the barracks, Tom James.

'Dickie, TJ here is just back off leave, and will show you the ropes for the next number of weeks. Commandant Reilly is back off leave this morning as well, and will want to meet you.' Dickie had heard of Commandant Reilly by reputation. A legend on horseback, an international show jumper, a fabled inter-county player in his youth, and a ferocious drinker. 'He should be here around 10 or so.'

'Do I get into SD1?'

'No, working dress is fine.'

Dickie left with TJ, a short, wiry man with a ranger tab on his sweater. He was prematurely balding, had an Errol Flynn moustache and a near permanent grin on his face.

'Well Dickie, you didn't top your class if you were sent to this godforsaken battalion!'

'I thought this was a good posting?'

'If you're a footballer, jockey, or an alcoholic. Do you *ride to hounds* like our Major Horace?'

'Horace?'

'Commandant Horace Reilly, Quintus Horatius Flaccus, Baron Killimore, and another four or five titles, Barrack OC.'

'Don't ride to hounds. Is that a problem?'

'Pulling your leg, Dickie. Let's get a cup of tea.' Dickie followed him upstairs to the company orderly room, where CS Culligan was seated behind his sparse desk. 'Now CS, have you gone over payroll with our shiny new subaltern?'

'No, sir, the second lieutenant has been hard to pin down for the last week.'

'Surprised at you, CS.'

The CS took Dickie through payroll, the procedure for absentees and deserters, the calculation of allowances and so on.

'Deserters?' Dickie asked, shocked. He thought that the presence of two deserters on the payroll must be a grave slur on the company. 'What's being done about them?'

'They're off payroll once they're been declared in Standing Orders,' the CS went on, 'then we pass their names to the Gardai.'

'But have we not gone out looking for them?'

'Yes, sir,' the CS continued, patiently, 'the P.A.s go out to their last known address a few times, after that it's a matter for the guards.'

TJ sat with the clerk, drinking tea and discussing who was returning from UNIFIL. The phone rang, and the adjutant ordered Dickie downstairs to meet the barrack commander. John marched him in, ordered the salute, while Commandant Reilly told him to take a seat.

'So, Richard, tell me about yourself.' Horace invited with a regal sweep of his hand.

Dickie explained about his upbringing and schooling, and his month in university before going to the Military College.

'A good school. Did you play any sport?'

'Played schools rugby sir, got knocked out in the semis by CBC though.'

'A pity, a pity. Did you play any *Gaelic* sports?'

'The emphasis in the boys' school was on rugby, sir.'

'I see, well, not your fault, I suppose. Girlfriend?'

'I was seeing someone when I went to the Curragh, but it broke up after a few months there.'

'I don't suppose a young man like you will have any problems finding a young woman in Killimore!'

***

His first ordnance check took more than two hours. CQ Hession was a porter-bellied, chain-smoking, officer-hating alcoholic with the street-smarts of a fox. Dickie started on the rifles. The CQ opened the ledger, while the store-man picked up the rifles and read out the number. Paranoid that the CQ might have 'borrowed' a rifle from next door, Dickie got up from the ledger and checked the serial number of every fifth or sixth rifle. Just in case. The rifles had dedicated slots in the rack, to which the CQ had affixed post labels with each serial number. The store-man chanced reading the number from the labels. Every time he did, Dickie insisted he pick up the rifle and read the serial number.

The CQ, too experienced to allow Dickie's actions grate, made himself a coffee. He stirred the cup as lugubriously as possible. Dickie got down as far as the support weapons on the ledger. There was a 60mm mortar on repair. The CQ didn't miss a beat.

'Here's the receipt voucher from the tiffy, sir.'

'I want to see it, CQ.' Dickie held visions of an IRA training camp, dozens of wide-eyed activists ogling the pilfered mortar.

'It's in the workshop, sir. Broken firing pin.'

'I want to see it, CQ.'

Silence ensued.

'Better go over to the tiffy's workshop, see if he's there, Mick.'

The store-man shuffled out. The CQ made his point though. Would he get off his butt and read out a single serial number? Would he fuck. Counting ceased. He sat there, slurping his coffee, occasionally dunking a ginger-snap biscuit into it.

It was nearly five o'clock when it finished. The CQ gave Dickie a wan smile. Honours even. The young officer had got what he was entitled to. And the CQ had shown his mule-like determination to preserve at all costs the sanctity of his stores.

***

'Congratulations, Dickie!' Captain Caple declared in his office after morning parade.

'What is it?'

'Nine weeks in the School of Engineering, you're nominated for the Assault Pioneer Platoon Commanders' Course.'

'By who?'

'Me.'

'What do I do?'

'Fill in the joining instructions, report there in two weeks, we'll see you back here in August.'

'This qualify me for anything?'

'Yes. In the event of World War III, you will be appointed to blow the first bridge over the Blackwater.'

'Oh. Is it a good course?'

'Second Lieutenant,' Caple waived the letter impatiently, 'I hadn't heard of an Assault Pioneer Course until ten minutes ago. Now fuck off and do some work.'

***

He was on duty Friday evening, meaning he'd be more or less stuck in Killimore for the weekend. He had to get himself a car fast. Getting out of Killimore on a Saturday morning by bus or train was painful. TJ was taking over from him in the morning. He figured it would make more sense to do a straight Friday-Saturday-Sunday duty occasionally. It would bugger up fewer weekends.

TJ had already run a four-mile circuit around Killimore when Dickie handed the gun over to him at breakfast. He changed into civvies and resolved to walk the town from top to bottom. He had lunch in a pub in town, and came back at five for dinner with TJ.

'Bit of a kerfuffle today, Dickie.'

'What's that?'

'No sign of Corporal Murphy for the barrack guard.'

'What happens next?'

'He'll be charged for AWOL on Monday.' He paused to lick soup from his moustache. 'Then I got a call from the cops, asking if one of our guys was missing. Turns out they've got a body in the morgue. Gunshot wound to the head. Dead about 24 hours.'

'Murphy?'

'That's what I thought, but the guys told me that he'd left barracks at eight am. Got a call from his girlfriend.'

'He's in the shit so.'

'I suppose. Cops asked us to do an ID.'

'You looking at me?'

'No. The spare foot growing out of your head. You tool.'

'What do I have to do?'

'Go to the hospital. See if you can ID him.'

Dickie didn't enjoy the rest of his meal. The stand-too driver took him to the hospital, a sandstone affair on the outskirts of town. Dickie produced his and was ushered down a brick corridor to a chilled room. A trolley at the far wall bore a corpse beneath a green surgical sheet. A doctor removed the sheet from the head. Dickie saw a man in his late twenties or early thirties, moustache, with a vaguely green-blue pallor to the skin. There was the smallest of entry wounds in his right temple, and no exit wound.

'He'd been dead at least twelve hours when he was found this morning in the park.'

'Oh.'

'Can you positively identify the deceased?'

Dickie looked at the corpse again, and compared it with the mental picture he had of the Corporal Murphy in Support Company, which was vague at best. He looked like every other soldier with a moustache. Dickie could draw no link between this man and anyone he knew from memory.

'No.'

The doctor drew the sheet back and showed Dickie out to the Land Rover.

***

'And that was it?'

'Yes, TJ. He asked me if I could positively identify him. I said no.'

'But it *might* be Corporal Murphy?'

'Well, I suppose it might be him. But I can hardly declare I've identified a bloke dead unless I'm sure of it?'

'Oh for fuck's sake, Dickie. We'll leave it until the morning. See if they identify him on their own.'

Dickie went out for a drink, then went to bed. TJ woke him in the morning, dropping the Browning hard on his balls.

'Cops called again. Asked if we're *really* sure nobody is missing. I'll go to the hospital.' TJ marched out of Dickie's room.

He was back in 40 minutes, Dickie had barely finished mounting the duties. He had a head like Vesuvius on him.

'You're a complete fucking arse, Dickie.'

'It was him?'

'Of course it was him.'

'What now?'

'Tell the adjutant. Tell the Boss. Come up with an explanation for how it took two formal identifications before we twigged one of our blokes topped himself!'

'Sorry, TJ.'

'Sorry my hole. You man the adjutant's phone, I'll use the one in the mess.'

Caple was in barracks within the hour. The three got together in the office.

'You fucking gobshite Mandeville! How could you not ID of one of your own NCOs?'

'Don't really know the man. Didn't want to say he was dead for sure.'

'Shut up. Make contact with the CS. Tell him the score, that we need to make arrangements for a military funeral. TJ, the boss is in Down Royal for the racing, so I can't send a Land Rover up for him. Tell Private Shivnan I'll get him mileage in his own car to get

128

up there now and drag the Boss out of the bar. I'm going to have to come up with some bullshit excuse for the Battalion Commander about Horace.'

TJ and Dickie nodded their assent to the plan.

'And Mandeville, consider yourself lucky that Murphy's an orphan. You fuck-up like this with someone who has next-of-kin, and your career in this army will be short and painful.'

***

Shivnan's mission across the Border to get Horace was a failure. He was back that night at ten. Dickie rang Caple. He didn't seem too bothered, Shivnan's mission was simply arse covering. Horace was always back around coffee-time. They'd have time to set up a morning conference. Horace would look like he had it under control all along.

Horace's Audi glided into barracks at 10:50 precisely. Caple gathered TJ and Dickie into the office.

'He'll go upstairs, get into working dress, and come down to coffee. Leave the talking to me.'

They followed Caple lemming-like to the mess and grabbed a coffee. Horace entered the ante-room at precisely 11:00hrs. Coffee was a great time to start the working week, and he hated tardiness.

'Good morning, gentlemen. A fine morning it is!'

'Indeed sir. I hope you had a good weekend in Down Royal.' Caple got through the pleasantries.

'Modest success John. Finished the weekend in the black!'

'Sad to say sir, but we had a tragedy over the weekend. I've set up briefing for you after coffee. Corporal Murphy shot himself in Cosgrave Park, with a pistol.'

'One of ours?'

129

'Yes, sir. The tall chap in Support Company. About six-one. Black hair. Moustache.'

Horace reddened instantly.

'Not the corporal, Captain Caple,' addressing Caple like a three-year old. 'The pistol. Was it one of ours?'

'No, sir. Apparently a .25" Beretta. Cops reckon he imported it illegally from Lebanon.'

'I understand.' Horace relaxed visibly. 'We have a funeral planned?'

'The CS is working on it now. We're waiting on an autopsy to finish and they'll release the body.'

'Have you given the funeral details to the CO?'

'No, sir. I thought you'd wish to do that yourself.'

'Very good. I'll put the call in straight away.'

Caple escorted Horace out of the ante-room, winking to TJ as he went. As the door closed behind the barrack commander and the barrack adjutant, TJ turned to Dickie with a smile.

'Quintus Horatius Flaccus! The survival instincts of a sewer rat crossed with a cockroach!'

'Is that the end of it, TJ?' Dickie asked, his own failure uppermost in his mind.

'Mostly. Whatever about you, it's trickier for the lads who saw Murphy's ghost on Saturday morning. The cops are asking them a few questions now. Smuggling a Beretta and hiding it in barracks is also a bit embarrassing.'

'That it?'

'Shiny shoes for the funeral!'

***

Caple and CS Culligan put together the funeral for Cpl Murphy. An orphan soldier, his girlfriend was the only civilian mourner in the garrison church. Horace Reilly and Caple sat with her in the front pew. The padre's obituary recalled a short but dignified life, enriched for having joined the family of the army, where his brothers joined him to bid him farewell. He asked that no one would question Cpl Murphy's decision or his method of going, only that they should remember him fondly.

***

They marched the last mile to the local cemetery, the Battalion pipe band playing laments. The service over, the firing party loosed their volley over the grave. The girlfriend winced, the only woman in a graveyard of green uniforms. She was older than Cpl Murphy, thirty-five at least. She was a striking woman, with shoulder length black hair. Dickie wondered, as she looked into the grave, if she had put thoughts of motherhood behind her. CS Culligan stepped forward as the padre finished, and invited her, the officers and men back to the NCO's Mess for lunch after the funeral.

***

It was one o'clock by the time they filtered back to the NCOs' Mess. The CO was in his element. He thanked the Mess President for the invitation, and gave a short oration that made feel they had just buried Caesar. Dickie had to admire the man. His only concern on Monday was that Murphy had smuggled a Browning out of barracks. A polite round of applause, his job done, Horace walked back to the knot of officers at the bar, and called for his usual day-time tipple of a large bottle of ale with a brandy chaser. Having told the Mess President he'd authorise a £300 write-off for the evening, all hands stayed in pockets. The privates plucked up the courage and followed him to the bar.

***

No one knew what to say when one of their number had killed himself. Tongues remained civil, at least while Murphy's girlfriend was there. By five, some of the married soldiers had started to head home. She noticed, and without ceremony stood up.

'Before you go, I'd like to say something.' She was clear and steady. 'Seamus had no family, but he had you. I don't know why he did it, but I'm glad he had you to say goodbye to him. You gave him a lovely send-off. Thank you, all of you.'

She sat down. The soldiers began to shake her hand before they left. Dickie wondered what would become of her. Horace worked the room, talking to almost everyone before he came back to the bar.

'Gentlemen, I think it would be appropriate for us to have a quiet drink together in the mess afterwards.' Dickie caught Caple rolling his eyes to the ceiling. The six officers filtered out of the NCOs Mess, through the archway and into the Officers Mess. The waiter had been tipped off, and welcomed them in the hallway.

'Will you be eating first, gentlemen?' he asked Horace.

'What's for steak, waiter?' Horace replied.

'Chef has six nice T-bones prepared, sir.'

'Splendid, I think we'll eat then.' They sat in the dining room, Horace at his usual place at the head. 'And bring a bottle of that nice Rioja.'

***

The Assault Pioneer Platoon Commander's Course began the following Monday at the Engineer School. Clay and Nolan were also on the course, along with two very senior captains. Dickie vaguely remembered the pioneer platoon in the organisation chart of the mobilised infantry battalion.

The officers were billeted in Connolly Barracks, home to the Third Battalion. Ryall was already making a name for himself in 'The Bloods' with insane levels of enthusiasm.

The course consisted mostly of building bridges, blowing them up, with some mine warfare and booby-trapping thrown in for good measure. It culminated in a day of demolition in the Glen of Imaal, exploding large quantities of PE4. The largest was a cratering charge, requiring a full 30kg of PE4 to be dropped into a deep hole and blown.

The students were too focussed on the explosion site. From the rear the sergeant instructor roared the engineer's mantra 'Look Up!' after blowing the big charge. To Dickie's horror, an enormous boulder was rocketing skywards, arcing towards them. The demolition party were almost a kilometre from the blast site. The boulder reached its apogee in the air before them. It seemed to stop and pause in mid-air, before crashing to earth in a splash of soil.

Even the senior captains thought it the most enjoyable day's work they had spent in the Defence Forces.

***

Caple had posted the Killimore duty list to Dickie in the Curragh. The pioneer course finished on a Friday, Dickie was on duty for the weekend back in Killimore. He'd had no orderly officer duties in six weeks, so couldn't complain.

***

Battalion HQ ordered Support Company to run the battalion officer's range practices and shoot in September. Everyone would get their rifle, pistol and Gustav ARPs done on the one day. There would also be a competition against the battalion senior NCOs in the pistol.

Horace decided to go the whole hog, with a white linen service for lunch in a large tent.

Caple reckoned he hadn't fired a weapon since he was commissioned in the early sixties, as he'd spent so much time in the Equitation School.

His staff car whisked him onto the range just before the CO arrived. Dickie thought he looked a little unsteady on his feet. Caple looked at him.

'Racing in Listowel last night.'

They finished the rifle and Gustav before lunch. They sat down in the tent to an excellent lunch of salmon. At Horace's insistence, wine was served. Most of the officers took their cue from the CO and stuck to water. Horace quaffed half a bottle of Chablis.

They repaired to the pistol range after lunch. The Battalion QM was range officer. Horace was on the first detail. He lined up for the first practice, standing at the 15 metre point beside Dickie. The QM roared at them to load, cock their weapons and fire. Horace looked at Dickie to his left, and saw him inserting the magazine into the butt. He did the same, though with the rounds facing to the rear initially. He twisted the magazine around, and slapped it home. Then he pointed the pistol at the target and pulled the trigger. Nothing happened. He pulled it again. And again.

'Make this work, CS!' he shouted to CS Culligan, hovering paternally behind.

The CO and the other officers saw him. He knew it, and didn't care. He was Horace! Quintus Horatius Flaccus, Baron Killimore! All-Ireland Champion, Olympian. His place in the firmament was guaranteed. He'd make it to colonel on seniority, before some beguiled minister would ensure he was promoted general, brigadier at the very least. The CS took the pistol, cocked it carefully, and returned it to Horace.

As the detail marched off the range, Caple whispered to Dickie 'At least now he knows the difference between a Webley revolver and a Browning automatic.'

From Katanga to the Mess

She had shown up at a few of the Killimore home matches. A sister of Jim Fitzgerald, the 2nd XV's scrum-half, she cheered wildly whenever her brother played. She was petite, five foot five-ish, strawberry blond hair dropping to the small of her back. Her name was Ciara. She was absolutely stunning. She was also very young. Dickie didn't realise just how young until Fitzie's mother dropped him to training one evening. Ciara sat in the back seat, still in her school uniform.

Towards the end of the season, Sundays brightening, Ciara wore increasingly eye-catching clothes to the matches. Her Leaving Cert exams approached. She came to the drinks after each match, and drank Sprite among a few of the younger women. Whenever she passed, he could detect a hint of Charlie fragrance. When Dickie was at school, Charlie was a teenage cliché. On Ciara, the mere suggestion of it from her neck was spellbinding.

The season drew to a close and Dickie arranged to hold his twenty-first birthday in Killimore RFC. Fitzie approached Dickie over a drink in Lonergan's, and asked if his sister could go. Keeping sisters away from colleagues was an elementary military precaution. Dickie asked about her age. She wouldn't be eighteen until December, but it was a private party. She could be on the clubhouse premises.

Dickie shrugged. Every dog and cat in Killimore who could squeeze into the clubhouse would be welcomed. That was the deal, all Dickie had to do was pay the DJ for the night.

***

'You haven't been on this one before, sir?'

Imprinted at cellular level in the Irish soldier was the need to impress upon young officers how ignorant was the Irish officer. This was most prevalent among drivers, who had junior officers as a captive audience.

'68 Dwyer, one of nine Dwyers or O'Dwyers posted in Killimore, was one of the great proponents of educating young officers. His numerical moniker being one below titillation, he was subject to double entendres such as 'sniff', 'one-short', but usually 'foreplay.'

'No, '68, I haven't.'

'This is the biggy, sir.'

Dwyer was referring to 'Kilo 5,' the longest cash escort route in the country, descending into the bowels of Kerry and West Cork. It took up to fifteen hours to complete. An enormous milk-run of banks along the Atlantic peninsulas of Kerry, they never knew how much was in the cash wagon, which on Kilo 5 was always a large truck. TJ told Dickie there was probably over eight or nine million on board.

Kilo 5 had another distinction. In all the years that the Army had escorted the bank runs, none had been robbed, with one exception.

A few years back, IRA spotters had noticed that after a long series of bends on the road southwest out of Glenbeigh, the cop car speeded up on a three-mile straight stretch that preceded another set of bends. Like cars on a Formula One circuit, this concertina spread the convoy out. As the cop car entered the next series of bends, it was far ahead. The cash wagon entered the wooded chicane on its own, and the raiders struck. With the squad car and first escort vehicle out of sight, they set up a mock road-works and diversion. The cash wagon was directed up a quiet road, hijacked and looted.

When the FFR at the rear of the escort caught up with the convoy, there was no cash truck. The cops tried to make radio contact with the cash wagon drivers and the crime was detected, too late. A tidy, bloodless and highly lucrative job successfully carried out.

Dickie had rehearsed the anti-ambush drills with the escort. The soldiers in the back of his FFR had to watch for tailing vehicles or spotters.

It was an uphill task maintaining vigilance on cash escorts. The Army was covering millions of miles per year following cash wagons, with nothing happening. Keeping soldiers tuned in day in day out was difficult.

The escort climbed the N21 to where it banked west overlooking Knockaunatee. North Kerry opened up below them. This was a view usually blanketed by rainclouds. Today, it was laid out in all its glory, the farmland in indigo and green beneath the few roaming clouds. The peaks of the Mangertons gave way to the graphite teeth of the peaks around Killarney. Ireland's little Monument Valley, it always took his breath away.

The other difficulty encountered on long escorts was FFR syndrome. Also known as escort horn or Land Rover langer, this was an erection of mahogany hardness and indefinite duration. Dickie wasn't sure of the cause. His mind tended to wander when stuck in vehicles for long spells, inevitably towards things that would stimulate the end result. A thirteen-hour drive in a Land Rover gave ample scope for the mind to drift.

Some said it was physiological. It didn't happen in trucks, for example. The fixed, upright, spread-legged seating position in the front of a Land Rover, combined with the psychopathic determination of drivers to maintain the heater on full blast, provoked a semi-permanent engorgement of the organ.

Inevitably, it was at its most prominent just before a cash-drop. Dickie had to squirm in the seat, pointing it upwards, before he alighted from the FFR, lest he frighten some passing female.

Kenmare was difficult. His arousal was very tardy in subsiding. The town was thronged with shoppers. Dickie leaned forward against a wall but his member refused to retract. If he could bottle this, every pensioner and porn-star in the world would kill for it.

'Alright, sir?' Dwyer shouted from the Land Rover. 'You look a bit... peaky.'

'I'm outstanding, '68. Outstanding.'

***

Dinner was finished Dickie when got back that evening. Ollie Fielding, the old civvie waiter, sat at the table, thumbing his way through the Irish Times.

'Lieutenant Mandeville. You must be starving.'

'All gone, Ollie?'

'Orderly officer's just finished. Chef has left a nice steak in the oven for you, and I have a slice of Mrs Fielding's apple crumble for afters.'

'Thanks, Ollie.'

Ollie brought in the steak and garnish, and sat at the other dining table as Dickie ate. He'd heard Ollie's story from Caple, but never from Ollie.

Ollie was a one-man institution. A young Tipperary man with nothing to do after the war, he figured the British Army was the safest bet, as it had just finished in Korea. He joined up and was posted to Cyprus before he realised he was about to invade the Suez. Having nothing against the Egyptians, and having joined up without the slightest intention of fighting, he deserted.

He found himself back home in the service of 'a Protestant lady of means' in Dalkey, where he was her driver, gardener and general dogsbody. The arrangement was unhappy. Though wealthy, her aspirations far exceeded her income. She struggled to maintain the staff to which she had become accustomed. The household staff contracted, the workload was distributed among the remaining.

'The fact that she was a complete wagon had nothing to do with her persuasion, sir!'

'Point taken, Ollie.'

The rancour climaxed one Friday evening. Ollie had arranged a return to Tipperary for the weekend. Madame needed a chore completed on Saturday. Ollie reminded her he would not be working, by her prior agreement. She cancelled his weekend off, at which point he threw his hat on her kitchen floor and left.

Life in late fifties Tipperary was dull. Ollie felt drawn to uniformed life again. He joined the Irish Army this time, figuring his chances of involvement in conflict were nil. He was but six months a private soldier when the first Irish troops went to the Congo. He reckoned the Niemba massacre was 'a bit of a blip' and that peace would soon break out across Congo.

As the big US Airforce Globemaster bringing Ollie's battalion to Elisabethville circled the airfield, it was riddled by ground fire before landing. Ollie finished a six-month combat tour in Congo, with no chance of escape from the heart of Africa.

He returned to Ireland unscathed, and never again fired a shot in anger, retiring as a corporal.

He spotted a job for a civilian waiter in Killimore officers' mess, and took it.

On top of receiving his army pension and waiter's wages, Ollie was now a civilian, beyond the grasp of Horace, who hated him. The soldier waiters could be charged at will, but Ollie the civvie was outside the scope of military law.

***

Dickie's 21st finally arrived. Classmates, friends, and Killimore RFC players started to congregate in Lonergan's Bar. The only problem would be clearing Lonergan's at closing time.

It was quiet at the clubhouse. Uncle Fester Fennessy, the local Garda Sergeant and 2nd XV tighthead prop, was on the door.

'Expecting many, Dickie?' asked Fester.

'There's a big crowd in Lonergan's. Just hope they come up before too long.'

'They will. One of the lads will do a walk-through at half-eleven.'

'You're going to raid Lonergan's?'

'A walk-through, not a raid!' Fester chuckled to himself.

'Thanks.' Dickie busied himself.

Fester's mini-raid on Lonergan's worked a treat. The clubhouse started to fill quickly as midnight approached. He recognised quite a few. The two girls from Bank of Ireland. One with an elfin bob of blonde hair and gorgeous. One who looked like she played too much camogie without a helmet. Both great company. There was Elizabeth, that girl going out with Paul the flanker. She always held Dickie's gaze a bit too long.

Fester produced mounds of salty cocktail sausages at half past midnight. The bar was mobbed again.

Dickie found himself amongst a group of unknown women. One of them fixed him with an immobile stare when she realised he was the birthday boy. Not much to say, but she wasn't shy about body contact. Dickie asked McEvoy, the club captain, the lie of the land. McEvoy replied that her name was Maeve, and 'she wouldn't die wondering.'

***

Just as Dickie plotted, he looked up and saw Ciara in the corner. Perched in the shadow of one of the DJ's speakers, on her face a look of abject dread.

She was stunning. She wore boots over blue jeans, a long white angora sweater, meshed with holes the size of fifty pence coins, through which he could make out her bare skin. Too nice to feign cool indifference, her brown eyes met his like a faithful Labrador.

Only then he realised the girl was besotted with him. Weeks away from her Leaving Cert, and the grown-up world had intruded into her life. Fitzie hadn't just been trying to sneak his under-age sister into a late party. She had ordered him to get her there to meet Dickie.

One am, there was still time.

He walked casually towards her. Her eyes brightened as he approached.

'Hi, Ciara. Just saw you. Thanks for coming.'

'We're just in. My friends were slow to leave Mulcahy's.'

They chatted for a few minutes. She gazed at him. It would have been uncomfortable were it not a very attractive gaze to return.

'I'm boring you.'

'No!' she placed her hand on his arm. 'No. It's just that I have to be... home.'

He'd forgotten she was a schoolgirl. 'I can give you a lift home. If you like. If...'

'Yes!' she placed down her glass, whispered to a friend, and was back to him in less than thirty seconds. They emerged from the clubhouse into the light over the car park. Its intensity penetrated the mesh of the angora sweater. He could make out the line of a bra strap over her pale skin. She strode confidently beside him to his car and slid in.

She lived in an affluent estate in the north of Killimore. The lights were still on in the sitting room as he pulled up.

She grabbed the door and jumped out, smiling to him to follow her to her gate.

A hedgerow obscured the sitting room and front door. She turned towards him. The big brown eyes were happy, expectant. All that was wanted now was a promise to meet. He thought of the girls in Ciara's league he had pined for in his own school days, to no avail.

Kissing her would be a promise he would never keep. Walking away would break her heart.

He kissed her. The whisper of Charlie he'd first noticed in the car, filled his head.

A flash of resentment shot through him. She would have laughed at his seventeen year old self.

She was thirteen years old as he was joining the Army. He was ashamed of his petty resentment.

She pulled herself tight against him and kissed him hard, offering a sweet tongue. He felt her heartbeat, pounding rapidly beneath her sweater.

He could see her road laid out ahead, a couple of years of chaste dating, a big white wedding, kids before he was twenty five.

His road was different. Three years university in Galway, Lebanon if it was still going, captain, a whole other life.

God damn it. He was twenty one years old. No longer imprisoned in the Curragh. His own room. Money in his own account. And a clubhouse full of women celebrating his birthday.

Grown women. Women with cars. Women without cars who wanted guys with cars. With their own apartments, and jobs. No parents waiting for them to come home. With double beds, in bedrooms not plastered with Duran Duran posters. Beds that didn't have cuddly toys in them. Where they didn't want to show him scrap books, or pirate cassette tapes.

Suffering Jesus, what was he doing here? He had to get back to the clubhouse. A wave of panic shot through him. He wondered if she mistook it for passion.

There was only one way to end this without appearing a fraud. He held her tighter, kissing her harder. She groaned. He ran his hands up her bare back towards the bra strap, and fumbled as if to undo it. Her hands detached from around his neck hand pushed him away. The big brown eyes were bewildered.

'No!'

'I thought you...'

'No! I just...'

'Sorry.'

'Were you going to...?'

'Ciara...'

She looked into his eyes and saw only lust. The ship of teenage fantasy crashing on the rocks of male desire. Her eyes welled with tears.

'I thought…' and her thoughts were too much to express. She hurried towards her front door, wiping tears from her eyes.

He drove back to the clubhouse, unsure whether he'd been selfless or heartless.

The clubhouse was heaving to the sound of the Bangles. The heat and smoky fug of the place hit his face like a slap. He couldn't see Fitzie. He a grabbed a drink.

'You went off with Fitzie's sister?' McEvoy asked.

'Long story.'

Maeve Reilly was still there, drinking a glass of lager. He waited till he caught her eye.

She lived in a farmhouse a few miles north of Killimore, where the valley gave way to the hills. Killimore cast a faint dull sodium glow above the trees, as she directed him to park up the lane. They jumped into the back seat.

She was undressed to her open blouse, he with his jeans about his knees, when the rap of the hand-torch jolted Dickie.

'Move on!' shouted some duffer in a tweed jacket. Dickie scrambled into his jeans, and jumped into the front seat.

'Jesus! That your father?'

'I think so.'

'You think so?'

'Turn left up Tubber Lane. Half a mile. Pull in at the shed.'

Dickie hadn't yet met a woman more determined to get laid than he. He parked by the shed, and clambered into the back seat. Maeve hadn't budged. She sat in the middle of the back seat, and moved her right knee around him as he knelt down. She was as wet as an otter's pocket, and was trying to pull him inside quicker than he could don his rubber NBC suit.

143

'Hold on, hold on!' he felt the ring roll down his member just in time for her to sink her nails into the cheeks of his arse, and haul him hard inside her. She shouted loudly. Dickie was distracted by the thought the farmer might stride up, torch in hand, at any moment. They grappled, sweaty and urgently with each other. It was over very quickly, and they sat side by side in the back seat.

'You better get me home, so.'

'I suppose so.'

'Will I see you again?'

'I'm sure you will, Maeve.'

***

Ollie walked into the dining room just as Horace left for the races. He carried three plates, and served Captain Caple, whose wife was at her mother's, first.

'Fine looking steak, Ollie,' said Caple, looking at a T-bone half the size of the plate.

'Sure is, Ollie. Serving the good stuff while the boss is away?' said TJ.

'Gentlemen,' began Ollie in dramatic fashion, 'you will be delighted to know that the standard of meat the mess is purchasing from the butcher has risen considerably since Lieutenant Mandeville started donating pork to Maeve Reilly, who runs their delicatessen counter.' Verbal hand grenade thrown, Ollie turned on his heels and was gone.

TJ and Caple broke into laughter. How in hell had Ollie found out about Maeve Reilly?

'There's one lieuy who's glad he's off to Galway.' Caple said sagely to TJ.

***

Dickie finished packing his car for Galway on Friday afternoon. He was as giddy as the night before commissioning. For the next three years, he was posted to USAC, a student in University College Galway.

The class were meeting that evening in Galway, officially reporting to the OC on Monday morning for briefing, and enrolling in college on Tuesday. The MP Corporal saluted him as he drove out the gate, the Eagles blaring on his stereo.

***

Dickie, Morgan, Healy, Commons, Foster, O'Leary, Doyle and Clay pitched up in Garvey's Bar on the corner of Eyre Square. They discussed the virulent strain of chastity infecting large swathes of college females.

The small cohort of women who were freer with their favours developed a reputation. A frisson of shame attended association with a woman known for nothing other than her willingness to conjugate. Particularly if her bed had recently been vacated by one's comrade.

Commons had fallen victim the week before, lying in the arms of Emer in her bed in Nun's Island (Emer loved her address).

He was awoken by a banging on her door at two a.m. A strapping Donegal girl, she'd had the misfortune to spend the night with a visiting naval officer the previous month. She was instantly christened 'The L.E. Emer,' on the basis she was always full of Irish seamen.

Commons answered the door, to be confronted by his brother, a fourth year engineer. The elder Commons muttered 'best be off now' and walked back to the carful of students who had brought him there.

As Commons admitted later, when he got back into bed, Emer threw her arms around him and uttered the immortal 'I love lads who chat me up first.' The reputations of Emer, and the Commons brothers, were sealed at coffee the next morning.

***

'It's the Catholic Church!' Foster decided.

'Opus Dei,' Morgan qualified. 'They're recruiting "consecrated virgins" around the college.

'Jesus wept.' O'Leary groaned.

'We need a few Proddie birds to dilute the gene pool,' said Healy, looking at Dickie.

'Mick, Church of Ireland girls don't wander about, trying to relieve Catholics from the burdens of their fucked up church.' Dickie reasoned.

'When's your sister coming to college, Dickie?'

'Don't even think about it, Foster.'

Doyle was in the corner, itching to start a sing song. It was only ten p.m. on a Wednesday night. The front door opened. The Lee sisters were from Kildare, two of the most 'obliging' girls west of the Shannon, walked in. Like many of the dimmer progeny of wealthy parents, they found their way to Galway, where the entry points for pretty much every course were lower. They wouldn't grace the cover of Cosmopolitan any time soon, but they were outrageous company, self-deprecating, armed with sailors' tongues when required. On the evening of their first sighting in Galway, Foster christened them 'Ug' and 'Port.'

'Hello, boys!' they shouted at the doorway. They went to the bar, and ordered drinks.

O'Leary was on his feet. 'Let me get those for you, girls.'

'Bit early for that sort of thing.' Foster said to no one in particular.

'It is. It is.' Clay agreed, joining O'Leary at the bar.

146

They stayed put until closing time, and headed to Salthill, minus Clay and O'Leary.

***

Dickie had successfully avoided computers thusfar in his career. They appeared to be slowly infesting the Army; Battalion Operations, the QM and the orderly room were now using them. There was no avoiding them now.

They were a required part of the first-year commerce course. He was required to turn them on and off without the intervention of a sergeant. They even had to write simple programs in Basic.

So, with the other four first-commerce students in USAC, he bought his floppy disks in the college shop, and booked sessions in the little Nissen huts which housed the banks of computers. He wondered if moving to Arts was still an option.

***

Eamon Cole was holding court in the college bar in the Quad, pint glass some seven feet in the air. A young female supporter of the football team asked him to explain his overheard compliment her on her 'excellent conformation'.

'Of course, my dear! But before I do, I must know your name.'

'Mary' she giggled.

'And I'm Eamon. Now Mary, I don't want you to be offended, because offence is not intended, but conformation is the description of the profile and content of an animal!'

Offended or not, she was wide-eyed in fear and wonder, as Cole's free gesticulated wildly.

'You're comparing me to meat?'

Dickie kept his ear cocked to hear how Cole would get out of this one.

147

'No, no! Conformation describes the convexity of the carcass; and the ratio of flesh to bone. Too much flesh, there's no structure, too much bone, and there's no meat!'

'Really?' She wasn't sure where he was going.

'Perfect form and conformation is always worth the premium!'

Cole could read the phone book, and make it sound like Yeats. She settled on a barstool beside him, drinking a rum and coke.

'So what am I?'

'E3, or even E4L I'd say, a perfect blend. If my father spotted you he'd steal you away from me.' From what Dickie knew of Cole's father, that much was true.

Cole made his move at eleven. He availed of a hubbub in the conversation and ushered Mary quietly towards the door. He didn't escape Corrigan's attention.

'Showing her the Ring of Kerry, Eamon?'

Cole had already pushed her ahead into the Quad. He bowed theatrically from the door and disappeared into the night.

'What's the Ring of Kerry Jack?'

'I'd have to kill you, Dickie.'

***

They got into their 'syndicates' at the end of March. The syndicates were loathed and admired in equal measure by the civilian students. They took the same form as those in the Military College; a group took a problem, dissected it into portions, and divided it between the syndicate members. Thus were college subjects carved up every year in USAC.

The syndicate went beyond a mere study group. The intelligence gathering component required each member to get his or her hands on the best study notes, advice or tips from fellow students, lecturers and staff. Past papers were subject to statistical and regression analysis. A list of primary questions, and likely runner-up questions was produced. These were divided among the group, who were individually allotted questions.

The syndicate was sacrosanct. No civilian could be admitted, nor sample its fruits. The secrets of the syndicate were inviolable.

That was the theory anyway.

***

'These notes aren't even in your own fucking handwriting!' Morgan was studying Healy's Geography notes. They first aroused suspicion not because of their feminine cursive script, but because they were photocopies.

'They're good fucking notes!' retorted Healy. While his contribution to the *Principles of Human Geography* was of high quality, the only way any civvie had parted with these was in trade.

'Do your own fucking notes, Healy, or you're out of the syndicate!'

Dickie hadn't seen Ryall this agitated through 18 months in the Cadet School. He was the brains in the Geography syndicate, and didn't appreciate having them spread among the citizenry in UCG.

Ryall stormed out of the TV room, leaving Healy to watch 'Neighbours.'

'You Arts boys have that syndicate malarkey cracked!' shouted Commons.

***

'Anyone heading into College?' Healy asked at coffee. He was carless since his recent self-inflicted disqualification. Upon being challenged at a Garda checkpoint as to why his tax disk was for another car, he explained that he'd 'had a few pints.'

'Yeah, I've got a 12 o'clock.' Dickie said. He needed an excuse to go to Accounting. Healy might as well be it. Behind him, Commons leapt to his feet, his Irish Times a ball of flame.

'For fuck's sake, O'Leary!' Commons shouted at O'Leary, underneath his easy chair with a Zippo.

The CO walked into the ante room, offering a breezy good-morning to all. The cigarette smoke was insufficient to camouflage the smell of freshly burnt newsprint. He ignored it, and poured himself a coffee.

'Studies going well?' He said to no one in particular, but looking at Dickie.

'Pretty well, sir. On the run into the exams. Be good to have them over.'

'You'll soon be back in your unit, wondering where the time went.'

***

The newsagents half way down Renmore Road was run by a Pakistani family. With inexorable Army logic, it was known as the 'Paki Shop.' The proprietor, Mohammed, was a softly spoken man of legendary discretion.

One of the First Battalion company commanders made a regular pit-stop at the shop to get his Racing Post. One sunny morning, locals phoned the cops when an Opel, incarcerating three distressed children, was found parked beside his shop. The Gardai attended within minutes, and were about to start enquiries when a horrified Mohammed emerged and solved the problem straight away. A quick call to the Barrack Adjutant saw the flustered company commander reappear, and take his traumatised offspring to school.

The shop was open until eight nightly. It stocked all the toiletries, washing powder, pain killers, and snacks required by the young officer. And rulers. 12-inch, balsa wood rulers, marked on one side only. Whether by accident or design, Mohammed had sourced rulers that were printed only on the front.

Perhaps they were cheaper. But someone, somewhere realised that a blank ruler had 12 square inches of space to fill, on a piece of wood that could be brought into any exam hall. Mohammed sold a lot of rulers.

Unauthorised Use of a Balloon

With no semester one exams in first-year Arts, Commerce or Science, the main difficulty for OC USAC was keeping young officers on the straight and narrow until they got into second year, and the academic work started in earnest.

The boss focussed the mind with the occasional room-inspection. He also insisted on a full service dress inspection, during which he demanded to see their dress uniform and great coat, otherwise he would refuse to sign their uniform allowance claim.

The threat to withhold the uniform allowance was serious. Most of them couldn't afford car insurance without it. Healy might not have a car, but was overdrawn to the tune of five years of uniform allowance. For him, it was merely cutting his losses. Except he didn't have a greatcoat.

They lined up in Service Dress No 1 outside their rooms. The boss started on the top floor, working his way down. Healy had arranged to take greatcoat from one of the engineers on the top floor who was of similar build. As the boss moved along the top floor, the engineer dropped his greatcoat out the window to the waiting Healy below. Healy removed a pip from each shoulder to coincide with his current rank.

The boss made it to the second floor in 30 minutes. Entering Healy's room, Dickie heard him admiring the dress uniform and the greatcoat.

'Recently demoted, second-lieutenant?' the boss asked casually.

'I bought it from my brother, sir. He out grew it.'

'Very good, Healy.'

***

For first years with exams, the return to unit for Christmas was pre-ordained. There was no pretence that this was for anything other than giving other officers a break from the duty list. Dickie would spend a lot of the two-week break with a BAP tied to his hip, counting soldiers, bullets and guns.

The Christmas Dinner was on Saturday night. The battalion commander decreed it would be in Killimore. Dickie had no partner. He'd have to move fast.

Thursday saw a scheduled visit from a youth group to barracks for a weapons display. These normally took place in the summer, but Horace knew the leader of this group. Battalion HQ in Wolfe Barracks would have been closer for them, but Support Company had the bigger guns. CS Culligan set out a fine display, running from pistols up to a .50" IIMG, a 90mm anti-tank gun, and an 81mm mortar.

Checking for live ammunition was always a priority. The first thing every youth did when they picked up a weapon was to point it at their best friend and pull the trigger.

Accompanying them was a young woman of unsurpassed architecture. Dickie, as orderly officer, hovered to the side.

Her name was Keelin Roche. She would love to attend the Christmas Dinner on Saturday. She jotted down her phone number.

Dickie was in self-congratulatory mode after the display. He was headed for the adjutant's office, when the CS appeared, white as a sheet.

'Sir, there's a Browning missing!'

Dickie looked back towards the main gate. The last of the youth group were filing out, on the way to mount their coach. He sprinted as fast as he could towards the gate. The gate policeman was surprised to see him run out the gate, still armed. The coach door was open, the first youth stepping in.

'Stop! Against the wall now!'

They moved with surprising speed against the wall. Keelin looked on, agape.

153

'If you hand it over now, we won't call the cops!' Dickie threatened, and started to frisk the first startled youth. Four teenagers down the line, a shell-suited specimen with galloping acne and gelled hair stepped forward.

'Left it in me pocket, by mistake.'

'Anything else?'

'No.'

The sullen youth handed it over. Dickie turned for the main gate. CS Culligan took the Browning from him.

'Best not to say anything about this, sir,' he said, tapping the side of his nose.

'Absolutely, CS.'

Dickie and the CS walked back in the main gate. The BOS, an obsequious cavalry sergeant, was waiting.

'Everything alright sir?' he asked archly.

Dickie checked his watch. Just after three-thirty.

'Flag down, sarge.'

They made their way to the main square of the old British barracks, which overlooked Sarsfield Avenue through a cast-iron railing. They saluted and lowered the flag. Outside, a young boy accompanying his mother, and saluted them solemnly.

***

'And would this young lady's name be Keelin Roche, Dickie?'

'It would, John.'

How the fuck did Caple know this already?

'A few things you should know. First, she's the Battalion 2i/c's daughter. That's the only reason Horace agreed to host them. Second, she tried to get a cadetship this year. Third,

154

she is a corporal in the FCA field signals company in Wolfe Barracks. And fourth, she is *allegedly* having an affair with the married PDF cadre officer.'

'Oh.'

'Other than that, she's a lovely girl. You'll have a great night.'

Dickie made for the door. He couldn't seem to take a dump in this place without Caple knowing.

'Everything okay at the weapons display?'

'Yes, John,' Dickie replied, immediately worried his voice had risen an octave.

'Two things will land you in front of a Court Martial, Dickie. Ordnance and money.'

'Yes, John.'

***

Dickie installed Keelin in a B&B on the Cork road for Saturday night. He thought the Battalion 2i/c would bring his daughter to and from the dinner, but she came up with some cock and bull story about staying with one of her school friends on Saturday night.

The toasts and speeches were interminable, but Dickie's mind was elsewhere. During the droning orations from the top table, Keelin smiled sweetly towards her father on the top table while stroking Dickie's groin with her bare foot.

The 2i/c announced he was heading for home just after midnight. He offered his daughter a lift to the B&B. She told him Dickie would drop her to the B&B later. The 2i/c eyed Dickie suspiciously, grabbed his coat and wife, and left.

There were just a few junior battalion officers left in the bar. The barman was dismissed. TJ worked the chit-book behind the counter and dispensed drinks. Dickie was fixated on the zip at the back of Keelin's dress. An oversized silver ring contrasting with the black of her dress, it twinkled at him provocatively. She saw the look in his eye.

'Time to take me back to my B&B, Dickie,' she said, loudly.

'Good night Dickie! Good night Keelin!' TJ waved from behind the bar.

As they entered the hall, Dickie pointed upstairs. She took off her shoes and tiptoed up.

'Right and right again. Room three.'

They closed Dickie's door and in what seemed fractions of a second, they lay naked on his bed. Keelin straddled him unceremoniously.

'I'm not on the pill. If you come inside me I'll fucking kill you.'

Dickie nodded, and stuck rigidly to his task beneath her, until thoughts of turning the battalion 2i/c into a grandfather overwhelmed him. He remembered his wallet.

'Hang on! Hang on!'

He grabbed it from his trousers and opened the pocket. Bare. There had been two rubbers in there the previous week.

He remembered Healy pleading with him in the Oasis. Healy had finally scored, condomless. Dickie, in his cups, had handed over not one, but his last two prophylactics. The big, useless, gobshite.

Dickie cursed Healy, and the whole catholic-run, priest-infested country. His next trip to Dublin he would buy fifty boxes of the bloody things in the Family Planning Centre, and sell them to feckless bastards like Healy.

'I know who has one!' he pronounced with absolute confidence. She looked at him; smiling, bare and carnal.

Bulging like a rolling-pin, he pulled on his boxers and edged out onto the landing. No one there. TJ's door was open. He checked the top drawer, nothing.

He crept down stairs. The mumbling from the bar was audible. Lining the ceiling of the hall was a garland of balloons. He took a chair and removed two of the long white ones, and shot back upstairs.

Standing out of sight, he bit end from one of them, deflating it slowly. The flaccid white sausage of rubber looked not dissimilar to an unfurled condom. This just might work. Inserting his middle finger inside, he rolled it carefully back up to his fingertip. The rubber was firmer and thicker than the contraceptive variety.

He went back to his room, his erection starting to flag. Keelin, lying uncovered, brought it instantly back to life.

'Sorted,' he said, starting to roll the balloon over his member.

'Looks odd.' Keelin said in the dim light of the bedside lamp.

'American, apparently.'

'There's no teat.'

'Amazing!'

The rubber was also less yielding than the latex species. Pulling the thing on was an effort. He rolled it down an inch without Keelin seeing his exertion. As it rounded his glans, it tightened like a garrotte. Perhaps the moment would pass.

It didn't. The blood continued to flow to the tip of his penis, but seemed unable to flow out again. Dickie's glans started to swell. Impressively at first, then alarmingly. As the tip expanded, the shaft contracted and became soft, leaving him with an inflated golf-ball of hardness, atop a flaccid lollipop stick of skin. It grew. Now the size of a mandarin orange, the deep purple colour was visible through the white of the balloon. He had to get it off. He felt about looking for the base of the ring. Horrified, he realised he could no longer feel it.

'Jesus, get it off!'

She sat up on the bed and tried to pull it off. No good. She grabbed Dickie's nail scissors from the sink.

'Christ, what are you doing?'

She dug the long nail of her left index finger into the side of his penis and got it under the tight ring of rubber. He squealed. With her free hand, she picked up the scissors again.

'Trust me, Dickie!'

She held the end of her finger under the ring and slipped the tip of the nail scissors under it. Snip, snip, and it was gone. The relief was instantaneous. His manhood, hung traumatised and lank between his legs.

'Poor baby!' Keelin said, caressing it. 'Teach you not to play with balloons...'

She had the most wonderful hands.

***

The evenings lengthened towards the end of February. Ireland was in with a good chance of winning a Triple Crown with an away match in Edinburgh. Lyons and Cole announced they had secured a 'really good deal' from a travel agent for a package to Scotland. Eight of them duly coughed up the £250 required, and took a coach from on Friday morning for Dublin.

Cole led his little posse to the back two rows of seats. Of Dickie's class, he, Healy, Drury and Foster travelled. OC USAC had cleared their absence from lectures for the day. The bus groaned its way out of Eyre Square for the four-hour journey to Dublin Airport, with pit-stop in Kinnegad.

They joined a knot of Irish fans in the bar in the airport. The barmaid encouraged the fans to participate in a draw for a children's charity, putting their business cards in a large glass bowl. Corrigan and Lyons spotted the bowl, and shouted 'Russian Roulette!'

Lyons dipped his hand in the bowl.

'Right, lads. It goes like this. You take a business card. You are that man for the weekend. You score, you leave the card with the bird and tell her to call you soon. That simple.'

'That's fucking evil!' Foster said, hand deep in the bowl.

'Hugo Barrington. Veterinary Surgeon. What a name! That's me! That *is* me!' Cole was beside himself as he put the card in his wallet.

Foster pulled a card up in disgust. 'Darren Bradley. Rentokil. Jesus!'

'Suits you, Henry!' Drury grunted into his pint.

'No fucking way can I be a 'Darren,' from 'Rentokil.' He's not even a manager.' Foster was having second thoughts.

'Rentokil might come in handy with some of the things Healy rides...' Corrigan said.

'You should fucking talk, Corrigan!' said Healy, annoyed that *Corrigan*, of all people, would look down on his scoring.

'I want another one!' Foster declared.

'If you forfeit your card, you buy the players a round.' Lyons shouted.

'My round anyway!' he put his hand back in the bowl.

'Conor McDermott. Chartered Accountant.' Foster announced, deflated.

'Serves you fucking right, Foster. Try scoring with that!' said Lyons.

Dickie's turn. He inserted his hand into the bowl, glimpsing down.

'No looking!' Corrigan shouted.

He withdrew a card with a plain white reverse. 'Vivienne Holland. Mortician.'

Laughter rang about the bar.

'Perpetually stiff!' Corrigan shouted.

'Free go if we pick a woman's card?'

'Vivian is a bloke's name,' Corrigan said.

'It's spelled with an E-N-N-E.'

'Free go if you draw a bird's card!' Cole adjudicated, and Dickie drew again.

'Oliver McCracken. Used Car Sales, Cavan.' There wasn't even a decent make of car on the card.

'On your bike, Mandeville, sell some metal.'

Cole lifted the bowl out to Corrigan.

'Doctor Alan Woods, prosthodontics and cosmetic dentistry. Classy!'

***

The match won, spirits were high. The Scots partied as well in commiseration as in celebration. They made their way to Queen Street and gained a lodgement in a bar. There was an especially large pocket of women to the rear of the bar. Cole installed himself. Returning from the bar holding his signature four pints, he shouted to Corrigan.

'Doctor Woods! It's been too long!'

'Hugo, my man! How are the horses?'

***

Gormlaith looked prettier than her name. She told him it meant 'princess.' She had waist-length hair, blue eyes and freckles. Unprompted, Dickie launched into the genetic qualities their offspring would have.

At the pace the others were drinking, he wouldn't be fit to stand too much longer. It was time to go.

She lived somewhere off Glenogle Road, but the house was full of partying students. Dickie hailed another cab, back to his hotel. He was rooming with Foster, who would just have to find a woman with an empty house.

***

'That's enough sleep for you!'

She nudged him back alert. It took a while. He hadn't planned on more than one performance tonight. She grappled, kissed and pulled at him for several minutes before Dickie felt the throb of an erection.

She rolled a condom onto him and straddled him. She thrashed wildly on top of him for a while, agitated that her efforts were not bearing fruit. He was weary. Weary of rugby, of bullshitting and of drinking. He wanted to enjoy his *petit mort*.

She held him by the shoulders, and began grinding her pelvis athletically into his.

'Jesus Oliver, what is wrong with you?' accused the Glaswegian twang.

'Oliver?'

'What?'

'That's me.'

'What are you on about?'

'I'm sorry, Gormlaith. My real name is Dickie. I'm actually a... detective with the RUC. If I'm travelling with a lot of Irish, I have to use a cover name.'

'Oh. Is that a cover accent?'

'Gormlaith, Gormlaith, Gormlaith,' he said as soothingly as he could.

He grabbed her thighs. He thrust vigorously, knowing the well was dry. There was no other way out. Squeezing her waist tightly, he thrust as manfully as he could for a minute or two. She settled into her stride. Waiting until her head and voice dropped, he feigned a mighty release.

'That's better, *Dickie*,' she rolled to his left, and reached down for the condom. The bedside light was on. She'd see the empty latex sac. Laughing and pushing her away, he whipped it off, and threw it under the bed.

'So tell me all about this RUC undercover work,' she whispered. He was already asleep.

He woke up to an empty bed. Foster, in the next bed, grinned like a cat.

'Good morning, Dickie.'

'Henry. Where's…?

'Gormlaith?'

Foster feigned urbanity, but was just a dirty young man.

'Yes.'

'She had to go.'

'So have we. Bus in an hour.'

They washed for breakfast. 'Doctor Alan' was already sitting at a table with a blonde. She looked like she'd been dragged from page 3 of 'The Sun,' and had tied two table-napkins together to cover her ample mammaries.

Cole was breakfasting alone. He stifled laughter as he demolished a plate of bacon and scrambled eggs.

Corrigan slipped the business card across the table. 'I can't wait 'til you come over to Dublin, Tracey! Those veneers are on the house!'

***

It was hard to get back into the military game when he returned to Killimore for the summer. The Army was now deep in budgetary 'cutbacks.' Dickie resigned himself to long periods of detention in barracks with a BAP strapped to his waist. He volunteered to do consecutive days mid-week, once someone let him out for a run at lunch time. He was, at least, getting £20 per weekday on duty before tax, defraying his bulging overdraft. He wouldn't be back in the black by September, but the red ink on his current account would go from four digits to three.

***

Dickie and the CS Culligan, who was BOS, approached the guardroom. Dickie had just cleared the Private's Mess, and was on his way to deposit the takings in the guardroom safe.

Orderly officer and BOS crossed the darkened square. No challenge came from the soldier on sentry beat. Dickie walked up to the Perspex window overlooking the Inner Square. The sentry stood slumped on the sandbag wall, head resting in the fork of his arm. Dickie and Culligan exchanged angered looks. Dickie removed his bunch of keys and rapped the Perspex. A stir, but the soldier did not rise. He pulled the fat bunch of keys back further and swung them hard at the plastic. The soldier raised his left hand in an emphatic 'halt!' He raised his head, then stood up straight, and made the sign of the cross.

'Sorry, sir. I always finish a decade of the rosary before midnight, sir. Not your cup of tea, I know.' '68 Dwyer declared, piously.

Dickie mulled the cheek of the bastard, and whether he'd make a charge stick. He knew he wouldn't; Dwyer had prefabricated his defence as he woke up. Dickie admired his thinking under pressure.

'Next time, do it in the guardroom, not on the beat, soldier.'

'Certainly, sir,' said Dwyer, with a salute that would do the Sergeant Major proud.

***

Finding A.N. Other

163

Dickie awoke in USAC head pounding. He was still nauseous. Marketing Research in the Cairnes Theatre in thirty minutes. The smell of urine from his wardrobe was rank. The bastards had taken the u-bend from his sink the night before. He'd pissed in the sink. He took the soiled clothes from his laundry bag, threw them on the fetid puddle. He screwed the u-bend back on. He dragged a razor across his face, brushed teeth and ate some toothpaste. He was in his car in fifteen minutes.

He was still pickled. He was over the Quincentenary Bridge at five past nine, driving as fast as his gin-befuddled mind allowed. He skidded down Distillery Road, through rain-filled potholes.

The car bounced into one of the bigger craters, sending a spume of brown water onto the pavement. Professor O'hUigín, Dean of the School of Business, was doused in filthy water. Come rain or sunshine he always wore the same flasher's mackintosh. Dickie was goosed if O'hUigín recognised him. He caught the angry wave of the Professor's umbrella as he swung into the campus. He took the service road under the Arts Concourse, and parked.

09.10hrs. Fuck. He pushed through the double-doors of Cairnes. The place was absolutely heaving, as usual for Rosie Dillon's lecture. She was in her late twenties, a girl of wondrous architecture, and not a self-important arse like most of the faculty.

But of Rosie, there was no sign. Every single seat, bar the one right in front of the lectern, was taken. Dickie needed an end seat... might puke, or soil himself...

Where was Rosie? The inconsiderate, indolent bitch. He had a good mind to report her to the Dean. He stumbled down to the front row, and sat beside an unkempt civvie. He'd give it ten minutes, then head to the shop for Anadin.

Some had started leaving when the door swung open, and Rosie burst in. She was more dishevelled than he. She scampered down the stairs, clutching her shoulder bag.

It looked like her boyfriend's idea of foreplay was dragging her through a hedge. She normally sported a perfectly manicured, jet-black bob. This morning she looked like she'd been electrocuted. She reached the lectern and flicked on the projector. The light stung him viciously. She found a sheet of acetate in her bag, and slapped it on the projector. She searched in vain for a marker pen, glancing up and down at her class. She smiled as she retrieved a marker pen from her bag. She regained her composure and bade good morning. She started to scribble on the acetate. No lines of wisdom emerged. It was not an acetate marker, but her wet toothbrush, projected two-feet long on the screen.

She met Dickie's smiling stare with a sheepish grin.

***

Dickie ended up at the Arts Ball as Paddy's wing-man. Paddy had been invited by Erin, who was in her final year.

The Great Southern Hotel hosted. Erin, a big fan of history lecturer Professor Maurice Hicken, had wrangled the seating plan to place herself beside him. Dickie found himself one place away from the great oracle, sandwiched between his date, Erin's acne-riddled friend Maureen, and Eleanor Cleland, an economics student who had spurned his advances in the Oasis some three weeks previously. He assessed the emotional proximity between Eleanor and her partner.

Erin gushed over the professor throughout dinner. Paddy became bored with her patter, and intoxicated on red wine. He despised Hicken.

Erin's fawning flattery would have embarrassed a weaker man, but the professor was made of stern stuff. He bore every verbal garland with manly resignation. Their exchanges were almost intimate. Dickie wondered had they gone further. He doubted it; the

165

professor always struck him as somewhat effeminate. He was married with children. Presumably his own.

The professor passed a remark about the handsome young army officers at their table. The lick of condescension was unmistakable. Hicken loathed the army. He associated all who served in it with the execution of his uncle during the Civil War. Hicken couldn't have been born before 1940, but the family scar remained.

The conversation somehow got around to World War II. Dickie tried not to ignore Maureen, but enjoyed exchanges with Eleanor.

'Bollox!' grunted Paddy.

Dickie caught the end of a patronising observation by the professor about Hiroshima and Nagasaki.

'The Japs should be grateful! Olympic and Coronet would have killed two or three million of them.'

'Excuse me?' the professor spluttered 'Coro...'

'The invasions of Kyushu and Tokyo Bay. They were going to be twice as large as Normandy. Those civvies were spared by the bombs.'

'That remark is as absurd as it is obscene, young man. Almost two hundred thousand people were incinerated in a country already beaten.'

'With *all due respect* professor,' Paddy retorted disrespectfully, 'no one told the Japanese they were beaten. Not the Emperor. He was a god.'

'A beaten people could have been left in peace.'

'Peace my arse. They'd have attacked again.'

'That is unknowable.'

'I'll tell you what's knowable, Professor. The Allies killed 35,000 French invading Normandy. Half the death toll of Nagasaki, and the Frogs were allies! You think they'd have spared more Japs than Frogs?'

166

Paddy loved facts, even as his speech slurred. The professor realised a graceful exit was impossible.

'Let's hope the world will never be faced with such choices again,' he said, with a regal wave of the hand.

Erin shifted uncomfortably, conflicted between admiration for the professor, and support for Paddy.

The altercation had the pleasant consequence that the professor found conversational refuge in Maureen. Dickie found Eleanor unattended, her date immersed in debate on the strengths of the college senior football team.

***

Freddie Lane was cornered at the breakfast table by Corrigan and Cole. Dickie sat down at the head of the table, munching a bowl of cornflakes. Lane hadn't graced The Oasis in a month. Something was wrong.

'People are talking, Freddie.'

'Your absence has been noted.'

'Jesus lads, a man just takes a break…' Freddie reasoned.

'Rumours abound you've been loitering with that young engineer, Sally Henderson.' Corrigan continued.

'Who says I'm "loitering" Scut?'

'Holding hands?' Cole sounded paternal.

Lyons sat down at the table.

'Morning, Teabag.'

'Morning, Freddie.'

'Freddie was just telling us why we've seen so little of him,' Corrigan continued.

'Holding hands with Sally Henderson.'

'Sally Henderson in third eng?' Lyons asked.

'Indeed.' Cole intoned.

'Sally Henderson, tour guide through the land of Sodom and Gomorrah?' The cutlery hit the table with Lyons' remark. 'Allegedly.'

***

Dickie awoke stone cold sober at nine on Saturday morning. On Thursday he had pinned his 3rd XV team sheet to the Rugby Club notice board. The 'A.N. Other' brothers filled four positions, including loose-head prop. All four Club teams were on the field on Saturday. The seniors were playing Sligo in a Connaught Senior Cup match. The Under-20s were playing Trinity away. The seconds were playing Ballina, the bus was leaving at ten.

His efforts on Thursday and Friday to fill the four berths had been in vain. Dickie had five hours to assemble a starting XV. There would be no poaching from any other team.

He started his prowling in USAC. He heard snoring in Commons' room. A heavy Guinness fug hung over the place.

'Phil,' Dickie shook him. 'Phil.'

Commons groaned. No sign of consciousness beyond a few simian grunts.

'Phil, I need you for a match this afternoon.'

'Fu… go way… me alone…' He turned into his pillow and fell back into unconsciousness.

'Useless fuck.' he shouted. McGuinness's car was in the carpark. He headed for the top floor. McGuinness lay in bed, reading a book, enveloped in a Rothmans cloud.

'Fuck off, Dickie!'

'Wouldn't be here unless I needed you, Rob.'

'I've never played a game of rugby in my life.'

'Life begins today.'

'Go away.'

'Look, Rob, you'll be playing on the right wing. If by some mad chance the ball gets that far, run with it until you're tackled. No one'll pass to you anyway.'

'No.'

'There'll be pints in the Skeff tonight.'

'No.'

'Place will be crawling with rugger huggers. All four teams playing today.'

McGuinness paused. Dyed in the wool soccer player he might be, but he had a deep appreciation of the female rugby fan.

'Good man,' Dickie patted his shoulder as he got up. 'Bring your boots and shorts.'

Dickie took the jerseys out of the tumble driers downstairs. McGuinness and he shovelled down a breakfast of scrambled eggs and coffee, and made for Dickie's car.

'Right, Rob. All we need now is a centre, another winger, and a loose-head.'

'What positions do they play, Dickie?'

Dickie drove to Tirellan Heights, the rabbit-warren of student infested houses overlooking the Headford Road.

'Where are you off to, Dickie?'

'Sally Henderson's house.'

'Freddie?'

'Freddie.'

The architects of Tirellan Heights decided street names were superfluous. There were at least four hundred houses in the place, numbered with meandering randomness. No one knew where number one was. Or if it existed. Dickie navigated his way to Sally's house. Drunk, he could find it without difficulty, having deposited Freddie there before. Sobriety and daylight compounded his confusion.

Sally's house was distinguished by its lawn, last mown in the mid-seventies. A black sack of empty bottles and cans nestled against the gable wall. Dickie rang the bell and waited.

Freddie answered the door in a pink, floral satin dressing gown.

'Dickie, what brings you here?'

'I need a winger, Freddie.'

'I'm honoured the thirds have chosen me to play this fine day!'

'Will you tog, Freddie?'

'Gimme five. I need a shower.'

'Freddie, you're going to play rugby, against Connemara.'

'Quick shower, Dickie, and I'll be with you.'

'Does Hank the Bank live near here?'

'I think he's in 329.'

'Ready in five?'

'For you, Lieutenant Mandeville, four.'

Dickie went back to the car, already putrid with cigarette smoke.

'For fuck sake McGuinness, you've to play a match in three hours.'

'Where's Freddie?'

'Having a shower.'

'Taking Sally up Chocolate Boulevard again?'

'Does everyone in UCG know?'

'I'd say the college chaplain knows.'

'Jesus wept. Where's 329?'

'Down there, turn right, third house.'

329 was almost as decrepit as Sally's place. Dickie knocked on the door. It was answered by a tired looking Hank the Bank in a pair of grey boxers.

Henry Brennan was a third year arts student, whom providence had unjustifiably plopped into UCG. With the demeanour of a 1920's dandy, Henry should have been born six decades earlier into wealth and title, should have gone to Harvard or Oxbridge, should have socialised with thin and dim home-counties girls, one of whom he would marry, to sire some more. Instead, Henry was born the second son of a second son of a large Cork farmer. His father died young, leaving his mother, a teacher, to fend alone for three children. Dark rumours followed, of modest wealth squandered before the father's death, through drink, gambling, or worse. Henry though, had never lost the vestigial sense of entitlement that hung about the Brennans. He led a social life beyond his means, financed by regular fund-raising trips to his widowed mother, and continual borrowings from anyone in UCG with a few quid. His credit in USAC alone was the best part of £1,000. He'd been christened Hank the Bank, or, just as often, Hank of Ireland. Athletic, charming and good-looking, he got away with it, most of the time.

'Henry, I've got a game with your name written on it at half two.'

Hank immediately started to rub his quads.

'I'd love to, Dickie. Had a match yesterday. Legs are fucked.'

'You'll be grand. We'll get you warmed up.'

'I was planning to stay in Saturday. Funds a bit low Dickie.'

'You don't have to go out if you don't want to,' Dickie said. Hank shrugged and started to close the door on him. The club funds were healthy, but any talk of pay-for-play among the civvies and there wouldn't be a penny left.

'A tenner, Henry. Best I can do. Strictly for expenses.'

'Twenty, Dickie, or I'm back to bed.'

'Fifteen, for eighty minutes.'

'Done.'

'I'll be back in two minutes.'

They drove back to Sally's. Freddie stood outside with a kitbag, and jumped in.

'I still need a loose-head, Freddie,' Dickie said as they went back for Hank.

'Cawley is in The King's Head.'

Cawley drank like a fish but always stood his round. He was studying a European-funded course in the Institute of Technology under an assumed name to claim drinking income, while he lived with his parents.

'What the fuck's he doing there at this hour?' Dickie looked at his watch. It was now eleven.

'Hard night last night. He said if I was thirsty he'd have the hair of the dog this morning.'

'Can Cawley even play rugby?'

'Dickie, half your team can't play rugby. Including the captain.'

'Harsh, Freddie,' McGuinness offered.

Hank jumped into the car, and they made for town.

'We go in there, grab Cawley, get a few coffees into him, and head to the grounds,' said Dickie.

'Man has a serious fucking drink problem,' Hank said.

'Steady, Hank,' Freddie reasoned 'I used to have a serious drink problem.'

Hank fidgeted, embarrassed. 'Really?'

'Yeah Hank. Couldn't afford it!' Freddie slapped Hank's knee.

'Fuck you, Freddie.'

They parked in Church Yard Street, in front of St Nicholas Church, and descended into the gloom of The King's Head. Cawley was sitting down to an enormous mixed grill, with a pint of Guinness. Beside him sat Rick O'Meara, Bostonian, third med, and hooker on Dickie's starting fifteen, which was so far only fourteen. Or maybe thirteen. Rick was also tucking into a mixed grill with Guinness.

'Rick, what the fuck are you doing? You're playing in three hours.'

'Gotta get my head straight, Dickie. Late one last night.'

'Rick, we're down a loose-head and my hooker is on the piss. Jesus.'

'We got us a loose-head right here.' He put his arm around Cawley. They both downed another draft of Guinness.

'Pearse, you can't play rugby, you're about to scrummage against a thick Connemara fucker, and you're drinking.'

'Connemara don't have a tight-head, Dickie.'

'What?'

'I was on the piss with him in the Skeff last night. He drove back out to Spiddal on a skin-full. Put the car through a ditch. He's in the University Hospital with two pins in his left leg.'

'How d'ya like them apples, Dickie?' Rick roared, slapping him in the shoulder. 'Have a drink!'

'Finish those and we'll go.'

'You might as well. The boys are.'

Dickie turned to see McGuinness, Hank and Freddie take large mouthfuls from fresh pints. Freddie slid a glass of Jameson down the bar towards him. Can't get any worse, he thought, as he picked it up.

'Ladies and gentlemen' Rick shouted at the German couple nursing a small Guinness and a coffee in the other corner. 'To the glorious Thirds!'

***

Six in Dickie's Peugeot was a tight squeeze. They made the sports ground at 1:30. The referee was already there, a school teacher from Athenry who knew Pearse Cawley well. The motley fifteen gradually wandered in to the dressing room.

The sight of fifteen bull-necked Connemara men getting off the bus was not a morale-boosting sight for the pimply undergraduates in Dickie's team. Last year they'd been playing rugby against school boys. Now they looked like extras on the set of *Deliverance*.

'So you don't see their loose-head?' Dickie asked Cawley.

'I don't know who the guy is, but I know he's not their loose-head.'

They togged off, and started warming up. The referee asked for Dickie, who stepped outside. 'I wanted a quick word with you because I see you have Pearse Cawley on your team.'

'Yes, started playing with us this season.'

'Position?'

'Loose-head.'

'I didn't know he'd taken up rugby, still less the front row.'

'Mad keen, sir,' Dickie said. 'By the way, I heard their loose-head is in hospital. Don't know if they have a sub prop.'

'No one is getting hurt for a J2 fixture. Understand, Dickie? And we're not going to have a match of uncontested scrums. Go back talk to your front row. I'll be calling the captains out in five minutes.'

Dickie briefed the troops. With Connemara fielding a J1 team in Athenry today, Dickie had hoped they'd concede the lesser match. Now they looked set to take the field.

Dickie's game-plan revolved around keeping the ball away from the non-players as much as possible, avoiding scrums, and using the younger legs to keep the Connemara men running as hard and as long as possible. They started a loud warm-up. Dickie got Rick to keep it going when the referee reappeared.

The Connemara captain looked like the bastard issue of a boar and a sheep. Squat and bulky, he had hair sprouting from every orifice of his body. Inside the home dressing room,

Rick sounded like he was warming up the entire roster of the New England Patriots. It was impressive until Dickie realised Rick sounded pissed.

'Listen to me at all times. Any problems in the front row, I'll order uncontested scrums.'

'We won't need uncontested scrums, sir,' the Connemara man grunted.

Dickie said nothing.

'Keep it clean or I'll ping you off the park. Kick-off in five minutes.'

Connemara kicked off. Dickie caught the ball cleanly, delighted with himself. He passed it to his right, then watched in slow-motion horror as the backs spun the ball all the way out to McGuinness. Faster men would have tackled them in mid-field, but the Connemara men moved like shire horses. McGuinness looked boggle-eyed. The nineteen year old centre spun the ball like a bullet at him. By this point the burly farmer opposite him had moved up. McGuinness, his brain processing both the speeding ball and the on-coming hulk, froze. Surprised, he caught the ball. He wanted to get rid of it as quickly as possible. Rooted to the spot, he flung it infield just as the Connemara-man tossed him over the touch line like a sack of potatoes. The on-rushing Connemara centre almost intercepted the ball, but it bounced forward off his head.

Fifteen seconds played. Scrum. Fuck, Dickie thought. Game plan out the window. McGuinness was trying to get up when Dickie pushed him down again.

'Alright?'

'Okay, Dickie,' he replied.

'Scrum down' the referee shouted. Dickie and Rick noticed that the unknown Connemara prop had moved around to loose-head. This left Pearse Cawley to confront an enormous tight-head with no visible neck. They rotated their own props in retaliation. Dickie saw the disgust in the opposing front row. They scrummed down, Cawley having moved left to face the other virgin prop, a porcine-looking man. UCG's scrum-half put the ball in, straight down the middle. This resulted in an unplanned contest for the ball. The Connemara hooker's thick leg flew up to hook the ball. On the left of the scrum, Cawley and his opposite were getting intimate. The Connemara-man screamed. From the opposition front row came a grunt.

'Ginger can't scrum. Break his fuckin neck!'

It was whispered, but loud enough for the referee to hear. The Connemara men put on an eight-fat-men shove. Dickie saw the flash of a fist below, and the Connemara front row went straight to the ground. Cawley and his man traded punches on the left. The referee blew his whistle frantically.

'Up! Up!' he shouted as the packs slowly got to their feet. All bar the Connemara hooker, who was out cold. Cawley was still swinging as he stood up. 'Stop!' the referee shrieked.

'You two have never played a minute of rugby in your lives! Captains!'

Dickie and his opposite shuffled forward.

'I need a doctor for this man,' he said, looking at Dickie. Dickie turned to Rick and indicated the prone hooker.

'I'm not treating that fucker!'

'I can send you off right now!' said the referee.

Rick bent down over the unconscious man and slapped him hard in the face.

'Get up you cunt!'

The c-word definitely sounded worse in a Boston twang. The hooker opened his eyes, and slowly rose to his feet.

'One minute and thirty seconds on the clock and neither team has a full front row!'

Dickie and the Connemara captain stared at the grass like children.

'Has either of you got a sub?'

'No, sir.'

He stuck the whistle in his lips and blew a long blast into their faces.

'It's a draw. And a complete waste of my Saturday afternoon!' He turned and jogged away back to the changing rooms.

The two teams stood around for a moment. Dickie looked at Rick.

'Do we clap the fuckers off, or what?'

'Ninety seconds of rugby, I think we just get the fuck outa here.'

Dickie shook hands with the Connemara captain, and led his fresh clean team back to the dressing room. At least he wouldn't have too much washing to do tonight.

'Next time Rick, stay out of the pub on a Saturday morning.'

'I wanted jazz, man. I thought The King's Head played jazz?'

'Sunday mornings only, Rick.'

***

She always sounded like she was in bed when Dickie called.

'Dickie, you can't just phone me when you want a shag.'

'I don't want a shag, Keelin, I want you to come to come to the Spring Ball.'

'You *don't* want to shag me?'

'I don't *Just* want to shag you. There's a considerable difference.'

'I'll have to check my diary.'

***

Except for the engineers, it was the senior class's final year in college. The Spring Ball was looked forward to with excitement among the student officers, and with trepidation by the staff.

The CO and his wife wisely exited the ball just before midnight. The DJ, in the middle of his 'classic' set, had *Mustang Sally* on the turntable. Jack Corrigan abandoned his girlfriend at the bar and made straight for the DJ. Grabbing the mike, he stood on a chair and started dancing to his own lyrics.

'Muck-shoot Sally, think you better close that muck-shoot down!'

On the dancefloor, Sally Henderson froze in horror. Freddie Lane shrugged his shoulders with all the innocence he could muster. The slap across his cheek was audible. She stormed out the door, Lane in rapid pursuit.

Corrigan returned to the bar. His girlfriend stared, open-mouthed, at him. Una Compton was in fourth engineering, two classes senior to Dickie. He had met her for the first time in USAC. When or where Corrigan had first squired her was a mystery. Several of Dickie's class thought her sexy. Dickie thought her masculine to the point of butch, which was forgivable. The fact that she was a nasty, aggressive bitch wasn't. What attracted Corrigan to her was beyond Dickie. What attracted her to Corrigan was beyond everyone.

Corrigan's reputation was ubiquitous, yet Compton ignored it. Corrigan managed surreptitious liaisons behind her back in UCG, which she was either unaware of, or overlooked. She was infatuated with him, and Corrigan appreciated a warm mattress in USAC on those nights a younger filly in UCG did not oblige.

Compton held a large gin and tonic in one hand, and poked Corrigan in the chest with the other. She knocked back her gin and left room, tears streaming down her face. Corrigan returned to the dance floor.

Dickie was doing his best to shower attention on Keelin while watching proceedings. Robbie Lyons put his girlfriend into a taxi. He returned to the bar and ordered a large Jameson.

'Right lads, time to mix up the gene pool.'

The night was wearing on. Keelin was unusually frisky, while Robbie Lyons, Eamon Cole and Jack Corrigan were womanless. It was time to get Keelin behind a locked door.

'You still seeing that married captain?'

'You still chasing everything with a skirt in Galway?'

'Keelin!'

'Dickie!'

She removed his bow tie before he got the door open.

***

The CO was known to enforce the 'no guests' rule in USAC, but the knock on Dickie's door at eleven am on Sunday was unexpected. Keelin didn't awaken. Dickie pulled on a pair of boxers, and opened the door an inch. More startling was the sight of a military police captain standing in the corridor.

'Lieutenant Mandeville?'

'Yes.'

'Captain Rooney, 4th Field MP Company.'

'Yes?'

'I'd like a word. In the dining room.'

'Now?'

'It is important, lieutenant.'

Dickie glanced back at Keelin. She was stirring awake.

'I'll be up to you in a minute.'

The captain turned on his heels and walked back towards the public rooms. Dickie didn't know the man from a bar of soap. He threw on a shirt, chinos, and a pair of deck shoes.

'Who's that?'

'MPs. Want to talk to me.'

She sat up with no thought to modesty; a glorious sight on a Sunday morning.

'About what?'

'No idea. Best you get dressed. Lock the door behind me.'

Dickie walked to the dining room. The CO's car was in its spot. Jesus Christ, what sort of purge was under way? Robbie Lyons sat at in the small TV room, being quizzed by a military police commandant. The MP captain sat at a dining table at the very far corner. Privacy was assured.

'Sit down, lieutenant.'

Dickie wondered how long he was going to keep up the 'lieutenant' crap. He opened an A4 notebook. There were some interviews dated that morning. He couldn't make out the names.

'What's this about?'

'We're investigating an alleged sexual assault at the spring ball last night.'

'Who by?'

'Not important, lieutenant, I just need to establish some timings.'

'Okay.'

'You attended the ball last night, Lieutenant Mandeville?'

'Yes I did.'

'What time did you leave?'

'Let me see... I...'

'If you're worried about the young woman in your room, lieutenant, that matter is not part of the investigation.'

'About two fifteen. Didn't check my watch.'

'And you returned to your room.'

'I did.'

'And while you were at the ball, whose company were you in?'

'My girlfriend.'

'Anyone else?'

'Yes. Not particularly. It was a ball.'

'Were you drinking in the company of Lieutenant Corrigan or Lieutenant Lyons?'

'No.'

'I understood that you were.'

'If you mean was I within ten feet of them at the same bar, I was. If you mean was I in a round with them, I wasn't.'

'Did you see an altercation between Lieutenant Corrigan and Lieutenant Compton?'

'No.'

'Lieutenant Compton says you did.'

'I saw Lieutenant Compton and Lieutenant Corrigan speaking at the side of the dancefloor. Afterwards she left. It was midnight. I thought nothing of it. She lives here.'

'Did you see Lieutenant Lyons leave the ball?'

'No.'

'Did you hear Lieutenant Lyons say anything before you left?'

Dickie wondered where the hell that had come from.

'About what?'

'About anything?'

'I can't recall all the conversations last night.'

'No need to get defensive, lieutenant.'

'You're classifying a straight answer as being defensive.'

'You're not in a position to get smart with me, lieutenant.'

'Have you any other questions for me?'

'Did you hear Lieutenant Lyons make a remark about "diluting the gene pool"?'

181

'No.'

'Did you hear anything from Lieutenant Compton's room after you returned to yours?'

'No.'

'Did you hear Lieutenant Lyons return to his room?'

'No.'

'Thank you, Lieutenant Mandeville, that's all for now.'

***

The MPs returned on Monday. The allegation against Robbie Lyons was that he went to Compton's room after she left the ball, and sexually assaulted her. He agreed he went to her room, he denied sexually assaulting her. The three other females in her class accepted her version. A few of Lyons' class stuck to his. The vast majority of USAC residents were neutral on the matter.

There was no rape, no witnesses, and no evidence. The atmosphere in USAC remained toxic. The investigation would continue for the summer. It eventually concluded with insufficient evidence to bring any charges. Lyons was formally admonished by his CO back in his unit, for having been in Compton's room without her consent.

***

Deep in the confined lunacy of the final week of exams, a group of them sat watching TV in the main ante-room. An unofficial apartheid was now in place, where the females watched TV in the small ante-room, and the rest confined themselves to the main ante-room. There was some intermingling, but when any of the males attempted entry to the small ante-room, there was a frisson of tension.

Dickie padded past the glass door of the small ante-room. It was just as well the girls were where they were. The seniors were in the main ante-room, watching *Once Upon a Time in America*. Noodles eyed Deborah in the shower, and raped her in the car.

'Jaysus, Teabag, that's a bit like you and my ex.' Corrigan sneered at the defenceless Lyons. A snigger went through the group, no one wanting the females next door to hear them.

'Fuck you, Corrigan!'

Cole planted his hand on Lyon's shoulder. 'Teabag is dead! Long live Noodles!'

A car-horn tooted outside. Lyons patted his backside in search of his wallet.

'You got a fiver, Eamon? You can have a slice of my pizza.'

Cole pulled his wallet out and handed it over. Lyons extracted a fiver, and was about to hand the wallet back when he looked into one of the pockets.

'Well, well boys, what do we have here?' He pulled his index finger out, with a blue rubber ring around the base of it. 'This, gentlemen, is the first confirmed sighting of the "Ring of Kerry!"'

Cole was on his feet in a split second.

'Hand that back you little fuck!'

Lyons retreated, the ring held aloft on his finger.

'When a young lady, in the throes of passion, asks Eamon here if he's wearing any protection, he puts her hand on the base of his todger, where this little baby sits. She thinks she's covered. Cole shoots his goo!'

Cole was still in pursuit.

'Lyons!'

'So if you see any enormous little bastards running around Galway in a year or two...!'

'Jesus. That's brilliant!' Healy turned to Foster. 'Why didn't I think of that?'

Dickie and the rest of his class were glad to be out of USAC for the summer, and back to the daily grind of military life. Rumours were rife in Killimore about what had gone on at the ball. Dickie was asked on more than one occasion about the incident. He said nothing. There was nothing to say.

***

Dickie had heard of coursing back home in Wicklow, but knew no one who coursed. It was a way of life in Killimore, and attracted monstrous crowds.

Dickie still found time between numerous barrack duties to get out for a run and see the coursing spectacle for the first time. Horace made an appearance. Caple even took a night off on Wednesday while his wife went home to her parents. They headed for the coursing, and the County Arms afterwards. Dickie didn't realise that poker players followed the great coursing caravan.

The main lounge in the County Arms had been cleared, and laid with card tables. There were four 'small stakes' tables, with maximum bets of £100, and two other tables, with a maximum bet of €1,000 or half the pot. A crowd had formed around one of these, where the pot now stood at £45,000. Back home, that would get Dickie a decent house and a few acres. The hand fell to a spectacled gent. A roar of applause went up from the crowd.

'If there's 45 grand on a table down here, how much are they playing for in the private sessions upstairs?' whispered Caple.

They grabbed a steak and Caple headed back to the mess. Dickie wandered back to the Arms. There was a disco on the first floor. He got a drink.

'Hi Dickie, long time no see.'

It was Ciara Fitzgerald. He hadn't seen her since his twenty first birthday. She looked stunning, and seemed unburdened of her former virginity.

'Didn't recognise you, Ciara.'

'Not a school girl anymore.'

'No.'

She wore a tight sleeveless black top over black jeans and boots. Her hair had darkened somewhat. She sipped a rum and coke. A few of her friends gossiped behind. She had filled in every direction. In her boots, she was almost at eye-level to him.

'What are you doing these days?'

'First arts, UCC. You?'

'Going into third year in UCG. Business.'

'And then?'

'Probably Lebanon next winter.'

A glimmer of alarm in her eyes, but she gave nothing else away.

'Be careful.'

'About the last time... I wanted to say...'

'My fault. Schoolgirl stuff.' She batted the memory away with self-deprecation.

The room heaved to the beat of Salt-N-Pepa. Dickie moved close to her to be heard. She held her head by his cheek. He could smell her hair.

'Ciara, could we ...?'

In the smoky fug of the dancefloor, he hadn't noticed her. Maeve Reilly, in what passed for Killimore's version of the Salt-N-Pepa dance routine, rubbed her buttocks into Dickie's groin.

'Hello Dickie!'

'Maeve! Excuse me, but...'

Ciara turned to her friends in disgust as Maeve continued her frottage.

'Ciara!'

'It's okay Dickie, we were leaving anyway.'

She made her with her friends to the cloakroom. Dickie followed. A queue of hackneys formed outside.

'Dickie Mandeville, you really are pathetic!' She climbed into the back of a hackney, and was gone.

The bouncer let him back in the door. The Proclaimers were playing to loud booing. It was the last song of the evening.

'Haven't seen you in a long time Dickie.'

'Maeve. Why did you do that?'

'You weren't like that last time.'

'I was talking to someone.'

'I thought you were more interested in women than girls.'

'I'm going.' He finished his gin.

'So am I.'

She left her drink and followed him downstairs.

'I'm staying in the barracks tonight Maeve.'

He walked down the river, towards the main gate. She followed at a trot.

'You can give me a lift in the morning.'

'No.'

They were almost at the gate. She grabbed his arm, her other hand squeezed between his legs.

'I know you want to.'

His blushed as he hardened in her hand. What the hell.

The worst thing arriving at the gate with a woman was the careworn look of concern from the gate policeman. He wished Dickie a leery good night, a pause between the words.

The lights were out. Caple and the orderly officer were in bed. He padded quickly upstairs, Maeve behind him. They fumbled with each other at the side of his bed. Dickie, sour-tempered and conscious he had to have her home in less than six hours, was peremptory.

'Take it easy.'

'What?'

'Slow down.'

She stood in an open white blouse, he was down to his boxers.

'Slow down? You practically pulled my cock out in the street.'

'You think you can have anyone...'

'This is your idea.'

'It's not. I want to go.'

A red mist of bitterness, of lust for Ciara, of shame for standing here with someone he didn't want, descended over him. He forced himself on her. She resisted weakly.

'Take me home now.'

The got dressed without a word. The gate policeman smiled wanly as Dickie drove out the gate.

He stopped down the lane from her house.

'Fuck you Dickie Mandeville.'

***

'No way lads, I haven't a fucking bean!' Paddy pleaded, sucking earnestly on his pipe.

'All work and no play makes Paddy a dull boy.' O'Leary was determined to get at least one partner into Galway for a drink. Macroeconomics II had defeated Paddy. Worse still was the fact that the lecturer who failed him was a corporal from the Barracks. He was a part-time lecturer, who had secured the post following award of a doctorate in the US. Paddy

187

endured the ignominy of changing into civilian attire, strolling up to the Barracks, and sitting down with Private Lehane at the back of the cookhouse, where the mysteries of the IS-LM model were explained to him.

'Summer School' took place in August of every year. Those who had failed an exam the previous semester congregated in USAC for repeats.

The shame repeating exams was one thing. The fact that the repeats took place during Galway race week was worse. USAC was thronged with visiting officers on the piss for a week of gambling and socialising at the country's best, and longest, race meet.

Students were allowed two days study per exam, plus leave on the day of the exam.

'I'll go in with you Richie,' Healy announced. 'I've fucking had enough.'

Healy and O'Leary were repeating Geography.

'Good man Healy. You drive, Dickie!' O'Leary was on a roll.

'Overdrawn to hell. Seriously.' Dickie just want to keep the head down and pass.

'Bank manager wrote to me. Monthly spend limit of a hundred quid, no more cheques,' said Paddy.

Paddy's MO was to cheque for £40 in the Skeffington. This he would drink down to pocket change, before repeating the process the following night. He did this most nights of the week, and was still at a loss why his overdraft was equivalent to half his salary. The Skeffington, well used to his antics, dutifully held his pile of cheques until the 16th of the month, after the officers' mess bank lodgement. They didn't want him to bounce a mess bill, and face military charges.

'I'll buy you a pint.' O'Leary, sweetly.

'No cheques left, lads.' Paddy shuffled through his paperwork. 'I thought there were 25 cheques in a book?'

'There are, you plank.' Healy shouted across the corridor.

'No. This one ends on 517. Starts on 500.'

'What fucking bank are you with Paddy?' O'Leary asked.

'Allied Irish.'

'Same as me,' said Healy, fluttering his chequebook. 'There, 25 cheques.'

They congregated in Paddy's room, sure of catching this pathetic attempt at malingering. The chequebook had a narrow metal spiral binder. Healy produced his. 25 cheques and stubs. Paddy offered up his. 17 stubs, all made out to £40 cash.

'That's pretty fucking unusual man,' O'Leary declared. 'Never saw a cheque book with 17 cheques.'

'The bank manager's hardly going to remove eight cheques,' Dickie said, eyeing his own Bank of Ireland chequebook. A flat booklet, with a pressed spine, it was easier to fold into his arse pocket.

'Yeah. I've 25.' Healy checked.

'Jesus lads. You're paranoid,' O'Leary pronounced, retrieving his cheque book. '273', he said, warily. 'That's fucking odd.'

'Literally,' Dickie sniggered.

They inspected it. Another Allied Irish Banks cheque book, with a spiral binder. There were no paper stub remnants in the ring binder.

'I'll ring them tomorrow,' O'Leary said. 'This is something we need to war-game over a drink.'

'Jesus Christ O'Leary! I'm not going out!' Paddy pleaded.

'This sounds serious, lads.'

McDuff, of the junior class, was returning to his room from the toilet. He was back in Galway for a failed archaeology paper.

'How's the study, Cyril?' Dickie enquired.

'Study's shite. I've been racing for the day. The gee-gees are good.' McDuff pulled a wad of ten-pound notes from his pocket. '£140 pounds on *Major Disturbance* in the 2:30. I think we should celebrate.'

They piled into Dickie's car and headed for town. The road was a carpark. They stopped at the Huntsman Bar.

The plan was two pints, and back to USAC. After four, Healy announced they were going nowhere until they'd had a gallon. O'Leary spotted the race results on the TV news. *Major Disturbance* had come in second. McDuff told him it was an each-way bet.

***

The Court Martial was over very quickly. The banks faxed copies of the missing cheques to USAC the next day. The cheques and stubs had been removed from the book, and cashed. McDuff had even signed one of them with his own name. It had still been cashed.

He pleaded guilty to all charges, brought a counsellor in from Gamblers Anonymous, and brought the Padré from the 1st Battalion in as character witnesses. He got an admonishment, reduction in rank from lieutenant back to second lieutenant, and reduction in seniority to last place in his class. As McDuff had been second-last in his class, this was not an overly severe punishment.

Though he denied it, he was now prime suspect for the hoisting of the overalls on the Military College flagpole.

***

The duty corporal called Dickie to the payphone in USAC. The tremor in Keelin's voice was unmistakeable.

190

'I'm pregnant, Dickie.'

He almost dropped the handset. She must have heard his audible exhalation.

'It's not yours. It's Colin's.'

'What are you going to do?'

'We're moving in together.'

'His wi... has he left home?'

'Monday.'

'Does your father know?'

'Yes.'

'Is this what you want to do, Keelin?'

'No,' a mordant laugh down the phone, 'it's what I'm going to do.'

'Anything I can do?'

'Bit late for that, Dickie,' she sobbed.

'I'm sorry, Keelin.'

'So am I, Dickie. Bye.'

'Bye.'

Night Swimming

'She's Suki, that's Lulu, and she's Vicki,' Bo Laski showed the Polaroids to Dickie at the bar. The girls were old Vietnamese flames of his. Dickie had doubts about Vicki. A hint of a moustache. More Victor than Victoria? They were in the Cottage Bar, at a table-quiz with Doyle, Drury, and O'Leary.

Bo was a legend, the sort of student any college with pretentions to renown would have to invent if he didn't exist. He'd spent his first decade after Vietnam ingesting every psychotropic substance conceivable. Someone convinced him to avail of his GI Bill rights and get an education.

Most reckoned he picked Galway for its relaxed attitude to recreational drug use. Bo was of indeterminate age, but looked mid-fifties.

He was unaccompanied, but was rumoured to keep the company of a Phillipina nurse in the hospital. He'd pop up anywhere that served Wild Turkey with his Guinness. He drove a Series II Jaguar XJ of mid 70's vintage. He had replaced the 4.2 litre petrol, which he couldn't afford to fuel, with a black-could belching diesel. It egested two vast plumes of black from its tailpipes everywhere it went, in a low threatening rumble.

Five years in UCG, Bo had yet to exit second year. He held some left-field theories. His principal one was that the Vikings conquered Ireland not because they were better fighters, but because of access to automatic weapons. According to Bo, the writings of the Irish monks could be interpreted in support of this theory. The absence of archaeological evidence Bo explained as a Plantagenet cover-up to ensure that the Irish couldn't access the technology to counter the Norman invasion.

If one inhaled deep enough, it all made sense in a Capricorn-One sort of way. Any other student would have been politely ushered out years ago, but the GI-Bill cheques just kept coming. Tears of regret would flow down the cheeks of the Dean of Arts the day Bo Laski graduated.

From the back of the lounge, the quiz-master shouted 'What is the main ingredient in the Japanese dish, Hochi Wichi?'

Dickie looked down at his puzzled team-mates. Bo returned the photos to his wallet, and mumbled to Dickie 'Hedgehog, man, it's hedgehog!'

***

'Hi there, Dickie!' Amanda Carberry regarded Dickie with a look of friendly curiosity, a Camel burning in her left hand. She was 22 going on 31, in the best possible way. She carried herself with a poise beyond her years, the Grace Kelly of third arts. She was recently separated from Tony McClean, sometime UCG RFC centre, her boyfriend for all three years in college.

'Amanda, wow, hi.' Dickie checked mentally if he'd said 'wow.' He had.

'Final stretch now, Dickie.'

'I know. Last night out before I hit the books.'

'Sure, Dickie!'

'Out all alone, Amanda?' He asked hopefully.

'Well, I was out with *those* two, but they're busy!' She pointed out to the dancefloor, where Hank the Bank Brennan and Billy Cummins from Dickie's junior class were dancing with her friends Kirsty and Jayne. 'Isn't he something to do with you?' she asked, pointing at Cummins.

'My junior class.'

'Lady-killer!'

'So he tells everyone.'

'Dickie! Oh captain my captain!' Hank planted himself beside Dickie. 'We're going skinny dipping on the prom. You coming?'

Amanda returned his gaze with a smile. 'Sure, why not?'

He squeezed them into his car, and drove down to the promenade. They climbed over the low sea wall onto the rocks. The tide was all the way in beneath an unusual sea fog. The night was crystal clear, stars visible above. The lights of Clare winked on the far shore of Galway Bay. But as far as the eye could see, the water was blanketed in a fog no more than one or two feet deep. The bay was invisible, the only hint of water beneath was the gentle lapping of waves.

'Come on, Dickie!' Hank had handed his shirt off to Jayne. Amanda removed her pumps and walked in the water. Dickie followed suit. She held his hand for balance. Jayne paddled in her feet while Hank, determined, stripped naked. Stacking his clothes on a rock, he walked in. Billy and Kirsty looked on. Dickie's feet were already turning numb.

'Dickie, there's no way I'm getting in there.'

'I was hoping you were going to warm it up for me.'

They turned towards Hank as he walked into deeper water, milk-white buttocks disappearing into the fog. He waved, and dived in. The water was no more than eight or nine degrees. The drink was keeping him warm. That wouldn't last long. He executed a creditable front crawl, arms sweeping out of the gloom in a succession of Nazi salutes. He swam for about twenty yards and ran towards his clothes. They cheered him loudly.

'Sad, don't you think, Dickie?' She said, lighting another Camel.

'What is?'

'Six months, this'll all be over. Get a job. Married. Kids. We'll have years to look back on this and wish we did more.' A hint of melancholy in her voice.

'Can't have that, Amanda.'

'Coming back to our place?'

Hank was clothed, and asked for a cigarette. They made the house in five minutes.

A mature three-storey on Sea Road, it was typical student gigs. Half a dozen Mateus bottles tarted up with candles, ash trays that looked like bar jetsam. Amanda didn't look the thieving type, not so for Kirsty and Jayne. Kirsty fingered a three-in-one system. Grace Jones' *Island Life* filled the room.

Hank's bravado had faded. He sat quietly on the sofa, Jayne beside him.

'Drink, Dickie?'

'Whatever you're having, Amanda.'

She emerged from the kitchen with two Bacardis and coke, no ice. She sat down beside Dickie on a faded two-seater. In the corner, Billy and Kirsty were getting on famously.

'So soldier, what's next for Dickie Mandeville?'

'Oh Jesus!' Jayne shouted from the other sofa. Hank's eyes rolled back in his head. 'He's having a seizure!'

Dickie touched his forehead. He was clammy. The fact the heating wasn't on in the house didn't help. All three women were on their feet, flapping.

'He's got hypothermia.' Dickie spat.

'I'll get him a hot whiskey!' Kirsty started for the kitchen.

Jayne loosened her clothing. 'Aren't you supposed to use body warmth to heat them up?'

'No alcohol! He needs blankets, a hot water bottle, and sweet tea.' As fate shat in his eye once more, Dickie started to sound like his old CS Moran.

Cummins sat in the corner, smoking.

The girls swaddled Hank in a blanket, thrust a hot water bottle onto his belly, while Jayne dribbled tea into his lips. He started to come round. Dickie and Amanda regained their position on the two-seater. After a few minutes or so, Cummins and Kirsty tip-toed out of the living room. Dickie was jealous, Amanda seemed more social than frisky.

Hank started to mumble semi-coherently.

195

They finished their Bacardis. She fixed another. The night was slowly righting itself. He looked into Amanda's eyes and hoped she might reciprocate.

The thud on the floor above came in two distinct parts, followed by a scream. Dickie wasn't well acquainted with Cummins, but knew of no violent episodes. He ran upstairs, followed by Amanda and Jayne.

Kirsty was covering her naked body with a bathrobe. Cummins lay unconscious on the floor, naked. A waning erection was covered by a condom. Dickie sniffed the air. It smelled only of alcohol and cigarettes.

'What the fuck happened him?'

'I dunno! He just… He was… Then he…'

Dickie knelt beside Cummins. His lips and face were swollen.

'Need to get him to hospital.'

Amanda flashed a filthy look at Kirsty.

'He was putting *that* on.' She pointed at the condom. 'We were just … Then he fell over.'

'No wacky-baccy?' Amanda sounded dubious.

'That's it, Amanda. I swear!'

'Can't bring him to A&E with that thing on.' Dickie pointed at the condom.

Kirsty looked stupidly at his groin and shrugged her shoulders.

'Oh for Christ's sake Kirsty!' Amanda shouted. She pulled the condom off with a loud pop.

'Get your clothes on!' she shouted at Kirsty.

Dickie and Amanda pulled on Cummins' clothes. They manhandled him downstairs. Hank started babbling. Amanda shouted at Jayne to stay with him. The hospital was no more than 500 yards away. They threw him into the back of Dickie's car and drove to the A&E.

Dickie could tell by the speed the staff that Cummins was not a well man. An American female intern took his vitals.

'What happened him?'

Dickie and Amanda looked at Jayne in unison.

'Nothing. He just...'

'Did he take anything?' The young doctor pulled up Cummins' sleeves.

'No!'

'Ingest anything?' Urgency now.

'No!'

'Alcohol?'

All three shouted 'yes.'

'He was naked on the floor wearing a condom. Nothing else.' Dickie added.

The intern put an oxygen mask on him and spoke with another doctor. The doctors asked

the three of them to leave. Dickie looked over his shoulder and saw a syringe.

Staff took whatever details Dickie had. He didn't know Cummins' date of birth. He gave his

address as USAC.

'What now?' Amanda asked.

'Go home. I'll wait for him.'

The girls had a cigarette at the door. Amanda walked back to Dickie.

'We better go.'

'I know.'

'See you around Dickie.' She kissed him gently on the lips and was gone into the night.

***

'Mr Mandeville?'

Dickie was asleep in reception. The nurse shook him gently. It was 07:30. Staff were

stepping over his outstretched legs. His mouth was sticky.

'Yes?'

'Mr Cummins is awake now.'

'Is he okay? What's wrong with him?'

'Acute anaphylactic reaction to latex.'

'Wow.'

'Lucky you got him in here quickly.'

She led him into a small ward with Cummins and three other curtained beds.

'Billy.'

'Dickie.'

'Okay?'

'Yeah man.'

'How the fuck did you not know you were allergic to latex? You nearly died!'

And the fact he'd pretended to be God's gift to women for the last three years.

'Didn't know, Dickie. Sorry.'

'You want me to call someone?'

'No. I'll call my folks from here.'

They're going to call the MO in Renmore. I gave your address as USAC.'

'I know.'

'I'm going back.'

'Please don't tell the lads.'

'I won't.'

His eyes welling with tears, Cummins implored him.

'I'm serious, Dickie. Don't!'

'I won't, Billy. Seriously.'

He wouldn't. He was the only one who knew anyway. The girls would be too embarrassed to admit what happened. He looked at Cummins. A drip in his arm, electrodes stuck to his chest, barely alive four hours earlier; and the only thing he was worried about was his reputation as a ladies' man.

He waved Cummins goodbye, and left.

***

Amanda was safely back in the arms of Tony before Christmas.

***

University for army officers was not introduced because the nation's thinkers thought it a good idea to have an educated military. The Department of Defence had been forced to admit it couldn't attract people to become army officers. In one class in the mid-sixties the Department had fixed a provision for twenty army cadetships. The army interviewers declared themselves happy with only fifteen of the candidates. The Department insisted on twenty. Nineteen were eventually commissioned. Ever since, the identity of the four 'no-hopers' had been kept a closely guarded secret.

While the introduction of college education had attracted a better calibre of candidate, the downside was the fraternisation of the officer corps with the liberal, arty, students of Galway.

For this reason, the Army Ranger Wing appeared in USAC every Easter, just before the Semester II studies. Their mission, to coax the soon-to-graduate young officers to volunteer for the summer selection course, before they settled into their post-college careers.

Andrew Salter-Day was the officer in charge of the Ranger party. A Ranger for two years, Salter-Day sported long blonde hair and a matching Viking beard. Dickie suspected his mother was lining him up with Andrew's younger sister. Solid Church of Ireland family, indeed, decent land-holding, certainly, desirable daughter, no. Emily suffered that most lethal of Irish compliments; she had 'a great personality.' She also had a face of a second row who'd played too many matches without a scrum-cap.

The Rangers had taken a few dining tables into the rear TV room, and laid out their Aladdin's Cave of weapons, sights, night vision devices, specialist radios, and eavesdropping kit.

Dickie toyed with a HK MP5 sub-machine gun. Its torch-light aiming point lined up precisely with the iron sights. Very dinky.

Bang. All eyes turned, and McDuff stood rooted to the spot, a smoking .38' Smith & Wesson revolver in his hand, a hole in the TV. The Rangers didn't utter a word. They started to gather the weapons into canvas holdalls. Salter-Day produced a pocket-knife and extracted the slug from the wood panelling behind the TV. The last Ranger left the TV room no more than sixty seconds after the shot.

The assembled students kicked about for a few moments wondering what to do next.

'Jesus lads! It works!'

Healy played with the remote control and Sky News filled the silence. The bullet went through the cabinet without hitting any vitals.

'Siemens. Some fucking TV lads!' O'Leary patted the television, and returned to his room to study.

***

Dickie awoke at 07:30 on the morning of his final exam. He breakfasted with the four commerce students. There were six on their last day of arts, and two on their final for engineering. USAC would soon be no more than a shared recollection at a bar.

The waiter served him bacon and eggs, and wished him good luck.

Returning to his room, he chose the most battered jeans and shirt-top to wear. It would be a long evening. He packed his soon-to-be-disposed of writing material, and noticed a green signal smoke grenade at the bottom of his wardrobe...

***

Dickie gave Healy, Morgan and O'Leary a lift to the exam centre. On the way into the Hall, Healy spotted Professor Ó'Murchú, Dean of the Department. Ó'Murchú was renowned as a perambulating bollox of Olympian standards, whose brother was a full Colonel in Athlone. The academic did not like the soldier. His dislike extended to all officers. Nothing would give him greater pleasure than to catch a young officer cheating.

'Oh shit! Ó'Murchú!' Healy declared in the lobby. He walked over to the bin, and broke four of Mohammed the Paki's finest rulers into it.

They took their seats in blocks by faculty and year. Geraldine O'Dea, postgrad, and member of the Diving Club with Dickie, was invigilating. Dickie smiled at her, she winked back. Four or so years older than Dickie, she was universally admired for the manner in which she filled a pair of jeans. 'Oh my GO'D' was the standard refrain on spotting her arse. Concentrate Dickie... No repeats. A summer repeat would interfere with his posting to UNIFIL.

There were quite a few of them in the big gymnasium in Salthill. Geographers Morgan, Healy and Ryall sat behind him. O'Leary and the Spaniards were to the left. The Fourth Engineering were in there too. Some three hundred all told.

Last exam in Galway. The fairy-tale was over. Next week they'd be back to the barrack grind for good. Dickie took his paper from a female invigilator, her figure unknowable beneath loose dungarees.

There was a minor kerfuffle among the geographers an hour later. Healy was involved. Nothing serious. Everyone back to their papers. The funereal march of invigilators. The hurried turn of page, dry coughs. The raised arm for another answer book. The girls with childhood tokens sitting on the exam desk. The involuntary tapping of pen. He wouldn't miss it.

Fingers aching from almost three hours of continuous writing, Dickie checked the clock. Ten minutes to go. He looked at the fourth question again. There was nothing else to write. He looked back over the other three, and the strategic two empty pages he'd left in his answer booklet after each one. He had egested every single thought he could muster onto the page.

He thought of rising. No, he would stay here to the bell.

12:30hrs crawled around. He handed his answer books to the unknown postgrad, not a single additional word written in the last ten minutes. He made his way out to the lobby. Students conducted pointless post mortems.

O'Leary lit up a Rothmans.

'Warwick for a few?'

The geographers exited the lobby onto the steps. Morgan, spitting rage, grabbed Healy by the scruff.

'You stupid, ignorant, fucking prick!'

Healy had a sly grin on his face.

'You could have had us both caught in there!'

'Calm the fuck down. Nothing happened!' Healy pushed him away.

'What the fuck?' O'Leary asked.

'Invigilator asked for my ruler during the exam,' Morgan explained.

'So what?'

'The one with cogs for four essays on the back.'

'You get caught?'

'No.'

'So fucking what?'

'Ruler was for that fuck,' Morgan jabbed a finger at Healy. 'Healy broke all his rulers on the way in. Realised he needed a ruler. Asked the invigilator. She took a ruler from some random bird. Healy says no. He wants *my* ruler! I nearly shat myself. Kept my ruler for an hour. I had to make shit up for two questions!'

***

The afternoon exam crew joined them in the Warwick just before six. They convoyed back up to the college to the student bar in the Quad. A steady stream of pints and garlic chips kept them fuelled until closing time. Salthill would be mobbed tonight. It was time to get to the Oasis.

'What the fuck are you going to do with that?' Healy asked, patting the smoke grenade.

'Jesus! Forgot that!' Dickie grunted. 'We'll never be back.'

'Never will!' Healy was laughing his head off. 'We going?

Dickie pulled the pin and rolled it under a bench.

'We are now!'

They made quickly for the door, leaving the Quad bar for the last time.

From the lawn, they watched the thin plume of smoke grow into a thick, green belch.

Students started to run, screaming, into the Quad.

'Our work here is done!' Healy always loved *Animal House*.

Dickie drove to the Oasis. They went in the side door, escorted by Timmy the boxing bouncer. Healy ordered pints, and was gone. Dickie gradually discerned the other exam goers from USAC.

'Hi, Dickie,' Geraldine, the invigilator at the morning's exams, tapped his shoulder.

'Hi.'

He thought she was being social. She wasn't.

'Tell your friend if I ever catch him cheating again, I'm turning him in.'

'Who?'

'Healy.'

'You caught Healy cheating.'

'Several times.'

'You didn't turn him in?'

'She wouldn't let me.' Geraldine pointed out onto the dance floor. The hands of the dungaree-clad invigilator were thrust deep into Healy's arse pockets, while she buried her tongue in his mouth.

***

'My office, Dickie,' Captain Caple said after morning parade. 'Bring the puppy with you.'

Dickie gave the nod to the recently commissioned Odhran Higgins to follow him.

'Start shining your swords and smartening your privates.'

'What's up?' asked Dickie.

'You're off to the Park next week, ambassadors' credentials, American and Hungarian.

'I thought Eastern Command do all that stuff?'

'They do, but they're flat out with the EU presidency, a Lebanon rotation, and a Council of Ministers meeting. They've decided to share the joy with their rural cousins.'

'Great.'

'The CS will get them ready for first rehearsal at 11:30. Better pull your finger out.'

'When is it?' asked Higgins.

'Depart here Monday morning 10:00hrs, rehearsal in the park at 15:30, overnight McKee, parade at 08:30 Tuesday morning, US ambassador at 09:30hrs, Hungarian at 10:30hrs, Depart for Killimore at 12:00hrs.' Caple rattled off like gunfire.

'Okay, John.' Dickie and Higgins went to B Company stores to draw swords. The CQ handed them out with a cheery grunt.

'You ever done flag-officer before, Higgins?'

'No, wasn't tall enough.'

***

Dickie was conscious of a bell sounding, starting to hurt his ears. Through the slits of his eyes, he could make out yellowing wallpaper, and a leatherette armchair.

'Dickie, Dickie,' something was moving him, he wanted to be left alone. 'Dickie, it's six-thirty am, you wanted me to wake you.'

Higgins knelt on the side of his bed, nurse-like.

'Go away, Higgins.'

'I've got Solpadine and water.'

Dickie tried to get up, but the floor was unsteady. His mouth tasted of decaying Liebfraumilch. Still images of his night out with Lyons in Dublin played at the back of his eyes. What was he doing going on a bender the night before a guard of honour? He wondered would he be better off shoving two fingers down his throat.

'Where's the bog?'

'Down here, on the right,' said Higgins.

He reached the toilet and tried to unzip his fly before he realised he was naked; he felt a mighty contraction in his stomach. He just got his head into the bowl just in time.

'You all right, Dickie?' Higgins asked from the shower.

'Tasted better on the way down,' Dickie groaned. He got into the shower, staying until the shower cubicle stopped moving. 'What time did I get in at?'

'I heard you around five.'

'I'm going to meet the CS. You can order me a fry.'

'Okay, Dickie.'

Dickie took his time shaving, his hands were still shaky. He walked to the cookhouse, and saw the CS outside having a cigarette with two of the sergeants.

'All okay CS?'

'Fine sir, fifty men present and correct. You okay sir, you look a little pale?'

'Bit of a head-cold, CS.'

'You sound poorly.'

'Pretty heavy head-cold.'

'I didn't see you bring any civvies with you sir.' The CS wasn't letting go.

'I didn't bring any civvies with me, CS,' said Dickie, technically true.

'Armoury at 08:00hrs?'

'They'll be ready sir.'

He flashed a smart salute. Dickie headed for the mess, hoping there wouldn't be any senior officers there. Higgins was on his own, in the far corner of the dining room. Dickie looked at the cereals, couldn't face them, and took a glass of orange juice.

'You order me a fry?'

'On the way, Dickie. Who were you out with?'

'That baboon Robbie Lyons, my senior class. He found a set of civvies for me somewhere.'

They finished breakfast just as some commandant wandered in. He sat at another table reading the paper. They went upstairs to change.

'I need a dump,' said Dickie.

Dickie shivered as a satisfying effort emerged from his backside. A tug at his shoulders. He parted his legs and looked past his wedding tackle into the toilet bowl. A dark crescent of faeces glinted on the tail of his only shirt.

'Fuck! Jesus! No! Higgins!'

No answer.

'HIGGINS!'

'Dickie, are you Okay?' Higgins said, running into the ablutions.

'No I'm fucking not well okay! You got a scissors?'

'No.'

'A knife?'

'No.'

'Bring me my sword!'

'Okay, Dickie.'

Higgins was puzzled, but thought better of questioning. He came back and pushed the blade under the cubicle door. 'I wiped the brasso off the hilt, Dickie.'

'Okay.'

The hilt jammed under the door.

'Fuck it! Pass it over the top.'

Dickie grabbed the hilt. He removed his shirt, trying not to spread the offending stain. He attended to his own backside, then took some tissue to his shirttail. He draped the shirt over the cubicle door, then stabbed the blade into the tail just above the stain. He pulled the shirt sideways, expecting the shirt to tear horizontally. It didn't. With a loud rip, the shirt split vertically up to the shoulders.

'Fuck!'

'Dickie?'

'Shut up, Higgins!' He grabbed each brown shirttail, tearing at right angles to the vertical split. He threw the soiled flaps in the bowl, wiped his hands and flushed. One tail stuck insolently in the u-bend.

'Bollix!' he shouted, donning his bifurcated shirt.

'Okay now, Dickie?'

'Fuck off and play with the soldiers!'

***

'But I did the Officers' Mess audit last time.' Dickie looked pleadingly at Caple, who'd just produced the Barrack Routine Order with Dickie's name on the audit board.

'You did, Dickie, but the only other junior officer in the barracks is the Mess Secretary, and he can't audit himself. I'm the adjutant and I'm doing the NCOs. Tough shit.'

***

The overseas party in Killimore was Dickie's idea. He stood alone in a corner of the County Arms disco, head spinning. Why he'd stayed in a round for six hours with Cole and Lyons was beyond him. They had left him in pursuit of women. The corners of the room danced left and right, out of sync with the back-beat. And then she appeared.

'Dickie.'

'Maeve.'

He hadn't seen her since that night. Her eyes burned. She leaned forward. He retreated. She locked her arms around his neck and started to kiss him. She pushed her groin hard into his. He had no idea if she was interested in getting back in bed with him, or was luring him somewhere to kill him. He ran towards the residents bar, down the stairs and out. She didn't see him. Nor did the lads. He stumbled along the river and back to the barracks.

He awoke on Sunday morning feeling poorly. He pieced dissolute strands of the previous night together. Location, day of the week, the County Arms, Maeve Reilly; why was his bed wet? Maybe he'd pissed on his pillow. Wouldn't be the first time. Why no smell? He checked his watch, 12:25pm. He heard noise downstairs, lunch. He grabbed a towel and staggered towards the shower. He could hear Ollie shouting his head off downstairs because the officers had hangovers.

He donned what clean clothes he had left and crawled downstairs.

'Ah, Lieutenant Mandeville graces us with his presence,' Ollie brayed. 'Would a mixed grill be in order, sir?'

'Great, Ollie, thanks.'

'Chef! A mixed grill, four Dispirin and a pint of milk!'

'Go away, Ollie.'

'Don't mention it, sir. Always pleased to help the wayward officer.'

He sauntered off into the kitchen, tea cloth draped over his arm. Pete Clay, Mick Healy, Dick O'Leary and Henry Foster were already sitting at the table, along with an FCA orderly officer.

The fearsome foursome had also come to Killimore. Cole, Lyons, Arnott and Corrigan ploughed through the mixed grill lunch at the next table, grunting, and sniggering like none of them had anything stronger than orange juice the night before.

'You didn't have the salad, Teabag?' Pete Clay asked, beaming.

'The hair of the dog, so to speak?' Henry Foster chimed in.

Dickie had no idea what they were talking about.

'Decorum please, gents.' Lyons intoned.

'Cucumber disagrees with me the next day.' O'Leary eyed Foster.

The orderly officer placed a fork of egg mayonnaise in his mouth. Figuring he was the butt of some obscure joke, he finished and headed for the anteroom. Healy and O'Leary snorted in a fit of laughter.

'What the fuck's going on?' asked Dickie.

'The lads are wondering if the orderly officer whiffed bearded clam from his salad.' Foster explained.

'What?'

'Or got pubes in his teeth.' Healy added.

'Is that a pube, beside the tomato?' Foster pointed his knife at the vacated salad.

'Lads, please...' Cole put on his senior face.

'What the...?' Dickie was clueless.

'Helena...' Clay pointed his fork at the ceiling.

'Broderick?' asked Dickie.

'Yes.'

'She's still up there?'

Clay and Foster nodded.

'I saw her last night. Drunker than I was.'

'Indeed she was,' said Clay.

'After you wussed off, O'Leary brought her back to the mess,' continued Foster. 'Drunk as a wheel-barrow.'

'She was grand.' O'Leary dismissed him.

'I shifted her first.' Corrigan said.

'You said hello, I sealed the deal,' replied O'Leary.

'You didn't seal the deal, you pulled her out the door, tosser.'

'Having squired Helena back to the mess,' continued Foster, 'O'Leary opens the bar and plies her with a large whiskey. Then falls asleep.'

'Enter the fearsome foursome!' Healy declared dramatically.

'Corrigan here reclaims what's his and takes Helena upstairs.' Clay said.

'He who hesitates, masturbates...' Corrigan whispered.

'Sleeveen,' snarled O'Leary.

'After all that,' said Foster, 'Scut couldn't produce the goods.'

'Less of the 'Scut,' Henry.'

'Limp as a wet rag...' said Foster, for dramatic effect.

'She did everything. Pulled it, licked it, and sucked it, no joy. Never happened before.' Corrigan sounded mystified.

'Along comes Teabag,' intoned Foster, 'and spied Corrigan's door. Decides to see what the action was. Spots the cucumber on the floor.'

'What?' asked Dickie.

'Scut figured Helena deserved a little stimulation.' Lyons chuckled.

'What did Helena have to say?' asked Dickie.

'Not a lot.'

'I told him it wasn't the best thing to leave around,' continued Lyons 'So he puts the cucumber back in the fridge!'

All eyes fell on the salad plate, almost finished.

'Thank Christ I wasn't there for that,' said Dickie.

'We tried, Dickie. Two pints of water on your head, not a budge.' Lyons laughed.

Ollie emerged from the kitchen with the mixed grill.

'Discussing undetected crime?' Ollie enquired.

'Fuck off, Ollie.' Healy grunted.

'Great craic lads, but what if she remembers?' O'Leary asked.

They heard movement upstairs.

'Could be Paddy,' Dickie said.

'Could be her,' said Healy. 'What'll you say?'

'About what?' smiled Corrigan.

Dickie started into his grill, craving protein.

Footsteps descended the stairs. Clay hummed the bridal march.

'Dickie!' Helena gushed.

'Helena,' Dickie greeted her. 'Tea?'

'Mixed salad?' Foster asked.

'No, no!' she said, 'I'll have lunch at home!'

'Sorry I wasn't …'

'I know, Dickie,' she giggled, 'but Richard and Henry and Jack looked after me.'

'Lift home, Helena?' Corrigan's eyebrow arched to his hairline.

'No thanks, Jack, you're too good!' She said, walking towards the front door. 'Give me a call when you're in town the next time.'

She waved through the French windows on the way out. Corporal Ramsbottom opened the gate, grinning back towards the mess.

'Always thought she was a quiet girl.' Dickie said.

'Not looking forward to the drive back,' said Healy.

'What about Paddy?' wondered O'Leary.

'Fuck him, he's still in bed.' Foster sympathised.

'Better shake him, he's no lift,' Clay said.

'Pit-stop in Abbeyleix?' Healy asked.

'Just the one,' said Foster, 'straighten the road.'

***

Goat-Shit, Gas, and Saddam

With so few young officers being commissioned, there was no waiting time for overseas volunteers. Dickie's name appeared on the Gazette for UNIFIL just after graduation. His UNIFIL company commander was Barny Ryan, who had been the battalion adjutant in Wolfe just prior to promotion. The company 2i/c was Mark Baxter, a classmate of Barny's. The battalion commander was a Lt Col Gibson from the west, a former military policeman with a reputation as a stickler. Sean Ryall would also be in B Company, along with Sean Pearse, two classes senior as weapons platoon commander. Pearse's middle name was 'Alan,' he was forever 'Sap.'

***

Cadet Dickie had pondered the likelihood of having to fire his weapon in anger. It happened occasionally, invariably overseas. Never, though, through the long, sweating, claustrophobic hours of chemical training in the Curragh, did he think he would ever use NBC kit in anger. Saddam Hussein's threat to bomb Israel after his invasion of Kuwait changed all that.

***

For no reason other than he still had his Cadet School notes, Dickie was nominated by Barny as the company NBC instructor. He and Mark Baxter then had to figure out how to get their hands on respirators, canisters, NBC suits, and all the other paraphernalia Dickie never thought he would see again.

30 sets of used NBC gear arrived for B Company a few days later. Each set had the full monty: inner cotton and outer rubber gloves, rubber over-boots, Fuller's earth bottles and pads, and dummy combo pens. Training by platoon, Dickie repeated the training four times to complete the whole company.

***

Four weeks of formation training passed quickly. Everyone had to be able to use all the support weapons. There were crash courses on the 84 anti-tank, the 60mm mortar, and the .50" HMG. They had to learn minesweeping drills, and how to operate the detection equipment. They had to conduct range practices, nominate next of kin, and complete wills. For the old hands, it was old hat. For Dickie and the other first timers, all new and exciting.

***

The departure of the Chalk I gave Dickie a free week. Thursday night in McKee was a gathering for Commons' 'engagement' party. He was barely out of college, and was going to get hitched. She didn't approve of 'stags.' Thursday was just a few drinks and making sure Commons was serious about going through with it. McKee had organised the usual spread of cocktail sausages and chicken curry.

'Things just won't be the same without you, Pete. No session would be complete without you there in the corner, spouting wisdom, opening your foul lunchbox every few minutes.'

'Go fuck yourself, Foster.'

Cole stretched himself to full length at the fireplace. 'And the Lord God said, "It is not good for the man to be alone. I will make a helper suitable for him."'

Robbie Lyons continued in Genesis. 'And the Lord God put Adam to sleep, and removed a *boner* from Adam, and behold: Jack Corrigan!'

'Now that you're getting married, you can practice Ring of Kerry contraception!' Healy shouted, standing by Cole with his hand aloft. In the bar light it was tricky to see, but he held a white rubber ring on his index finger.

Cole looked down on the mantel piece, and saw his wallet was open.

'Give me that!' he roared.

'I can't believe you are still using that thing!' Corrigan shouted.

'I can't believe you haven't been caught.' Commons said.

'Haven't heard from your sister in a few months, Commons?' Cole was getting dirty.

Lyons stretched out his arms in cruciform. '...and the truth shall set you free...'

'Cole, my sister wouldn't touch you with his!' Commons said, pointing at Healy.

'Actually lads, it's a momento from my late father. He gave it to me as a souvenir...' Cole roared across the room, holding the ring aloft '...of the night he had rubber failure 24 years ago! Riding Teabag's mother! Come here to me brother!'

The barman discretely shined glasses behind the counter. Two military police commandants, in full SD1, with holstered pistols, came into the bar and ordered a whiskey.

Dickie turned to Lyons, his eyes conveying the question.

'Il Duce lost a vote of confidence today. Won't resign. The leader of the opposition rang the Chief, and asked that the Army would 'assist' Il Duce into his car and bring him to the President for resignation.'

'That's bollox, Lyons!'

'Serious, Dickie!' Lyons slapped him on the leg. 'Chief tried to duck. Yer man said that Il Duce was acting unconstitutionally, and it was the Chief's job to uphold the constitution. God's truth. They're on the way to the Dáil now!'

'Jesus!'

The MPs knocked back their whiskies and left the bar. Lyons waited until they cleared the door and shouted.

'Any chance I can have your Sam Browne, sir? You won't need it after tonight!'

***

15th October

They formed up in the Curragh at 20:00hrs. Dickie was the only B Company officer on Chalk II. No one was AWOL, the convoy left for Dublin at 23:30hrs.

Dublin Airport was a strange place at one am on an October morning. A few shadows moved about, tending to airside vehicles. Dickie's chalk was trucked onto the tarmac. A biting wind cut across the apron.

The civilian posse travelling was known as 'Swan-Batt'. Various civil servants from the Department of Defence, Foreign Affairs, and elsewhere. Officially, it was to understand the mission and form an appreciation of the Middle East theatre. In fact it was about sunshine and a week of duty-free shopping.

The admin, checking and rechecking finally over, the jumbo heaved skywards at 04:30hrs. He tried to kip as much as possible on the way over.

Israel looked surprisingly lush and green from the air. They landed at 07:30hrs local. A neat pile of baggage and stores sat on the tarmac. Not a lot else happened. The IDF liaison hadn't arrived. Without him they couldn't without him.

Four hours passed. Morning warmth yielded to the forenoon sun. It beat down on them, a shock contrast to Dublin. They joked about feeling the 'Israeli love' already. Dickie looked at the Swan-Batt party, some already dishevelled and puce. A hundred metres away, and forbidden to approach, were Chalk II of the homeward-bound battalion. Tanned, carefree, laughing and waving at the winter battalion.

Eventually, when the Israelis were happy, the incoming Irish were directed towards a convoy of Swedish busses. They exited the gates of the airport at 13:30hrs.

The DFHQ brief said Ben Gurion Airport was just 140km from the Lebanese border; it seemed to take an age. As they approached the north of Israel, the road rose gently, giving them a view of the Mediterranean. There was another delay at the Roshaniqra border crossing. Then they were through, and into South Lebanon. The convoy stopped a few hundred metres inside the border. A fleet of UN-white trucks and jeeps was parked by the roadside. They exited the buses, which returned to UNIFIL HQ.

The first thing that struck Dickie was the smell. Israel smelled like any other Mediterranean country, reminding him of summer holidays in Greece or Spain. Here, less than a click across the border, was another olfactory universe. The smell of diesel vehicles baking in the afternoon sun mingled with that of flora Dickie knew nothing of, and goat-shit. An old man whipped a donkey slowly past them, reddish dust rising off the donkey's rump.

Jack Salmon from his senior class, stood grinning.

'Well slap my thigh if it isn't Dickie Mandeville!' he roared down the road.

Laid out like corpses at the roadside where two hundred flak jackets, with a chipped blue helmet atop each one, a half-litre bottle of water, and a sandwich wrapped in cling-film. They mounted the trucks by Company. After a drink of water and a roadside piss, they were on the way.

Dickie climbed into the rear of Salmon's P4, allowing him some view of the road ahead. Naquora mingy-street was long; the variety of the shops and restaurants at the force HQ enormous. They passed through a swing gate manned by a sullen DFF militia man.

A short distance on, they came to a UN checkpoint. An enormous Fijian opened the gate, snapped to attention, and slapped a salute on his rifle. With a wild grin he mouthed 'on the ball Irish!' to the drivers as they passed. They were in the UNIFIL AO.

At 19:30hrs, the B Company convoy came to a halt outside a three-storey whitewashed house south of the village of Haddathah. Their baggage wouldn't reach them until tomorrow.

The local mingy-men opened their shops, and quickly sold out of soap, hand towels, shampoo, razors, and toothbrushes. The CS had allocated the incoming soldiers to various posts. Dickie headed off with a section to Bayt Yahun. This would be his platoon HQ for the next two months.

With Salmon in the rear hatch of a Sisu, Dickie tried to get his bearings. The big diesel engine blew warm air back on Dickie as Salmon shouted directions. They drove down to the checkpoint at Haddathah village, turning right towards Tibnin. A lone soldier manned the checkpoint. A winding stretch of roadway took them to the village of Ayta Az Zutt. The Irish on the checkpoint waved. They turned into the labyrinth of village streets, the driver inching through ancient laneways.

Post 6-46A was a ten-man position, run by a platoon sergeant. They dropped six of the new B Company arrivals, and headed for Bayt Yahun.

They drove through Total, home to the transport workshop, and the only regulation soccer pitch in IrishBatt. He could see the lights of his post on a hill about a kilometre to the south. To the east, he pointed at another dim point of light, post 6-20, the 'Black Hole.' It was inside the DFF lines, close to the single point of dim yellow light that was Brashit DFF Compound.

The soldiers in 6-21 locked the chain link fence behind them. Two of Dickie's own platoon were on duty on the roof. Platoon mates cheered in recognition of one another as the new arrivals jumped out of the Sisu.

Dickie checked watch. 22:30hrs, 00:30hrs at home. They'd left the Curragh 25 hours before. He made up his single cot, drew the mosquito net around him and was asleep in seconds.

***

Trooper 'Foxy' Fox collected Dickie at 08:00 to take him on the minesweeping course in Recce Company. The IrishBatt Engineer Officer was running a crash course in the new mine and command-wire detection equipment. It hadn't been available at home during the formation, and had been shipped out direct to UNIFIL. DFHQ had a knicker-fit about the state of detection equipment following a roadside bomb that had killed three soldiers in C Company that summer. The last ripe red cactus fruit were falling from their spiny flat branches by the roadside.

They drove up though Tibnin to Recce Company HQ at Al Yatun. Recce manned a few checkpoints on the main roads, and acted as the battalion reserve.

The Banduki Arms, their small officers' club, bore a close resemblance to a real bar, and dispensed a broad range of beers and spirits. Dickie had been warned by his boss to keep away from the place.

The engineers carried themselves with a certain swagger in the AO. All civilised existence for the soldiers in UNIFIL was dependent on the 'whingeneers': washing, showering, toiletry, lighting, cooking. Fall out with the engineers, and you had to pray nothing went wrong in your post.

Some of them, with specialisms such as plant, generators or water filtration, could come out to Lebanon as often as they liked. Their military lives consisted of a rolling one-month formation, six months in Lebanon, a month's UN leave, and four months at home before the cycle started again. One of the sergeants in the current Engineer Platoon had the

220

numerals '12' on his UNIFIL ribbon. Another allegedly ran two happy families, one in Athlone, the other in Tibnin.

The students met at the Engineers' stores. There was no missing them: they were beside well-appointed billets, which bore a seven-foot Goofy cartoon. The dog carried a mine detector above their unofficial motto: *semper in excretis.*

***

The engineers took them through the simple drills for detecting command wires and looking for mines. The old detector was a bitch to carry for anything more than a few minutes- the weight of the detector head caused the bicep to start to twitch and burn after a while. The new Vallon was like picking up a toothpick in comparison.

'Make sure your bounds go at least fifty metres to the side, and a hundred metres ahead of the road team. You'll minimise the chance of both teams being hit if something does go off,' the engineer summarised, confidently.

***

'Couple of Almaza tonight, sir?' One of the departing B Company soldiers was leering wildly at him in the back of the Sisu. He was duty officer tomorrow, and would do his first, understudy mine sweep up to Hill 880 in the morning.

'One or two. My first early-bird in the morning.'

Dickie stood up, head out of the hatch. He was glad he wouldn't be on the canner run later. They were in 6-38 in about thirty minutes.

Dickie joined up with Ryan, the Padre and the orderly room corporal to put in a fairly dismal performance, over three bottles of Almaza. The local beer wasn't bad. The choice

221

was that, or Maccabee or Goldstar from Israel. The bottles came in threes because there was no dollar coinage, so it was three beers for two dollars.

Canteen rules required the barmen to take the cap off all bottles sold, to prevent 'repatriation' of alcohol to dry posts, which all the OPs were. Dickie perched his three bottles on the table in front.

***

Dickie's first duty officer passed off without incident. In the little ops room next door to the orderly room, the signaller sat with two 46-sets, one on the B Company net, the other on the battalion net. He took in the various shoot-reps, move-reps, firings-close and administrative traffic from the OPs and checkpoints, and recorded them in the journal.

***

They still only had one working buried-wire detector in B Company. SOPs required that it was used on the right side of the road up the Hill. This side gave most cover to anyone laying command-wires. It was bright, sunny and cool. Overhead, an Israeli drone buzzed quietly.

Bill Kenna, a Lieutenant with the homeward-bound B Company, oversaw Dickie. They formed up outside the stores at 05.45. The soldiers tested the RDK on a strand of phone cable running out of Ops.

The tarmac-metalled road ran only about two hundred yards south of 6-38. Then it turned into a stony dirt track.

Several attempts had been made to set bombs along this route. The unspoken history was the young officer blown up a couple of years previously between Hill 880 and At Tiri. Eyes open. You can relax when you get to the Hill.

Most of the houses beyond the end of the tarmac were shuttered and unoccupied. Olive and orange trees grew among the other vegetation. Bill and Dickie walked along the track, behind one of Bill's squaddies carrying the Vallon mine detector.

About a kilometre up the Hill, the ground rose steeply. They came to a swing gate, with a spotlight run by a small generator. The first man to arrive at the gate unlocked it, and turned off the generator. In the scrub to the right, Dickie could see metal signs with the skull-and-crossbones, warning of buried mines. He saw no sign of them among the dried yellow-brown vegetation.

The track was steep, and swung to the right. They lost sight of Haddathah village and they were also out of sight of Hill 880. To the left, the wadi dropped away to a series of steep terraces, beautifully constructed by the locals over centuries past to create ground for tillage. There was no tillage now. After another few hundred yards, they got a wave from the sentry on the Hill. The Sisu drove up, and Dickie was inside 'The Hill.'

The soldiers moved about in shorts and tee shirts. He could smell eggs on the pan, and freshly brewed tea from the portacabin cookhouse. The post was laid out in a do-nut, with a large bunker slightly off-centre. The driver of the Sisu turned the car nose-out to the gate, where the guns could cover it. To the immediate left of the entrance gate was a small cabin which turned out to be the post commander's. Next to his, the cookhouse and the rec-room. The easterly tip of the post watched over Haddathah Compound, and was an OP hut, a cupola for a 90mm anti-tank gun, and a concrete-covered observation point. There were two billets for the soldiers, the generator shed, and an ammo bunker. A gabion-protected enclosure above the ablution block was the gym with bar bells tipped with cement-filled tin cans.

The occupants of the OP descended on the Sisu, grabbing the mail bag, the Irish news telex, laundry bags, and rations.

It was 07:30, and one of the soldiers was running laps of the OP. He didn't stop for the visitors.

***

'You can see it, you know.' Sean Ryall slurped a Sprite over dinner in Haddathah.

'I thought you couldn't see infra-red?''

Dickie figured he might be talking though his backside.

'Most of the time. But if they light it up on misty or rainy nights, you can see the beam.'

Ryall was talking about the infrared searchlight on the T54 tank in Haddathah Compound. The standard DFF drill, when something went wrong, was to drive the T54, drive it out and point the barrel down into the valleys.

'Spotted it last week. Bit of drizzle on the Hill. I was looking through the night scope at the tank. I saw steam coming off the searchlight, so I knew it was on. Then, I saw the beam. Really faint, pointing down into the wadi.'

'I'll wait until I see it.' Dickie said. Ryall was still prone to bullshit. Most officers from the Curragh were.

***

Some UNIFIL battalions had never carried out NBC training. The Force Commander required the trained to assist he untrained, for a possible bio or chemical attack on Israel. Dickie was despatched to NepBatt. Fred Lane got FijiBatt. The Finns had to train GhanBatt.

Dickie and Fred Lane made it to Naquora on the Monday convoy. They had arranged a 60hr together over the field phones three weeks previously. They deposited their uniforms, and made arrangements for the Swedlog bus, which was going to drop them in Haifa. Then they headed out to Mingy Street for a real breakfast.

***

Hearing the English-speaking voices at the bar in Haifa, a middle-aged man approached them. 'Can I buy you guys a drink? Don't hear too many Irish voices in here these days.'

Eric had come to Israel after the war. The accent was unmistakeably London East End. His father, who had fought during the war, volunteered to fight for the new state in 1948. Eric had fought in 1973. Now he had two daughters and a son.

Dickie and Fred spoke with him for a good hour. He and his family had carved their life here from the same rock as that a few miles north across the border, and in the face of odds far greater. He and his would never give this up, for anyone, or anything.

Fred nodded and smiled, and got his round of beers in, and wanted to know the name of the nearest nightclub. Eric asked what sort of nightclub they wanted.

'One your daughter won't be in tonight, Eric,' said Fred, draining his glass.

***

A crowd gathered around the Sisu in Bayt Yahun. There was post on this evening's convoy. Foxy hopped out with the blue nylon sack, the soldiers followed him children.

225

'Lieutenant Mandeville!' Dickie went back to his room, and opened his letter. UCG Alumni cordially invited him to a theatre night, tonight, Tuesday 20th November. He binned it impatiently.

Dickie was on the OP tonight with Conheady and the medic. The sky was cloudless. The sun dropped like a stone behind the Tibnin hills. It was a beautiful, moonlit evening. He didn't need his sweater until 10pm. Nothing stirred. Any move by Amal or Hezbollah on a night as bright as tonight would be suicidal.

Conheady was great on duty. His was quiet; not prone to the endless yammering of the younger soldiers. Dickie came up onto the roof with three cups of tea to find the two soldiers looking at the moon through the 20-power binoculars.

'Jaysus, sir, look at that,' Conheady whispered. 'You'd never see that at home.'

Dickie took a look skywards. Through the big surveillance binoculars, the moon was bigger and clearer the Dickie had ever seen it. Every crater and crevice was crystal clear.

Inside the stairwell, the BBC World Service news crackled. The headline was the UN resolution permitting use of force against Iraq, if it didn't vacate Kuwait.

***

Christmas leave planning was under way to allow the maximum number of married men home. He would be duty officer in Haddathah on Christmas Eve, and back in Bayt Yahun for Christmas dinner with his platoon on Christmas day.

All the talk was of a deadline for the Iraqis to withdraw from Kuwait by the second week of January. Battalion Ops staffed a plan to evacuate UNIFIL through Tyre to Cyprus. The Battalion QM announced that full NBC kit issue would be ready in January.

***

The Battalion shoot was scheduled for the 18th of December. Dickie, bored and determined to win something in the competition, set up a small range just north of fence in Bayt Yahun. His target was an A4 paper sheet. He'd fired a dozen rounds when a burst of .50" HMG slammed into Target House. Buckley was on duty on the roof.

'Sir, you're making them nervous.' He said, nervously.

Dickie took a look through the binoculars, and could see the DFF scurrying about, and watching earnestly northward towards 6-21. He decided they were jumpy, so made himself and Buckley a cup of coffee. They stopped scurrying after twenty minutes or so. Dickie headed back to his little range. He had loosed just two rounds when a long burst of HMG went straight over the house.

'Sir, I think that's a firing close,' Buckley shouted down, He had the Very pistol, and was shaping up to fire a flare. Dickie was about to ignore the insolent bastard, and was back into the aim, when he heard the jangle of the field phone.

'Sir, Lieutenant Ryall for you.'

Dickie cleared the Browning, and marched up to roof.

'Dickie, what the fuck is happening over there?'

'Practicing for the Battalion shoot.'

'IDF Liaison in Naquora has asked if there's AEs near you.'

'Well there aren't.'

'Stop firing before they drop a 155 on you.'

'Alright. Tell them it's a young lad hunting.'

Dickie put down the phone. Buckley put down the Very pistol, maintaining a superior look.

'I'm going for a read and a crap soldier!' he yelled at Buckley from downstairs.

'That's what we all say, sir.'

Baxter collected the shooters from their posts at 07:00hrs. The convoy reached the ranges in Ghandiriyah at 09:00hrs.

Dickie competed in the pistol but came up firmly in the rear. His own Corporal Clooney, a serving Ranger at home, won the competition, with Rangers in second and third.

He fared better in the rifle, taking third place individual. B Company also won the Falling Plates and the Combined Weapons trophy.

Back in Haddathah, Barney announced that the Falling Plates team could stay there for the night. They hit the canteen to celebrate. Dickie had beer with them before heading back to Bayt Yahun.

***

The gas alert was underwhelming. Barney opened the lieutenant's bedroom door at 01:30hrs, and was stifling a yawn as he said 'gas, gas, gas.' Dickie ran out to alert the soldiers in the billets. He was in the recce billet by the time he realised he wasn't wearing his own respirator. He alerted the three billets, and headed back to his room for his own gear.

Nerve agent would leave no smell, no warning before the convulsions, sweating, and involuntary defecation set in, followed by unconsciousness and death. If it was mustard, then blistering, choking and blindness awaited. Saddam had them all, probably some more besides.

He stopped thinking about it. Haifa was miles away. If anything got this far, its concentration would be too low to be harmful. Probably. Unless a Scud went the wrong way. He recalled Spike Milligan not fearing the bullet with his name on it, but being scared shitless of the one stamped 'to whom it concerns.'

The company assembled in the cookhouse in NBC gear. The Velcro rank markings for the NBC smocks had not arrived. Army wit took over.

'Where's the CS?'

'That you?'

'No it's me'

'Who?'

'Spartacus!'

'Waterford Spartacus or Tipperary Spartacus?'

If this alert didn't end soon, someone was going to piss their suit. Dickie found the boss in the Comcen.

'Probably a false alarm. But make sure everyone is in full NBC gear.'

'Will do, sir.'

'Make sure no-one whacks themselves with a combo pen... all we fucking need!'

'Yes, sir.'

Most soldiers recognised Dickie for no better reason than he was lanky and wearing a BAP. The battalion net was filled with chatter about whether the Israelis had confirmed it was gas. Dickie got an APC crew ready to alert the villagers about the gas alert. Barney came out of the Comcen with word the Israelis had confirmed the Scuds were carrying high explosive only.

Dickie told Foxy to park up the Sisu. The alert was over.

'Degas! Degas! Degas!' shouted Foxy.

Dickie went to the Comcen, to check in with Sgt Spollen in Bayt Yahun.

'Ambrose is in a bad way, sir.' Dickie could hear the smile in the sergeant's voice.

'Well?'

'We opened the NBC suits. Ambrose opened up his smock and there was another pair of legs in it. Lads told him he was going to die. As a joke, like.'

'Oh.'

'Didn't take it well. Said he'd never see his girlfriend or daughter again. Started crying.'

'What did you do?'

'Said I'd give him my smock if it came to it. Alert's over. Now he feels like a gimp.'

'Let him in on the canteen run tonight.'

'Will do.'

'You alright?'

'Never better. Excitement is the spice of life.'

'Back to bed now.'

'Nighty-night, sir.'

'Jaysus!' shouted the signaller.

'What's up?'

'Helivac for NorBatt. Two Norwegians with atropine poisoning, Whacked themselves with combo pens.'

'Ouch. I hope the Swedes can treat that one in Naquora.'

'Don't think so. Swede's are asking the Yids can they fly them to Haifa.'

'Stop earwigging and get back onto the IrishBatt net, Radar.'

＊＊

Dickie, still giddy, took an hour to get to sleep. He was groggy when his watch alarm sounded at 05:30hrs. He shaved quickly, and joined the mine sweep crew outside.

Dickie walked with Smith, the blonde basketballer from weapons platoon, on the bounds to the right of the road.

'100 yards short of the swing-gate,' Smith shouted to his buddy on the other side of the road.

Dickie knew the soldiers tried not to follow established paths through the fields, but there was only a few places they could meet in the middle. In places, the thistles and cacti were chest-high and impenetrable. In practice, there were just six or seven places the soldiers could meet on the road while the APC crew caught up.

They met a few minutes later and stopped on the road. The road crew walked ahead of the APC and swept the tyre tracks up the Hill. They caught up, and Smith and Dickie set off again to the right. They rounded the minefield past the swing-gate. Dickie could see the DFF guards move about behind their fortifications in the distance. One scared, stupid, or just bad DFF man firing a volley of HMG, and they'd be dead without even hearing the bullets.

They were on their last bound, under their own sentries on Hill 880. Dickie could smell coffee and eggs from the cookhouse.

'Morning, Dickie!' Sean Ryall shouted from the fence. 'Good fun last night?'

'Great fun. Got two hours sleep.'

'I was on watch. Hitting the wankin' chariot soon as you go!'

'DFF done the sweep to Bint Jubayl yet?' asked Dickie.

'No. Lots of activity last night. We thought they'd try to take our NBC gear. They told us that the Israelis gave them none.'

'Hear about the Norwegians last night?'

'No'

'Two of them whacked themselves with combo pens.'

'Ouch.'

Dickie grabbed a tea and ambled around 880 as the lads emptied post and supplies from the Sisu. He was next up on the Hill, for the final two months before rotation. The Hill was a pain in the arse. Every diplomat, clown and VIP in the AO wanted to come to the highest point in the south of UNIFIL, for 'the brief'. Despite the fact that At Tiri had seen more action and casualties than anywhere else in IrishBatt, it was deigned to be the platoon sergeant's post because *the officer* had to give *the brief* from Hill 880.

***

'Sir, problem at the checkpoint.' Radar was manning the comcen during Dickie's duty.

Four armed Amal men were hanging around the checkpoint. It was near midnight. Dickie put down the phone and rolled out of bed.

They were in the village five minutes later.

He and Corporal Clooney jumped out of the Sisu, and spoke with the militia men. Clooney had a smattering of Arabic. The Amal claimed to be looking for a rabid dog. Big dog, Dickie reckoned, looking at their combat gear.

The field phone jangled. The comcen had routed a call from the Hill. Dickie found himself talking to Sean Ryall.

'Dickie, is that you at the checkpoint?'

'Yup, Amal blokes looking for a dog.'

'DFF must've spotted the dog. Barrel of the T54 pointed at you.'

'Fuck.'

He wondered if they had a round up the spout. He ordered his men into the bunker. He pointed at the Hill, said 'tank' and told the Amal to fuck off. They scarpered. The field phone jangled again. Battalion Ops wanted to know what was going on. Dickie told them.

Sean Ryall came up in clear on the company radio net.

'Two-zero this is six-four-one, shots fired Saff al Hawa, over.'

Fair fucks to Ryall. He knew the lads were exposed. Time of flight for a 155 was under a minute.

Dickie told the lads to stay in the bunker. He jumped into the Sisu as it roared back up the road. As they drove through the gate, three star shells popped over the checkpoint.

Illum shells were the polite Israeli reminder that they could to blow the shit out of the place. No artillery followed. Dickie went to bed.

Amal didn't. They opened fire at Haddathah and Bayt Yahun compounds at 03:30hrs. The return fire from the DFF was heavy. Haddathah and Bayt Yahun posts went into groundhog. The real pain with these incidents came afterwards, when the reports had to be collated and sent to Battalion Ops on what had happened. Establishing who fired what, how many, at whom, from where, estimating casualties or damage, and logging it all in Zulu Time, was not easy to do.

A lot depended on the signaller, and whoever was manning Battalion Ops. If Freakin' Frank Mullen, the Battalion Ops Officer was in there, all hope was lost. Like a demented Commander Queeg, Freakin' Frank stalked the Battalion Ops room, deluded that he could morph violent events by force of his personality. No detail was too insignificant for Frank. The signallers' in-joke was that Frank didn't want shoot-reps as IDF artillery landed, he wanted them as the rounds left the muzzle.

***

It was one of those things he'd prefer to pretend he didn't see. Dickie looked over at Corporal Davis, who looked right back at him, wide-eyed, and he knew he couldn't pretend.

They were on an APC patrol to Bayt Yahun at 01:30hrs. They, were in Total when they saw it. Both were standing in the rear hatches of the Sisu.

They saw it at the same time. High in the sky over Tibnin, a green fireball silently tumbling across the sky. Impossible to tell if it was high and fast, or low and slow. They followed its

233

downward arc until it disappeared over the hills to the south. Seconds later, they saw a faint greenish glow on the Israeli horizon.

Dickie looked at Davis momentarily. 'You saw that?'

'Yes... sir.'

'A plane?'

'No fucking idea.'

'Crashed, though?'

'I... think so.'

Foxy was manning the HMG. He had his helmet on, was facing forward, and had seen nothing. There'd only be a sergeant on duty in Battalion Ops. Freakin' Frank must be in bed...

It seemed so high, and disappeared so fast; maybe he and Davis were the only two to see it. He wondered what he was going to say on the radio, or write in the Ops journal. The words 'Unidentified...' and 'Flying...' formed involuntarily in his head. Freakin' Frank would ask if he'd been to the canteen. Davis read his mind, as he willed the thing away.

'What if there were people on it sir? Or under it? When it landed?'

Dickie would have to bite the bullet. It would be easier when he was writing the journal, the tricky first bit would be making the call on the net.

'Hello two-zero this is two-five-bravo, over.'

'Two-zero, send over.'

'Two-five-bravo, possible aircraft... fire heading south over position 6-41, over.'

'Two-zero, say again...'

Dickie cut him short, he'd straighten it out as soon as he got back to Haddathah. 'Two-five-bravo, you heard it, we're on our way to your location, out.'

234

On his return to Haddathah, Dickie wrote as asinine a description as he could, omitting the letters U, F, and O. He told the signaller to send it in on the landline, not on the net, and went to bed.

Battalion were pretty happy next morning. When UNIFIL Ops initially reported it to the IDF liaison, they said nothing. By eight a.m. they said that a 'non-hostile object' had landed in Israel. By lunchtime, Israeli radio reported that a Russian spy satellite had fallen to earth. The skies above were full of prying eyes watching the build-up to war below.

***

The report of the beating in Ayta Az Zutt came in while Dickie was on patrol in At Tiri. He'd no chance to speak to Sgt Spollen before the boss door-stepped him getting out of the Sisu.

'Upstairs when you're ready, Dickie,' Barny said.

'Always nice when the boss welcomes you back sir.' Foxy said

Dickie removed his throat-mike and followed the company commander into the house. Inside was Sean Pearse, a message pad in front of him.

'Dickie,' enquired the boss, 'any chance that your lads are selling beer to the locals in Ayta Az Zutt?'

'None sir, lids off every bottle in the canner before the barman hands them over. All lids into the bin. All bottles on the table before the canner closes. No bottles in the APC on the canner run.

Dickie looked over at Sap for some inkling of what was going on.

'What if someone had a stash they'd bought elsewhere?'

'Easier for someone who's in camp.' Dickie lobbed that one at Sap. His recce section was permanently in camp. 'Trickier for the guys in the outposts. What's up, sir?'

'Your lads have reported a beating and kidnapping from Ayta Az Zutt.'

'Amal police drove into the village,' Sap finally took his head out of the message pad, 'grabbed a young lad outside the checkpoint, beat him senseless, threw him in the back of the car. Told Cpl Davis "This is what happens to Muslims who drink alcohol." Locals think they've taken him to Sila Prison.'

'Who is he?'

'Sgt Spollen's getting the name now.'

'I better get down there.'

Dickie grabbed his flak jacket, helmet and NBC gear and headed out again. Sap walked him into that one, he thought.

He went into the recce billet and roused the duty crew. They'd just settled into a cup of coffee and a Jean Claude Van Damme movie.

'Ayta Az Zutt gents.' Dickie ordered.

'Just sat down, sir.' Cpl Murrihy whined. 'What's up?'

'Kidnapping.'

'Jesus.' Murrihy started running to get his gear.

'Local civvie,' Dickie explained, and Murrihy immediately slowed down again.

Murrihy drank his coffee and grabbed his kit. The Sisu groaned out the gate to Ayta Az Zutt. Ed Spollen was on the checkpoint with Cpl Davis.

'Well, what happened?'

Spollen went through the arrival of the Amal, the beating, and the 'arrest' of the teenager, a local trouble-maker named Murtada. The story tallied closely with the version Dickie got in Haddathah.

'Ed, any chance this guy got drink from us?'

'No fucking chance, sir. I check them back in off every canner run, if I'm not on it myself.'

Dickie, the sergeant and two soldiers did a foot patrol through the village, finishing up at the café below the checkpoint, where they sat down for a Turkish coffee. The locals didn't know anything bar the fact that Murtada was gone. A few were happy to see the back of him. He'd produced a handgun during fights with other young men recently, though he hadn't fired.

Still, they were nervous about what Amal would do to him. They'd be happy for Amal to scare the crap out of Murtada, and hand him back. Dickie finished his coffee and headed back up the hill to Haddathah.

Ryan was chewing his pipe, and freshening the B Company map.

'Battalion Commander's on the way, Dickie.'

'Problem, sir?'

'Just said he's dropping out for a coffee.'

Lt Col Gibson detested informality. A coffee was not going to be just a coffee. Dickie explained the Murtada situation to the company commander. With a Naquora convoy, leave, and Sap gone on a food distribution to At Tiri, Dickie and Ryan were the only two officers left in Haddathah.

The battalion commander's escort got to B Company at 10:30. Gibson was on his own, no Freakin' Frank in tow. Ryan took him up to the anteroom, where coffee and biscuits awaited. He went through his company commander's brief pro forma. Gibson cut him short.

'Thanks, Barny. About this Murtada fellow in Ayta Az Zutt, I hear he's been attracting Amal attention.'

Ryan, tapping his pipe into the ashtray, was just about to reply. Gibson turned to Dickie, and without pausing for breath, continued. 'I want you, Lieutenant Mandeville, to get Sergeant Freyne from four platoon, he's a Jiu Jitsu expert you know, down to Ayta Az Zutt this afternoon, lift Murtada and hand him over to the Amal Police. They know how to sort that sort of behaviour.'

Dickie was momentarily flustered. Ryan stepped in.

'There's been a development on that front this morning, sir.'

'Yes?' replied Gibson, half quizzical.

'Amal entered Ayta Az Zutt this morning at 08:30hrs, and lifted Murtada. Took him to the prison in Sila, apparently.'

Dickie hoped the consummation of his plan would satisfy Gibson. It didn't.

'You didn't cover that in your brief.'

'I sent a sitrep as soon as Dickie returned. I was about to address current operational issues when…'

'Ayta Az Zutt is in your platoon's area, isn't it, Lieutenant Mandeville?'

'Yes sir.'

'And Murtada was lifted from under your noses in the village?'

'They did it outside our checkpoint area sir.'

'Not good. Not good at all. I want a full report on the incident.' The Amal had jumped the gun on Freakin' Frank's plan, and Gibson wasn't happy about it.

'I'm working on it, sir.'

Gibson contemplated a Rich Tea biscuit deeply.

'Lieutenant Mandeville, as I passed though Haddathah village on the way here, I couldn't help but notice again the paintings of those Saad cousins on the meeting hall.'

Dickie and Ryan exchanged glances again. The Saads were ancient history. They were shot dead in a confrontation with soldiers in a previous IrishBatt. In an inspired decision, the battalion commander had despatched his Int Officer to Haddathah on the evening of the shooting with $40,000 in cash. He met with the Mukhtar, who agreed the settlement of $20,000 for each family.

238

He took the money from the payroll credits, causing a stink both at home and with the short-changed soldiers about to go on leave. The families honoured the blood money payment. No more was heard about the killings. For his unauthorised ingenuity, the battalion commander's career ran into the buffers, and he retired in rank.

'This is glorification of thugs who died because they got into a fight with professional soldiers. I want you, Lieutenant, to paint over those murals.'

Dickie imagined himself atop a ladder, expunging the images of the Saads as AK rounds hopped around him. He wondered what photo his friends would produce for his memorial portrait. Freakin' Frank Mullen's fingerprints were all over this brain-fart of a plan.

'Their anniversary service is a few days away, sir. The locals don't exploit it. As far as they're concerned, it's two-nil to us, and should be left that way...'

Dickie wondered if Gibson would consider him insubordinate.

'Indeed. Best as it is then.'

Gibson relaxed and exchanged pleasantries with Ryan. Dickie was surplus to requirements, and could just sit there. He wondered at what precise point in the life cycle of the senior officer normal brain-function ceased.

***

'Rocket's hot!' shouted Hennigan, in his *Top Gun* accent. He had a hand towel wrapped around his waist as he entered the rec room.

Dickie dragged his eyes away from *Star Trek the Next Generation*. There was a running bet with O'Dwyer on how many 'Gods,' 'Hells' and Damns' were bleeped out of each episode by Lebanese Christian TV. *MacGyver* suffered the same censorship. They were the only programs in English, other than a bible worship program that the lads insisted Dickie should be interested in because of his 'persuasion'.

Cpl Davis's dreaded collection of Jean Claude Van Damme videos was on hand if he complained about program.

O'Dwyer, with four trips to the Leb under his belt, claimed the Lebanese would never show repeats of the original Star Trek, as it was too "raunchy" and "Captain Kirk kissed black birds and green birds" which was too much for Lebanese of either Muslim or Christian persuasion.

**

'I promised not to tell! I promised!' Paddy McCoy and Robbie Lyons from the senior class were nursing Almaza beers at the officers' mess in Tibnin. Col Gibson was holding one of his social nights. Up to 20% of the officer strength were permitted to attend. Gibson would consume the sum total of one Almaza for the evening. On principle, McCoy insisted on getting pissed.

'Tell what?' Lyons rose to the bait.

'Loftus'd fucking kill me!' McCoy rasped. Now Dickie and Lyons were interested. Sean Loftus, Dickie's classmate, was in Recce Company with McCoy and Lyons. Something seriously juicy had happened.

'Spill yer guts you cock!' Lyons ordered.

'The gas alert... Loftus... I promised him I...'

Dickie was getting impatient. 'For fuck's sake, McCoy!'

'The night of the gas alert, we were having a few beers in Al Yatun. For Loftus' birthday.'

Tears were forming in McCoy's eyes as he fought the urge to laugh.

'Sean had a few too many beers, conked out at midnight. When the alert came, the signaller rapped on our billet door. I decided to get into the full NBC clobber before I woke him. I got into the suit, boots, respirator, the works, and put on the helmet for good measure. Woke Sean. He had a complete knicker-fit! Started crying… Said he was going to die… Said if he lived, he'd never touch another drop … Asked me to tell his bird he loved her… Asked for his mother… I started to shit myself laughing. He sobers up… Starts thumping me… The boss comes in the door, looking for all officers in the Comcen. Tells us to get the fuck up… After it all dies down a couple of hours later, Sean pins me to the wall and makes me swear not to tell anyone.'

'You're some wanker, Paddy!' Lyons declared, before doubling up in laughter.

'Quality war story,' said Dickie. In the corner, he spied a glowering Sean Loftus. 'I think you're fucked though!'

***

'He's volunteered to do checkpoints until the rotation, sir.' Spollen told him gravely outside the cookhouse in Haddathah, referring to Pte White. White was one of the older soldiers in Dickie's platoon. He was married with a kid, quiet, did what he was told, never caused trouble.

'What's up?'

'Burnt his balls, sir.'

Dickie walked straight into Spollen's trap. The NCOs hanging about the cookhouse broke into laughter at Dickie's expense.

'Go on!'

'Wanted the all over tan. Put a sock on his cock. Turned over onto his belly, fell asleep with his legs apart. The sock was on his cock, not over his balls. Burnt the sac off himself.'

'Will he go to the RAP?'

'Won't see the Doc, sir. Just has a problem sitting down. Happy to do checkpoints.'

Private White no longer.

***

Dickie's last two months were in camp. By the end of April, he started planning the repatriation of mingies and hooch.

Chalk two was always the quiet chalk in both directions. In a 747, a judicious officer could almost import a car. But Dickie was on Chalk three. Full of Battalion staff and assorted odds and sods from Naquora. He'd would have to do some serious work on getting his booty back to Dublin.

Most prized was a Sony three-in-one stereo system he bought in the Battalion PX. He would have saved a few shekels if bought it in FinnBatt, but buying in the Irish PX was an Army Canteen Board purchase. His his receipt was good back home if anything went wrong.

At home the Sony would set him back £400. With the dollar exchange rate on the day he bought it, gratis President Bush and the Gulf War, he'd got it for less than £250. A week's Leb money would pay for the best stereo he'd ever own. The only drawback was that the system was big.

Ali Strawballs stocked a four-foot by three-foot by two-foot cheap plastic suitcase that could fit a small Lebanese family inside. The thing was a tacky, blue affair, costing $12. It had the added benefit that Customs wouldn't think it belonged to an officer. The speakers and tape deck would fit in Strawballs' suitcase, wrapped in clothing. He got a shoulder kit-bag from Hafif the Thief, for six bucks. Not much of a bag, but he'd his clothing into it. He'd 'gift' his wog-jacket and wellington boots to the incoming B Company.

This left room for two cases of officer-grade hooch in his kit box.

***

Il Duce

The 747 did a lazy anti-clockwise arc over Dublin Bay, and banked west around Howth Head. The MO was pissed and singing. The flight was dry, but he'd injected a bag of oranges with Smirnoff Blue, and consumed fresh screwdrivers all the way home.

A CQ jumped into the aisle, wagging his arse rearward.

'Ladies! Prepare to enter a world where you're no longer attractive just because you've got a vagina!'

The stewardess cleared her throat over the tannoy, and told him to retake his seat.

***

Within hours of arrival in Killimore, Dickie was told he was on the audit board for the NCO's mess, and he was going on his Infantry YOs course in two months. He was pulling five or six orderly officer duties per month, including one weekend. It meant a few quid by way of duty money. In all other respects it was a pain in the arse.

Caple called him into the office one Thursday.

'Dickie, we just got word from the Department of Foreign Affairs.'

Dickie sat up.

'They said your Guard of Honour for the US Ambassador was so good they'd love to see you again.'

'Fuck you, John. What is it?'

'Il Duce is opening a supermarket in Killimore next week. You and Higgins are to give the man the ceremony befitting his high office.'

***

The car park of a new shopping centre was unimposing for state ceremonial, but it was wide, open, and quiet.

They had a band rehearsal on the main square in Killimore, now it was the real thing. The guard of honour fell in outside the 'Animal Magic' pet super store. The local councillors and glitterati were present, as were the Battalion Commander, Battalion Adjutant, Horace, and John Caple. Dickie stood the guard of honour 'at ease' and they waited. And waited.

Dickie figured thirty or forty minutes had passed. From the corner of his eye, he spotted Ciara Fitzgerald, a vision in a red top. She spotted him, but made no gesture towards him. A murmur of excitement through the crowd, and Dickie heard the growl of a motorcycle escort.

Dickie called them to attention. As local barrack commander, Horace escorted Il Duce to the saluting point. As Dickie handed over the guard to Il Duce, he realised how horrified the man was to be here. He who walked among Doric columns, discussed the construction of passage tombs, who graced great libraries and galleries; taking a salute outside Animal Magic pet super-store. Nothing concentrated the mind like next year's general election. He'd struggle to hold two seats in the constituency. He looked like Socrates contemplating a cup of hemlock.

Dickie marched him through the guard to the click and whirr of the photographers. He returned him to the saluting point, and asked for permission to dismiss. Il Duce granted it, with a patrician bow of the head.

The VIPs disappeared and Dickie marched off the guard. As he unbuckled his scabbard to mount the truck, a photographer tapped him on the shoulder.

'Jasper Parry, *Examiner*,' he said, handing over a business card.

'Hi.'

'Give me a call tomorrow with your details, and I'll send a shot or two up to you.'

'We won't we see it in the paper?'

'No. He's never published in photos with taller men. You won't make it into the *Examiner*.

Or any other paper. Sorry.'

'Oh. Thanks.'

***

Healy organised a session around the England International match. Clancy Barracks in Islandbridge, not usually on the party circuit, was holding an event because there was an Ordnance YO's course on. Drury was on it. Foster was the only regular mess member among them.

Since half of them had no match tickets, they agreed to drinks together before kick-off. The ticketless would stay put, and all would RV in the Lansdowne Hotel for nine. Dickie didn't have a ticket. Foster, Doyle, and Drury were in the same boat.

Eleven of them sat down to watch the France-Wales match in the bar, as hailstones rattled the sash windows. The barman threw more turf on the fire. The second half of the French match started, Healy started blustering for the match-goers to get a move-on. Clay, Hackett, Commons, and O'Leary looked content to stay put. Only Morgan was keen to move.

'I wonder how much I'd get for this?' said Commons, looking at his ticket. 'Barman, would you like to see Ireland and England from the West Upper?'

'I have to mind the bar, sir.'

'I'm an officer. I'll mind the bar. You can trust me.'

The little barman regarded him with a sceptical look.

'Soccer man, myself, sir.'

'For fuck sake Commons, give it to one of the lads if you don't want to go. We need to get taxis,' Healy grumbled.

'Mick, I don't think we're going to win today. Let's think before we take any rash decisions. Barman! Six hot toddies,' Commons shouted to the barman.

Healy reddened. 'Barman, don't touch that fucking kettle! Get the phone and call two taxis!'

'Mick, that sort of language is uncalled for. Six toddies when you're ready barman!'

The barman retreated into the storeroom.

'I can't find the phone book sir.'

'Commons, you stupid fuck!' Two rotund ordnance commandants looked up from their table. Commons warmed to the task.

'Let's watch the first half here. See what way the wind is blowing?' Healy rose and went for him.

'Bisto Healy, thickening nicely,' said Foster, turning to Dickie.

Morgan stepped in.

'Commons, I don't know about you, but I'm off to the match.'

'I'd love to go to the match with you Lieutenant Morgan. A man who knows a bit about rugby. Let's call a taxi.'

They left for the gate, Healy seething.

'Five black ones, chaps?' Foster asked. They nodded. 'Billy, you can come out now,' he shouted.

'Jaysus sir, let me know before you bring those gentlemen in again?'

'Billy, what else would you be doing on a wet Saturday?'

'I should be under the duvet with Sharon, making little Billies.'

'She nice, Billy?'

'My Sharon is just lovely, sir.'

'Better make sure those six wretches are heading to the match then.'

'They wouldn't get a look-in with my Sharon, sir.'

'I don't think it's a look-in Lieutenant Healy is after, Billy.'

'Ah please, sir!'

Dickie rowed in. 'You can take the officer out of the bog, but not the bog out of the officer, isn't that right Billy?'

'True indeed, sir.'

'Very hurtful,' replied Foster.

'Lads, shut the fuck up!' Drury was glued to the match. 'Good man Condom, you big blond sperm cell!' he roared as the French lock swatted a Welshman.

***

'Billy, call us a big taxi, the five of us are heading for town,' Foster announced theatrically, in his cups. The barman nodded and went back into the mess office to call the usual cab companies.

'It'll be an hour before they get anything here, sir,' he said when he eventually returned. It was one am already.

'Bollox, Billy,' replied Foster. 'Get back on that phone and be more assertive. Tell them we're officers for God's sake!'

The barman spent another five minutes being rebuffed.

'I'm sorry sir, still an hour.'

'Take my car.' Drury offered.

'Shut up, Charlie, you're gee-eyed,' Foster replied.

'There isn't a snow-ball's chance of a cab at this hour on a five-nations Saturday.'

'All right so,' said Foster.

They grabbed their jackets from the cloakroom and started for the square. The cold February air was like a slap in the face. Drury's ancient Peugeot 106 was nearby.

'Jesus. The smell!' Dickie gasped.

'McCoy barfed into the air vent. Can't shift it.'

'Christ, it's vile.'

'Girlfriend isn't mad about it either.' Foster and Doyle barged into the back seat.

They turned right towards town, Dickie opened the window to suppress the smell. The dashboard rattled loudly.

'What's that fucking noise?' Foster bellowed from the rear.

'I think it's dried peas. McCoy had a curry when he puked.'

'Would you not have the fucking thing cleaned out?'

Drury pulled out a cloth to wipe the windscreen. He was moving the water in a clockwise direction when the impact occurred. Doyle bounced forward and head-butted Dickie in the back.

'What the f...?' wondered Drury, unsure of what had happened.

'Gobshite, Drury!' shouted Foster.

'Oh shit,' said Drury. He'd just rear-ended another car.

'He pulled up at the red light there,' Dickie realised.

'Shit, shit, I'm pissed as a fart. I'm done...' Drury yammered.

'Say nothing, be nice, give him your details, straight to Strings,' said Foster, helpfully.

The impact felt worse than it was, Dickie saw. The other car was a Fiat 127. Drury had broken the left rear light cluster, now twinkling on the ground.

Drury's Peugeot fared worse. The rear bumper on the Fiat had damaged the front end of the 106. The other driver opened his door slowly to get out.

'Say nothing, Charlie,' Foster whispered.

'Are you okay?' he asked carefully.

'I think so. What have you done to my car?'

Late fifties, Dickie thought. He walked to the rear to assess the damage.

'My window was fogged up. Had a few drinks. I'll pay for the damage.'

'Shut up you tit!' Foster slurred out the passenger window. Mr Fiat grabbed the back of his neck with his hand, and fell to one knee.

'I think I'm going to be sick. Call an ambulance! Call the Gardai!'

The lights were on in the Conygham Road Bus Depot. A vending machine threw a glow onto the roadway. Drury called out and three fitters ambled appeared in overalls.

'Can you call an ambulance?' Drury asked.

'And the cops! This driver is drunk! I want him breathalysed!' Mr Fiat lay on the ground.

One of the fitters returned to the Depot, the others shuffled out to the road.

'Sweet divine fuck. What'll we do now?' Foster thought out loud.

'We better bugger off, Charlie,' Dickie told him.

'Can't leave a man behind...' Doyle was in expansive mood.

'You want to sing them a fucking song, Paddy?' Foster sneered.

The cold was biting. In the distance, Dickie could see blue flashing lights.

'Fuck it lads, they're here,' he said, before realising it was an ambulance.

'My neck...' Mr Fiat groaned as paramedics strapped him to a body board. 'Where are the cops?'

'On their way,' said a medic, pushing him into the ambulance.

The four of them exchanged banalities with the fitters as the ambulance left. Ten minutes passed. The fitters tired of waiting. Freezing fog moved up the Liffey.

'Cops are on the way. We'll be inside, okay?'

'Thanks.' Drury answered.

'It's half-one, lads,' Dickie said after a while. 'I don't think the cops are coming.'

'You realise, Charlie, the fucker didn't take your details?' Foster announced.

'What?'

'He was so keen to squeal like a pig that he didn't take down anything.'

'Neither did they.' Dickie pointed at the Bus Depot.

'Let's go,' said Doyle.

'Jesus, I'll get done for leaving the scene of an accident.'

'Only if you're caught.'

'Five more minutes,' Drury said.

'Strings!' Foster shouted, still not giving up on a night out.

'Fuck off, you bollox.' Drury was having none of it.

They looked around. There was nothing but freezing fog. Drury took the wheel of the Fiat.

The others pushed as Drury steered it towards the footpath.

'Push you fucks!' Drury hissed. They heaved as hard as they could, and the Fiat jumped

onto the pavement so hard that it hit the Phoenix Park wall before stopping.

They parked it close to the kerb, threw the keys onto the floor, and locked the doors.

Drury did an about turn for Clancy Barracks. The gate policeman looked askance at the car,

and gave desultory salute.

'Bar's still open.' Foster gestured at the lights.

***

Foster called him about the house party on Thursday. Penny, his latest squiring, lived with

a group of other women in Harold's Cross. The ladies were celebrating a birthday. Foster

was instructed to bring Dickie along.

Dickie ditched his car in Collins Barracks, taking a bed in the Ball Alley.

The party kicked off in Bongo Ryan's, before taxis to the house. These girls knew how to

party. The stereo played basso nova instead of chart music. Penny, obviously the new girl on the block, did a few laps collecting spent cans and bottles. The male to female ratio started off poorly, the ladies having invited a disproportionate number of men. As the night wore on, the men thinned out, and a small congregation filtered between the sitting room and kitchen.

She was perhaps a year or so off thirty; blond, shoulder length hair, black, high-heeled boots, and the finest pair of leather pants ever painted on a woman's thighs. She bumped into Dickie more than once.

'Grainne's friend Ita, fiancé ditched her last month.' Foster arched his eyebrows.

Dickie acquired an armchair in the sitting room. A bottle of Heineken dangled from his hand. The seating was all taken when Ita returned from the kitchen with a rum and coke. She was about to sit on the floor, when Dickie patted his lap. Gamely, she walked over, and sat down.

Dickie remained as nonchalant as he possibly could, as Ita slowly pressed her leather-clad buttocks into his lap. An involuntary tingle in his loins; he hoped she couldn't feel the swelling beneath. A trace of Opium teased his nostrils. He'd never liked it. Ge did now.

'We have to stop bumping into each other!' She clinked her glass off his bottle.

'I hope not!' he replied.

She pressed her thigh deeper into his groin, her right hand behind him. His heart throbbed so hard he thought he'd burst a blood vessel. She leaned down and kissed him.

The last partygoers left as Sunday morning awoke. Foster and Penny had disappeared upstairs. Ten, then eight, then six were left in the sitting room. She leaned into his ear, the open top of her blouse filling his face her warm scent.

'We better get upstairs while I still have a room.' She stood and held his hand. He followed her upstairs. The leather pants wiggled carnally up the steps.

She kicked her boots off, and lay on the bed to let Dickie remove the leathers He thought they'd slide off, but they were reluctant to descend. She laughed as he grunted in determination. She opened the belt and buttons of his 501s. No longer restricted, his erection popped proud of his boxers. She took it into her mouth, then dragged him under the duvet, where they finished undressing each other.

He was about to mount her when she whispered that she had heavy 'goings-on' tonight. Her head migrated south; Dickie was happy again. As his excitement rose to a crescendo, her head popped up and she announced politely that she didn't like the taste. He worried he'd be left nursing a teak erection by himself. She crawled slowly up beside him, pressed her buttocks back into the palm of his right hand, and breathed in his ear.

'I'm just going out to grab a bath towel to put under us.'

***

An impromptu session developed in Dublin the Saturday before a few of them were due to head to the Curragh for the Infantry YOs. Drury, still on his Ordnance course, showed up. He was especially pleased that he'd sold his beaten Peugeot to the Ordnance School for £20 as scrap. It had been blown to pieces as part of a car-bomb exercise in the Glen of Imaal the previous Wednesday. The grievously injured Mr Fiat would have great difficulty in tracking him down now.

Dickie, Foster, Clay and Drury had a few libations before heading to the gate policeman's hut while Corporal 'Robbo' Robinson hailed them a cab for the city centre. He chatted to the resident officers Clay and Foster, over a cup of tea. The conversation was interrupted by a knock on the door, and an accent as soft as a head-butt.

'Robbo darlin'!'

'That you Maxine?'

'Yeah. Can you mind this for me?'

The shoe-polish lid covering the spy hole pushed sideways. A roll of five-pound notes, bound with a small elastic band, was pushed in.

'No problem Maxine.'

'Thanks Robbo. You're a star.'

Robbo wrote 'Maxine' on a brown envelope, shoved the cash into it, and placed it in the pocket of his greatcoat. Clay and Foster had seen the transaction before.

'Stops the punters robbing them.' Robbo explained to Dickie. A taxi honked outside.

What consideration he received from the ladies of Benburb Street, no one knew. But as Clay remarked in the taxi, Robbo was the happiest-looking corporal in Dublin.

***

'Your Est-of-Sit was flawed. You didn't differentiate between the commander's specified and implied tasks. This reduced your courses of action. You need at least two workable, viable, courses of action before you can compare them, and war-game each action, reaction, and counter action. If you don't understand the commander's intent, you can't develop relevant courses of action!'

The rest of the YO's class sat riveted as Finn Lambert filleted Lane. To some, this was merely unpleasant. To the ambitious, like Ryall, this was the secret sauce of advancement. He scribbled notes furiously. Six years commissioned, he already had a serious case of career priapism.

Lane feigned interest as only his classmates knew he could. It was like being back in the Cadet School. Which, in a way, they were. Looking out the window, they could see the latest litter of cadets spinning to and fro. And here they were with an instructor from their Cadet School days. It was all 'Dickie' this, and 'Sean' that, but Lambert was by now a commandant, thus remaining a 'sir' to the students. The Military College still ran on the twin fuels of ambition and fear, as it had in Dickie's Cadet School days, and ever before.

Lambert's most annoying trait was his tendency to pepper his classes with the latest and most irritating acronyms. Just returned from the US staff course in Fort Leavenworth, demonstration of his new-found erudition was of the utmost importance. Thus MOUT replaced FIBUA, a perfectly adequate, Ronseal-like acronym which had served the Army well for years; but deemed too British. No doubt one of the instructors would soon find his way to Camberley for the British staff course, and battle would commence to reinstate FIBUA in the Irish military lexicon.

Lane nodded slowly as Lambert finished dissection. Dickie knew that behind the concerned exterior, Lane was pondering the fastest way to get his submissions done before slipping out to Newbridge for a beer.

A late beer in the college mess was an acceptable diversion after the completion of submissions. There was a C&S Course on at the same time. The commandants never seemed to make the bar before 11pm. Morning PT for the YOs at 07:00 tempered the desire to stay on.

Further entertainment was available from an International Peace-Keeping course being run by the College for overseas students.

Cole was a junior instructor to the group as well as being the course admin officer. This made him general dogsbody for the foreign students; an Indian, two Brazilians, a Ghanaian, a Nepalese, a US Marine, a Chinese, a British Army Air Corps pilot, two Egyptians, a Pole and two Italians. The Irish supplied four army officers and two civil servants from the Department of Foreign affairs to bulk up the numbers. Bar the Egyptian major, all seemed to be getting on pretty well. The Chinese major was polite, but spent most of his time taking notes on the international students.

Lane hated the college bar. No matter how late he finished, the overriding concern was to jump in the car for a late pint in Newbridge. Lane wasn't destined to remain long in the Defence Forces; his mission was to gently educate the more senior types of this fact.

***

The afternoon lecture on fire-planning inched, mollusc-like, to a close. An Artillery School instructor droned through a handle-bar moustache from the lectern. Dickie read the hand-out as the lecture noise emanated from the front. The words entered his left eyeball, skated the back of his retina, move to the right, and exited without impression on his mind. The topic was especially gratuitous, as the YO's course didn't have a full module on fire planning. Artillery planning was reserved for the captains' and commandants' courses. Dickie was tempted to shout the executive summary; 'if your final assault line is within the danger area, and you reach it within the time of flight of your supporting fire, you're fucked...' That was the extent of knowledge required on the YOs. Why this pompous gunner had to waffle fifteen minutes into their dinner time was beyond him.

There were two students from Dickie's junior class, and two pretty senior captains who had dodged the YOs for years. No Infantry YOs, no place on a Standard Infantry. No Standard Infantry Course, no promotion to commandant. So the captains had six weeks on the YOs, followed by four months on the Standard Infantry.

They finished a hurried dinner, barely more tolerable than seven years previously. Thursday was the day even the most ambitious ventured into Newbridge for a drink. But first they had to visit their pigeon-holes, to see what the Infantry School pigeon had egested for tonight's course work.

They had to produce a company-in-attack trace; a move plan for a mounted infantry battalion advance-to-contact, and describe the legal requirements for a cordon-and-search operation in conjunction with the police.

It was well after ten when most finished. They stuck to the plan. There were only two more weeks left on the course.

It was inevitable that someone wanted to go to Pharaohs nightclub. It was 00:30. What harm could it do? Clay, Lane, Hackett and Dickie decided to club. Ryall demurred.

Two drinks, back in the cars. What could go wrong?

The hen party was about twenty strong. Hackett took a shine to the bridesmaid. The feeling was mutual. Driving back to the College lines in Hackett's car, Dickie cursed the fact that he hadn't driven himself. The bridesmaid's buttocks bounced gleefully in his lap in the back seat. She was no oil-painting, but had a great body. They were back to the lines in ten minutes, Hackett disappearing upstairs with her.

The class fell in at 07:00 for morning PT, awaiting the instructor. No sign of Hackett. Lane, who'd had a few whiskey chasers in Pharaohs, had eyes like a road map of Ireland. Hackett's car skidded to a halt in the inner square. The cadets opposite looked on in bemusement. He was already in his tracksuit. He joined the class.

'Where's the bird?' Clay asked.

'Ballymany Cross. She'll get a bus.'

'She's in a mini-skirt!'

'She'll be grand.'

'What happened your neck?'

'What?'

'You've got a hickey!'

'Fuck off, Clay!' Hackett blustered, but the poppy-sized *purpura* was clearly visible below his Adam's apple.

257

'The wife will love that!' Lane was coming too.

The instructor's car pulled into the square as Hackett pushed away curious onlookers. PT was a pretty tame affair, though Lane puked the whiskey up. They were back in the inner square at 07:45. Hackett was in the shower before most of them had their PT kit off.

They walked to the cookhouse for breakfast, the C&S and the Peacekeeping courses already sitting. Hackett came out, a slice of toast between his teeth, his LA30 under his arm.

'If I'm late, tell them I had to go to the hospital!'

Dickie got eggs.

'I mean, what the fuck am I doing here? Six weeks learning how NOT to kill people!' Larsson, the big US Marine remarked loudly to the British pilot.

'I'm a Goddam US Marine Corps Officer!' According to Cole, his outbursts were legendary, his regard for his fellow students scant. The Brazilians were 'natives,' the Egyptians 'camel-jockeys', and he couldn't bring himself to describe the Chinese major in public. His most famous declaration was 'I love my God, my corps, my country, and my wife! In that order!' They wondered if a sardonic sense of humour was at work, but the man lacked a single Irish chromosome.

Hackett arrived twenty minutes late into their first lecture. He sported a small bandage taped to his neck.

'Well?' Lane enquired, after class.

'Told the doc I needed her to cut me. She said she couldn't. I told her I'd be dead by tonight if she didn't. She nicked it with a scalpel, gave me three stitches. Sorted.'

'What'll you tell Karen?' Clay asked.

'On a patrol exercise last night. Caught it in barbed wire. Right lads?' More a command than a question.

They shrugged and agreed. Six more hours until they escaped the mad orthodoxy of the Military College.

Four weeks down, two more to go.

***

Harrington was on the verge of tears. A married captain, he was patrol commander. They had been dropped off on a forest track, to put in an assault on a position at Knickeen Ford, in the Glen of Imaal.

He had planned his route out with a one km march due west, dead-reckoning to a featureless spur. Two classmates had tried to talk him out of it before he wrote his orders. The DS for the exercise, a wiry Ranger Wing Sergeant Major, politely poked holes in Harrington's plan.

Dickie was equipped with a Trilite. A beast of a night scope, it was almost as heavy as the rifle. But it gave Dickie a clear view of Harrington's navigation. They should have been descending gently towards a square stand of forestry. Instead, they were heading far to the right of it. Dickie asked Harrington to check the ground on the night sight. Harrington told him to fuck off.

He blundered along this route for half an hour before changing bearing on some random spur. This brought them to one of the breast-like hillocks between Lobawn and Table Mountain. Harrington finally gave up when he came to a river that wasn't on his route.

He and the Sergeant Major were studying the map beneath a poncho. The rest were close enough to hear him sobbing that he thought he knew where they were. The Ranger, who probably knew where they were to the nearest half an inch, delicately suggested Harrington might take a southerly bearing. Harrington agreed. He lifted the poncho before extinguishing his torch, receiving a chiding from the Sergeant Major.

Dickie saw a flicker of *Schadenfreude* cross the Ranger's face. On the side of a mountain with 12 infantry officers, hopelessly lost.

They got under way. The assault planned for darkness at 03:00 went in at 06:00 in morning light. The 'enemy' had fallen asleep, expecting the assault hours earlier.

The Sergeant Major's debrief, on a forest track before they mounted up, was polite but devastating. A chastened Harrington was mute all the way back to the Curragh.

***

The course was to culminate in a pretty ambitious exercise. With troops from the Third Battalion, they would carry out an advance to contact, followed by a deliberate attack on a position in the Glen, with live supporting fire from two 105mm howitzers.

The 105mm guns wouldn't actually be firing on the objective, but at a target 90° to the west, and 1.5km away. The final assault line for the 'real' and the 'target' objectives were the same distance from the objective. In theory, the DSs could adjudicate if the assaulting troops had been fired upon by their own artillery.

Dickie was in charge of the 'point' platoon. He advanced on foot with the 105mm gun following up to the rear. The engineers had organised 'enemy' pyrotechnics.

Dickie reported contact while the artillery lieutenant, who was under test on his own YO's, deployed his gun.

The rest of the company started to move through Dickie's position. The young gunner officer dug in the spades of his gun.

As the gunners prepared to fire, Dickie was confused. He expected the barrel of the gun to be pointing in broadly the same direction as the axis of advance. His platoon was moving west to east. The barrel of the gun was pointing west. He pulled out his compass, and checked his map.

He whistled at the Artillery School DS, pointing at the gun. The loader rammed a HE round into the breech, and shouted that he was ready. The DS, realising what was wrong, dropped his map and ran over to the gun crew.

'Stop! Stop!' he shouted frantically.

The gun crew stood fast. The DS ordered the gun unloaded. Dickie's radio crackled, asking what was the hold-up on the artillery fire. Dickie bluffed.

He looked on as the crew rotated the gun through 180°. Thus were the good folk of Dunlavin and surrounds spared an unfortunate delivery of 105mm high explosive from the students of the Military College.

***

The full course debrief was held on the last Thursday afternoon. It was followed by the end of course dinner, where everything (not committed to a course report) was forgiven and forgotten. The dinner was a tame affair. They adjourned to the bar after, and found themselves in the teeth of a full-blown diplomatic incident. The College Commandant did a rapid situation estimate and exited at speed.

Dickie had never seen Cole anything other than unflappable. Now he was holding Larsson, the US Marine, by one arm, and the Egyptian major by the other. In the corner, the Egyptian captain smoked manically over an orange juice.

The YOs class and instructors edged carefully into the corner of the bar and ordered drinks, as Cole continued an animated discussion with the two protagonists. Eventually, the American extended his hand to the Egyptian. The foreign students started to disperse among the others filtering in. Cole, flustered and flushed, made it to the bar.

'Pint of stout please, Johnny.' He called to the barman.

'What the fuck was that about?' Lane asked, for once delighted he was in the College bar.

'Fuckin' yanks!' Cole whispered. 'The Egyptian asked yesterday when the students were going to get their course medals. Apparently they get them in Egypt. The rest of the class started cracking up. Over dinner the yank presents him with a medal he'd made from a 20p coin. Egyptian had a shit-fit.'

Cole drank half the pint. 'Threatened to call the Egyptian ambassador. I asked Larsson to apologise. Said he wouldn't apologise to a "sand-nigger camel jockey". I told him yer man was going diplomatic. Talked them into shaking hands this evening.'

'Lord Cole of the Foreign Office!' Clay exclaimed, clapping him on the back.

***

They packed their cars next morning, and left the Military College. Dickie pointed his car towards Kilimore. Just the Standard Infantry and the C&S Courses stood between him and his inevitable rise to Chief of Staff.

He had to get a girlfriend. It'd be a long winter without one.

***

There was an informal gathering in Galway at the races in August. It was like he'd never left. He cut his losses at £100 on the course, and headed for town. The Great Southern was a sweating, heaving mass. The unwashed vied with cabinet ministers to attract the attentions of the circulating waiters; anything to avoid the bar.

Corrigan, Lyons and Cole entertained a group of young ladies in the basement bar. Hank of Ireland was in the far corner; Dickie avoided him, money was tight. Eleanor Cleland appeared from nowhere, a Barbour coat over a tight top. He tried to remember if it was three or four years since he'd lusted over her at the Arts Ball.

'Hello, Dickie.'

'Eleanor.'

'Nursing losses?'

'My father told me not to back women or ride horses.'

***

They were still kissing at one am when Corrigan shouted at them to get a room.

***

An Unexpected Proposal

Summer gave way to winter; and Killimore was even quieter as the sole second lieutenant left for college. Caple told him he was nominated for the next summer trip to Lebanon. Form-up training would start in the Curragh in March.

After the previous escapade, Killimore no longer seemed the wise place for an overseas party. A quorum gathered in Broderick's Bar, Kilreekill. They planned a few quiet libations to celebrate Clay's engagement, and Dickie's impending departure, after which they would adjourn to Galway for louder entertainment. There was something solemn, profound and spiritual, watching the old man pull slow pints with his arthritic hands, surrounded by Dithane 945, Ivomec, and Chenountion.

'What do you want to do now?' Dickie asked, to no one in particular, but looking at O'Leary. He knew he was mellow when he started getting philosophical.

'Meaning what, Dickie?' O'Leary sounded bolshy.

'Career wise? Life wise?'

'Get laid as regularly as possible. Get overseas. Get promoted.'

'Then what?'

'You're working pretty far ahead there, Dickie.' Clay said.

'Well?'

'Get married, drop sprogs, go overseas again, get promoted again.' O'Leary wasn't bothered by this line of questioning.

'Is that it?'

'Dickie's having an existential moment,' Foster announced. 'What are you whining about, Dickie? You're going overseas again. Clear your overdraft before me...'

'Just wondering if that's all there is. I just thought there'd be more to it...'

'For fuck's sake!' Healy swallowed the remainder of his pint. 'Here's to the Israeli shell that shuts that fucking mouth!'

***

The DFHQ briefing was different when one already sported a UNIFIL ribbon. The DFHQ Ops and Int types wouldn't be able to justify their jobs, Dickie supposed, unless able to define some new and menacing threat to the next battalion. Hezbollah was more active, Amal was on the wane.

There had been one fatality in the unit they were replacing, but it was the result of Israeli rather than Lebanese fire.

More significant for junior officers was the fact that promotion on seniority had ended. Dickie's battalion, like the winter battalion preceding it, would be stuffed full of middle-aged men sweating to improve their career profile.

The average age of the senior captains and commandants had jumped in just one year. Old hands, realising they wouldn't be interviewed unless they had another operational tour under the belt, appeared from under every crevice in the Army. For some, old as the hills, it was their first to UNIFIL. Others had clocked up impressive years abroad in New York, Damascus or Jerusalem, without ever having to suffer the indignity of service with the soldiery.

None more so than Dickie's new company commander, James Reihill. Seven years abroad, Africa, New York, and Middle East without a sniff of an enlisted man. Now he was about to command a rifle company in the most difficult part of the Irish AO.

Dickie nearly choked to see Horace smiling down on him from the back row. Baron Killimore gave a regal wave of welcome to Dickie, as if born to the Hills. Upon his chest, the single blue ribbon of a service medal. Twenty-five years commissioned, Horace had never served a day abroad unless astride the back of a horse, or atop its female owner.

The battalion commander Bill Goodwin had a solid, intelligent reputation, and was his own man. He was also rabidly anti-alcohol.

The staff officers droned on about water, fuel and electricity, possible access to Beirut Airport, and so on until every sheet of acetate had been projected, briefed, and slotted back into its folder until the next brief.

They had lunch in the officers' mess. An Eastern Command commandant sat down at the B Company officer's table, as he'd been in Haddathah before. He expounded in detail on how he and one of his sergeants had despatched a local militia man who had confronted soldiers of their company.

They all filed out into the sunshine for the battalion officers' photograph.

***

Things with Eleanor had moved beyond Dickie's usual three-month itch. His free weekends involved going to Dublin, where she was working for a business consultancy. Promises were made to meet upon his return from Lebanon.

***

Dickie could immediately recognise the reporters sent to the Glen to cover their 'battle inoculation.' They looked like surplus and oversized fatigues had been dropped randomly on their heads from the top of a building.

266

Engineers simulated bombardment while the battalion took cover in the sunken railway line for the tank targets. As the warning came over a radio set to stay down for incoming machine gun fire, a corporal to Dickie's shouted 'Targets UP!'

Dickie had a quiet flight to Ben Gurion. The convoy seemed quicker this time; he could pick out landmarks he knew on Highway 2.

At the border, he recognised Morgan. He would be taking over from classmates in Haddathah, as Morgan and Healy were about to head home. Morgan's winter trip had not been good. His unit was the first to travel with 'meritorious officers,' and was packed with senior captains and commandants, like Dickie's. His company commander and 2i/c were great buddies, and professional tossers. They had lost one corporal to gunfire near Bayt Yahun. Dickie wanted to hear the unofficial version.

They got the soldiers on the way to the posts, and headed for the canteen. Healy greeted them there.

'Boss is away! Let's play!' he shouted, ordering more Almaza. The company commander was *in flagrante* with a nurse in SWEDMEDCOY. He'd taken Morgan's convoy to Naquora for his last night with her before returning to his wife and family.

With the clock nearing closing time at 21:30, Dickie went to the bar to buy his round. He got a sharp elbow from a lanky corporal beside him.

'I was in front, sir!'

Dickie didn't know whether to punch him or charge him. Healy interposed himself between the two.

'Get your beer, Smithy, and fuck off.'

Dickie brought the beers back to the table. Twenty minutes drink-up time before the canteen run. One of the home-bound squaddies asked Healy for a song. He stood up and gave a word-perfect rendition of 'Do-Re-Me' from 'The Sound of Music'. Unprompted,

Morgan followed up with '*Climb Ev'ry Mountain*.' The canteen erupted in cheers. Dickie hadn't realised the winter trip had been so bad.

They waited until the canteen run before leaving. Healy turned to Morgan.

'Bunker bevvy?'

'I think so.'

They checked the coast was clear, and descended into the HQ bunker. Healy motioned Dickie to sit down. He opened what looked like a sealed rations box. Inside was a bottle of Jameson and four shot glasses.

'Wasn't here last year!' Dickie remarked.

'Had to get away from the boss at night.' Healy said.

'A fucking Anti-Christ.' Morgan added.

'Gone to Naquora to create baby Anti-Christs.' Healy thought he was hilarious.

'A bit late for her to be making a baby anything.'

'You saw her?'

'She was waiting for the convoy.'

'What's she like?'

'She actually asked him 'is that a gun in your pocket?' when he was handing over his BAP.'

'What the fuck is she like?'

'You know Ursula Andress?'

'Yeah!'

'She's nothing like her.'

'For fuck sake, Al!'

'Late forties, hair dyed off her head, high mileage, too much sun, big knockers.'

Didn't put off Healy, who lay back and contemplated his whiskey. 'I'd love a bit of that. Might pull a sickie to Naquora next week.'

'Ask them if there's a cure for pulling your plum.'

'Fuck you!' Healy hissed. 'Anyway, to the married man.'

He and Morgan clinked glasses and drank.

'You're?'

'Almost.'

'Didn't hear. Congrats. When did…?'

'Cyprus. February. Doing the deed in September.'

'No hanging around for you.'

'No point, Dickie. Love the girl.'

'I'll miss the wedding.'

'I know. But you're an honorary member of the guard of honour. Give your money to Healy.'

'One of the greats goes down. Not that way. I mean.'

'Shut up, Healy.' Morgan whispered to him.

'Soon be just you and me left, Dickie.' Healy almost sounded maudlin.

'What the fuck was that in the bar?' Dickie asked.

'You just ran into the 2i/c's pet signaller,' Morgan smiled.

'Pet?'

'When Cunningham got shot in November, the 2i/c was duty officer on the night. Smithy was signaller, the boss was down in Naquora riding Helga.'

'Is that her name?'

'Mick, I've no fucking idea what her name is.'

'Okay.'

'The lads in the Black Hole spotted some movement near Bayt Yahun village, radioed it in. 2i/c ordered a foot patrol out to see what was going on.'

'Inside the Enclave?' Dickie couldn't believe it.

'Yup. The lads walked from the Black Hole to Bayt Yahun and did a recce. We heard gunfire, and lost the patrol on radio. 2i/c sends me in the Sisu to investigate. We drove past Bayt Yahun compound. There was an Israeli tank there, the yids looked jumpy. I kept the orange light flashing the whole way.'

'Amal, Hezbollah, was there a fire fight?'

'The yids had their own foot patrol out. Ours patrol got close to them. Must have been a jumpy conscript in the tank, sees all these guys and guns, and opens up with a HMG. Our patrol scattered. The yid patrol spots our medic and drags him over to one of their men. Had a point-five bullet-hole in the chest. Medic did his best but the yid was fucked. The yids scarpered.'

'So there was no one else?'

'Nope, only the Israelis opened fire. Killed their own.'

'What happened then?'

'I found the medic behind a wall, covered in blood. Thought he was hit, but it was the yid's blood. Then we found Cunningham. Got a point-five in the head. We went back to Tibnin, dropped Cunningham's body at the RAP. Battalion Ops interviewed me, I told them what happened. Then I headed back to Haddathah. 2i/c was in a panic.'

'I'd say so,' said Dickie.

'He's on the phone to Naquora, found the boss about to go out for dinner with Helga. They agreed to change the ops journal.'

'Why?'

'Smithy had it all down in print; when the first report came from the Black Hole. He wrote down the 2i/c's order for a foot patrol.'

'What did they do to the journal?'

'2i/c changed it to read that the sergeant on post ordered the foot patrol. 2i/c came down to the comcen later.'

'I see.'

'2i/c took the original page out of the journal and burned it. Smithy said he expected to have a third stripe by Christmas!'

'How the fuck will they organise that in Cork?'

'That's the 2i/c's problem. The Court of Enquiry should be kicking off by then, and he won't want Smithy saying anything out of school.'

'Fuck me.' Dickie could see why there might be a bit of tension.

'All good clean fun, Dickie, when you're knobbing a nurse while one of your squaddies gets shot. And all because your 2i/c didn't read the UN SOP forbidding night patrols in the enclave!' Morgan downed his whiskey, and went to bed.

***

Haddathah was quiet on Tuesday morning. Dickie had read the three-week old papers in the anteroom, and went for a walk. He fancied a new pair of sunglasses. Ali Strawballs' shop was empty. His wife Amaal dusted video cassettes outside the shop. She produced her best smile for customers when Ali was away.

'Good morning, Lieutenant Mandeville,' she said softly, putting the duster aside. She pronounced his name slowly, sounding almost French. 'Is there something you would like?'

She never flirted overtly like some of the separated women. Dickie knew her English was good. She was well aware of her *double entendre*. He also knew she didn't do it with the soldiers, or with older, or indeed most, officers. Dickie looked into her eyes longer than he should. She held his gaze, returning a smile.

'Just looking for a new pair of shades...'

'You like Ray Ban, Diesel, Oakley, Gucci...?' The newest Ray Bans were there. Dickie didn't fancy the porn-star Guccis. He pointed to a pair of aviators. He considered himself in the mirror, but was unsure.

'I think you'll like these better,' she said from behind. As he turned around, she reached up and wrapped a pair of Wayfarers gently onto his face. Her hands touched his temples and cheeks. His face flushed.

She wore a light fragrance, floral, mixed with the smell of her own skin. He turned quickly to the mirror, a moment to collect himself. The veins in his temple pulsed, and he felt his chest pound.

'They're very nice...' he sounded like a cretin. 'How much?'

'Fifty two dollars, Lieutenant Mandeville.'

'Special price for me, Amaal?' he turned and smiled at her, the Wayfarers still on, as he regained his composure.

'For you forty seven.'

'Amaal...' he smiled.

'I'd love to, Lieutenant Mandeville, but you know, Ali...' The flirtation was over. Amaal was sealing the deal. 'They look really good on you.'

He handed her the cash.

'See you soon, Lieutenant Mandeville,' she said as he walked up the street.

He couldn't believe his juvenile reaction to her. Not as cool as he thought.

***

He went with the CQ on the rations run to the Black Hole. The Sisu overtook Lebanese civilians at the DFF checkpoint, and Foxy waved to Jalboot at the swing gate. Dickie was swanning out the rear hatch in his new Ray Bans.

272

Jalboot motioned at the convoy to stop. Jalboot was unpredictable at the best of times, but Dickie could see that his eyes were swollen red.

'Marhaba Lootenant, qi fack?'

Dickie always motioned a salute to Jalboot, who loved it. In his ZZ-Top beard, he affected a John Wayne salute in response.

'Israelis shelled the compound last night. Killed two.'

'Israelis?' Dickie asked, pretending he didn't know what happened last night.

'Hezbollah fire RPGs from Target House at our compound last night. Rounds went over top. Hit Israeli tank in Bayt Yahun. Israelis thought it was us. Fired two rounds at compound. Killed two sentries.'

'I'm sorry, Jalboot. Did you know any of them?'

'Hassan was my brother in law. Hopefully they will let me north to bury him today.'

'Will that be safe for you?' Dickie couldn't believe this DFF murderer could go safely to a funeral north of the DFF area.

'Yes, yes, no problem.'

'If I can help.'

'Thank you, lootenant.'

***

Dickie's convoy got into Naquora at 09:15. He handed over the convoy paperwork to the Irish Sergeant Major, got rid of his pistol, and headed to the International for breakfast. As he walked through the row of billets near the Irish Officers' club, a figure walked towards him in UN whites. None other than Baron Killimore himself.

'Good morning Dickie. How are you?' extending his hand. 'How are things in the AO?'

Horace's complexion was even more florid than it had been before.

'A little busy over the past few nights. No-one hurt. Good to get a day in Naquora.'

'Good, good Dickie. Whatever you do, avoid the International Mess like the plague. Food damned near killed me last week. Just spent three days in Swedmedcoy.'

'Thanks for telling me sir, just on the way there for breakfast.'

Dickie dropped his swimming gear in the Officers' Club. He headed for the gate, flashed his ID, and headed out onto the street. Might as well try some Lebanese pancakes, the smell of fresh baking filled the air.

Some HQ folk never dined in the International, taking breakfast, lunch and dinner among the Lebanese eateries.

The traders were honourable to a fault. They made a point of telling the buyer whether something was 'mingy', 'good mingy' (for quality knock-offs), or 'genuine'. While they were skilled in the production of good quality clones of the best-selling scents, the packaging and spelling them down. A counterfeit batch of *Poison* and *Lou-Lou* perfume arrived in South Lebanon the previous month in beautifully rendered boxes marked 'Poisson' and 'La-La.'

Dickie had booked a call from the International Exchange. His mother was home, he told her and his sister that all was well, before hitting the sea for a swim.

***

Dickie was early for his meeting in Battalion HQ, half an hour to kill. Strolling along the officers' lines boardwalk, a familiar voice from one of the billets. To an accompaniment of female giggles, he heard Brian Arnott shouting parade orders from the dentist's billet. Dickie peered through the window netting.

'*Ar ais! Ar aighd! Ar ais! Ar aighd! Socair!*' Arnott was in jungle greens, boots, and shirt, his shorts thrown over the top of the bed. The dentist was on all fours, naked from the waist down, and in full service dress from the waist up. Arnott, on his and knees taking her from behind, held her tightly buckled Sam Browne like reins. Her dog-tags jangled rhythmically on the pillow.

'Afternoon, sir!' Dickie roared up the lines, in a 'senior' voice.

'Fuck off and get your own, Mandeville!' Arnott shouted back.

Dickie started back up the lines towards the mess. '*Bogaig tuailimí*!' Arnott roared.

Dickie decided it was time for a beer. He went into the bar. Alan O'Loughlin of his senior class was reading an old copy of the Times over a coffee.

'How long has Arnott been shagging the dentist?'

'How long do you think I've been reading at lunchtime?'

'Almaza?'

'Strict Ramadan on the bar from the boss. No beer before seven'

'Balls. I'm parched.'

Arnott walked into the bar about two minutes later.

'Well well,' said Dickie, 'The sergeant major of billet nine...'

'Squinting through windows, Dickie?'

'Filling the dentist's cavity?'

'Done that, my friend!'

'Are you going to the CO's dinner tonight, you tosser?'

'Done that too, last Saturday. Better get back to Al Yatun. I need a beer. Mouth's as dry as my sack!

***

Dickie was assigned as LO to the Irish reporter for his two days with B Company. The four company LOs were briefed by the IO in Tibnin on what could be shared with him. The

275

Press Office in Dublin laid down the law for media policy. 'The mushroom treatment' as it was universally referred to in Tibnin, feed'em shit and keep'em in the dark. And get them shit-faced if expedient. In B Company's case, the IO spelled out that the pet reporter could not be told of the Hezbollah mortar that hit the observation tower in the Black Hole last week. No expressions of opinion on the IDF, the DFF, Hezbollah or Amal. No comments on the UN postal system, or the cost of telephone calls home.

He was a stringer for several dailies, including some UK papers. He was also thought to be writing a book. DFHQ was therefore according him all reasonable assistance.

***

As he returned, Comdt Reihill and the company 2i/c were discussing their officers' night the following Saturday. This was the night Dickie was babysitting the reporter.

Bollocks and damn. Another dry night for Dickie in the middle of an Olympian piss-up on Saturday night.

***

Dickie picked him up in Brashit, and brought him to Bayt Yahun first. They watched the slow procession of humanity into DFF territory. Then on to lunch in Haddathah. Reihill had wine on the table. After an abstemious single glass of wine with his lunch, Reihill made the usual afternoon announcement that he was going "East of Eden," and took siesta on the veranda. The 2i/c hadn't touched a drop over lunch. So Dickie was surprised when he announced how lucky they'd been over the last four months not to take casualties from shell or gunfire. Dickie wagged his head frantically. The 2i/c ploughed on regardless.

The reporter went to his room after lunch 'for a nap.' Dickie could hear him scribbling down the 2i/c's babbling while it was still fresh in his head. He bit the bullet and went into the Boss's room. Reihill lay on a camp-bed on the veranda in a pair of micro-speedos.

'Sir, the 2i/c may have said a bit more to the reporter than we were authorised to disclose.'

'How much?'

Dickie listed off the incidents.

'Jesus. Why didn't you stop him?'

'If I told a captain to shut up at lunch, sir, it would raise even more interest.'

He said nothing in response, dragging himself back into uniform.

'What'll we do now?' Dickie asked.

'Keep him moving, I'm taking him to the Hill now. Get him blotto at the party tonight, get him up on the early bird in the morning.'

'Okay, sir.'

'Have the early bird at five in the morning. Not six. And bring the fucker on the bounds.'

***

Dickie deposited the hung-over and thistle-torn reporter in Al Yatun the next morning. He returned to Haddathah to find a commotion outside Company HQ. A woman was crying uncontrollably at the foot of the steps. Commandant Reihill came down to see what was happening. Mohammed Sauli had left his shop to translate.

'Her daughter is getting married tomorrow. Her dowry is a plot of land beside the house. The groom's family has refused to accept it. They say there's an Israeli bomb in the ground.'

'Is there?' Reihill asked.

Sauli questioned the woman, who became more agitated, hands flailing over her head.

'She isn't sure Commandant. The land was shelled in February.'

'What does she want?'

'She asks the Irish to blow it up. Or else no wedding.'

'Tell her we'll see what we can do.'

The engineers arrived in Haddathah after lunch. The engineer commandant was accompanied by corpulent sergeant and a translator.

They drive to the field. It was burned dry of vegetation, just desiccated scutch grass and thistles.

'Where did it land?' the engineer asked one of the locals.

'About here,' said the translator, taking directions.

The circular depression might have been the entry point of an unexploded 155mm shell. Or a dog chasing quarry.

The engineer asked for the mine sweeper. He started in the general area of the depression. The sergeant sat down beside Dickie while the commandant swept the area, marking it with a few sticks.

'There's something down there. How big, how far down, I've no idea.'

He and the sergeant returned to spot with spades and a probe. They dug carefully downwards, until the hole was four feet square, and about two feet deep. The base of a shell was visible.

He called the sergeant forward with the demolition box. Dickie followed.

'It's gone a little rusty Sarge. Not going any lower. Fill a few sandbags.'

The sergeant retired a few yards away and started to fill earth into sandbags. The commandant taped four sticks of PE4 around a primer, through which he threaded a length of detonating cord. He placed the charge gently onto the buried round and filled earth on top of it. He placed the sandbags on top of the mound. He taped a detonator to the detonating cord, and cut a length of fuse.

'Right, Dickie, get them all down the road.'

Dickie shepherded the onlookers down the road to the graveyard, and returned to the engineer.

'All ready, sir.'

The engineer held a storm-proof match to the fuse. Dickie remembered the ordnance course mantra: walk, never run, from a burning fuse. There was time enough for everyone but the man with the broken leg.

Keeping an eye on his stopwatch, the engineer joined the others at the graveyard junction. The explosion was muffled, only a thin column of smoke heading skyward.

A crater about ten feet across scarred the field. The mother of the bride was clapping with some other women.

'You think we'll get an invitation, sir?' Dickie ventured.

'Will we fuck, Dickie.'

***

Another early bird. Dickie was up at 05:30 after a sweaty night's sleep. He needed a cup of coffee before the mine sweep. The Padre normally said his office in his room. He was standing at the window holding his Liturgy, looking up the street, as Dickie walked in.

'Morning, Father.'

'Morning, Dickie.'

'Keeping an eye on the early bird this morning?'

'Could say that, Dickie. I'm keeping a pastoral eye on Amaal.'

Dickie went over to the window. Amaal had lifted the shutters, and was putting out the shop's wares, dusting the boxes with a coloured duster. She wore a white hijab over a pastel abaya. The abaya wasn't particularly tight, but clung to her back and legs as she crouched down.

'Easy on the optic nerve alright, Father.'

'Easy on the optic nerve my arse. She'd put a horn on a dead Franciscan!'

***

The change in Hezbollah as a fighting force in just one year was remarkable. He was about to report an Israeli/DFF foot patrol in the wadi one afternoon. They were moving tactically, staying in dead ground, giving very little away. The AKs were no giveaway, since the DFF always used them; the Israelis occasionally so. He was about to transmit a moverep when the sentry glanced up from the 20X binoculars.

'Sir, they've all beards.'

Dickie went over to the binos. The DFF had beards, but not the Israelis. Every single one had a beard. The camo patter, though hard to discern, was strange. They stopped in cover. One of them took out his own binos. They were looking at the DFF Compound in Bayt Yahun. One of them transcribed into a notebook.

If he called this in over the net now, there would be a 155mm fire-mission from the Israelis. He rang Haddathah on the field phone and called the moverep down the line.

***

'What was that, sir?'

280

He was on the midnight shift with McClaverty, the farmer's son from Roscrea. His platoon had just started their stretch in At Tiri and the Hill.

'What?'

'Saw something hitting the front of Haddathah Compound.'

There was no sound following the impacts. Dickie trained the binos on the earthworks. Nothing. Then a small wisp of luminous green from the bank. Then two more.

'See them?'

'Yeah. I see them now. What the fuck are they?'

'Dunno, sir. No noise.'

The hill lit up. Two streams of 0.50" HMG sailed down into the valley. He composed a shootrep, but wasn't sure what to call the incoming fire. The signaller in Haddathah said there were reports of automatic cannon fire over the net on R'Shaf and Brashit Compounds. It was a coordinated attack; a matter of time before there was an Israeli response.

'Think I see muzzle flashes now, sir.' McClaverty was outside on the 20X binos. Dickie radioed down to Haddathah that there was incoming from the Israeli artillery compound in Qiryat Shimona.

'Four more muzzle flashes, sir!'

Dickie jotted them down, and sent his shootrep.

***

The MO decided to have a blood-bank in the MAP after a request from Tibnin Hospital. Dickie was going down the Hill for duty officer, McLaverty wanted to go to the canteen, so the QM took a dozen in to offer a pint of red for the civilian casualties.

Pete Clay was sitting in the chair opposite, giving blood. A Company, based in Tulin to the north, was normally the quietest part of the IRISHBATT AO.

'How did last night go?'

'No more volley-ball for Post 6-11!'

'What?'

'Got a 155 slap in the middle last night. Big hole in the tarmac where the net used to be.'

'Israelis aren't into net-sports.'

'God help the Muslim who gets this stuff, sir!' said McClaverty smiling at Dickie.

'Why's that, Mc?'

'He's going to get an arm-full of Israeli beer and Irish bacon!'

***

Dickie thought the night's activities would have gotten it out of Hezbollah's system. They were just warming up. He'd had a few Almaza over the table quiz in the canteen, and gone to bed at 22:30 for the early bird.

They got the callout for groundhog at 04:00. Dickie headed for the bunker with his helmet, flak jacket and pistol. All-clear at 05:00.

Battalion Ops cancelled the early-birds for the morning; there was concern about unexploded ordnance, and jumpy DFF men. The duty officer was sent on a mounted patrol to Ayta Az Zutt. Reports started to some in from all over IRISHBATT of AEs on the move. The Israelis had made a formal complaint to New York about the ease with which AEs were moving about the UNIFIL AO. The Force Commander issued an edict about stopping AEs at all checkpoints. Part of the UN mandate was to 'Confirm the Israeli withdrawal;' stopping any locals attacking a force that wasn't meant to be there was problematic. And preventing their retreat afterwards was worse. Nonetheless, Goodwin insisted that AEs be denied movement through Irish checkpoints.

Dickie sat down beside Signalman Binchy, listening to the intense radio traffic on the net.

'Something's up in A Company, sir.'

'What's up?'

'Al Jurn. Shooting at the checkpoint. They're sending a C Company armoured car to it.'

Dickie listened to the controlled confusion of signallers criss-crossing messages from NCOs and officers on the ground.

'They're looking for Starlight, and a medevac.'

He couldn't remember what Starlight stood for.

'The MO, sir.' Binchy said, flicking over to the A Company net.

It was alive with traffic from Post 6-10 in Al Jurn. There was a casualty. C Company, nearest to 6-10, had a car on the way. Binchy flicked back to the battalion net.

'Now there's a casualty in C Company.' Binchy made sure there was nothing incoming for B Company, then flicked over to the C Company net. Someone manning the radio in a Sisu was in distress.

'Take your time. He doesn't need you anymore!' was the last, bitter message.

Dickie brought Binchy his breakfast. Both listened to the unfolding story from Al Jurn.

'One guy shot in the stomach in Al Jurn. Sounds like he'll make it. One guy dead in C Company in an armoured car.'

Dickie and Binchy checked that the shoot-reps and move-reps were in from the Hill, the Black Hole, Ayta Az Zutt, and Bayt Yahun. Reihill hovered in the background, and let them get on with it.

The duty officer's patrol found a fully mounted anti-aircraft cannon in the village. Battalion Ops told him to stay put until the IO got there. They didn't get back until 09:00.

Dickie grabbed a shave upstairs. Binchy appeared in the bathroom.

'Boss wants you, sir.'

Reihill was on the field phone.

'Right, Pat.' He hung up the phone and spoke to Dickie. 'Hezbollah fighters heading back to Haris via the graveyard. We've to stop them. Checkpoint at the graveyard, Dickie. Off you go.'

The CS had a patrol ready. As they mounted the Sisu, Dickie could see word had spread about that morning's casualties. The soldiers looked more than happy to level the score if Hezbollah asked for it.

The graveyard was on the far side of the village. A road skirted it to the north. All was quiet when they got there. Dickie parked the Sisu broadside on to the road, and ordered the soldiers to open the rifle ports. It was 09:30. An old man approached, walking a donkey. It had no panniers. He waved absentmindedly. A farmer drove towards them on a battered Massey Ferguson. He had no trailer, or cargo box. They waved him on.

The sun rose higher. A few hundred metres away, a tan seventies Mercedes slowed and stopped. After a few minutes, it drove slowly towards them and pulled up fifty metres short of the Sisu. Dickie told the patrol to cover it from the rifle ports, and jumped out the back. He cocked his BAP and slid it into his right pocket. The gunner manned the MAG in the front hatch.

The windows of the Merc were open, cigarette smoke curled lazily into the September morning.

'*Marhaba.*' Dickie was about to extend his hand when he realised he was holding the BAP. He extended his left, knowing it was insulting. Part of him wanted to provoke them. The driver shook his left hand anyway.

'*Marhaba.*'

'*Kíf hálack?*'

'*Mabsút.*'

No tension in their eyes, two buddies out for a morning coffee. Their hands were visible. On the back seat was a mound of something, covered with a blanket. Dickie had forgotten the Arabic for 'I want to search your car;' he pointed to the back seat.

'*Min fadlak?*'

'*Lá*,' the passenger's response, polite but firm.

Dickie walked back to the Sisu. The Irish waited. The Hezbollah finished their cigarettes, then turned the old Merc around and headed back into the village.

***

The Force Commander, a Norwegian Lieutenant General, left Naquora that afternoon for Cyprus to go on holidays with his wife. Lt Col Gibson lifted the order that Hezbollah were to be stopped at Irish checkpoints the following day. The body of the C Company soldier was repatriated the next.

***

The Lebanese summer gave way to golden October. The afternoons were more pleasant and bearable. The CS fixed names for chalk rotations, and canteen conversation bent towards home. Vindicated by their electoral success, Hezbollah activity had waned.

Captain Holmes, the battalion junior ops officer, decided to rotate the weekly company ops officers' meetings around the company areas.

Foxy sounded the P4's horn at 07:30hrs. They headed off to Brashit in glorious sunshine. C Company's ops officer Bernie Carter was standing at the door of the house. Like theirs in B Company, it served as officers' mess, cookhouse, and company HQ.

Bernie had tea, coffee and biscuits ready on the officers' dining room table. Dickie admired the framed .50" HMG bullet stuck in the dining room wall. It had passed through the outer wall and run out of steam just as it emerged into the room. Its deformed brown snout jutted out of the plaster, pointing squarely at the centre of the table.

The then company commander had photographed the diners eating lunch when it struck, and framed the picture and bullet in situ. He inscribed it: 'Presented by Major Ackal Hashim to the Officers of C Company. Attending the presentation were…'

Bernie saw Dickie eyeing the picture and affected his Colonel Blimp impression.

'Of course those wretched Swedish engineers tell us the new T walls will stop those little blighters from interrupting lunch in future. Not a lot of use if the perfidious yids start firing tank-rounds…'

'That's why the cunning B Company officers dine on the opposite side of the house,' said Dickie.

'Quite, quite, Richard, but C Company officers aren't stupid enough to sleep yid-side of the house. Like you.'

'I'd rather die dreaming of Amaal than eating with the company commander…'

'Gland in hand… Coffee, Dickie?'

They settled down to the weekly drone of operational statistics. Afterwards Bernie announced they would visit two outposts either side of lunch. The first was a local house almost directly below Bayt Yahun compound. As they wound up the road to it, Dickie could scarcely believe it was inhabited. It was far more badly damaged than Target House, the southerly walls holed by tank and HMG fire. They lived only in the rear of the house, the front acting as a shield of sorts.

As they pulled up, a woman in her early forties came out to greet them. 'Ah, Lt Bernie', she smiled. A small petrol generator hummed by the gable.

There were three generations of women living there, and no men. The grandmother sat impassively in the corner, stitching a tablecloth. The mother called towards the kitchen, and three girls emerged, carrying the accoutrements for tea and Lebanese coffee.

Dickie was unprepared for the vision that was the eldest daughter. Unusually tall for a Lebanese, about 5'10' or so, and slim, she was darker in complexion than the average. She had gold-brown hair falling in ringlets to just above the small of her back, and wore a dark floral dress extending below the knee. It failed to obscure long, olive legs. She looked straight at him as she placed a tray on a small table. She was breathtakingly beautiful. Bernie, sitting in the corner, sniggered quietly at Dickie.

'My husband is working in Riyadh, and spends most of the year there. The girls stay with me and his mother. Their brother had to go to Beirut.'

Dickie had never been in a private Lebanese house without a male family member being present. Small talk didn't seem appropriate.

'Looks like you have bad neighbours...' said Holmes.

'Yes,' said the mother, quietly. The remark redundant as it was tasteless. 'This is Ilham, Rafa, and Maryam,' she said, motioning last to her eldest daughter who was pouring a cup of Lebanese coffee for Dickie.

They exchanged pleasantries. The mother expressed her gratitude for the occasional Gerry-can of kerosene for lighting, and for the occasional patrols that dropped in. Dickie spied the young man's photo on the dresser.

'Your brother?' he asked Maryam.

Maryam locked respectfully back towards her mother, who nodded imperceptibly.

'Ali, yes. He had to go. If he stayed here... the DFF...' she pointed her palm towards Brashit Compound. Dickie understood. There were no neutrals beneath a DFF Compound. Ali would have been press-ganged by the DFF, or else would have had to join Amal or Hezbollah. The daughters' English was evidently better than their mother's. Grandmother had none at all. They chatted amiably, looking for reassurance every now and then from mother. The atmosphere relaxed, though grandmother, while comprehending none of the conversation, policed the girls' behaviour nonetheless.

'What will you do here?' Dickie asked the mother.

'They will stay here until they get married.' The girls smiled as she replied.

'You never know, ma-am. They might marry a nice Irishman.' Dickie said impishly, eyes falling on Maryam. She sat upright beside her mother, hands clasped on her lap, bare calves crossed below her.

'If you raise our children in the Book, I will marry you and go back to Ireland with you, Lieutenant Mandeville,' Maryam said, looking him square in the eye. Her own eyes were the darkest pools of brown; he thought he'd fall into them. She glanced left to her mother, whose gentle bow of the head signalled approval.

Gentle laughter rose from the officers, the Lebanese women smiled, Maryam remained perfectly serious. Dickie had no witty rejoinder; the moment passed.

After another ten minutes or so, Bernie expressed their gratitude, and they moved out to the vehicles.

As the P4s kicked up dust on the track, Dickie looked back. Maryam stood linking arms with her mother, her hair blowing gently in the breeze. The most beautiful girl he had ever set eyes on had just proposed to him. He would be back in Ireland in a few weeks, and would never see her again.

Eleanor was on hand to give him a proper welcome home. His parents could wait. He stayed in Dublin with her until the weekend, when she went home to Galway.

The All-Blacks were in town. After Ireland's Triple-Crown in the spring, some held out a hope for a decent Irish performance.

'Not a fucking snowball's, Dickie,' Healy told him down the phone, when he enquired about a ticket. 'Why don't you try Killimore?'

'Sold their allocation again, Mick.' They'd made £1,800 towards the new clubhouse.

'Try the GOC's lunch in Rathmines.'

Dickie hadn't heard this route before.

'If you get in, look for RSM Hitchcock, Second Regiment. He's in charge of stewards on the day.'

Dickie rang the mess office in Rathmines and booked a plate at the GOC's lunch.

Saturday morning in the Officers' Mess, the place was thronged. About fifty assorted alikadoos, liggers, fans, old gents, toadying Eastern Command staff officers, Healy, the GOC, the Garda Commissioner, and the RUC Chief Constable, the US Military Attaché. Ownership of a ticket was presumed in such exalted company. No one asked him to produce his.

'*Dobriy vyecher,* Colonel Richardson!'

'*Kak pazhivayesh,* Lieutenant Morgan!'

Healy and Dickie looked askance at Morgan as he rattled off in an apparently decent impression of Russian with the Director of Intelligence and Russophile Richardson.

'What the fuck was all that about?' Healy demanded, when he returned to the knot at the bar.

'Only one other guy in the Army speaks Russian besides Richardson,' Morgan thought this was useful information.

'So fucking what?' Healy continued.

'Thought geography was your thing?' Dickie was trying to nudge him back to the cheating episode, but realised Healy was his partner in crime.

'And that guy is on a new European mission in Georgia. Per diem of $220 per day, tax free for two years. Followed by a guaranteed job in Int in Dublin when you're back, rpice of a house in your arse pocket. And Mrs Morgan has just got a job in Dublin.'

'Well fuck me sideways if Morgan hasn't just developed a career horn,' said Healy. 'What's Russian for "it's your round you useless tit?"'

After the obligatory beef stroganoff and pints, they were off in a coach with Garda motorcycle escort.

The convoy was at Lansdowne in twenty minutes. Dickie trotted down the steps after Healy, who wanted rid of him as quickly as possible. Healy had a muttered conversation with a man in a black Crombie, holding a Motorola. RSM Hitchcock leaned over to Dickie, a look of some annoyance on his face.

'Head for the touchline, Havelock end. Watch out for Spud. Six foot. Red hair.'

The RSM patted Dickie on the back, as much a dismissal as to wish him luck.

It wasn't too hard to spot Spud. He had a head like a traffic light. He told Dickie to stand in the touchline area, and not to go far a half-time drink.

The match was good, but the result was inevitable. Dickie made quickly for the Berkeley Court. Foster and McGuinness were propping up the bar.

'Bit of a bummer, thought it'd be closer in the end.'

'We didn't go. It was a bit cold,' said Foster. 'Kept you a spot at the bar.'

'Welcome home, Dickie.' McGuinness lifted his glass.

Dickie shouted three pints before the crowds got too big. He had a hot whiskey chaser; he couldn't feel his frozen feet.

'One or two here and vamoos?' suggested Foster. 'This place will be Calcutta.'

The rogues' gallery slowly congregated. Cole, Arnott and Lyons appeared. The crowd at the bar degenerated to a scrum. They made their exit for the Lansdowne Hotel. McGuinness insisted on food. They gulped hot-dogs *en route*.

The Lansdowne served pints through a snug on the entrance terrace. Through the basement door Dickie could see Healy, glued to the England-Australia match. Morgan was engaged in intensive conversation with a pretty little thing in an All Blacks top.

'Bit early for that sort of thing, Al!' Foster roared through the crowd at him.

Clay, Drury and Doyle appeared. A few senior types from Command HQ waved at them from the terrace.

Dickie spotted a girl from third arts in UCG whose smalls he'd unsuccessfully attempted to remove one night. He couldn't remember her name, and thankfully she could not seem to remember him. Healy was ensconced among a group of Kiwis, telling them how their team could up their game.

It was close to ten pm, and the crowds had abated. The occasional taxi pulled up, reducing the crowd infinitesimally each time. They needed a plan. There was no way they'd get as far as Bad Bobs.

'Straight to Strings!' Doyle declared.

Entry to Strings was an art form perfected by Clay and Foster. On a night like tonight that could be relatively early, perhaps before midnight.

In the event, it was still nearly one am when they got there. The pints continued to fly like Frisbees until Foster shouted that he mightn't talk them through the door. After abusing him for panicking, they left and meandered up Leeson Street.

'Brian' the bouncer was his usual, obsequious self. He looked at his watch. At least twenty loitered hopefully at the top of the stairs. Foster threw him the shrugged-shoulder look of a long-lost Mafiosi. Brian was having none of it.

'We're full, gentlemen, full nearly two hours ago.'

'We'll only stay for one,' offered Foster.

'I think I left my coat here last night, Brian,' said Clay, warmly wrapped in his coat. These were Healy's 'championship minutes,' when the bouncers sized you up, decided if you were too pissed, estimated how much drinking capacity you had left.

Brian nodded to his partner, and opened the gate. Abuse rose from the other expectant punters.

'Members, members,' he chided gently.

Foster and Clay led the charge down the stairs. The place was heaving, a thick fug of cigarette smoke obscuring the end of the bar. Lyons and Cole headed into the sweaty maw. Lyons' eye fell upon an unguarded bottle of Liebfraumilch and two glasses. He did a fast recce of the dance floor and grabbed the bottle and glasses.

Clay spotted a girl with whom he had enjoyed unencumbered couplings, and was gone. The group split up to find space in the packed cellar. Foster pulled out a packet of Rothmans.

'Well isn't it great!'

Cole pinched two more glasses, and Lyons poured the requisitioned wine.

'Stand back, Eamon, and watch the master,' Lyons shouted at Cole.

'You couldn't pick fluff out of your hole, Robbie!' Cole roared back.

'Guided tours of the Ring of Kerry tonight.' Lyons laughed.

McGuinness was already stuck into a girl who looked like she'd just left her beat on the Grand Canal. Stiletto heels, ridiculously short red miniskirt, and a white blouse that looked like it was painted over voluminous breasts. McGuinness smiled guiltily at Dickie and returned his gaze to his *inamorata*.

Two tearful girls walked around the bar towards Foster and Dickie. They were looking for a lost bottle of Liebfraumilch. Cole's large forearm reached out.

'What's wrong, girls? Ye look very sad.' Cole asked with a feigned earnestness that never failed to sound sincere.

'Someone stole our wine!'

'We've only our taxi fare left,' said the other. Lyons winked at Cole, before putting his hand on the shoulder of the prettier girl.

'A terrible thing. Have some of ours. Henry, two glasses quick!' shouted Lyons, tending to his victims.

The girls cheered as they quaffed rancid Liebfraumilch, surrounded by men, two of whom were in the advanced planning stage for the rest of the night.

'Jesus!' Foster mouthed to Dickie. 'If they think wine theft is bad, wait until Cole is heat!'

Lyons' arm extended with the empty bottle of Liebfraumilch.

'Mandeville, it's your round! I got that one! Ask for the special price!'

Dickie went to the bar. The 'officer' price was a one-pound reduction in the standard bottle of Strings gut-rot. In all his nights in Strings, he'd never seen anyone part with more than £20 for the stuff, but Lyons insisted this was a special price for officers.

In February he'd spilled some of this stuff on a pair of dark green chinos. He woke up next morning to find the spot was bleached to a pale khaki.

Dickie returned to the corner, rationing out as little as he could to Lyons, Cole, and the girls. Foster was already talking to two women to his left. The shorter one was cute and busty, the taller one dark and Amazonian; they introduced themselves as Catherine and Elizabeth respectively.

'What's a South African doing here?' he asked.

'I live here. And you?'

Elizabeth was athletic, with raven hair, and the darkest of brown eyes. The Afrikaans accent was pronounced but didn't grate.

A roar went up from the front of the club. Dickie thought the place was being raided by the cops. The entire, victorious All Blacks team entered. They did a predatory lap of the club. One of them did himself no favours with a lecherous look towards Elizabeth, by now contracted to Beth.

McGuinness was soon womanless. The protuberant mammaries of his erstwhile squeeze were directed at the Kiwi number eight's face.

McGuinness extended an empty wine glass. Dickie poured.

'Wouldn't happen after a soccer international Carl,' Foster teased.

'Don't allow soccer players in here for a start!'

'Very funny, Mandeville.'

The club started to empty. Cole and Lyons had the wineless girls close to the door.

'Look at those awful women.' Beth nodded at the pair with Cole and Lyons.

'Awful?' Dickie asked.

'Must have talked three guys into buying them wine with some sob-story about theirs being stolen.'

'Shocking, Beth.' Dickie grunted.

McGuinness was still chatting beside Dickie, Foster and the two rugby fans. Miss stilettos-and-breasts wobbled back to him.

'Sorry about that, Carl. Yer man insisted on talking about some football match. Boring bastard. Couldn't understand a word. Want a dance?'

'This is Elaine, by the way,' McGuinness introduced. He pronounced her name with two syllables; she enunciated with three.

McGuinness pulled in his gut and hit the dance floor. He danced like a man recovering from a motorbike accident. Elaine had a repertoire of well-oiled dance moves, occasionally putting out her arm for an absent pole.

'You can take a girl out of the Northside...' Foster whispered to Dickie. They watched, fascinated, as the courtship ritual continued. After a while, McGuinness headed for the bar, then turned in bewilderment and made for Dickie.

'Dickie, I need some Leb money.'

'What?'

'Ordered a bottle of Champagne at the bar. Put down twenty quid. Barmaid asked me for another thirty. I give her this,' McGuinness held thirty pence in coins. 'She wants fifty pounds!'

'Pour Sprite in Blue Nun. She won't know the difference.'

'Go fuck yourself, Henry!'

Dickie withdrew the cash from his wallet. 'Return spring on cash.'

'Definitely. Thanks, Dickie.'

'I hope the Kiwi doesn't take it personally!' Foster grunted.

McGuinness made for a corner with Elaine. The cork popped loudly.

A group of as yet womanless Kiwis came towards the dance floor, to see what pickings were left. Catherine checked her watch. The girls were heading home. Dickie leaned forward to ask Beth for her number.

'Aren't you coming with us?'

He looked at Foster, who nodded towards the door.

Elaine collected her things and came back to McGuinness.

'She's a lovely girl.' McGuinness declared. As he followed her to the door, she wiggled suggestively past the Kiwis. The number eight exchanged looks with McGuinness.

'Fuck you Zinzan!' McGuinness shouted, and disappeared upstairs.

The taxis were a little easier to get at four in the morning. They soon arrived at Catherine's house, a redbrick in Glasnevin. She made tea, deciding Dickie and Foster had had enough to drink. Catherine asked for a sing-song; Beth surprised everyone with a Zulu lullaby. Foster and Catherine disappeared.

Beth left the sitting room, returning with a mattress and duvet for the floor. She undressed and slid her olive body beneath the cover. Dickie, in keeping with his day so far, did exactly as he was told.

***

He rang Eleanor on Sunday afternoon, and told her he missed her.

***

'Fuck this one up, Lieutenant Mandeville, and it'll be on Sky News.'

Dickie had just been briefed in Battalion Operations. Senior IRA bod, wanted for a bombing in London, had been captured. He was to be escorted to court to face an extradition warrant. The goon squad of local supporters was already circling the station.

'And take no crap from the local cops. They do it our way or they can escort the bastard themselves.'

'Yes, sir.' Dickie and the sergeant saluted, and went down to join the escort. They had three cars, two for the escort, and the sergeant would shadow in the third as a reserve. They exited Wolfe Barracks at speed.

Dickie was shown into the Chief Superintendent's office without fanfare. The plan was simple. The escort would assemble behind the steel gates of the station. The prisoner would be loaded, the gates would open without warning, and they would exit for the

Special Criminal Court. Dickie couldn't have asked for more. He agreed the positioning of the prisoner vehicle in the convoy, and left.

He recognised the little man who entered the office as he left.

He was relaying the plan when an inspector arrived and told him there was a change. The prisoner would be brought out the front door. The inspector turned on his heels and was gone. A cop opened the gates and motioned them out. Dickie recalled the CO's words about taking no crap. The Chief Super was unlikely to change his plan again.

The three cars moved out in front of the station. There were two hundred or more protesters outside. Tricolours and placards everywhere. Stuck in the middle was a TV crew. Dickie got the picture now. The little man was a reporter. He'd turned producer, and was grabbing his prime slot straight after the six pm headlines. The mood was ugly. A protester with a loud-hailer whipped republican slogans from the crowd. The reporter joined his crew. It was about to happen. Dickie got a nudge in the arm.

'You in charge of this escort?' a bullet-headed guy in a Crombie who could only be a cop.

'Yes.'

'We'll be following you in the Ford.'

This was against everything Dickie had been drilled with on mixing uniforms and plain clothes. Why they looked for an army escort, only to put two detectives following with handguns and an Uzi was beyond him.

'You're not supposed to be here. Any shooting starts, stay back. My lads will shoot anyone in civvies with a gun.'

The detective snorted and returned to his car. The rising commotion told them the prisoner was on the way. He came out the front door of the station, handcuffed left and right between two uniformed Gardai. A few beer bottles tumbled towards the steps of the station. The crowd started to jostle with the cops. The reporter was recording a piece to camera, action-man capturing a confrontation of his own making.

The cop cuffed to the prisoner's right hand took a hard punch to the face. They made it to the open door of a cop van, the prisoner was bundled inside. The blue lights came on, and Dickie's men gunned their engines. A few protesters tried to impede the escort's exit, but a patrol car in front parted the crowd slowly and they made their way out of town. At the edge of town, two motorbike cops waited, and they maintained a steady 80mph all the way to Dublin.

***

The Battalion Adjutant spotted him as he made his way to the mess for coffee.

'You're improperly dressed, Captain Mandeville.' He shouted from the steps of Battalion HQ. Dickie turned and looked quizzically at the Battalion Adjutant. 'Gazette was published this morning. You're a captain. Get a third pip on your shoulder before coffee!'

***

It couldn't be. He pulled the philtrum down hard with his left index finger. There it was, glistening proudly beneath his right nostril. The embryonic stage of a bright, silver-grey hair. It didn't seem to want to grow downwards like the others. It stood erect and obstinate, announcing its arrival. He ran his razor hurriedly over it, decapitating it, dressed quickly and got into uniform. Perhaps it would be gone tomorrow.

***

'But I haven't done an 'A' Course, sir.' Dickie stated to the CO.

298

'So you're perfectly qualified. Almost no one who does a unit administration course becomes adjutant. They usually make them QMs, or Ops officers. You'll do fine.'

Dickie didn't want to complain too much. It was an honour to be asked, but he was a captain barely a month.

'I'll be the most junior staff officer in the Battalion. By a long shot.'

'Adjutant is going to Angola. Ops Officer is getting promoted in three months, and will be getting A Company. QM is going to DFHQ. Complete clear-out of my battalion staff.'

'That's pretty bad, sir.'

'Par for the course for Officers' Records. They couldn't plan a bowel movement.'

***

'Calm down, Duncan. Tell me what happened.'

Duncan was on the phone from Killimore Barracks. Dickie was orderly officer in Wolfe, had finished the Times crossword, and was settling down to a morning coffee in front of BBC rugby highlights. The CO was on leave. Eleanor was travelling from Galway to spend the evening with him in Wolfe. Orderly dog didn't get better than this.

'One of the stand-too just put a round through the roof of the stand-too. When I went over to check it out, they put another round through the door. Nearly hit the BOS.'

'Two NDs in one morning. What were they up to?'

'I'd told them to clean their barrels, they were filthy.'

'So they cleaned them. How'd they get live rounds up the spout?'

'I told them to clean them in the stand-too room, after mounting.'

'You *what*?'

'Well that's the way we did it overseas. Two of them were just back from the Leb with me.'

Duncan was just back to duty after his UN leave.

'If we all did at home what we did in the Leb, Duncan...'

'I know, Dickie. I'm sorry. I was just...'

'Have you two buckshee rounds?'

'Won't work, Dickie.'

'The Battalion Adjutant just asked if you've a couple of spare rounds, Duncan.'

'The CDO knows.'

'What? Who told the fucking CDO?' Dickie exploded. He was pacing the TV room to the length the phone cable would allow. Saturday was officially over.

'I did. I, I thought it was the right thing to...'

'You rang the CDO first, before ringing me?'

'I didn't know you were on duty today, I...'

'Oh for fuck sake, Duncan...' What was the point? One last chance maybe. 'Who's the CDO?'

'Coffey.'

No chance. 'Okay, Duncan. Have you sent him a written report yet?'

'No.'

'Fax it to Battalion HQ first. I'm letting the boss know now.'

Dickie rang the CDO. The baritone drone of his old IrishBatt ops officer oozed from the other end of the landline.

'Good morning, Dickie,' the "Grinder" Coffey intoned when Dickie identified himself. 'I'm so glad there's a staff officer on duty.' Dickie presumed it was a compliment. 'A serious matter in Killimore, I've informed the GOC already. We're lucky no one was hurt.'

Marvellous, Dickie thought. That would cheer up the CO no end.

'Thank you, sir. I'll be phoning the CO after this call.'

'Have you arranged to replace the orderly officer?' Dickie hadn't given it a moment's thought.

'I've alerted the stand-too officer. The CO will decide if the orderly officer is to be relieved,' Dickie replied, realising he'd have to find out who the stand-too officer was before he rang the CO.

'Very good. Could you let me know the CO's decision for the CDO's duty log? I'll let you get along, I'm sure you're busy.'

'Will do, sir,' said Dickie, beating the phone back into the cradle.

***

Dickie was in his office at eight am on Monday. This morning, the CO would probably turn in on time. He'd been remarkably sanguine about it on Saturday. When Dickie sounded him out on Grinder's query about replacing the orderly officer, he laughed. 'Do we have a choice now?' The stand-too officer was at a football match, and couldn't replace Duncan until three. Every soldier in Killimore knew by dinner time that Duncan had been stood down.

The CO arrived at eight-thirty and came straight into Dickie's office.

'Nothing further from Cork or Killimore?'

'No sir, now that it's a Command matter, we'll have to see how the GOC wants to proceed.'

'What can he do?'

'He could send the MPs to investigate, he could send the Command Adjutant to investigate, or he could get you to investigate here.'

'And if he directs an investigation here?'

'Sgt Lafferty's working that now sir. It looks straight forward.'

'Thanks, Dickie.' He turned on his heel and went upstairs to his office, directly overhead of Dickie's. He was in surprisingly good humour. The advantage, Dickie presumed, of knowing his career was over. He'd retire a battalion commander, and there was nothing the bastards could do to stop him. Dickie took the morning parade, and waited for Command to decide the next move.

Sgt Lafferty dropped the post into his in-tray, smiling. Dickie could see the top letter was closed, marked personal, and addressed to him in a ministerial envelope.

'Going up in the world sir, and you only the adjutant for a few months,' Lafferty smirked.

The salutation on the letter was 'Dear Capt Mandeville.' Dickie scanned to the bottom. It was signed by the Defence Minister in person.

Dickie had never seen a parliamentary question that wasn't addressed to the 'Adjutant,' or the 'CO'. The letter described the circumstances of one Private Emmett, a constituent of the minister, 'victim of a hasty court martial,' who had deserted under duress, and sought to put right his legal status. Emmett's service number looked pretty senior. There weren't too many of that vintage in barracks. Dickie called in the Sergeant Major.

'Emmett? Jesus, sir, that's a bit of a stretch.'

'Can you remember anything? About the court martial?'

'There was no court martial. We had a bit of a laugh about it. It was '71 or '72. He went AWOL as a recruit, never even made three-star private. Surrendered after six months, and was due for CO's orders. He was standing outside the CO's office, and just did a runner. Hopped the back wall. Never seen again. He must be looking for a state pension or a job now.'

'How's that?'

'The criminal conviction stays on your file. Even if you're never locked up. It would be flagged if he went for a job with a local authority, or looked for a disability claim.'

'He's getting his affairs in order.'

'Sounds like.'

'Okay, thanks.'

The sergeant major left, and Dickie called the Command Legal Officer.

'Good morning, Captain Mandeville. Bit early to be calling me. The GOC hasn't made up his mind on the incident.'

'Not about the incident, sir. I've just received a letter from the Minister for Defence, addressed personally.'

'Congratulations.'

Dickie briefed him on the contents. He could hear the CLO chuckle as he went through the story. The CLO dictated a few short sentences for Dickie to drop into his response to the Minister.

**

The unfortunate Duncan fell victim to a GOC determined to set an example, and a CO who couldn't care less. Dickie had gone over the CO's options with the CLO on a confidential basis. He had absolute authority to dismiss a charge, refer it for summary trial by an authorised officer, or refer it for full court martial.

Dickie tried to persuade the boss to dismiss, and give Duncan an admonishment in his confidential report. Still a hefty sanction for a young man due promotion to captain, but not a conviction on his record.

'I agree with you, Dickie, but the GOC directed I'm to refer him for trial, where he'll get a severe reprimand. He wants to show NCOs that officers will be disciplined as well as the men.'

'Nice to know the punishment in advance of the trial, I suppose.'

'Captain...'

'Sir, I've checked with the CLO. There is nothing the GOC can do if you dismiss the charge.'

'I have no intention of going against the GOC's decision.'

Sergeant Lafferty brought in two cups of tea with the admin file for the morning.

'Are you sure about this letter to the minister, sir?' he said, drawing up the chair on the right of Dickie's desk. 'I've done a few in my time but...'

'The CLO dictated it to me himself, Sarge. It's the law. Apparently.'

'And apparently, the minister will still be a minister after the next election.'

'Private Emmet remains legally classified as a deserter. Should you know of his current whereabouts, or should he return to your constituency clinic, please notify a member of An Garda Siochána or the Military Police, immediately.'

The Practicing Thespian

The transfer to Dublin hadn't been too hard to arrange. He got a copy of the Gazette every month, and was able to track who was going where. He managed an artful three-way swap with Dublin and Donegal. He would be ops officer of the Second Battalion, in Rathmines, the 'Vikings.'

***

Robbie Lyons was the man who suggested the house. Dickie had his single officer's room in Rathmines, but figured it was time to move out. Lyons was already assembling a property portfolio, source of funding unknown, and never wasted an opportunity to tell everyone they needed to be on the property ladder.

The Stoneybatter house, he was told, was in an up-and-coming area. It was just a walk away from McKee Barracks and DFHQ. Rathmines was a short car ride, cycle, or a decent walk away. The house needed work, but he could live in quarters for the duration.

Lyons secured him a solicitor off Mountjoy Square for the conveyancing. Dickie arrived on a Wednesday afternoon to complete the paperwork.

'So you know Robbie Lyons?' Dickie enquired of the solicitor.

'Sort of. I've done a bit of conveyancing for him. Cyril, my junior, knows him better.'

'McDuff?'

'You know him?'

Dickie almost guffawed. He had no idea if the senior knew of McDuff's past.

'Junior class. Haven't seen him in years. Must say hello.'

'Sign… here, last one. Congratulations, Dickie,' he said. 'Cyril's office is across the hall.'

Dickie emerged into the dimly lit corridor, and picked out the door opposite. His knock was greeted by a loud 'Yeah.' McDuff was annotating one of a large pile of manila folders on his desk.

'Dickie. How the hell are you?'

'Cyril. Haven't seen you in a long time.'

'Lucky you!'

'How ...?'

Words failed Dickie. McDuff had rammed third year, and left USAC without a degree. To top his court martial in Galway, he had been involved in the disappearance of a bank lodgement for the NCO's mess in Kilkenny. He had taken the hint before the Military Police came a second time, and resigned. There had been rumours of credit card fraud, otherwise McDuff had never been heard from again.

'I had a few things going on. Figured best to make a clean start. No contract, so I left. Studied part time. Got a job here doing P.I.'

'P.I.?'

'Personal injury. Slips, trips, falls and such. Hearing as well. You've done a fair bit of competition shooting, haven't you?'

'Yeah. No problem with the lugs though.'

'Sure? Even a small loss is five grand, guaranteed. More than your house deposit, I'd say?'

'Sure is. Hearing's fine though.'

'Loud and clear, Dickie. We can't sue where there's no disability!' McDuff rolled his eyes to the ceiling and smiled. 'Married?'

'No. Significant other.'

'Good for you.'

McDuff was already returning to his paperwork as Dickie left.

The battalion commander, affectionately known as Uncle Pester by all ranks, called Dickie to his office to inform him that he would be training the three-star platoon due in August. There was no point in giving it to one of his two lieutenants, he said, as they were off to college in four weeks.

At least Pester was giving him Sgt Mulholland, ex-Ranger, partially sane, as the platoon sergeant. The platoon was large at 54, with eight women thrown in, a first for Dickie and some of the NCOs.

***

O'Boyle, a would-be articulated truck driver, was driving Dickie's Land Rover to the Glen.

'Thought you weren't due back off that course for another week, O'B?'

'Fuckin' failed me in the S&T School, sir.'

'For what?'

'Bit of an altercation between my truck and a lamp-post.

'The lamp-post's fault?'

'Fuckin' right it was sir. No way it should've been there!'

'Going to apply again?'

'Nah. Fuck it, sir. Don't see myself in the truckin' business when I do me twenty.'

'Handy job in civvie-street though. I hear some tanker drivers make forty K a year.'

'Know a few of them. Miserable fucks.'

'Stay in, do the potential NCO's Course?'

'Fuck that shit, sir. I'm tryin' me hand at acting.'

Dickie grunted.

'Fuckin' serious, sir. Sergeant Keavney in the Squadron introduced me to Rose Henderson.'

'What's he got to do with acting?'

'He's a talent scout. For Rose Henderson.'

'Who's Rose Henderson?'

'Biggest casting director in Ireland.'

'What does Keavney have to do with her?'

'His wife's her first cousin. Met her at a weddin'. Happened she was looking for extras as British Army squaddies. He got the gig. I got a few nixers as an extra before moving to speaking parts. Rest is history.'

'O'B, but what the fuck do you know about acting?'

'Well, *she* says my aesthetic is informed by my military milieu, but my delivery is authentic.' Holding his cigarette between thumb and forefinger, he jabbed the word 'aesthetic' at the windscreen. 'Says I have to move on from the literal, but I'll grow with experience. She's auditioned me twice.'

'For what?'

'A few of those IRA films. Lots happening in Dublin at the minute, you know. Tax reliefs and all that.'

'What are you playing?'

'You know- Heavy number 1, Cop number 2, that sort of shit. Once you speak few words you're on a different pay scale.'

'You have an Equity card?'

'Not yet. But Sergeant Keavney has a bit of a fix while your application is pending.'

'Well...' Dickie was dumbstruck. 'Best gig so far?'

'That IRA film, *Satan's Legion,* finished last April.'

'With that yank from *Sally and Jane*?'

'The very one! Got no lines, but got a solid three weeks as a uniformed extra. Good money.'

'Bit of a tit, yer man?'

'Arsehole of the highest order sir. Self-important twat.'

'Jesus,' thought Dickie out loud. Private O'Boyle, actor, despised thespian royalty.

'So Sergeant Keavney got you a paying gig on *Satan's Legion*?'

'Well him and Corporal Woodward.'

'Support Company Corporal Woodward?'

'The man.'

'What's he got to do with *Satan's Legion*?'

'He bought a couple of Humber Pigs in a British Army auction a few years ago for a couple of hundred quid. Rented them to them movie for five-hundred a day, and drove one of them. For the Belfast scenes.'

'Jesus.' Dickie didn't know what to say. Half the Battalion seemed to have an alternate line of work outside the gates.

'Last day of shooting in Ringsend, Sergeant Mulholland gets thirty of us around his trailer, fuckin' huge motor home. We're all in British Army clobber. Mulholland gets a camera, grabs '48 O'Shaughnessy, with the shit teeth, and bangs on the Yank's door. We hear him potterin' around getting' his make-up on and shit. He opens the door. Mulholland roars at him 'Hey Bud, I want a picture of the two of us for me daughter!' As he's gettin' out of the trailer, Mulholland pushes the camera in his chest and says 'Not you! Me and Shocko!' He pulls O'Shaughnessy into him, and the two of them smile while yer man takes the photo. Fuckin' disgusted he was. Fucked off into the trailer with the lads pissin' themselves laughin'. Last we saw of him.'

'Harsh, O'B.'

'Fuck'im, sir, wouldn't piss on him if he was on fire.'

'Where are you appearing next?'

'Well... I need an agent. That's the tricky bit. No agent, no speaking roles. No speaking roles, no agent.'

'The dilemmas of the modern infantryman, O'B.'

'I'm serious, sir.'

'And you reckon this is a job, after you've done the twenty.'

'If I position meself, sir. Rose says Irish television and film is about to experience a golden age. Just got to position meself...'

'Don't try the speak-to-my-agent routine with the Sergeant Major.'

'No way, sir. Man's a fucking philistine. Absolutely no appreciation of the dramatic arts.'

***

Dickie was nominated as the next Portlaoise Prison platoon commander. The soldiers liked it because of the security duty allowance and the time off. Officers liked it because of the time away from unit. As a high-security facility for paramilitary prisoners, it was strictly run, with onerous SOPs.

Number 1 Security Prison Company ran the guard with four platoons, two in and two out, one platoon on post, the other resting. A minimal kit list was permitted, wash gear, gym gear, and change of underwear only. All carried in an army kit-bag, which was thoroughly searched on entry to the prison.

***

The second toothbrush in the glass was disconcerting at first. Dickie had left home as a teenager. The only time since them he'd shared a room since was for six months in the Cadets' Mess, and for four months in Lebanon.

There had been no big-bang decision that Eleanor would move in. One week she was renting her own place, the next they decided it was best if she moved in. The fact he had found a suitable Church of Ireland girl was welcomed by his mother.

The little things threw him at first. The compromise over meals, that laundry had to be done just so, that the TV was not exclusively his. But he had someone to come home to. Not literally, as he usually got home before she did. He no longer needed to find someone for weddings. It was… nice.

***

Dickie's first briefing before taking in the guard platoon was in Brigade Operations. Second Battalion volunteers were vetted thoroughly; an ex-soldier was in Portlaoise for murdering three Vikings in Lebanon. The Brigade Ops officer finished his briefing with a wink and a warning about the current Portlaoise commander, a commandant unknown to Dickie. His prison brief was in a week's time.

'Make sure your ID card is in date,' the ops officer warned. With that, Dickie trundled off to coffee in the mess.

***

The timings of the three-star training and the Portlaoise guard platoon training started to chafe. Sgt Mulholland took his young charges out of the camp in the Glen for a four-day base-camp exercise, leaving Dickie to wonder what he'd get up to in the mountains

311

without an officer in base camp. Dickie and Sgt Burns, his guard platoon sergeant, went to Portlaoise for their formal prison brief.

They went through the search area on at 09:30hrs on a wet August morning. Burns was led away by the QM for his admin briefing, while Dickie went upstairs to the small officers' mess.

***

Dickie lay under the poncho bivvy in his shell-scrape in the Glen. Crane, a young two-star from Tallaght, was beside him. Boundlessly enthusiastic about soldiering, he was enjoying every minute of the exercise.

This was the three-star platoon's final exercise. Eastern Command had organised that all three of the Dublin training platoons would occupy the Glen at the same time, facilitating wider patrolling, 'live' enemy from opposing platoons, and good testing of navigation. Dickie's platoon had been allocated the area just south of Cemetery Hill for a reverse-slope defence. He chose an intersection of ditch-lines for his triangular platoon base, affording use of the ditches for cover, and ensuring they would be relatively dry if the September skies opened on them.

***

The fighting patrols had gone well the night before, Holland was back in his Ranger element again, attacking the Second Regiment platoon in their base to the north. He'd come back from the patrol trying to control hysterical laughter.

Holland had navigated his patrol to within twenty metres of the Regiment's position undetected. He told his patrol they would carry out a recce before their attack. They were so close, they could hear every word spoken in the 'enemy' camp.

The Regiment's platoon sergeant, 'Lugs' Tracey, had been on the same Ranger Wing selection course as Holland. Holland passed, he failed. He had spent the rest of his career investing in top-end boots, alpine climbing gear and the like, but Holland always had the red-piped Ranger flash on his shoulder that could never be acquired in a mountaineering store.

The Regiment's own fighting patrol being led by a young gunner officer had gotten lost in the forest. Holland could hear the crackle of pine branches as they tried to return to base. Tracey was whispering loudly to his charges, getting them ready.

Holland's men heard what sounded like the Regiment's fighting patrol galloping back to base. Louder it got, Holland incredulous that anyone could run at that sped through a forest in the dark. Tracey stood up in the centre of his platoon, shouting: 'Ready lads, here they come!' The first ripples of automatic fire started from the Regiment's patrol base. Through his night scope Holland watched a flock of sheep, disturbed by the other fighting patrol, make a run south to safety. Tracey, John Wayne-like in the centre of his platoon, shouted fire orders. He reached for a Schermuly rocket-flare in the pocket of his very expensive Gore-Tex raincoat. Unfortunately, he had already removed the safety cap from the Schermuly. He pulled the firing ring, setting the rocket off, and a stream of burning propellant into his armpit. The phosphorous flare ignited in his pocket. He screamed for help and rolled on the ground trying to extinguish his burning raincoat.

Ever the Ranger, Holland chose this precise moment to press his attack. As the young two-star soldiers of the Second Regiment struggled with screaming, panicked sheep falling into their slit trenches, Holland and his patrol threw smoke grenades, thunder-flashes, and charged. Pandemonium ensued. While Holland's patrol methodically threw thunder-flashes into every trench they could find, young soldiers of the Second Regiment were manfully heaving kicking sheep out of their trenches. The sheep were spooked literally shitless as they were manhandled out of the trenches, depositing warm, black nuggets onto the uniforms of the equally frightened soldiery. Violent kickings followed for the young and agriculturally ignorant city kids.

Dickie, a mile away and on the lee side of Cemetery Hill, had seen the fire fight. Flares and Very lights floodlit the sky, and continuous automatic fire could be heard. Holland himself called 'Endex' when he noticed Tracey writhing in pain. The unfortunate lieutenant commanding the Regiment's fighting patrol returned to his patrol base to find Lugs Tracey being loaded into the back of an ambulance with third-degree phosphorous burns to his right hip. Holland bade farewell and took his warriors back to Cemetery Hill non-tactically.

**

A desultory attack from the Fifth Battalion's platoon on Dickie's position had followed. Hearing them clumsily approaching, Dickie called theatrically on non-existent soldiers to reinforce number three section on the westerly ditch. 'There's fuckin loads of them!' he heard a young two-star shout. They fired a few shots, shot a flare or two, and were gone.

**

At 04:00hrs, festivities were over, and Dickie repaired to his bivvy beside Crane. The night was dry. He looked forward to at least a couple of hours of warm sleep. Crane had mastered the art of falling asleep the moment he lay down. Dickie's mind was still alert as he burrowed into his sleeping bag.

He knew what he *didn't* want to do for the rest of his life, but he didn't know what he *did* want to do. He couldn't recall the time he'd decided to become an officer. Was it in primary school?

He'd have ten years' service come November, and knew there was no way he'd do another decade. There was still time to enrol for a master's degree in business school this year. He'd graduate in two years, thirty years old, qualified for a small pension, and ready to get a real job.

IT? He could barely turn on a computer. HR- they said it was the coming thing... Finance- he might have a shot. The civvies he knew in UCG were all making a little money. Some guy the year ahead of him was leasing jets in Shannon. Had to be something better than a £300 increment each year, waiting for promotion to commandant.

He thought of the cynical, shrivelled, half alcoholic commandants who populated the mess, stealing the Irish Times to save themselves a pound. He'd sooner die than turn into another Statler or Waldorf.

Too late to back out of Portlaoise Prison now. Business school would have to wait another year.

A hint of orange glowed on the horizon. His breath condensed on the cold poncho above him.

'Jaysus, sir, this the fuckin' life!' Crane smiled in pure teenage sincerity beside him. Dickie felt ashamed, a cynic at 28.

'Can't beat it, Crane!'

***

Dickie attended his final security briefing in the prison while Sergeant Mulholland took their charges for combat swimming off Dun Laoghaire Pier. Dickie had been able to organise a safety boat quite quickly with his diving contacts. He'd planned to be there, but Portlaoise Prison dictated he'd have to leave it to his platoon sergeant.

He returned to barracks just as Mulholland brought back the recruits from the sea. There was mischief in the air, two of the corporals giggling at the sight of Dickie by the Admin Block. The corporals shepherded the recruits back to the lines, while Mulholland debriefed Dickie.

'How did it go, Sarge?'

'There was a bit of malingering by Buttimer,' Mulholland referred to the female, eldest in the platoon, who was a bit too world-wise for her own good. 'Claimed it was her time of the month, so she couldn't swim. I told her wars wouldn't stop because she was on the rag, and jump!'

'She jumped?'

'Sure did, sir. Then I told her sharks could smell blood for two miles. Johnny Weissmuller wouldn't have made it back to the steps as fast, sir!'

***

Dickie left Dublin with Sgt Burns and the guard platoon. The first rotation was a day longer than the rest. They had to draw and zero weapons, and throw stun-grenades. They stayed in the Curragh that night. There were no absentees, all the subs were returned to Dublin in the morning.

***

Commandant Donovan, 'The Sultan,' OC No. 1 Security Company, was a particular man, by both reputation and habit. He affected the bonhomie of the high-flying DFHQ staff officer. He was as renowned for his practiced, considered malevolence, as he was for his galloping career priapism. Most senior officers were happy with a well-performing crew of subordinates. Donovan on the other hand enjoyed failure among his juniors. He had a Darwinian view of career progress. There were winners and losers. He was the winnower of losers.

***

'*Ljubimaja moja,*' Morgan was mouthing slowly into his mobile, the latest Nokia gizmo. She insisted he have one. '*Lju-bi-maja mo-ja,*' the lesson wasn't going down so well.

'Morgan! What the fuck are you at?' Healy ranted across the bar. Morgan raised his middle finger, and continued on as discretely as he could.

'*Ja poljubila tebja s pervogo vzgljada...*' Morgan was going as slowly as he could; it sounded like it was being written down at the other end. Then he hung up.

'Scut Corrigan has got some Russian hooker in a hotel in Pristina and he's trying to charm her. I tried to tell his he didn't have to charm her.'

'Thought you were trying to get a job as a spook in Int, not a pimp in Kosovo,' Healy was in witty mode this evening.

'So Dickie, Portlaoise Prison with *Oberst* Donovan?' Morgan was keen to move the conversation on.

Hourigan, the only signals officer in Dickie's class, had warned him well about Donovan. His reputation as a professional tosser was so well established that nick-naming him became a drinking game during an All-Army in the Curragh.

'Has to be the greatest wanker in the Army,' O'Leary kicked off.

'Defence Forces.' Foster joined in, 'No one in the Air Corps or Navy tops him!'

'I'd top the prick.' Healy was nursing a pint by the mess fireplace.

'Two charges this year!' said Clay.

'One YO done for a cracked case on a 77-set, the other coz he was five minutes late on morning parade,' Hourigan filled in.

'El wanko di tutti wanki,' Morgan was chuffed with his wit.

'Onan the Barbarian!' Paddy Doyle piped up from the bar, pleased with that one.

'You mean Conan?' Healy shouted at him.

'Read a fucking book, Healy,' Foster shouted.

'The Sultan of Onan!' O'Leary roared.

It was a good one, and it stuck. Onan the Barbarian might have worked on a sporty type, but Donovan was short, squat, and given to the occasional package holiday. It befitted a man who frequently sported an oaken hue. It had the further advantage that it could be contracted to 'The Sultan' in the presence of senior types.

This was so successful that when it got back to Donovan that he'd been named 'The Sultan', he was flattered.

***

Dickie munched the side salad that had arrived with his beef stroganoff. The other platoon commander was McCarthy, a young lieutenant from Cork. The 2i/c was a transport captain from the Curragh. The Sultan was fondly recalling his time recently in charge of a large group of reservists involved in an action movie in the Curragh. He affected the raconteur's bonhomie, chuckling at his own waggishness.

'He was not impressed when I told him he couldn't do a third take at 16:00hrs on a Friday evening.'

'Will you get a movie credit, sir?' Dickie enquired, with all the sincerity he could muster.

'Safe to say I won't be mentioned in Oscar speeches!'

Lunch ticked slowly by. The Sultan quizzed Dickie's knowledge of the SOPs.

'Have you gone over the protocols for opening fire?'

'Yes sir, warning shots, followed by containing shots, followed by firing ball ammunition to hit where necessary to protect life.'

'And make sure to fire more than one shot! Bit tricky at the Court of Enquiry if the only shot fired penetrates a prisoner's cranium.' The Sultan and 2i/c chuckled, but Dickie wasn't sure if this was walking him into a trap. He nodded.

'And don't worry about opening fire if it's prison officers making an unauthorised exit. The last escape attempt, they were all in Prison Officers' uniforms. You could spot the IRA men because their uniforms were pressed! The sentry fired at the only real prison officer. Turned out he was a hostage. That impressed the IRA. Worst case scenario, you kill a screw. The world is a better place! One thing the Army, the cops and the IRA agree on. A screw's a screw!'

***

The detectives arrived in Rathmines as the bus left for Portlaoise on the sixth rotation. Dickie wouldn't have paid too much attention, but the platoon sergeant pointed out Private Keegan's reaction. He looked like a man haunted.

Dickie got a call in the prison. The detectives were after Keegan. As a doorman outside a disreputable Dublin nightclub, he saw a punter being dragged out of the queue and beaten with a nail-festooned baseball bat. The victim had developed acute amnesia, but the cops had found a soldier-witness, and wondered if he could supply an identification.

Keegan feigned ignorance, but the cops were persuasive. Especially when it came to witnesses who had legal difficulties elsewhere. Keegan had plenty.

Keegan, Dickie and the platoon sergeant were called in on a rest day to sort it out.

'They want to interview you, and they want you available for the trial.' The CO read from notes.

'I know, sir.'

'They're aware you've been told not to testify, but if you don't, they'll prosecute you.'

'Sir, if I testify, I'll get my legs broken.'

'You've been threatened not to testify?'

'Sort of.'

'How?'

'They sent me a Thompson winter sun brochure and a bank draft for two grand. Told me to take the family to Australia for three weeks from the 15th of October.'

'Really?'

'Yes, sir.'

The sergeant started to chuckle.

'Is that how they do it now, Sarge?'

'Dunno, sir. Wouldn't mind an Australian holiday myself!'

'Wouldn't we all, Sarge! Best I can do is a winter trip to UNIFIL Keegan. If you were an NCO, I'd get you to Naquora or Cyprus.'

The CO understood that soldiers needed nixers from time to time, but he hated bouncers. Late nights and regular injuries meant too many of them were AWOL or sick.

'Don't want to go to the Leb, sir.'

'Then I suggest you get your evidence ready, Private Keegan. Dismissed.'

***

Ten of eleven rotations had passed off peacefully when Corporal Woodward came to him in a panic as they exited the bus in Rathmines. Bespectacled, well-read, Woodward had met his wife on a Kibbutz. He was an utterly reliable NCO. Which made his approach even more bizarre.

'Sir, I can't go back for the last rotation!'

'What's wrong?'

'Qatar! Qatar!'

'If it's medical, you need to see the MO. I can't sign you off.'

'Qatar! The country!'

'Let's go upstairs.' Dickie led him to Battalion Ops.

'Sir, my wife's business got a contract for two thousand SINCGARS backpacks for the Qatari army. Has to be ready in six weeks!'

'I see. Can't it wait? You saw all the crap over Keegan.'

Woodward had a reputation as something of a Heath Robinson. At first, he noticed officers dropping their pistols from their holster. The issued webbing holster was rubbish. He fabricated a comfortable, padded web belt, and a sturdy, quick-release holster for the Browning. Most officers, and sergeants had bought one, or clubbed together for a 'duty' belt and holster they would share in barracks. He graduated to a quiet line in bespoke webbing for the Ranger Wing, and the Garda Emergency Response Unit, who liked their kit just so.

Along came the SINCGARS radio, replacement for the venerable 77-set. Small, frequency-hopping and encrypted, it came with a comically bad backpack. Woodward took the dimensions of the radio, asked the QM if he could borrow one of the backpacks, and went away to develop his own prototype.

He advertised his new SINCGARS backpack in *Soldier of Fortune* magazine, and received a call from the Qataris.

'Even if we work day and night for the next six weeks, we'll struggle.'

'I thought war movie vehicle supply was your line of business.'

Woodward looked surprised that Dickie knew.

'Just a hobby sir. Don't really make a lot on it. But the wife's business needs this.'

'Sounds like you need a good ailment for Doc Moran tomorrow. He'll believe you. No-one goes sick off Portlaoise.'

'Thanks, sir.'

***

Collins Barracks was winding down. There was talk of turning it into a museum. Foster thought it already was.

The Officers' Mess in Rathmines was already fielding the bigger overseas parties, the barometer of the social factor in a mess.

The Rathmines barmen had a reputation for near wilful slowness, a trait dating back to the War of Independence, according to Tosh, the senior barman. Tosh regaled every officer's girlfriend with the story of the unfortunate barman accidentally shot while two drunken young officers argued over a Webley revolver in 1922. Realising the man was seriously hurt, the officers went behind the bar and reassured him that the padre Father Murphy was on his way. 'Tell Father Murphy to fuck himself,' the barman responded, and expired. The officers had shot the only Church of Ireland barman in the barracks. Tosh reasoned that slow service for junior officers was a mark of respect for their fallen comrade.

Dickie arrived with Eleanor, and met his brother and sister-in-law there. Tosh was holding court behind the bar, talking more than pouring. He got away with outrageous jokes by

322

preceding them with an impish smile, and following them with a 'sir' or 'ma'am' He spotted Captain Rooney, the Inspector Clouseau MP type who'd interviewed Dickie in USAC some years before, at the bar. Dickie hadn't seen him since.

'Lads were very innocent when I joined the army, ma'am.' Tosh confided with Eleanor, loudly enough for Rooney to hear. 'One of the recruits in my platoon asked the sergeant one night if prostitutes could have babies. The sergeant replied "Of course they can, soldier. Where do you think Military Police come from?"'

Eleanor snorted in laughter. Rooney pretended not to hear. Commons and Foster awaited gin in the corner of the bar.

'Tosh, aside from having a head like a blind cobbler's thumb, the difference between you and Tom Cruise is that he could actually pour a fucking cocktail!'

Tosh theatrically dropped slices of lemon into the high-balls, and solemnly pushed the gins towards Commons.

'Sir,' Tosh, right eyebrow raised for dramatic effect, 'when he pours... he reigns!'

'Cleaned! Cleaned!' Foster shouted at Commons, who skulked off to the bay window to molest some unattached women.

The party slowly warmed. At midnight, Eleanor went home, suffering from cramps. She insisted Dickie stayed on.

'Thank God for ovaries, Freddie.' Dickie toasted Lane.

'Freedom, Dickie.'

'Parole.'

Lane spotted Johnny Ledden, who was already stumbling into partygoers.

'You'd think he'd be keeping a low profile after his antics last winter.'

'What happened his head?' A two-inch square sticking plaster sat over his right ear.

'Didn't hear about his escapade on Tuesday?'

'No.'

'He was orderly dog, mounted the guard, marched over to the adjutant's office at half-eight. Adjutant and the orderly room sergeant were doing paperwork. He said "Do you have any fucking idea how bored I am?" opened the holster, then did his little Russian roulette party piece with the BAP, but chambered a round by accident.'

'I saw him doing that in the Leb. Tricky.'

'Trickier when you're hung over.'

'Good man Johnny.'

'Put the gun to his head, pulled the trigger. Stupid fuck wasn't actually pointing the muzzle at his brain, but the muzzle blast blew some scalp off anyway. When he hit the desk, the two lads though he was dead.'

'Jesus, I heard nothing about this.'

'He got an injunction against the Minister from reporting it, in case it screwed up his other legal action.'

'Gobshite.'

'Any arse, Dickie?'

'The regular, Freddie.'

'That's getting on for a while.'

'Sure is.'

'A terrible thing, when a man trails a good woman along...'

'She's nice...' Dickie nodded over to a girl in the bay window chatting to Commons.

'A girl of great strength, fortitude and resilience.'

'Off you go, Freddie, don't let me keep you here...'

A striking redhead approached them. 'You guys know how to get out of here?'

'Why would you want to leave?' asked Freddie.

'I was meant to meet friends. They haven't shown up.'

'You're among friends now. Freddie Lane, pleased to meet you.' Lane stuck out his stubby hand. Lane always got away with it.

'Margaret.'

'Dickie Mandeville.' From behind, a rasping cough. He turned to see his sister-in-law.

'Where's Eleanor?'

'Woman thing. Had to go home.'

'Poor thing. And you didn't go with her?'

'Just seeing the lads off. I'll be away soon.' From the corner of his eye, he could see the redhead walking slowly towards the door. He ducked out by the junior officer's TV room. Skirting across the lawn, he was pretty certain he couldn't be spotted from the bay window. He slipped nonchalantly into her trail.

'Margaret, isn't it?'

She turned towards him, a little confused. 'Derek?'

'Dickie. You realise you're heading for married quarters?' She wasn't.

'Oh.'

'Heading home?' enquiring the bleeding obvious.

'Well, yes. I thought I'd meet a few guys I from UCG. No sign. You?'

'Yeah. Thought I'd get a taxi. So hard to get them on a Saturday.'

He walked her down Military Road, onto Rathmines Road. A flurry of taxis passed, all occupied. Ten minutes passed before an empty cab pulled up.

'You take this one,' he said, holding the door. She paused as she sat in.

'Cup of tea?'

He tried not to look too eager.

'Harcourt Terrace,' she directed the driver. They pulled up outside an impressive Regency building that Dickie expected to be divided artlessly into flats. Instead, it was preserved in genteel decrepitude. They paused in the large hallway. Margaret evidently had no tea. She held Dickie's hand and led him upstairs. Her room held a respectably sized double bed and overlooked the street and the Garda Station across the road.

She pulled the curtains almost shut. A sliver of sodium light lay across the bed. She came back to him kissed him hard on the mouth. They undressed each other quickly and got beneath the covers. They rolled playfully around until the first bout was over.

Dickie was glad he hadn't drunk too much, he was good to go again. He discreetly felt the inner pocket in his wallet, which held just one more condom. She rested her head on his chest and held him while he stroked her back. He wondered who would break for the bathroom first. She hugged him. She was moving first.

Downstairs, the door opened; a male voice shouted up the stairs.

'You home, Mags?'

Dickie wondered if he'd intruded. That voice...

'Yeah, just in.' she shouted casually down.

Dickie could hear him climb the stairs and go to his own room.

'Housemate?'

'Yeah, that's Senan.'

'Met him at work?' he was fishing; that voice bothered him.

'No, UCG. He graduated a few years ahead of me, met him in Dublin, he was looking for a few friends to split the rent.'

He knew that voice. He knew Senan Richards. So did Eleanor. He was one of those suave, good-looking, detestable arse-holes who could squire the field, and remain on good terms with all of them. Dickie figured he might, possibly, trust Senan, but couldn't risk it. His heart galloped. He tried to relax. Minutes passed, and she stirred again. She rose to take a dressing gown from the back of the door. Dickie hadn't seen her properly since they entered the room. She was almost six feet tall, athletic figure. Long red hair fell to below her shoulder blades, but took a strange grey hue in the sodium light. She donned the dressing gown and went to the bathroom.

A silent morning dash was bad. Running thirty minutes after orgasm was contemptible. He had no choice. He donned the boxers, and felt around for socks, chinos, shirt, sweater and shoes. He patted his pockets for keys and wallet; this was one return journey he couldn't make. He opened the door and checked across the landing. A crack of light slithered beneath Senan's door. Margaret busied herself in the bathroom.

He padded down the stairs barefoot, holding everything in his hands. He reached the front door without audible creaks. The big old door swung quietly open for him. He checked for pedestrians, and movement from the Garda Station. None. He ran twenty yards down the footpath, and stopped to don his chinos. He made the corner with Adelaide Road still topless and barefoot. A taxi skidded to a halt on the corner.

'Get in! I always know a man in trouble!'

The taxi driver was one of the old reliables, sixty something, laughing heartily. He took out a packet of Rothmans and lit up.

'Tell me everything, from the beginning,' he said. Dickie obliged, knowing well the man would regale his next fare with it. He had Dickie home in twenty minutes, and wanted to give him the ride free. Dickie gave him a tenner and told him keep the change.

He sneaked into the hall, and relieved his bursting bladder in the downstairs toilet before washing his face and scrubbing his manhood vigorously with hand-wash to remove the stink of latex. There'd be a residual whiff of rubber from his boxers; he'd have to get a wash surreptitiously on in the morning. He padded upstairs.

'I thought you were going to stay in Rathmines tonight?' she groaned.

'It thinned out after you left. Thought I'd just come home.' He kissed her shoulder, lay down, and feigned relaxation until she went to sleep.

Conversations ebbed and flowed between blissful happiness and frustration things weren't moving along quicker. Dickie could never divine at which end of the spectrum she was; they always seemed to end up at opposite ends anyway.

A series of weddings followed in rapid succession. Foster's was first, followed by Commons and Bent. Wedding conversations turned inevitably to Eleanor and Dickie. Jewellery shops retarded her movement magnetically. She looked around the red-brick in Stoneybatter and wondered if there weren't more 'suitable' places on the Southside. The relationship had acquired its own personality, like a third person living with them.

***

'We need to talk,' Eleanor said. A long, meandering monologue followed, largely unnoticed by Dickie. All bar the last phrase, 'so I started seeing someone.'

'What?' Dickie said, incredulous.

'You heard me. Would you've even noticed if I hadn't told you?'

'When?'

'It's not that hard, the number of days you're away on duty, or diving, or shooting, or whatnot.'

'Who?'

'A guy I knew in college. Senan Richards. I don't think you know him. He was in my year. He's a nice guy. We're going to give it a try.'

She packed with military precision and speed. He thought she was going to ask him to drive to Harcourt Terrace. Instead, she stayed with a friend in Stillorgan. He was back in his house by eight. His toothbrush regained its solitary status on the washstand.

***

Aphrodite

Dickie faced the prospect of a womanless winter when the call came from DFHQ about Cyprus. Barny Ryan, his first overseas commander, now in DFHQ, was trying to plug a gap in the UNFICYP staff caused by a medical cry-off.

'You've done two trips to the hills, and you're single. You should be able to get your affairs in order quickly. What do you think?'

'Cyprus wasn't something I'd given any thought to.'

'Money isn't great, but you can buy a tax-free car, nice beaches, swimming pool on base.'

'Can't say no to that. Thanks, sir.'

'Drop up to DFHQ for a briefing when you can.'

What else was he planning to do? He'd be eleven years in the army when his rotation started. Half his classmates were married, the other half were studying. A third were gone to Civvie Street. He was going to Cyprus for a year unaccompanied.

He might go back to college on his return. A year out of the country would help him figure out what he was going to do.

***

A gold-embossed envelope sat beside his mess bill in Rathmines. Dickie, and friend, were invited to the marriage of Ms Ciara Fitzgerald and Lt Odhran Higgins in Killimore next March. He was glad he'd be away.

***

Cyprus was a UN mission very different to Lebanon. Half of the senior officers and NCOs were on accompanied missions with family. Camp Command was an administrative unit only.

The DFHQ brief was thorough.

Dickie's new boss picked him up at the airport in Larnaca, and drove him to Nicosia. The UN base was in the former RAF base and International Airport, on the western outskirts of the city. Fought over in 1974, the Airport was now the UN Protected Area.

He dropped his bags in his billet, a decent sized room, with en suite. It was just across the road from the all-ranks Irish bar, the Hibernia Club.

Two of his NCOs were assigned to the International Club, the Officers' Mess. Aside from running the Officers' Mess bar, sergeants Holden and Bailey also ran the International Club duty-free, which did a big trade at weekends. He was mess secretary, and a British major was the mess president.

Bailey was in his early forties, covered from the wrists upwards in tattoos. He was saving all his overseas money for laser removal when he got home. He worked out in the gym very afternoon, and was built like a brick shithouse. He was soft-spoken, gentleman to a fault, and as innocent as the day was long.

Holden was the senior sergeant; an oily, obsequious individual, who Dickie wouldn't trust across the street.

***

Nicosia was a unique town. With barely the population of Cork, it had a diplomatic presence from almost every country in the world. Ireland couldn't afford an embassy, and made do with an honorary consul.

Though nominally a modern democracy, the place was politically ossified. The president might change, but the rhetoric remained the same year after year, the same empty promises about reunification. The loyal populace enjoyed an effective welfare state created by a bloated civil service, and a banking system grown topsy for such a small island. The break-up of the Soviet Union fed the monster. Oligarchs removed cash by the truckload from the newly pilfered state assets to the safe Mediterranean haven.

After centuries of colonial domination by the Ottomans and the British, they were granted their chance at self-government and democracy in 1960. The British, seeing that partition wasn't the answer to every post-colonial problem, handed over a unified island, with the crown maintaining two sovereign bases in the south. Given the dispersed nature of the Greek and Turkish populations throughout the island, partition wasn't an option anyway.

The place disintegrated into intercommunal violence within three years. Most people thought the UN came to Cyprus after the Turkish invasion in 1974. They had been there since 1963, when sectarianism had escalated out of control.

Outwardly hospitable, with a huge tourist industry on the south coast, there was an unsettling hostility among many Cypriots towards Europeans. The married officers noticed this less, travelling with their families. But for Dickie, walking alone around Nicosia at night, the threat from the young Cypriot males was latent.

A young British captain had been bricked in the head outside an otherwise unremarkable kebab shop in Paphos the previous September. He was repatriated with brain injuries. No doubt most of the hostility Dickie felt was a residual Cypriot nationalism, directed at the former colonial masters and Turkish partition. The British were disliked almost as much as the Turks in some circles. The sovereign bases annoyed many. Yet most Cypriots accepted these bases as a necessary evil, bringing in British currency and visitors, and acting as some deterrent to Turkish aggression.

Whatever the basis for the animus, Dickie watched himself. In the old city he stayed away from doorways and the sides of the street, He kept to the centre of the alleys, where he had a chance to defend himself or run.

Puffed and self-regarding, every other one of them seemed to consider himself an Aristotle Onassis in the making, deporting themselves like Italians, without the skin, physique, self-deprecation, or charm of the latter. It was no wonder the Turks had kicked the crap out of them in a few days in 1974.

The bank vaults swelled with Russian loot, it was business as usual in the Cypriot ports. Those beautiful Mercedes Dickie had so admired in Lebanon hadn't driven overland after their theft in Switzerland, Germany or Austria. They moved in shipping containers with suitably innocuous paperwork supplied by Cypriot middlemen. The same agents were just as obliging with their services if the container held AK47s, RPGs, mortar shells, or cannabis from the Bekaa Valley.

***

UNFICYP was a civilian mission, and the military in the HQ offices were in a minority. The head of mission was a civilian, the 'Special Representative of the Secretary General.' An exalted human being, he maintained a large house on the base. He visited but once or twice a year, spending the rest of his valuable time in New York.

Despite the proliferation of air conditioning, the civilian offices opened at 07:00hrs, and worked on to a close at 13:00. Thereafter the mass exodus began. Those who dined in the International went for lunch, those who dined at home left the UNPA. In the summer months, most made for the pool, a RAF legacy, now under Dickie's wing in Camp Command.

The Force Commander kicked off every morning with a brief, the main part of which was the duty officer's brief from the previous day. This detailed any incidents requiring reporting back to New York by the mission. Dickie paid attention, as this was one of the duties he would have to perform in future.

***

It didn't take long for Dickie's dreams of Athenian beauties to be shattered in Nicosia. He'd be likelier to squire a Shia woman in South Lebanon, with the blessings of her parents, than ask a Greek Cypriot woman out on a date. Only one man was good enough for a young Cypriot woman, and that was a young Cypriot man.

The resulting inbreeding left a legacy of congenital skin conditions and orthopaedic problems among the locals. The only exceptions to the general prohibition on foreigner contact were divorced women. Their status in Cypriot society was almost as lowly as that of their Lebanese counterparts. He soon recognised the signs; the woman who smiled for more than an instant, or who returned his gaze, was invariably divorced. Even then, they didn't want to be seen with a Westerner in Nicosia; better to head to Larnaca or Limassol.

The same convention did not of course apply to the Cypriot male. Cyprus had a considerable population of British and Irish women who had fallen in love with Adonis some years in the past, to discover that the mythical Greek turned out to be just that.

Then there was the expatriate work visa. Unskilled workers required a visa, which was granted to the employer, not the employee. The immigrant worker was at the mercy of the employer, who was free to terminate the visa, and thus the worker's tenure in Cyprus, at any time. Thousands of Asians worked in low-paid positions under this arrangement, an almost invisible serf class.

Less than a hundred miles from Lebanon and Syria, the Greek Cypriots looked west to Greece as their home. The Greeks had given the world philosophy, geometry, democracy and drama. To all these, the Cypriots laid claim. Their contributions to civilisation were Ayia Napa, the toasted bacon and halloumi sandwich, and George Michael. In fairness, one of the British officers pointed out that the toasted bacon and halloumi sandwich was an outstanding addition to world cuisine.

The troop contributing nations were Argentina, Britain and Austria. These units also contributed staff officers to UNFICYP HQ, along with a smattering of others from Finland and Hungary. As a captain in camp, Dickie was expected to join the duty officer list in the Joint Operations Centre.

The British, quietly proud of their Falklands victory, spent their public hours apologising for it in front of the Argentinians. In conversation with Dickie, the subject of 'what do the Argies say?' invariably arose.

The Argentinians were more than happy to talk about the Malvinas. Even in defeat, it brought back happy memories of those days in 1982 when, for once, they were loved and admired by their own people. And it shone the spotlight away from the 'dirty war.'

***

'You up to speed on duty officer now, Dickie?' Crispin Gould, 11th Regiment Royal Artillery asked him over dinner. Dickie was understudy ahead of his first night as Force Duty Officer.

'Some of the stuff on that report seems trivial ...'

'If it's a violation, record it.'

'Roger. You guys do much UN work? I've never met a Brit in a blue beret before.'

'Just the mother ship keeping an eye on the old place, Dickie. Commonwealth and all that.'

'Really? You'd think the UK would want the Force Commander's job then?'

'Not interested. We've got the Chief of Staff and Chief Operations Officer. Force Commander's a figurehead only. London's happy for the UN to give it to wogs, slopes and neutrals.'

'I see.'

'Just Britannia looking after interests in the Med. No offence.'

'None taken.'

'The violations are numbered west to east along the line, irrespective of the time of occurrence.'

'Got it Crispin.'

Crispin had obviously been banished from the regiment up to UNFICYP HQ as captain of the reserve platoon because he was the most boring human ever to emerge between homo sapien thighs. He was proficient in German, which endeared him to the Austrians. His long-term girlfriend lived in Paderborn, where he was stationed with the British Army on the Rhine. In all other respects, he was the conventional British officer, middle class, with pretentions to upper, a grammar school boy, with the occasional affectation of a public school education. He hadn't been to college, but concealed it well. He retired to his room each evening, and ploughed through Kaye's and Malleson's six-volume history of the Indian Mutiny. Over the odd beer in the Hibernia Club, he'd hold forth on how much better off the Indians would be if they had remained in the British Empire.

***

Dickie was invited to a drinks reception in Ledra Palace on Wednesday night. Pimms was served in three different mixes, along a table crammed with canapés.

Lt Col Ian Hardgrave, the CO of the regiment, was determined to have the greatest drinks receptions on the island, even if he didn't much enjoy them himself. Aside from the luminaries in UNFYCYP, he had also invited the British High Commissioner, the commander of the British sovereign base in Akrotiri, and the Turkish and Greek army liaison officers, who maintained a discreet distance from each other all evening.

Working the room like a gundog, Hardgrave made it to Dickie, and was introduced by Crispin Gould.

'Irish Army ay? You must know Martin Glennon?'

Dickie nearly dropped his Pimms.

'You know Commandant Glennon, sir?'

'I do. Met him on the staff course in Fort Leavenworth. Top chap.'

'He was my class officer in the Cadet School. I haven't seen him in some time.'

'Do tell him I was asking for him.'

'Will do, sir.'

Having graced Dickie with twenty seconds more than warranted in Debretts, Hardgrave moved on. Dickie was accosted by two other British officers, apropos of nothing.

'Dickie?' The taller one, lanky, six three or four, offered his hand.

'Yes.'

'Harvey Rawcliffe, QM. This is Jack Fulton, Adjutant, I believe you play a little rugby?'

'Very little, Harvey.'

'Second row?'

'Occasionally.'

'Thing is, we've only got one.'

'One what?'

'Second row.'

'I see.'

'And we're playing RAF Akrotiri at the UNPA on Saturday. Hoping you might tog off.'

'Oh. Is that allowed?'

'It's a friendly. And we're all UN here I suppose. Good booze-up back here in Ledra afterwards.'

Dickie churned the myriad other exiting things happening on Saturday evening.

'Excellent.'

'Training tomorrow at two, your place?'

'See you then.'

***

Getting Crispin away from the Indian Mutiny, or the payphone when he was talking to Nina in Paderborn, was difficult. But bored out of their collective trees one November evening, Dickie convinced him to take a spin over the wire for a beer. His lads had told him of a modern bar just outside the camp in Egkomi. He found it without too much trouble.

The bar was nearly full, the tables heaving. Women danced on tables, flicking skirts in the Greek style at roaring men. Dickie heard the smash of a plate in the far corner; none of the staff appeared worried.

They found stools at the bar, grabbed a bowl of popcorn, and Dickie ordered beers. They were quickly served by a stunning woman sporting the nametag 'Natalia.' Crispin twigged she was Russian, with good German, in which Crispin was conversant.

They chatted between her answering the thirsty calls of the locals. Crispin was as boring after a few beers as he was without.

The place thinned out towards midnight. Dickie asked her if she wanted to go out. She smiled.

'I work until Thursday.'

'That's only two days away.'

'No, next Thursday, one week.'

'You mean nine days from now?'

'Yes.'

'No break?'

'Well, I don't start work until five. Finish at three am.'

'Wow.'

'My boss is... My visa... I...' She looked about furtively.

'Thursday week, then.'

'I see my boyfriend. He's American. Works at the embassy.'

'Lucky him.'

'Maybe some other time. He goes home in January.' She smiled mischievously, and was gone. Crispin yawned. They made for Dickie's car.

'Manager certainly knows how to work the staff.'

'Greeks really are a proper bunch of nobs, Dickie.'

***

The Ledra Palace was the jewel in Nicosia's post World War II crown. With a hundred rooms, two restaurants, and the finest interiors, its reign lasted only until the Turkish invasion in 1974, when it finished right in the middle of the buffer zone. Ever since, it had been the UN base for the troops in the Nicosia sector.

The once grand rooms upstairs were now soldiers' billets. Pipes and utilities had been hammered through adjoining walls without decoration or remediation. 60's grandeur was still discernible beneath the grottiness of a barracks.

***

As they got off their bus in the UNPA, Dickie immediately regretted his offer to play against the RAF Akrotiri team. With over 3,000 personnel on the base, the RAF had a lot more choice for a first XV than had 11th Regiment, who took to the field with just two subs, one forward, one back. Jack Fulton was the captain, and quickly went through the lineout calls.

The referee didn't seem too bothered with enforcement of discipline. Dickie, getting his only pass of the match in open play, was pinged as the pass was forward. He pulled up and was on his way back for the scrum when one of the RAF made a diving tackle into his side, nearly dislocating his shoulder. He threw an ineffectual punch at the squaddie, who laughed and re-joined his defence. Dickie's shoulder was screwed. He lasted another ten minutes.

They treated him to a session royal back in Ledra Palace. He couldn't quite remember how he got back to his billet, but the Audi was parked safely outside the next morning.

***

Dickie ambled over to lunch on Sunday, just before the kitchen closed. He took a large portion of roast chicken and rice, hoping the food would settle his stomach. Not as fit as he used to be. RAF thugs. He was disappointed to find he didn't have the table to himself. Kristine was sitting at the officers' table, peering at a two-day old *Daily Mail* while masticating some grilled halloumi.

Kristine was a civilian social worker and divorceé, employed by the British Army to look after the needs of the British squaddie that could not be confessed to an officer or NCO. She was painfully tiresome, disliked by every single Brit. Even Crispin hated her.

'Oh hallo, Dickie, didn't realise you were on the base today, you missed breakfast.'

Dickie figured she knew he wasn't feeling well, and turned up her forced jollity.

'Yes, Kristine, bit of a late one in Ledra last night.'

'I know, I know,' she said, in her best Sybil Fawlty. 'The Colonel rang me this morning. He's not best pleased.'

'Not best pleased? He was drinking with me until two this morning.'

'Not the point, Dickie. You don't know the appropriate time to leave.'

'I was drinking with the regimental rugby team. I didn't barricade them into the bar.'

'Ah, but you see you were a guest, and you didn't leave when the CO indicated it was time for you to go.'

'Indicated?' Dickie asked, two parts indignation to one part couldn't remember. 'Yes. He told me he got up twice and walked to the front door. That is the polite suggestion for guests to formally leave.'

'Formally leave.'

'Yes, you don't actually have to leave, you just go out the front door and return through the back door.'

Dickie gawped like a goldfish. 'I'm supposed to leave through the front door, but I can come straight back to the bar through the back door?'

'Yes.'

'Why?'

'So the CO can formally bid you goodnight, and retire at his leisure.'

'And who was going to fill me in on your bizarre rituals? Was someone going to tell me?'

'You should just know. It's good manners to know when it's time to leave.'

'I'm listening to a lecture from a member of the British Army on failing to leave politely when asked.'

'What do you mean?' She sounded perplexed.

'You lot were invited to Ireland in 1169 and haven't left yet. Despite invitations.'

'That's uncalled for.'

'Good God, Kristine! The next time the CO stands up at the bar, I'll follow the man to the door and bid him good night. Alright?'

'Very well, Dickie. I'll tell the CO this evening. I must be off now.'

Dickie was annoyed with himself for getting annoyed. The veins in his temple throbbed. She left. He finished his lunch in peace.

***

The British CO threw a regimental officers' dinner two weeks later. Dickie was invited as a guest. Dinner was followed by a long adjournment at the bar. After a while, Dickie saw him shifting uncomfortably over a brandy. He cleared his throat a little too loudly, then moved towards the door. The junior officers sniggered as Dickie stood up and walked out.

'Thank you very much, Colonel, a very enjoyable evening. Compliments to the chef.'

'A pleasure, Dickie.'

Dickie walked out of the mess, into the gloom beyond the porch. He turned right, and picked his way slowly along a rattan fence. He saw an open door and walked towards it. He stumbled into an empty beer keg. Laughter from the kitchen door.

'Dickie, fancy meeting you here?' the mess president was laughing with Andy.

'Looking for a nightcap. Nowhere else in Nicosia open at this hour.'

In the bar, the CO was warming the remains of his brandy in the corner. He raised his glass to Dickie, knocked it back, and was gone.

***

Gustavo and Dickie were alone at the dinner table on Friday evening. The long drag of a weekend on the base beckoned. Dickie gnawed on some foul-tasting Cypriot beef. Gustavo slurped a stew.

'Sod this,' Dickie said, and walked through to the bar to get a bottle of wine. Dickie poured the wine, and the two took a leisurely dessert, followed by cheese.

'And how is the Colonel's daughter, Gustavo?'

'As beautiful as ever, Dickie. She'll be in the UNPA on Sunday for mass.'

'Not much use to me, unless I convert.'

'She's worth it, Dickie!'

'She is easy on the eye, Gustavo.'

'Easy... on... eye?'

'She's attractive. Beautiful.'

'I see.'

Dickie had brought the *Daily Telegraph* into the dining room. The headline below the fold had caught his eye. An Argentinian Navy pilot and warrant officer had testified to a civil court about the disappearance of people during the Dirty War. Best say nothing yet. Gustavo needed a few glasses of wine to loosen up. They ate dinner, talked rugby and the Colonel's daughter. They felled the first bottle. Dickie ran back to the bar and got another. Gustavo's drunk tell-tale was obvious. He thought he understood much more English than he did, he found everything Dickie said hilarious, and he threw his head back to laugh in a toothy guffaw.

'See this in the *Telegraph* about the Disappeared, Gustavo?'

'Dickie, Dickie. *British* newspaper!'

'They're Argentinian airmen giving evidence. They say they were chucking them out of a Hercules into the Atlantic.'

'Evidence!' he shouted with an extravagantly Latin gesture.

'Is it true, Gustavo? Fifty thousand people?'

'Communist propaganda, Dickie! Ten... fifteen thousand, tops!'

***

The Argentinians supplied the two helicopters that made up UNFLIGHT. Their hangar was by the runway, more than a mile from the HQ. With virtually no money, the mechanics especially kept themselves around the hangar, fixed their craft, and drank maté.

The one element of the Argentinian armed forces held in high regard by the British was the Argentinian Air Force. Their willingness to hug the deck in the Falklands War was legendary, but Dickie didn't grasp just how low they flew as a matter of course. Not until the morning brief one Thursday, when AUSCIVPOL reported farmers' complaints that they were losing the top strand of barbed wire from their fences in the buffer zone. This was a big deal, because there were feral, rabid dogs in some of the minefields that would attack stock, or a man, without warning. Gustavo, sitting beside Dickie, chuckled.

'What was that about, the wire?' Dickie quizzed him after the brief.

'Nothing, Dickie. Jorge Acosta told me he hit a couple of strands, doing tactical flying on Monday night!'

'He hit a barbed wire fence?'

'Yes. They go pretty low.'

'At night!'

'They wear night goggles, Dickie!'

***

Gustavo brought Acosta down to the International on Friday evening. Dickie was buying. They reckoned they'd tease Crispin in if they let him talk about the Indian Mutiny. Crispin stuck to his room.

Wine with dinner, and beer in the bar, were followed by brandy sours.

'You're not married, Dickie?' Jorge was mystified. A 29 year old Irish man could not remain single.

'No, Jorge. The right woman I suppose…'

Jorge and Gustavo exchanged a meaningful look. Gustavo shook his head in the negative.

'So, Jorge, Dickie here was wondering if you would take him on one of your night flights to Sector One.'

'Of course, Dickie.'

'Love to Jorge, but Gustavo tells me you frighten farmers. My father is a farmer.'

'I didn't always fly low. I have the British to thank for it!'

Dickie looked at Gustavo.

'Jorge was a Pucara pilot in the Malvinas. Until the SAS blew up his plane!'

'Hard luck, Jorge.' Dickie sympathised.

'SAS saved my life! Stopped me getting my ass blown off by a Harrier! SAS shot down another one with a Stinger. Pucara can't outrun jets or missiles!'

'That's why you converted to helicopters?'

'No Dickie, not the Malvinas, the coup in 1983.'

'The coup?'

'Yes, Galtieri fell after the Malvinas. We had a civilian government. Then there was an attempted coup. The Army, the Navy, and the Marines deserted the President. He turned to the Air Force. The general said he would stand with the government. The Army sent a tank regiment to take the Casa Rosada. The Pucaras were scrambled to stop them. I spotted the tanks on Avenue Nueve de Julio. I was ordered to attack. I lined up my cannons on the tanks. I couldn't do it. So I fired into the trees on either side of the Avenue.

So did the other Pucaras. We couldn't kill our own cavalry. Then we saw all the soldiers

running out onto the Avenue, injured and dying. The infantry were in the trees. They

thought we were targeting them. So they all turned around, including the tanks. We killed

nearly a hundred of them. Our own soldiers.'

Dickie stifled a chuckle, but saw tears rolling down the pilot's face.

'So that's when I stopped flying the Pucara. I started flying the Hughes later in '83.'

'When will you come, Dickie?' Gustavo was determined to get Dickie into the chopper.

'I can't wait, Gustavo!' Dickie said, resigned. If he was going to go low flying, he might as

well do it with a semi-suicidal Argentinian pilot.

***

The Argentinian hangar was some 400 metres from the Australian police accommodation.

The runway enjoyed a fabulous view westward, into the setting sun.

The main runway was almost three kilometres long, and was overlooked by the barbecue

area of the Australian Kangaroo Club. This made it a superb location for drag racing,

preferably late at night, more preferably hammered. When someone produced a car with

a sunroof, like Dickie's Audi, the Australians insisted on driving it at full tilt down the

runway with the sunroof open. Their party trick was to stand up through the sun roof at

top speed, acting as airbrakes.

The airport itself was abandoned since the end of the fighting in 1974. An old Cyprus

Airways Trident, vandalised and gutted, stood near the terminal building. The terminal

was an eerie place, full of the ghosts of happy travellers and sad soldiers, all long

departed, in different circumstances. Large metal sun-lights punctured the roof,

illuminating the forgotten space below. No doubt the height of contemporary chic in 1974,

346

it was empty save for mounds of bird droppings, and the old advertising hoardings of the day.

***

Up close, the Hughes 500 looked even smaller than it did in pictures. All Dickie knew about them was that T.C flew one in Magnum PI. The sun was setting over the runway as Dickie pulled into the UNFLIGHT car park in his car. Gustavo stubbed out a cigarette before getting out.

Jorge was checking the chopper. A fresh-faced young man Dickie recognised climbed into the co-pilot's seat. Jorge finally came over to Dickie and offered his hand.

'Dickie, great to see you. Put these on.'

He handed Dickie a head-mounted night-vision binocular, and opened the back door of the Hughes. Gustavo was in the other rear seat, grinning. Dickie folded himself into the tiny rear seat and donned his belt.

There was a whirr behind Dickie's head, and the turbine started to spool up. As it reached a deep screech, Jorge nodded to his co-pilot, and Dickie felt the Hughes lurch upwards. Dark outside, the sun was an orange memory on the western horizon. The lights of Greek Cyprus contrasted with the darkness of the north. They rose a few hundred feet almost vertically, as Jorge eased west. Both pilots wore night vision googles. The tarmac of the runway disappeared behind them.

The Great Mesaorial Plain bisected the island, between the long, low Pentadactylos Range to the north, and the mighty Troodos to the south. It linked Morphou Bay in the West with Famagusta Bay in the east. Camp San Martin was some sixty kilometres west along the plain.

The land darkened below as they flew over the Buffer Zone. Jorge spoke with the younger pilot. There was a surge of negative-G as Jorge shoved the stick forward and the helicopter plunged to earth. Dickie lunged up into his seat harness. Beside him, Gustavo was grinning manically, the teeth glowing white in the image–intensified binoculars.

They levelled off. Dickie looked below him and could recognise features at their natural scale, walls, bushes, gates, fence posts, roads, tracks. They were travelling at 120mph or more. Jorge wasn't going over small obstacles like bushes and buildings, he was going around them.

It seemed to go on for ever, then it was over. The chopper rose in altitude, picked out Camp San Martin, flared and landed.

The CO, Lt Col Enrique Alessandri, and a few staff officers were on the tarmac to greet them. Dickie saluted, and the group were led to the officers' mess. Canapés and drinks were laid out for the guests. Gustavo introduced the colonel's daughter Veronica to Dickie with great theatre. Pretty, courteous, more mature than her 21 years, she was utterly uninterested in guests from Ireland. Unlike the staffers in HQ, the troops on the line were unaccompanied. Gustavo quietly explained that Lt Col Alessandri was a man of personal means, and had installed his family in a villa nearby for the duration of his trip to Cyprus.

An hour of pleasant small talk passed, with a non-committal promise to meet with Veronica in Nicosia, and they headed back to the chopper. The flight back to the UNPA was at altitude and uneventful.

***

The guards on the UNPA gate greeted Dickie with a funereal salute on his return from leave. He'd spent three weeks at home, attending his brother's wedding and some general family catching up.

He'd read about the security situation while at home.

He recalled, a year before, a DFHQ staffer who congratulated him on getting out to Cyprus "before Bill Clinton solves the whole mess and UNFICYP is no more!"

But in three short weeks, the place had gone tits up. The Greek commemorations marking the second Turkish Invasion, on 14th August 1974, had gone as they did every year until one Greek ran across the Buffer Zone to the Turkish side. He shimmied up a flag pole, and grabbed the Turkish flag. A Turkish policeman took out his pistol and drilled the Greek through the neck. He slid to the ground dead, still clutching the Turkish flag. Violence kicked off in earnest.

That was two weeks ago, and the protesting, rioting, and marching had been more intense than at any time since 1974.

**

The COO stood to attention for his moment of morning glory at the Force Commander's conference.

'Camp Command will have to restrict their admin duties and help with Camp Security. Permanent Force Reserve, that's PFR to our newly arrived officers,' the briefing room looked about to spot the new arrivals, who were all Brits, 'is carrying out constant patrols along the buffer zone to deter incursions by Greek Cypriots.'

Dickie's boss exchanged a scowl with him. It was alright a few weeks before, when the violence was at its height, to co-opt a few of the Camp Command NCOs onto garrison duties. But COO seemed intent on keeping them under his wing on a semi-permanent basis.

COO continued. 'PFR will carry out fly-the-flag patrols in Sector One, between here and here, and Sector Three from here to here.'

He looked like an out-of-work actor rehearsing a British Army training film. The exaggerated precision of the consonants, the ridiculous prolongation of the vowels; even the British Chief of Staff counted his own feet.

'It's important we give the civilians, especially the Greeks, the confidence that we won't tolerate any threatening military activity near the Buffer Zone.'

Dumb as he was, COO wasn't coming up with this on the fly. The COS had suggested it, or agreed with it.

Dickie turned to his left. Mercifully, Crispin had rotated home. The PFR commander from the new British regiment was the more sensible Marcus Rossiter. Dickie raised his eyebrows. Marcus returned the resigned look of generations of British officers before him when confronted with nonsensical orders. The briefing ended. Two Irish cops attending the brief looked to Dickie to decode this latest directive. He shrugged.

***

Dickie took a beer from his fridge, and sat down to watch the TV news. There wasn't a huge amount of choice, but he could get most channels. He nearly choked when he saw an 'advertorial' during an ad break on LOGOS, the Orthodox Church TV channel.

They had altered footage of the Greek protester being shot dead on the Turkish flag pole. The man was no longer sliding to the ground, dying. His right arm raised, Superman-like, he now slid *up* the pole. The Turkish flag had been airbrushed from his hand. Up he went, into a newly spliced background of sky; into rays of golden, biblical sunlight, beaming down through white clouds. He ascended into the heavens, and was gone.

***

'Jesus, sir, if they don't reopen the swimming pool soon, I'm going to have to start taking showers!' the CS in Camp Command joked. Two weeks into the "crisis" and the pool remained shut on the Force Commander's orders. The NCOs of Camp Command were still on operational rather than administrative duties.

'Starting to drag a bit, Harry. Hope this doesn't make it worse.' Dickie replied. They were drinking a beer in the Hibernia Club. Dickie was scanning the headline on the front of the *Cyprus Mail*. 'UN Patrols Deter Turkish Moves.' There was raucous laughter from the pool table, where two British soldiers were wiping the floor with their Austrian counterparts. The pot on the pool table looked close to thirty pounds.

'What's that?'

The civvies have spotted our PFR armoured cars zipping up and down the Buffer Zone. Put two and two together and got five. They think the Turks are planning to invade.'

'You're fucking joking, sir.'

Dickie slid the *Mail* across the bar top to him. Marcus Rossiter strolled in. The CS took the *Mail* and retreated to the corner to read. Rossiter shouted a lager.

'The Greeks are expecting those Turkish tanks any day now Marcus.'

'Not if we've anything to do with it!'

'What?'

'Whatever those Turks are planning, we'll put them off it.'

'Marcus! A, the Turks aren't planning anything. B, if they were, there's fuck all you could do about it with two clapped out Argentinian armoured cars. And C, we, the United Nations, are now scaring the Greeks into thinking the Turks are up to something, when they're not.'

'You don't know that for sure, Dickie.'

'Read a fucking newspaper, Marcus!'

'Sounds like Camp Command won't be there with us if the brown stuff hits the fan.'

351

'If green things with big guns come over the Pentadactylos, I'll be heading for Limassol with my car. Once I get it into a shipping crate, *then* I'll come back for the first Anglo-Turkish scrap since Gallipoli. Last one didn't go so well.'

'Low, Dickie. Low.'

'I'll buy your beer.'

'That's alright then.'

'Seriously though, when will COO stop these ridiculous patrols?'

'He's saying Independence Day.'

'Christ, Marcus! October 1st is six weeks away!'

Rossiter took a long lug from his beer and said nothing.

***

Lt Col Bellamy, the CO of the new British regiment, would afterwards admit that asking an Argentinian pilot to 'fly lower' was poor judgement on his part. He didn't know Jorge Acosta by reputation, and so could be forgiven.

The Greek demonstration at the Markou Drakou roundabout was getting aggressive. There were mutterings that they would move up to the Turkish checkpoint. Bellamy had a problem on his hands, and asked for the Argentinian chopper on stand-by.

There was always posturing in the Greek protests, especially with a TV camera around. The absence of Greek police didn't help. The stretch of road between Markou Drakou roundabout and Ledra was buffer zone. The Greek police weren't stopping civilians going past it. From the roundabout, it was less than 500 metres to the Turkish border.

Jorge landed in the Ledra car park and picked up Bellamy. Bellamy's men were spread across the whole of Nicosia, so he'd only 30 to spare for Ledra.

'Fly lower!'

Acosta reckoned he was at about 100 feet at that point.

'How much lower, sir?'

'Right down! Scare them off.'

Acosta took the Hughes down to little more than head height, edging the chopper along the line of protesters. Most backed away towards the roundabout. Some didn't. One of them decided to show the UN some manners. He jumped and grabbed a landing skid.

A lesser pilot would have crashed. Acosta hauled on the collective, taking chopper and protester skywards. They were now looking eye to eye with the Turkish police on top of Mala Bastion.

'What will I do now, sir?'

'Get rid of him!'

The space to manoeuvre was restricted by trees. Acosta flew high enough that a fall would put the Greek in hospital, low enough he'd leave it alive. He flew back towards the crowd, twenty feet or so, dropping slowly. A few of the protesters got their hands on the Greek's feet, and pulled him down.

'Would you like me to do it again, sir?'

***

The knot of staff officers belly-laughed in the International Bar as Acosta retold his story. Beyond the surreality of air bombing protesters with a live body, was Acosta's impersonation of Bellamy's accent. Sergeant Bailey's back was turned discretely, but Dickie saw a tear of laughter in his eye. Rossiter was laughing hardest of all.

'You've got to tell that story in front of a few Brits Jorge!'

'You tell them, Marcus!'

'I can't spread a story like that about my boss!'

Acosta's voice dropped an octave as he eyeballed Rossiter.

'You want me to spread a story about your CO? Such disloyalty.'

Rossiter looked about at the other poker-faced officers, Austrian, Argentinian, Canadian and Irish.

'I thought it might make an after-dinner anecdote,' he said, defensively.

The others started laughing at him.

'You bastards.'

***

The patrolling finally ended. One of the two Argentinian armoured cars broke down, needing a part from the motherland. It would not arrive soon. The PFR took to patrolling with the other armoured car and a Land Rover. The Cypriot press asked questions about the extent of the Turkish threat. They started to editorialise against UNFICYP. Not something a civilian-led force appreciated.

The Finnish Force Commander ran out of patience with his COO. A mild-mannered man, he took advantage of his imperfect English to ask COO slowly penetrating questions at the morning brief. Even the Argentinians started to feel sorry for the Brit.

The last patrol was on Friday. To save COO's blushes, the Force Commander said they'd review the situation coming up to Independence Day.

***

Marcus agreed it was cause to celebrate in Ayia Napa. They bundled into Dickie's car and took the motorway south. Half the NCOs in camp command were headed there as well. All stayed in O'Rourke's Inn. Dickie hadn't stayed there before, but Sergeant Bailey told him it was decent, clean, and just £15 per night. No money changed hands for the NCO's though. They each bought a bottle of Jameson or Johnny Walker in the Hibernia Club duty-free for six pounds, and handed it over in O'Rourke's. This paid lodgings for Friday and Saturday. Imported spirits retailed at about £45 on the island.

Dickie drove Marcus into the Sovereign Base in Dhekalia. There had been a rape and murder of a local girl some time before, and British forces were curfewed from ten p.m. nightly, even if they were with the UN. None were allowed stay in Ayia Napa. Marcus dropped his bag into a transit room, and they drove on to Ayia Napa. Dickie parked at O'Rourke's while Marcus looked for a cash machine.

***

O'Rourke's already buzzed. The band played a *Pogues* set. Dickie grabbed two beers and found standing room at the back. Cold lager cut nicely through the evening humidity; the coast was never as hot as Nicosia, but the humidity was worse.

The poke into his ribs was firm.

'Hallo, mate. She your missus?' Dickie wasn't good on accents, but it was East Londonese. He looked right. Two girls stood facing the band. Closest to Dickie was the taller one, jet black hair over a cropped tee-shirt, skirt and sandals. She looked vaguely Asian. She was also stunning.

'He wants to know if we're married?' Dickie said as casually as possible.

'Not yet anyway,' she replied, a glint in her eye. Dickie turned to the Londoner.

'We're working through a few issues.'

She heard him, and laughed to her friend.

'Noorsheena Sheridan. Sherry for short.'

'Richard Mandeville. Dickie for short. Unusual combination.'

'Nothing unusual with "Dickie." Or "Mandeville."'

'Smart-arse as well.'

'You're Irish?'

'Perceptive of you, Miss Sheridan. You?'

'I'm fifty per cent Malaysian, fifty per cent Irish, one hundred per cent Australian.'

'You come here often?' he asked, knowingly as possible.

'Last holiday before we go back to Uni in London.'

'Studying?' Dickie wondered if Aussies used the preposterous 'reading' term.

'Engineering.' She bore little resemblance to the hermaphroditic, Aran-wearing women who studied engineering in Galway. 'And do you come here often?'

'Oh, about once a fortnight during the summer.'

Dickie was glad Marcus was taking so long. Her father had met her mother in Kuala Lumpur. She grew up in Melbourne and studied electronic engineering. A third-year work experience had taken her to Europe, and she would graduate in London. Better work opportunities than back home. She had a filthy laugh. Her friend Suze threw looks about O'Rourkes that would make a Benburb Street hooker blush.

Marcus pushed in from the street. In new company, he affected the louche cad, the bastard offspring of Richard E and Hugh Grant. He generally got away with it until one got to know him. Suze looked very happy.

'Sorry, Dickie, met two chaps from Sandhurst down the road. Fancy meeting you here, Sherry! You've met our tame Fenian!'

'Hello, Marcus.' She was caught flatfooted, but there was none of the awkwardness of exes. Perhaps something briefer?

'Counting down the minutes to witching hour?'

'I'm on pass for the weekend, Marcus, staying with Suze.'

'I see.'

Suze cut to the chase.

'You guys must train a lot, do you?' she said, rubbing Marcus's bicep, her emphasis on the 'a lot.'

'Quite a bit, actually.' Marcus stuttered.

***

Come curfew time, Suze went back to Dhekalia with Marcus. Sherry took him to a disco he hadn't seen before. The dance music was non-stop, but the atmosphere was chilled. The crowd seemed to have consumed more M150 than alcohol. There was a welcome absence of wife-beater tee-shirts and drunken women in heels. The base beat of Tracey Thorn's 'Missing' moved through the floorboards. They stayed a while, she took his hand; they were on the street.

'You're really good. I swallowed every line of that bullshit in the bar.'

'Wasn't all bullshit, Dickie.'

They walked to a deserted Pantachou Beach. Most of the revellers would be clubbing for another two hours.

'British Army?'

'Australian.'

'Engineering?'

'Yes, but I'm a graduate. Commissioned into signals.'

'Marcus?'

'Met him on a course in England, before I came out here.'

'And now you're an Aussie spy in Cyprus.'

'Sig-Int in Ayios Nikolaos. You realise I have to kill you now.'

'Depends how you do it, I suppose.'

She pushed him away and glanced quickly around. She pulled off her sandals, wiggled out of her skirt, and dropped a white thong on top of it. She peeled off her tee-shirt, setting it down on the rest. She ran into the sea, front-crawling out almost a hundred yards before turning around.

'Brits always said you *Paddies* were afraid of water!'

He struggled out of his clothes and swam out to her. She was treading water. His toes found the bottom. She made her way over, and wrapped her limbs around him.

'Here, or back at your place?'

'Here, and back at my place.'

***

They found Marcus and Suze having coffee in Dhekalia the following morning. They decided to stay together for Saturday. Marcus rang his troop sergeant in Nicosia.

'I think we should get out of here!' Sherry announced.

'Paphos. My mum and dad have a villa there.' Marcus offered.

'First I've heard of it!' said Dickie.

'You didn't make me the offer Suze just did.'

'Gross, Marcus!' Suze thumped him in the arm.

Dickie cleared his room in O'Rourke's and they headed west for Paphos, getting there in two hours. The villa was in the old town, about a kilometre from Lighthouse Beach.

They spent the day on the beach, dining in a restaurant in the old town.

***

'You're oversexed and under-fucked.' Sherry whispered, as they lay in a communal pool of sweat in Rossiter's villa. There was no air conditioning. Even at full speed, the ceiling fan barely kept the mosquitos away. He followed a bead of sweat down the small of her back with his finger.

'Probably the closest to a dictionary definition of an Irishman. You should copyright that.'

'That bad, ay?'

'Buddy of mine put it beautifully- "an Irishman is like a camel, he can survive for months in the sexual desert, on one or two humps."'

'Irish girls must fancy a root from time to time?'

'Course they do. Once they stop thinking about their mother. You don't need chloroform or a ring, but it helps.'

'Irish women are crazy.'

'Double-oh Sherry, trying to charm me out of my secrets.'

'Don't tell me! Ireland's developed a new super-potato?'

'Down-right mean.'

'You'll get over it.' Her hand was already between his legs.

***

They didn't hang around on Sunday morning. Dickie had to drive to Dhekalia, then Nicosia. Sherry flashed ID on the way into the base. They pulled up at the officers' mess. Dickie took her to a corner of the hallway while Marcus said his farewells in the car.

'You'll be alright without me?'

'I'll manage.'

'Don't suppose we might...?'

'Don't think my fiancé would approve.'

'You're... quite the lady for surprises, Sherry.'

'Didn't want to spoil the moment. Sorry.'

'If he...'

'If he dumps me...' She kissed him hard. He didn't want to go.

'Promise you won't listen into my phone calls?'

'You've got a secret fiancée as well?'

He leaned over and kissed her.

'You'll never know, Miss Sheridan.'

***

Life returned to normal the following week. The offices closed in the afternoon, the pool

opened. The only cloud on the horizon was Cyprus Independence day.

Marcus lounged on a sunbed beside Dickie.

'I thought Lourdes was exclusively for papists.'

'Met quite a few of my own there. Royal Irish Ranger types.'

'Really?'

'Yes. Officer and sergeant were Catholics. The lieutenant was some chap called Hardiman.

Great stories about Sandhurst and Cyprus.'

'Told you the story about Queen Victoria I suppose?'

'Yes!'

'Oldest, lamest story in the book. Only works on foreigners!'

'The bastard. I thought that was a good one!'

'Who's she?' Marcus nodded in the direction of Madame Lemarie, who walked past the

bar looking for a free sun lounger.

'Claude Lemarie's wife. Swiss Embassy's senior bod on the island. Actual Ambassador is in Jordan. Claude is the man. A regular in the International on a Friday. Associate member of the pool as well.'

'They the daughters?'

'Yup. Genevieve and Dominique.'

'You seem to know a lot.'

'Saw their names on his application form. Late teens, early twenties, I think. First time I've seen them by the pool.'

'In the flesh...?'

'In the flesh.'

Some flesh it was. Mme. Lemarie was in her late forties. A touch too much sun, perhaps, but otherwise was a credit to the female form. Dickie rose and grabbed two cokes from the bar. The daughters laid their wondrous forms down on two loungers, safely away from mother. Dickie slowly regained his spot beside Rossiter.

'Right, Marcus. You're going over there, chat up the sisters, and invite them out to the pictures or something.'

Rossiter groaned and turned over.

'Dunno, Dickie. Busy week ahead.'

'Busy my arse. You've had fuck all to do since you stopped planning World War III against Turkey.'

'Why don't you do it?'

'I'm twenty-nine, horny, and the mother might think I'm after her. Now get up and do something useful.'

Another long silence.

'Marcus, I'm happy to let you have the nineteen year old, I'll take the older one. But if I have to chat them up, I'm taking the young one.'

'Off you go, so.'

There was no moving Rossiter. Dickie took a gulp of Coke, and strolled as nonchalantly as possible towards the sisters. Dominique it would be. Genevieve was a handsome girl, as they'd say in parts of Wicklow, but had the look of a girl who partied hard. Dominique was absolutely stunning, a Swiss Sophie Marceau with chestnut hair.

'Hi there.'

'Hi.'

'Dominique, isn't it?'

'Yes, hi.'

'We've met at the International I think, your father introduced us. Dickie.' The words were no sooner out of his mouth then he thought how perverted they sounded.

'Hi, Dickie.' She sat up, all eager, pert, and friendly. Dickie was glad he'd left his Speedos in the billet.

'Marcus and I,' he nodded in the direction of the prone Englishman, who wasn't even watching, 'were wondering if you and your sister would like to come out sometime, catch a movie?'

'I don't think so.'

'Really?'

'I'm not allowed.'

'Allowed?' What sort of family did Monsieur Lemarie run? Dickie thought to himself.

'I'm still at school.'

'University?'

She beamed the most beautiful, toothsome smile he had ever seen. 'Not university! School!'

'What age are you, Dominique?'

'Sixteen.'

'I see. Well.' He started to edge away. 'I'll see you. In the International. Sometime...'

'Yes, Dickie.'

He slunk away back to his lounger, mortified. Eyes darting right and left, he wondered had anyone seen him. Rossiter hadn't even the curiosity to turn around.

'Dinner for four?'

'Fuck off, you useless, oxygen-thieving, British bastard.'

'Crashed and burned Paddy. Crashed and burned.'

***

Dickie, Marcus and Gustavo walked into dinner. Two of the Aussie cops were already sitting down. Superintendent Sid Novak and Inspector Mike Menning were in from their normal beat in the Argie Sector Buffer Zone for a humanitarian conference, and giggling like children.

'You going to tell us what's so funny?' enquired Dickie.

'Yeah.' Menning struggled to speak without spitting out his dinner.

'Oh for fuck's sake Mike.' Marcus was very impatient when curious.

'We're in for Colonel Wilderberger's Humanitarian conference tomorrow, but we got a call from the police liaison to go to Nicosia General. Some bloke got the stuffin' knocked out of him at the Independence Day parade.'

'Oh.'

'He shimmied up a pole during the military parade, and pulled out a Turkish flag.'

'Jesus. Is he Turkish? Or just suicidal?'

'Neither.' They were laughing again.

Gustavo turned to Dickie, afraid he was missing something obvious.

'What is this?'

'Sorry guys. The guy was a Greek Cypriot. Climbed a pole. Unfurled the Turkish flag. Pulled out his lighter, and tried to light it. He was out of lighter fuel. The first assailant got his leg. The second broke his jaw before he could speak. The rest followed in for afters.'

'Christ,' Said Marcus 'Sounds like they did a job on him.'

'Broken jaw, broken arm, broken eye socket, four broken ribs, multiple soft tissue injuries, and they're treating him for head and internal injuries.'

'Will he make it?'

'Oh yeah, Dickie, nothin' terminal.'

'Especially after he hears his new name.' More sniggering.

'Do tell.' Said Marcus.

'Well, the bloke's name is Zinon Demetriou. Bill here calls him 'Zippo' on the way out of the ward. One of the Nicosian cops hears us, and looked a bit serious. Then he pisses himself laughing outside in the corridor and tells his mates. Poor 'Zinon' will ever be known by his real name again.'

***

Dickie and Rossiter found themselves in Australian company again on Friday night. Mike Menning and five of the other AUSCIVPOL cops had rotated home to the Federal Police, and been replaced by new blood. There was a general invitation out to the camp inhabitants to make their way to the Kangaroo Club for the welcome party.

Dickie drove up the camp. He and Rossiter reckoned they could hear 'Macarena' while they were still a good 200 yards from the Kangaroo. At 100 yards they could smell the steaks on the barbecue. It was shaping up to be an excellent evening.

They were confronted at the door of the Kangaroo by the burly Constable Preedy, armed with a full-size AK 47 water pistol.

'Open wide, Captain Mandeville.'

Dickie did as ordered. Preedy stuck the muzzle of the AK in his mouth and pulled the trigger. The hot sting of high-proof Bundaberg Rum hit the back of his mouth.

'Now you, Pom.'

Rossiter opened wide and took his punishment. They took a beer from a cooler and walked out onto the rear patio, where the party was in full swing, and the barbecue smelled enticing.

'Dickie! Marcus!' It was Preedy again, firing 'shots' from his AK 47. 'You haven't met Jacqui Lambie yet. Mike Menning's replacement.'

'Hi.' The woman offered her hand. Early forties, perhaps, toned and well-preserved. Dyed blonde hair, attractive, if masculine face. A wedding ring on the left hand that held the can of beer.

'Hello.'

Conversations rolled about the Kangaroo Club like pinballs. Party-goers filled themselves with the excellent steaks and burgers from the barbecue. The air was warm, the October sky cloudless. Above the runway, every star glistened. Rossiter was buried deep in conversation with one of his corporals. Jorge Acosta carried a t-bone steak the size of his foot onto the volleyball court. Dickie was trying to stick to beer, but Preedy did a further lap of the Kangaroo with a reloaded AK 47.

'It's a special place, isn't it? Couldn't wait to get back.'

Lambie had inserted herself beside him as he ate a burger on the apron, looking west over the airfield.

'You served here before?'

'Three years ago. As a station sergeant.'

'Got the t-shirt. Can't say I'll be running back to the place.' Dickie shrugged.

'Sounds like you haven't enjoyed yourself, yet.'

He felt himself being gently propelled across the apron, towards the first island of scrub that separated it from the main runway. The lights of the Kangaroo club faded behind them as they walked the 100 yards or so towards the green, or 'brown' as locally known, of the first hole on the UNPA golf course. Unable to support grass through a Nicosian summer, the 'browns' consisted of a hard, flat pan of carefully groomed fine sand. Dickie inhaled the eucalyptus fragrance of the weed that dotted the rectangle of scrub. He made a mental note to find out the name of the plant, knowing the note would be forever lost to memory the following morning.

'It's our own private universe here. Everything is different when you go home. But this is Cyprus.'

He had the sensation of being frisked as she kissed him. First, his Hawaiian shirt was open, next his chinos and boxers were about his ankles. She pushed him gently backwards. He lay on the sand, cooler now than the night air. She undressed quickly, just a white blouse, shorts and flip-flops to remove. Even in the dim light, he could see she was entirely smooth, not a follicle remained on her groin or beneath her armpits. She straddled him, and held him by the shoulders as she started a slow, rhythmic grind. Were it not for the dulling effect of the Bundaberg, it would have been over quickly for Dickie. As it was, it took several minutes for both of them; she seemed to enjoy herself. She lay quietly on his chest as they both recovered their breath.

'Isn't it great, being able to go back to a party with all that sexual tension relieved?'

'One way of looking at it!' Dickie laughed, as his manhood returned to jelly.

'Time we went back.' She stood and dressed. Dickie followed her back across the apron.

'You go in the front,' she pointed Dickie to the right, while she headed back to the party via the barbecue patio. She brushed sand from her knees as she walked.

Dickie strolled down the service road, and back in the front door. Preedy was still prowling with the AK 47.

'You been fighting again, Dickie?'

'Sorry?'

Preedy tugged at the left sleeve of Dickie's Hawaiian shirt, torn at the shoulder.

'Dirty devil. Two shots for you.'

Dickie opened wide.

***

His consciousness seemed to have retreated to a tiny, molecular point deep in his hypothalamus. He opened his eyes, slowly. The fan twirled on its axis above, yet he was still bathed in his own sweat. His buttocks were itchy. He reached underneath and found sand between him and the sheets. A wave of panic swept over him. The car? He stood up, immediately unsteady. He opened the billet door. The Audi was parked outside at a jaunty angle, but seemed otherwise unscathed. He had no idea how it got there. He retreated to the bathroom and regarded himself in the mirror. He looked like a mugging victim, his eyes pink, pallor grey.

He showered until he felt sensation returning to his extremities. A patch of dirty sand formed at his feet. The shower gel lather stung his groin. He looked down and was alarmed to see the base of his penis mottled a blotchy red.

He shaved methodically. His left cheek registered no feeling, as if he'd had a novocaine shot at the dentist. He brushed his teeth and spat. The toothpaste failed to clear his mouth, and dribbled warmly down his chin.

***

Sunday morning saw the end of Saturday morning's epic hangover, but not the unusual physical symptoms. The rash at the base of his penis had developed into a patch of angry-red pustules. He still couldn't feel his left cheek. Pinching it sharply caused no pain. He couldn't spit. When he ate, his left cheek retained a squirrel-like pouch of food, until he shifted it with his tongue or finger.

He avoided all company for the rest of the weekend. Panic on Saturday morning had turned to full-blown terror by Sunday evening. He was going home in six weeks looking like a drooling idiot with a galloping venereal disease. The fact he hadn't managed to write off his car on Friday night was small consolation. He cursed his stupidity. He nursed two double Bushmills in silence after dinner, to settle his nerves, and repaired to his billet. Alister Cooke's unguent Letter from America soothed him to a fitful sleep.

***

Dickie lay in his boxers on the gurney in the British RAP. Every minute until Capt Giles Greenwood commenced his Monday morning sick parade in the UNPA had crawled by like continental shift. He avoided the gaze of the medical orderly on the way in; a buxom corporal from Leeds who regularly drank with Dickie's men in the Hibernian. He strongly suspected she was *in flagrante* with Sergeant Holden, and hoped medical discretion would prevent her describing Dickie's recent visits to the RAP.

Giles looked blankly at him as he described his symptoms. The fact that he was sticking a needle into Dickie's feet and face, and asking him about his family's cardiac history was no less disconcerting.

'Sounds like the Australian party was quite a night.'

'Giles! This is fucking serious!'

'I take it no protection was worn during your... encounter.'

'No.'

'If anything shows up in your test, your partner…'

'I know. What is it?'

'The facial paralysis could be one of a few things, I'll need to send you to a neurologist in Nicosia General.'

'What sort of things?'

'Bell's Palsy, that's an asymmetric facial paralysis. You might have had a minor stroke on Friday night. Always possible where there's a large quantity of alcohol involved. I can't determine. You need to see a specialist.'

'And that?' Dickie looked down as Greenwood punctured one of the penile pustules with a needle, swabbed the discharge and put it in a sample bottle. He took a blood sample.

'Well first thing, it's not HIV. That takes months to even show in a blood sample.'

'So what is it?'

'Could be one of a few things.'

'Sweet Jesus.'

'Come back here on Friday. I'll have your bloods results.'

Greenwood picked up the phone and dialled a number form the rolodex.

'Nice chap. Qualified in the Royal College of Surgeons in Dublin. He'll be delighted to see you on Wednesday.'

***

Bombadier Snelling, a flame-haired lesbian from Rossiter's regiment, with biceps most men would envy, was signaller in the JOC for Dickie's duty on Tuesday.

'You alright, sir?'

'Yes Bomb Snelling, something wrong?'

'You sound a little strange, sir.'

So he did. If he spoke at his normal tempo, he slurred his speech, and dribbled spittle down his chin. So he slowed his diction somewhat, concentrating on deliberate word formation, and trying to speak from the right side of his mouth. Unfortunately he sounded mildly mentally retarded.

'Got a bang in the mouth rugby training yesterday. Bit of a think lip.'

'I see, sir.'

***

Dr Panos Antoniou really was very happy to see Dickie. He was a fan of the International Bar, McDaids, Neary's, and Captain America's. He was very keen to catch up on Dublin, which he'd left nine years before. As the doctor's enthusiasm to discuss Dublin's hostelries grew, do did Dickie's impatience.

'Can you please tell me what it is, Doc?'

'Most likely Bell's Palsy, or you had a minor stroke.'

'That's what Doctor Greenwood said.'

'Good!' Doctor Antoniou seemed unperturbed by Dickie's condition. He sounded like he wanted to return to the conversation about Dublin pubs.

'You can't be more definite?'

'No, but I'll give you a strong dose of steroids. That usually clears the cases of Bell's that don't go on to become permanent.'

'It can become permanent?'

Unfortunately yes.'

***

The cloud of depression overhanging Dickie had barely lifted by the time he returned to Giles Greenwood on Friday. The rash was still there, the pustules less prominent, but still visible to the naked eye.

'You'll be glad to know you tested negative for all the usual suspects Dickie.'

'Then what is it?'

'Do you mind if I ask if the young lady had a Brazilian?'

Dickie refused to give the game away by reacting to the 'young lady' comment, especially as Lambie was working in Ledra, where Greenwood was posted.

'I don't follow.'

'Was she shaven? Down there?'

'Yes. Bald as a cue-ball, actually.'

'There it is. Pseudofolliculitis barbae.'

'Pardon.'

'Beard rash. Well, not quite. You didn't shave. She did. More correctly beard burn, I suppose.'

'Beard rash?'

'Beard rash.'

***

The scrotal rash subsided. As did the Bell's Palsy, under the steroid assault. He also put on two kilos under the influence of the drugs. He quietly organised the repatriation of his car and kit, and avoided any further excessive inebriation. Inspector Lambie kept her distance in Ledra Palace.

***

At Last

Dickie had a lot of catching up to do in his time off after Cyprus. He was posted as adjutant 2nd Battalion. The previous was heading on some UN mission to Central America. He would be a month living in the mess before he got vacant possession of his house. He knew only two of the officers living in the mess this winter.

***

Real Madrid were playing Ajax in the Champions League. Dickie sat at the rear of the junior officers' TV room. There were eight or nine YOs in the room, planning their night out after the match. They were heading to bars Dickie had never heard of before.

'You coming out after the match, Dickie?' came the invitation, out of courtesy.

'I'll pass, thanks.'

***

He eventually got his possessions back into his house. The departing tenant, a biker with hygiene issues, left him a lot of cleaning.

In his absence, his sister had produced her first-born. Dickie was now uncle to Hugo. Sara announced she would be in Dublin that weekend to introduce him to the little man. They went for a drink and lunch.

Hugo was a fascinated with everyone and everything. His eyes rotated about as if on stalks, trying to imprint every impression on his little brain. He seemed much taken with Uncle Dickie.

Sara had some baby supplies to buy before she returned to Wicklow. Hugo enjoyed being pushed while seeing his mother walk beside him.

Dickie stayed on the ground floor at Mothercare while Sara went upstairs. Hugo grasped eagerly in every direction. He locked eyes on the tiny blonde girl in the buggy in front, waving wildly.

Dickie's eyes met those of the little girl's mother. Blonde, attractive, in a long black trench over a trouser suit. Was *déja vu* a symptom of hitting his thirties? She smiled at him, a flicker of recognition in her eyes. Her face flushed, and she spun the buggy about, stepping deeper into the store. Her husband must be there, Dickie thought.

Something as she pirouetted away... the curve of the thigh? Harold's Cross, six, seven years ago? Dickie finally recalled those leather pants, the way she took him to her bed, and invited him in the tradesman's entrance.

***

He got the phone call to his house on Sunday morning, and was glad as Barrack Adjutant he was no longer living in.

There had been an 'incident' on Saturday night. Hartigan, a married but living-in commandant, had attempted some degree of congress with Lieutenant Callaghan, a Second Battalion female, at two am. A lot of drink had been taken. The MPs hadn't been called, the incident had been 'addressed' by some of the male officers on the night, but there was now a 'situation.' Dickie filled in the CO by phone, and told him he'd meet him before parade on Monday morning.

Dickie sat down for breakfast with the YOs on Monday morning. There was no sign of Hartigan. Callaghan had taken a day's uncertified sick leave, and was gone.

He got over to the CO's office at 08:30hrs. Lt Col Peter Collins was the third battalion commander of the Vikings in 18 months. He had returned from Angola to take over from a man who'd been promoted full colonel. The boss sat behind his desk with a cup of tea, and waved the orderly room corporal out.

'Explain it again.'

'Lieutenant Callaghan appears to have had an altercation with her boyfriend in McDaids. Afterwards, she left for a house party in the company of another young man. In the taxi, she vomited. As the taxi driver was about to throw both of them out, the young man paid the soiling charge, plus twenty quid, and asked him to take her wherever she wanted to go. She was still conscious, and told him to take her back here. She was unconscious by the time they got to the gate. The gate policeman let the cabbie drive up to the mess.'

'We're not letting taxis into the barracks, are we, Dickie?'

'No, sir. A bit of discretion from Corporal O'Hare.'

'Go on.'

'Callaghan was still unconscious, so the cabbie went inside and banged on a few doors. Second Lieutenant Downs went out with a male classmate and carried Callaghan in.'

'She's the new arrival in the Cavalry Squadron?'

'Yes, sir. She undressed Callaghan in the ladies toilet, showered her, and put her to bed.'

The CO rolled his eyes.

'The commotion seems to have awoken Commandant Hartigan. He came into the corridor just as the junior officers went back to bed. He made his way to Callaghan's room, and got into bed with her. She woke up with Hartigan's head between her legs. He was attempting to...'

'Oh, Christ!'

'She screamed, he bolted. It woke some of the juniors who'd just gone back to bed. There was a confrontation with some of the male juniors, but Callaghan was too incoherent to explain what happened. Hartigan went back to bed, and Downs slept in Callaghan's room.'

The CO took a draft of tea and started to rub his temples.

'Where's Lieutenant Callaghan?'

'She's taken a day's USL. Seems to have gone home.'

'Did she call the MPs?'

'Doesn't seem so, sir.'

'Why not?'

'Worried how it'll appear, I suppose.'

'Tough. Should have thought of that before she got pissed.'

'Yes, sir.'

'Hartigan, why's he in quarters?'

'Wife chucked him out last year.'

'He's a gunner, why isn't he in McKee?' The intonation suggested the CO knew something.

'Officially, McKee is full. Unofficially, he had a similar encounter with a junior officer over there.'

'What did he do to her?'

'What did he do to *him*, sir?'

'Oh sweet divine...' Lt Col Collins was struggling. 'He's...'

'Never short of opportunity, sir.'

'I want him out of here today. Not another night in my barracks. Tell the GOC I'm not having him in the mess.' The GOC was the OC of the mess, but was unlikely to overrule the barrack commander.

'Yes, sir.'

'Tell Hartigan he can room in Baldonnell. The Air Corps are into *that sort of thing*.'

'Yes, sir.'

'Call the peelers first. I want them to hear it first from us.'

'Yes, sir.'

***

Two newly commissioned second lieutenants were brought to his office on their first Monday at work. One was coming to the 2nd Battalion, one was going to the S&T Company. Both young and wide-eyed, as Dickie was some ten years before. He did the quick introduction to the barracks, familiarised them with the orderly officer list, and introduced them to the CO.

Dickie saw that Peter Marsden, the Vikings second lieutenant, was almost 22 years old, but hadn't gone to college. He'd done the honours course in the Military College. Dickie would have to find out why.

Dickie and one of the S&T captains took them out for a drink later that night. They pulled into the International on Wicklow Street. The place was already heaving with students. The S&T captain got stuck into his new arrival, while Dickie gently tried to winkle out of Marsden why he'd spent nearly three years in the Cadet School.

'Well, sir...'

'It's Dickie, you're commissioned now.'

'Sorry. My first year didn't go so well. I knew that. The Glen, some of the exams. The School Commandant told me I was out, or back to the junior class. I just stuck the head down in the junior class and got on with it. Felt much better second time round, even going through the whole Stage I. Got through the two Glens and then the School Commandant told me they had decided they weren't going to commission me at all, and I was gone.'

'Oh.' Dickie tried to contain his surprise. They weren't going to commission this guy after two years in the College? And now he was a 2nd Battalion officer?

'It sounds bad.'

'Go on.'

'I asked the Colonel for an interview, just to ask why I wasn't going to make it second time around. He was very nice. Went over all the things that had gone wrong. I thought some of it was a bit harsh. Said nothing. He said my performance during the dig-in on the second Glen was the decider. He explained the things that went wrong. I saluted him and I was on the way out the door when I realised I hadn't done most of the dig-in. One of my class-mates, clocked me with a shovel by mistake during the digging. Got knocked out. They took me to the Curragh Hospital and stitched me here.' He indicated a small scar on his forehead.

'The Colonel was a bit surprised. I told him I was in hospital. He sent for my LA30. My admission and treatment were recorded, during the dig-in. But there were about six entries in the platoon diary for me over the same period. All bad. Colonel sent me back to my room. Turned out that there was some other stuff in there that she'd written about me that wasn't true as well.'

'She?'

'Yes. Female engineer. You might have heard of her. Una Compton.'

He said nothing.

'What happened then?'

'We heard some of the NCOs saying there'd be a Court Martial. Nothing happened. She got posted to the Naval Base. I got commissioned. Funny thing is, turned out her boyfriend was in the Navy. She never wanted to be posted to the College in the first place. So they gave her a shore job at Haulbowline. Near her boyfriend.'

'Interesting.'

Dickie would recall with picture-clarity the moment she walked into Ryan's of Parkgate Street. His stomach lurched. A friend of Morgan's wife, she was joining a group of UCG ex-pats for a TGI Friday before hitting the road to Galway. Dickie had heard of her, but never met her. A mane of dark hair falling just below the shoulders. She took a barstool beside Dickie and ordered a bottle of beer. His mouth turned to molasses. He resolved to say nothing, and smile agreeably if addressed.

He was glad he'd had two gins at the TGI in Rathmines. Enough to steady the nerves.

'Hi. I'm Laura.'

'Dickie. Nice to meet you.'

She chatted away among the group, while Dickie's head swirled. He wondered if his eyes betrayed the fevered workings of his brain. He tried to follow the conversation, appear relaxed and ready to offer a cool comment, while not vomiting with anxiety.

***

His mind flashed though past loves and lusts. He recalled a scorched Brashit, his jeep driving through the dust, away from a path not taken. What would have happened if he accepted Maryam's invitation? This girl wasn't quite as beautiful as Maryam, but she was up there. How faithful was memory? Was Maryam really that beautiful; or were his memories just an unspoiled fantasy of something that would never be? What the memory of Maryam really provoked in him wasn't regret for unrequited love, but anger that he'd done nothing. He hadn't taken a chance, hadn't dared. He'd left Brashit with a 'what if?' Laura was the here and now. He couldn't remember the last time he'd felt this way.

379

The evening passed pleasantly. She finished her solo drink before hitting the road. He'd done enough to register interest without making a fool of himself. As she'd waved her farewells, he ordered another beer. Morgan's wife clocked it though; his goofy grin as Laura left. Mrs Morgan flashed him a knowing leer, bothering him not a whit. His head was already working on how to next meet Laura.

***

Time slowed to a glacial crawl. He hadn't been this distracted since his subaltern days in Killimore, staring out windows, missing tracts of conversation. He wished every meeting to an end, every evening to nightfall. Meeting her was his only future.

***

Second Lieutenant Downs came into the Adjutant's office on Friday. She was tall, barely an inch shorter than Dickie. Dark-eyed and athletic, with a sports woman's figure, she was attractive, without being conscious of it.

'Can I have a word, Dickie?'

'Sure, come in.'

She sat down, fire in her eye.

'They're not going to charge Hartigan.'

'I see.' First he'd heard about it. 'It's a tricky one, Kate.'

'Dickie, he tried to rape her!'

'I know. Trying to prove it at a Court Martial is a different thing.'

'He did it before! With a guy!'

'I know, Kate.'

380

'Jesus Christ, Dickie!'

'Kate... did you carry her out of a taxi on the night?'

'Yes.'

'Was she covered in her own vomit?'

'Yes.'

'Was she unconscious?'

'Yes.'

'Did you shower her and put her to bed?'

'Yes.'

'Did you see Hartigan in her room, or coming out of her room?'

'No.'

'Did any of the other junior officers?'

'No.'

'Kate, you've just acquitted him.'

'Dickie!'

'Kate, he's going through a judicial separation. He'll fight it tooth and nail. He'll be lawyered up with some fancy big wig of a senior council, who'll ask you those questions and more besides. Your evidence alone would acquit him.'

'You could at least have charged the bastard! With anything! Let him deny it!' She knew it was hopeless.

She stood and brushed the creases from her skirt. She'd expected him to fight for Callaghan, and for her. Instead, he'd just spent five minutes defending an indigent Military Police investigation that would bring no consequences for Hartigan. She turned slowly and left. He felt wretched and cowardly.

***

'Jaysus, sir. You're away with the pookies!'

Sgt Mulholland was with Dickie on the firing point in Kilbride. The rain blew horizontally from the west as the first detail lay prone, waiting for Dickie's order to fire. Waiting.

'Wondering if the rain would make it through to the back of my bollocks Sarge. Range 200!' he roared, pushing thoughts of Laura out of his head.

The Battalion still had 42 stragglers who hadn't fired their range practices this year. Being adjutant saved no one from the ranges when there were so few junior officers in the battalion.

Enthusiasm for range practices was never high, but on a filthy day in October, it was sub-zero. They got ready for the kneeling snap at 200 metres. The butt-party were struggling to hold the snap targets upright in the gale. Dickie and Sergeant Mulholland weren't expecting too many hits anyway.

They finished at midday, and had a hurried tea with egg sandwiches in the back of a truck. Dickie finished the second detail by 14:30, and got to work completing the ammunition ledger while Sergeant Mulholland ordered the brass cleared from the range. They were on the road by 15:30, the brooding sun obscured by clouds.

***

He was home by seven, showered himself warm again, and rang Morgan to arrange a beer for that evening. Had to get some information on the Laura situation.

***

They went for a pint in the Angler's. He got the low-down. Just broken up from an odd-ball boyfriend. Not looking to meet anyone. Worked on the Southside. He got the name of her office. Dickie wanted to head home as soon as he'd finished Morgan's interrogation, but was duty-bound to stay for another two pints. Least he could do. He fell into bed at midnight, head spinning about what he'd do next.

***

Friday finally came. There were presentations in McKee for some young officer retirements. There was an autumn international against Australia in Lansdowne Road, and so a large crowd present. In a quiet corner, Dickie filled in Lyons on the Battalion's latest arrival from the Cadet School, and his problems with Una Compton.

'The fucking bitch,' was all he could manage.

***

The match against the Antipodeans was a close-run affair, the Irish doing all the close-running. Healy announced that they'd go for a civilised drink in the Berkeley Court Hotel. Lyons was celebrating the birth of his daughter. Corrigan was on hand to announce his young son would 'show her the ropes,' in a few years' time.

They made it to the Berkeley Court by six. Lyons regaled the crowd with tales of past glories.

'So we're having breakfast next morning when down comes *Doctor Alan Woods, Dental Surgeon*, and this unbelievable slapper called Tracey. She was like something out of one of Healy's Lebanese porn movies!' Lyons loved hitting multiple targets.

'She was a lovely girl,' Corrigan defended her honour weakly.

Lyons ploughed on.

'Anyway, after he shows her how to use a knife and fork, he says "Come on over to Dublin, those veneers are on the house!"'

The audience had heard the story a dozen times before, but erupted in laughter anyway. In the mirth, no one saw him coming. From about ten feet away, balding, late forties. He pushed his way through the knot, and threw a beautiful right hook, connecting with Lyons' jaw, flooring him.

'I was in Edinburgh that weekend. My *ex-wife* ran my reception. She took the call from *Tracey*. You fucking cunt!'

Healy was about to step in but security got to the guy first, ushering him out. The barman, preserving the dignity of the Berkeley, poured Lyons a Jameson. Corrigan, unscathed throughout the affair, came over.

'I'll get you that one, Teabag!' The two of them fell about the place laughing.

The bar took a while to settle down. Dickie looked over and saw Lyons, on the periphery of the group, quietly nursing his drink.

'Pissed off taking another one for Corrigan?'

'Nah. Poor fucker lost the wife. It's Una fucking Compton.'

'Forget it, Robbie.'

'Know what, Dickie? I wish I rode the bitch now.'

'No you don't.'

'I do. I'd have had some pleasure out of her. Everyone presumed I'd done something. Even my buddies. No smoke without fire. All that shit. Straight up- I was in her room. I was pissed as a lord. But I swear it was because I thought she gave me the eye. Soon as she told me to fuck off, I did. Never touched her.'

'I believe you, Robbie.'

'You do *now*, Dickie. Now she's a confirmed, lying, psycho, fucking bitch. You didn't then.'

Dickie said nothing. Lyons eyeballed him.

'Eight years I carried that one around. I figured 'if you can't beat 'em, join 'em.' When the dust settled, and I wasn't charged, I played up on it. Everyone thought it. All the birds. All the senior officers. Noodles. Robbie the Rapist. The fucking bitch.'

In a dozen years, Dickie had never seen Lyons in a single introspective thought. Lyons was the wild, mountainy West Corkman who never conceded defeat. He'd been beaten ragged by bigger men on a football field and shouted 'your sister loved it that hard' back at them. Now he looked a beaten man.

'I've 16 years done. With the wife, I've got seven rental properties. I've more coming in each month than the GOC. I'll be hanging up the musket myself in two months.'

He floored his pint, then his whiskey, turned, and was gone.

***

Most of the following week was spent on a Company Sergeant promotion board. There was one vacancy in the Battalion, 11 applicants, seven of whom were complete no-hopers. The form sergeant, in seniority and ability, was Sergeant Burns. Capable, diligent, and superbly turned out, he was also discreetly gay. The head of the promotion board was a DFHQ commandant, and the third member was a female captain from the Second Regiment across the Liffey, leaving Dickie as the sole Viking officer on the Board. The etiquette in these situations was that, within reason, the best sergeant from the unit with the vacancy got the job.

They finished their deliberations on Wednesday afternoon, totted their marks, and formally placed the candidates by score. Dickie was happy Burns would make a good CS, but could say nothing until the recommendation was cleared up the line. This required all the grown-ups to sign off prior to promulgation, a quasi-papal process that would take a few days.

***

Dickie was orderly dog on Thursday, a favour from the adjutant to make sure he'd be resting Friday, for a long weekend. By 17:30 all the escorts were dismounted, all the keys back, guns and bullets safely tucked away. Dickie was looking forward to dinner. The EOD officer and CDO were finishing dessert when he entered the dining room. Even better, he thought. Dinner to himself with Thursday's papers.

His satisfaction lasted five minutes, when Freakin' Frank Mullen came in, and sat down beside him. He had no idea what the man was doing in Rathmines at this hour. Now a Lt Col, he was Brigade IO, and as majestically incompetent in that role as he was as ops officer in Dickie's first trip to Lebanon.

'Dickie! How are you? Long-time no see!'

'What has you eating in, sir?'

'Maura's away with the girls at her sister's. Couldn't face cooking!' he blustered.

Frank settled himself at the dining table, slurped loudly at his soup, and said nothing until the waiter was safely past the kitchen door.

'How are things on that promotion board, Dickie?'

'Wrapped up yesterday, sir. Results gone to the Brigade Adjutant.'

'Well, hopefully you've got the right man. Quite a few worried with all that stuff on Sergeant Burns' p-file.'

Dickie looked up from his dinner.

'We had a closed-door run through all 11 unit files sir. Nothing strange on any of them. His file review was pretty good.'

386

'Not talking about the Brigade p-files, Dickie, I mean the DFHQ p-file. His full file.'

'Brigade gives us their files only,' he reminded Frank, the Brigade staff officer. 'That's all we're privy to.'

'Not your fault. Someone should have briefed the senior officer.' Frank never missed an opportunity to deliver a slap of the old seniority stick.

'Nothing of concern in there, sir?' He was worried Burns was some sort of IRA mole, or a moonlighting drug dealer.

'You must be aware of his sexual preferences.'

Frank saw anything less than supreme confidence in a junior officer as a sign of weakness, and Frank was, at heart, a little bully.

'I am, sir. I wasn't aware that was a basis not to promote him.'

'We can't have men like that as senior NCOs! Bad enough he made it to sergeant. A gay CS! Good God!'

Dickie chewed his food to mush while thinking.

'I don't see how we can discriminate against a gay sergeant, when we've been promoting gay officers for years, sir,' sounding as considered as he could.

'There are no gay officers in the Irish Army,' he said slowly, as if hypnotising himself into believing it.

'Sir, you had a gay company commander and a gay staff officer in the Second Battalion as CO. I thought you knew. Everyone else did.'

Frank's head leaned forward, veins bulging. The waiter entered with a beef stir-fry. Dickie wondered if Frank was about to ask him who they were. Even Frank wasn't that crass.

'Who were they?'

'Sir, if they chose not to tell you, or you weren't aware, I don't think it would be proper of me to volunteer their names to you,' Dickie said it in his most solemn, former-adjutant's delivery, leaving the suggestion that further questioning would be inappropriate at best. Frank was silent for the rest of dinner.

The rest of his duty passed uneventfully. Normally he spent the witching hours until five am glued to MTV in the orderly officer's cubicle. But his brain refused to go quiet. He strolled out past the sentry on the CCTV bank, and went on another barrack patrol. Sunrise suggested itself in the east, but the sodium lighting of the city still glowed. He pushed his hands into the pockets of his waterproofs. The butt of the BAP snagged in the lining of the jacket, the cheap material long since worn through, and the Browning's grip pulled and dragged the hole wider. He walked past the clothing store, by the School of Music, and Military Archives, and looked out onto the terraced houses beyond the railings. A dog come through the railing, and ran around the football pitch looking for something new to piss on.

He resolved to take control, contact Laura, and arrange a date. No big deal. He'd send her a bunch of flowers and a card. Clichéd as it was, it was the only bloody thing that didn't involve waiting around for some gathering organised by Morgan's wife, which Laura might, or might not, show up at.

***

CS Burns' promotion was noted in Command Routine Orders the following Friday. It took all of half an hour before Dickie got a call from Commons in the Second Regiment asking whether Burns had gone down on him, or he'd gone down on Burns.

***

She called him soon after she got the flowers. They met for a drink in Dun Laoghaire, she was as nervous as a gazelle. Morgan had warned him about the dodgy ex.

They met a few days later in Neary's, had a drink, and headed to a bistro off Grafton Street. The nervousness was gone. Dickie ordered a decent Barolo with the highest alcohol content on the list.

She had a self-deprecating sense of humour. She chatted easily. Dickie was happy to let her talk as long as she wanted. His physical symptoms abated, he was able to speak without changing feet. He could have listened to her all night, but both were working the next day. He walked her to her car.

'Thanks, Dickie, that was really nice.'

'My pleasure.'

'My turn next time.'

'You don't owe me dinner, Laura.'

'I know. It's still my turn!'

She kissed him on the cheek, beamed a radiant smile, and drove off into the October night.

***

Even the weights felt lighter for Dickie the following Monday. There was a competitive lunchtime gym scene in Cathal Brugha, especially since four of the Viking squaddies had set up a male stripper group called *Celtic Flex*. The spent their lunch breaks bench-pressing, curling and squatting with the others, but with an unusual degree of mirror watching, and industrial quantities of baby oil. Dickie couldn't figure if they waxed or shaved their chests, but there wasn't so much as a follicle between the four of them. His sister's new-born was hairier.

The other lads were laughing at the fact that the *Celtic Flex* foursome was down to three this afternoon. They had entertained a hen night in Mullingar on Saturday night when a group of women rushed the stage. One of them had caught Attwood, from HQ Company, and bit him viciously in the buttocks. He'd been taken to Mullingar hospital, where he got a tetanus shot, and had the pretty deep bite stitched. He wouldn't be doing any shows, or squats, for a couple of weeks, and awaited the results of blood tests. Corporal Leggett explained the seriousness of the problem to Dickie while bench-pressing.

'Women love scars, sir,' he said, brow furrowed in effort. 'But anything like bite-marks close to the anus, and you're stuck in the gay clubs for a while.'

'I see.'

***

Tuesday 11th November

Dickie got Morgan's call just after morning parade.

'Checking if you'd heard?'

'What?'

'That bird you were asking me about.'

Morgan was probably ringing to tell him she'd gone back with her ex, got engaged, or left the country. The fucking bitch; just when he thought he'd met the right one, at last.

'Heard nothing.'

'Shit man, sorry. That accident on the news last night. Outside Loughrea.'

'No.'

'She got hit by some bloke overtaking a truck.'

Morgan shook his head as Dickie looked for affirmation.

390

'Jesus.' He couldn't think what to say. 'Any...?'

'No. It'll be a few days. Has to be a...'

'Okay.'

'I'll give you a shout, man.'

'Thanks, Al.'

***

He was glad he no longer lived in the mess. He could retreat into his little shell at home.

It eventually made the death notices. Removal on Thursday night, she's be waked at home, buried on Friday. He couldn't face seeing anyone he knew from college. He'd go on Friday morning, and hide at the back of the church. What could he say? 'I was in love with a girl I met three times, who kissed me once on the cheek.' Plonker.

He told the CO he needed Friday off to take his mother to his aunt's funeral.

Dickie pressed his front door behind him, and fell into the armchair in the sitting room. A bottle of Jameson sat on the bookshelf, the ginger lady eyeing him. He grabbed a glass and opened it. 11 o'clock mass in the morning. He'd leave Dublin at seven-thirty just to make sure.

***

It was a grimy, dank morning as he passed through Maynooth. At least he was going the opposite direction to the drones heading for Dublin. Headlights stung eyes already bleary from the Jameson. He stopped in Enfield for some bacon, fried eggs and tea. He made Renmore by 10:30, and St Ignatius' church by 10:50. He recognised a few faces, but stayed at the back of the church.

The funeral made its way out of the church for Bohermore cemetery. Dickie couldn't face a box and a hole in the ground, a mumbled rosary and more pointless why-ing. He stayed seated at the back of the church, slowly breathing the forbidden incense. The occasional old woman interrupted his meditation, walking up to the offertory and lighting a candle. He remained invisible.

Two pm; they must be gone from the graveyard by now. He'd walk just in case. It drizzled incessantly as he exited the church. He walked back along Dominick Street and Bridge Street, keeping a slow pace. In High Street, an old beggar with an older dog eyed him and saluted him. He was in Bohermore by half two. No mourners remained. A sodden grave digger made his way slowly from the plots at the Eyre Square end. He threaded his way there along gravel and grass. It took him ten minutes to find it.

A rain-blackened mound of earth was all there was, rivulets of rainwater forming on it, and a simple wooden cross marking the spot. No words or thoughts intruded. The little cross of wood and the memory of a kiss on the cheek a few weeks ago were all that remained.

He retraced his steps back into town, going nowhere in particular. He walked to the Spanish Arch, and stopped to watch the Corrib ripple into the bay. Below his perch on the quay wall, icy brown water from the Maumturks met the Atlantic salt. He thought back to freezing nights in the Wicklow Mountains a dozen years ago. A few short minutes of cold would be replaced by perpetual warmth. He pinched himself at the sheer selfish inanity of it.

A damp echo of Sergeant Pond beside him in the mist; on the Curragh Plains, indifferent to suffering, reminding them what reserves remained in the human soul when all appeared gone. For Pond, no God but Darwin. Survival was a never-ending tote of the ledger between those who could endure, and those who could not. Pond wouldn't dwell on the passing of anyone at their own hand; they would merely join the forgotten tally of those who couldn't endure.

He looked south past Claddagh. The sea and sky blended in a seamless, soiled-cotton grey. The Burren was nowhere to be seen. The wet had long since penetrated his shoe-leather, his feet were cold and damp. Street lamps flickered into life. The end-of-week migration of students from the college down to the hostelries had commenced, as they took their places in front of bars, or in uniform behind them.

He walked back up High Street. He wasn't sure what he'd do. There was always a bed in USAC. He walked through the herbal fug outside Tigh Neachtain, and on past Freeney's. The door was open, few inside. He walked on by the King's Head. There was a thud on the window. Paddy Doyle stood among a throng who looked like they'd been there a while. He pointed at his pint glass, and moved out to the doorway.

'Dickie- what the fuck are you doing here?'

'This and that. You?'

'Two day course in Renmore. Implications of VAT registration for mess administration!' he said with a grin. 'Forty sergeants and admin officers in town. A few of us decided to stay the night. You having a drink?'

Not so much an invitation. Paddy saw the state of him, had an arm around his shoulder, and guided him in the door.

'Yeah, Paddy. Think I will.'

Glossary of Foot and Arms Drill

Aire: Attention

Aisiompaíg Airm: Reverse Arms

Ar Ais (Siar): Rearward (Backward)

Ar Sodar Máirseáil: Double March

Ath Dhéanamh: Do it again! (generic)

Athraíg Treo Fó Dheis (Chlé): Change Direction Right (Left) Right (Left)

Bogaig Tuailimí: Ease Springs

Clé (Deas) Iompaíg: Left (Right) Face/Turn

Garda: Guard

Pasáiste: Passage

Socair: Steady

Stad: Stop

Glossary of Other Terms

2i/c: Second in command

Adj: (pronounced as 'adge') Adjutant. Personnel officer, rank dependent on size of formation

AE: Armed Elements; generic term for militias in Lebanon

AF 451: Army Form 451, Officer's annual confidential report

AK/AK 47/AKM/Kalashnikov: assault rifle carried by most sides in middle-east

AN/PRC 46-set: Army/Navy Portable Radio Communications, vehicle-mounted medium range radio

AN/PRC 77-set: Army/Navy Portable Radio Communications 77 man-pack short range radio

AO: Area of Operations

ARP: Annual Range Practice

Arty: Artillery

ARW: Army Ranger Wing

AUSCIVPOL: Australian Civil Police (in Cyprus)

BAP: Browning Automatic Pistol, 9mm semi-automatic

Bn: Battalion

BOS: Barrack Orderly Sergeant

'Buckshee:' Unauthorised surplus or extra, especially ammunition or food

C&S: Command and Staff (School)

CDO: Command Duty Officer (usually a commandant)

CLO: Command Legal Officer

Colour: A ceremonial flag denoting a Brigade, or the Military College

Combo pen: Self-administered atropine injection (with single valium dose in the lid)

Comcen: Communications centre

Comhairleor: Mentor (chosen from the senior class)

Compounds: Fortified hilltop outposts operated by the DFF or Israeli Defence Forces

COO: Chief Operations Officer (UNFICYP)

Coy: Company

CS: Compound Smoke ('Tear Gas') or Company Sergeant (see ranks below)

DFF: De Facto Forces- Israeli surrogate forces occupying South Lebanon since the 1978

Israeli invasion and withdrawal

DFHQ: Defence Forces Headquarters

DFRs: Defence Force Regulations

DS: Directing Staff, officer or NCO instructors

'84:' 84mm recoilless anti-tank rifle

ED: Excused Duties, a temporary medical grading

Enclave: Colloquialism for the Israeli-controlled area in South Lebanon

EOD: Explosive Ordnance Disposal

'Est-of-Sit:' Estimate of the Situation. Planning and evaluation process

FCA: *Forsa Cosanta Áitúil*, (Local Defence Force) the Army Reserves

FFR: Fitted for Radio, a Land Rover with a 46-set mounted in the rear

FINNBATT: Finnish Battalion UNIFIL

FIBUA: Fighting in Built Up Areas

FN: Fabrique National, the manufacturer of the standard issue rifle, 7.62mm Nato calibre

GHANBATT: Ghanaian Battalion UNIFIL

GOC: General Officer Commanding

GPMG: General Purpose Machine Gun, also called a MAG; belt-fed 7.62mm Nato calibre

GS: Garda Siochána. Also an acronym for 'general service', a standard Land Rover without a radio

Greens: Colloquial for enlisted mens' service dress

Griddle: Basic manual substitution cypher used in tactical communication

Groundhog: Sheltering from shell-fire in a bunker

GTs: General Tests, the graded papers in Military College courses for students

Gustav: Sub-machine gun, 9mm fully automatic

HE: High Explosive

HF: High-Frequency, a radio set for long distance communication.

HK: Heckler & Koch, German weapons manufacturer

HMG: Heavy machine gun. Generic term for 12.7mm (.50" calibre) and above

IDF: Israeli Defence Forces

Int: Intelligence

IO: Intelligence/Information Officer

IS: Internal Security

JOC: Joint Operations Centre

LE: 'Long Eireannach' official designation for an Irish naval vessel

LD: Light Duties, a temporary medical grading

LA 30: 'Leabhair Airm' (Army Book) 30, medical record, all ranks

MAG: (Mitrailleuse d'Appui Général) GPMG

MAP: Medical Aid Post

MO: Medical Officer

MOUT: Military Operations in Urban Terrain

NEPBATT: Nepalese Battalion, UNIFIL

NBC: Nuclear, Biological, Chemical

ND: Negligent discharge (of a weapon)

OHP: Overhead projector

OP: Observation Post

Orders: Colloquialism for summary trial by Commanding Officer

PA: Poilíní Airm, Military Police

Padre: Radio appointment title for Chaplain, (and colloquial)

P4: Light Peugeot 4x4

PE4: Plastic Explosive

PFR: Permanent Force Reserve. Reserve element in UNFICYP Force HQ

Pl: Military abbreviation for Platoon

PT: Physical training

QM: Quartermaster. In charge of supplies and equipment, rank dependent of size of formation

RAP: Regimental Aid Post

RDK: Buried wire detector

RUC: Royal Ulster Constabulary

RV: Rendezvous

S&T: Supply and Transport (Corps)

SDA: Security Duty Allowance

SD1: Service Dress Number 1, best parade uniform

SF: Sustained Fire

Section 168: 'Conduct to the Prejudice of Good Order and Discipline', the catch-all charge under the Defence Act 1954

Sig-Int: Signals Intelligence

Sitrep: Situation Report

SINCGARS: Single Channel Ground and Airborne Radio System

SOP: Standard Operating Procedure

Starlight: Radio appointment title for Medical

Superfine(s): Heavy, patterned wool for officer's and senior NCO's service dress

SWEDMEDCOY: Swedish Medical Company (UNIFIL)

Tiffy Artificer: ordnance technician

TPT: Training/Practice-Tracer

UNFICYP: United Nations Force in Cyprus

UNIFIL: United Nations Interim Force in Lebanon

UNPA: UN-Protected Area (the UNFICYP HQ in the abandoned Nicosia International Airport)

UNTSO: United Nations Truce Supervision Organisation

USAC: University Students Administrative Complement, the unit (and building) that looks after and houses Army students in Galway

USL: Uncertified Sick Leave

Vikings: Army colloquialism for 2nd Infantry Battalion, Dublin

Wadi: Valley, river bed

YO: 'Young Officer,' a 2nd Lt or Lt

Zulu Time: Greenwich Mean Time. Standard time reporting format to ensure a common reported time irrespective of the time zone in which a unit operates

Army and Air Corps Ranks

Cdt: Cadet

Pte: Private (two-star or three-star)

Cpl: Corporal

Sgt: Sergeant

CQMS: Company Quartermaster Sergeant

CS (BS): Company (Battery) Sergeant

BQMS (RQMS): Battalion (Regimental) Quartermaster Sergeant

Sgt Maj: Sergeant Major

OFFICERS

2/Lt: Second Lieutenant

Lt: Lieutenant

Capt: Captain

Comdt: Commandant

Lt Col: Lieutenant Colonel

Col: Colonel

Brig Gen: Brigadier General

Maj Gen: Major General

Lt Gen: Lieutenant General

Printed in Great Britain
by Amazon